Sunday Meetin' Time

Book One: The Little Church on the Hill

Patricia McCullough Walston

WESTBOW°
PRESS
A DIVISION OF THOMAS NELSON
& ZONDERVAN

Scripture taken from the King James Version of the Bible.

WestBow Press books may be ordered through booksellers or by contacting:

WestBow Press
A Division of Thomas Nelson & Zondervan
1663 Liberty Drive
Bloomington, IN 47403
www.westbowpress.com
1 (866) 928-1240

ISBN: 978-1-4908-7393-0 (sc)
ISBN: 978-1-4908-7395-4 (hc)
ISBN: 978-1-4908-7394-7 (e)

Library of Congress Control Number: 2015904895

Print information available on the last page.

WestBow Press rev. date: 04/22/2015

Contents

About the Author

Atlanta native, Patricia Walston is a free-lance writer, historian, genealogist, teacher, parent and grandparent. She is all about family and has written award-winning articles that have been published locally and worldwide online. Her mentoring on family life is based on wisdom, experience, faith and Biblical principles. Patricia is a story teller.

She was born in 1941, just eight months before the attack on Pearl Harbor. Blessed with a close relationship with many grandparents and great-grandparents, she learned firsthand how people lived and survived through turbulent and bleak times in America.

Patricia listened to their stories of the "Good ole days," not realizing at the time they truly were the "Good ole times."

Both of her great-great-grandfathers fought in the Civil War. One was captured in the Battle of Atlanta and sent to a prisoner of war camp, and the other was seriously wounded in the Battle of Resaca in Gordon County, Georgia.

Both grandfathers registered for the draft during World War I. Her own father was drafted into the Army during World War II in 1943 while her mother worked in war plants packing supplies and parachutes for the American soldiers.

Patricia wrote this book based on learned and experienced history. She had the great advantage of having godly women influence her life. Any of them could have been the "Mama" in "Sunday Meetin' Time."

Growing up in the country without modern conveniences and before television, and before the electronic age ruled the world, Patricia loved reading. Later she enjoyed the thrill of research and genealogy.

When she was about ten years old, her family moved to the city, and she discovered the public library. Books opened up a whole new world for her.

Raised in a strong Judeo-Christian environment, she became a Christian at a young age and has been involved in various ministries throughout her lifetime.

Eventually, she created her own ministry to women and children called "Life Design." The premise of the group was to help women live Godly lives through mental, physical, and spiritual wellness.

For the past six years, she has been a prolific author writing over 2,000 articles for Atlanta Faith and Family Examiner You can these articles at http://www.examiner.com/faith-and-family-in-atlanta/patricia-walston

For more information, input, sharing of comments, etc. you may contact Patricia on Facebook under "Faith, Family, and Friends Gathering."

Like a sponge, she absorbed the stories of family folklore and family history; dating as far back as Ireland. She loved hearing the stories of her ancestors; how they lived; and how they did things.

The scripture where the older women were to teach the younger women was taken seriously by her mother and grandmothers. She was eager to watch and learn all that she could from these committed Christian women. She observed what they did as they went about their daily chores and routines raising large families. Today she is a mother, grandmother and great-grandmother to her own family.

This book, while originally a Sunday series in her newspaper column, emerged into a full-length book which characterizes those hard working, Christ-committed people who came before her. The roots of her Scot-Irish heritage spread deeply into her heart and soul. "Sunday Meetin' Time," was patterned after the small churches she often attended as a child. The stories were inspired by her personal observations and experiences.

Disclaimer

While things done and said in this book were actually authentic of the times, they are not recommended methods, ideas, or treatments intended for modern day usage.

These are merely depictions of the way people managed their life and times. None of these methods are recommended by the author.

These characters are vivid and loosely based on the author's family and upbringing but in no way are they patterned after anyone living or dead.

The names, like the characters, are fictional and not intended to reflect any person, living or dead.

The King James Version of the Bible is used and in no way disparages any other faith, creed, religion, or sect. It is in public domain.

The brand products and celebrities mentioned in this book are not endorsements of these products or people, but are intended to represent the times and activities of this era.

This book is intended as a memory book for those who lived during these times; and a peek back into history for those who did not. The author has artfully portrayed the history of this time by blending it into real life situations. However, it is totally a work of fiction except the Holy Scriptures.

"Not forsaking the assembling of ourselves together, as the manner of some is, but exhorting one another: and so much the more, as ye see the day approaching." Hebrews 10:25

Dedication from the Author

"All praise and honor belong to You, Lord, for the magnificent works of Your hands. You have made such beauty, and You have loved us enough to share it. We are humbly thankful!"

Before readers begin the wonderful journey through this book about the Alrod Family, it is the author's prayer that they will preface the reading with a personal prayer that God will open their hearts and minds so that they perceive the messages from God throughout the story.

This book is dedicated to those of yesteryear who were dedicated to the building and maintenance of those original small places of worship that so defined the beginning of our nation and influenced all future generations. This endeavor would not have been possible if it had not been for those who came before me, to those who have shared my life, and to those who will come behind me.

This book is also dedicated to the many pastors and teachers who planted spiritual seeds into my life. It is dedicated to others who came along afterward to water and cultivate those seeds to grow me into spiritual maturity. Much gratitude is due to those who prayed for me throughout the writing of this book; sometimes daily.

This is especially dedicated to the late Miss Annie Frances Flanigan, my fifth-grade teacher at Luckie Street School, who in 1953 predicted that one day I would write this book.

Special Acknowledgements:

Acknowledgement has to be given to my McCullough and Stephens Grandparents, who greatly influenced my life and whose stories were the inspiration for this book.

It is particularly dedicated to my husband, Ted A. Walston, Sr. who encouraged me over a lifetime of writing; and to Lynda Warf, my best friend, who pulled me kicking and screaming through the proofing of this book. Without her, this book could not have been published.

With much love, it is dedicated to the following:

My children, Rhonda Hall, Drew Walston, Jennifer Hall, and their families, and my brother Roy McCullough who would not let me quit. It is also dedicated to a beloved brother, Jim McCullough who recently departed this life; and two lovely sisters Bettie Long and Dale Cowart; as well as all their families.

The testimony of this book is dedicated to those committed people who came before us; to whom we owe a debt that we can never repay... unless we pay it forward. This book is dedicated to families everywhere; for they hold the key to our nation's survival. Let us be diligent in keeping the faith for those who come after us.

"Know ye that the Lord He is God: it is He that hath made us, and not we ourselves; we are His people, and the sheep of His pasture." Psalm 100:3

Church Covenant

"Having been led, as we believe by the Spirit of God, to receive the Lord Jesus Christ as our Savior and, on the profession of our faith, having been baptized in the name of the Father, and of the Son, and of the Holy Spirit, we do now, in the presence of God, and this assembly most solemnly and joyfully enter into covenant with one another as one body in Christ.

We engage, therefore, by the aid of the Holy Spirit to walk together in Christian love; to strive for the advancement of this church, in knowledge, holiness, and comfort; to promote its prosperity and spirituality; to sustain its worship, ordinances, discipline, and doctrines; to contribute cheerfully and regularly to the support of the ministry, the expenses of the church, the relief of the poor, and the spread of the Gospel through all nations.

We also engage to maintain family and secret devotions; to religiously educate our children; to seek the salvation of our kindred and acquaintances, to walk circumspectly in the world; to be just in our dealings, faithful in our engagements and exemplary in our deportment; to avoid tattling, backbiting, and excessive anger; to abstain from the sale of, and use of intoxicating drinks as a beverage; to be zealous in our efforts to advance the kingdom of our Savior.

We further engage to watch over one another in brotherly love; to remember one another in prayer; to aid one another in sickness and distress; to cultivate Christian sympathy in feeling and Christian courtesy in speech; to be slow to take offense, but always ready for reconciliation and mindful of the rules of our Savior to secure it without delay.

We moreover engage that when we remove from this place we will, as soon as possible, unite with some other church where we can carry out the spirit of this covenant and the principles of God's Word."

Prologue: The Old Country Church:
The Ole Country Church

As the new world in America was being founded, one of the first things the immigrants did was build their church...the building that is. They brought with them their church, which is the body of Christ; their faith, and beliefs.

In those formative years, the folks met in open fields or under shade trees much like Jesus and His disciples did. However, as soon as possible a proper building would be erected. These were simple structures made from the rock and wood that they found on the land. They were insignificant compared to the mighty edifices of today, but many large churches had simple beginnings.

The actual structure may have been built of rock, wood, and mortar, but the real foundation of the church was laid on the "Word of God."

There were no contractors; therefore, the congregation built the church by their own sweat and labor. Once it was finished, the congregation would dedicate it to the work of Christ.

The building was a convenience, but they knew that the church was not a building, but the people. They had escaped from state churches in their homeland, with their rituals and rules of the church hierarchy. They based their church teaching on the responsibility of man and his close relationship with God.

In the beginning, many churches only had a circuit-rider preacher to do their marrying and their burying, but sometimes not even for the burying - because that could not wait. They learned to depend on themselves... each other... but mostly on God. They put their trust in God when it came to choosing a shepherd to lead their small flocks. They considered this as no light matter.

He had to be a man of God. He had to have received the "Call of God" for that particular church. Most of all he had to be accepted by the congregation.

There were no assemblies, conferences, or conventions; they were on their own. These circuit rider preachers were paid a modest income; based on the offering each week. He often would be paid in goods such as eggs, potatoes, chickens and other staples.

As permanent pastors were engaged, they were often paid nothing at all because they provided for their own livelihood like Paul, the tent maker, in the Bible.

Sometimes these early preachers lacked much of what their followers had; and were often the recipients of used hand-me-downs for their family. The church people gave what they could afford, and if they didn't have money, they still gave.

If the church folks could not pay a cash tithe, they would give something in kind, like free labor. There were always repairs that needed to be done - wood to be chopped for the stove, and weeds to be cut around the churchyard.

The beloved minister in this story, the Reverend Herman James Alrod, was also a farmer. He worked his own land just like the other farmers. He was part and parcel of all that they were. He was affected by the same things they all were. Everyone shared in the upkeep and maintenance of the church; especially the dedicated deacons.

Herman Alrod was honored as their spiritual leader, and they understood that he was the shepherd of their flock but was also a fallible human just as they were. There were no paid staff members, organist, or nursery workers. Mamas kept their babies in their laps. Everything people did for the church they believed they were doing for God.

The communion bread needed to be baked only by a woman of admirable standing before the congregation and God. Since they were abstainers from all alcohol, they used the natural sweet juice of the vine for communion.

They were extremely particular about the serving of the Lord's Supper. In order to partake of the broken bread and the fruit of the vine, which represented the body and blood of Christ, they had to be a baptized believer and a member of the church in good standing.

These settlers came from many countries, backgrounds, and denominations. They gathered around their own kind and those who shared common philosophies of life and religious practices.

It was their custom to establish and grow a community by building churches that were like-minded. Close-knit families and friends often traveled to these different areas together in covered wagons. They were a strong and stubborn generation who carved a nation from the wilderness. What they didn't have, they either made it or did without.

As soon as they settled the area, the church and school became a priority. They knew intellectual and religious education would be the wood, rocks, and mortar that would become the foundation of their children's lives.

They also knew the necessity of connection and unity. They needed to know there were people nearby they could depend on in hard times and could celebrate with them in times of joy. They wanted people of honor and moral character to be in their community. So this is what they taught in the church.

As they grew, businesses began to open. They would hire a doctor, establish a bank, and persuade the trades to move into the area such as grocers, barbers, dry good and feed stores. However, the church and school came first.

Traveling back and forth to church was difficult over dirt roads – rutty and dusty in the dry seasons; muddy in others. The churches grew largely from within as they produced their own members by the birth rate. As others moved in, the population grew... and so did the community and church. Most of the time in a small area there would be only one church. However, down the road a few miles, there may be another group and another church.

Membership was not assured. Those wishing to join had to profess a belief in Jesus Christ, and be baptized in "Believer's Baptism." If they had been a member in good standing of another like church, a letter from that church could be requested. With the mail so slow, it often took months to receive the answer back. Until then, they could join by a statement of their faith.

Often when a family moved on further west or returned to their former town, they would request the church to send a letter along with them stating that they had experienced baptism and had been a member in good standing.

In any case, they had to agree with the mission statement of the church, and promise to be committed members through their church covenant. After satisfying the deacons and the preacher of their devotion to God and the church, they had to be voted on by the congregation.

Once voted on, they would be introduced and presented before the whole church. The pastor would make his recommendation for approval, and the congregation would respond by either "ayes" of "nays." Anyone with a "nay" had to be ready to stand and defend their vote. Once approved, the new members would stand down in front of the church to receive the "right hand of fellowship" and would become a member.

These early settlers, our ancestors, knew what it was like not to be able to practice their faith, and their chosen ways of worship before coming to America. America afforded them a freedom like they had never known. They cherished, practiced, and protected this right.

Many would come to fight and die to preserve that freedom. They raised their children in the nurture and admonition of the Lord and taught them to love, honor, and respect God, others, and their country.

Dr. William S. Pitts immortalized one such early church in a song. In 1857, he happened upon a place that he felt in his soul would be the perfect spot for a church. He had been traveling through Iowa on the way to see his sweetheart.

He said he was restless in his soul until there was a church in that special woodland. He felt that area just beckoned people to come and praise God. On a return visit to the vicinity five years later, he discovered a church was being built on that very spot; just like the one in the song he had written.

His song, "The Church in the Wildwood" later became known as the "Little Brown Church in the Vale." It was called that because it was painted brown. However, the color was not the significance of the small church, but the peace and serenity that it represented.

Today, when people visit that little church, and so many other small churches, that have survived storms, war, and every pestilence known to mankind, they feel the tranquility and peace left there by a century or more of God's presence.

> *"There's a church in the valley by the wildwood; No lovelier spot in the dale; No place is so dear to my childhood; as the little brown church in the vale."*

His song represented many such small country churches. In order to finish medical school, he sold it for twenty-five dollars, and it is now public domain.

The solace and peace of this song about the little church built there in the wildwood has lived on for many generations and stands as a monument to the small churches everywhere, and their impact on American life.

After the colonial days, and the settling of other states across America, many churches sprang up. Some grew into larger congregations. However, many always remained small churches. Countless people, even now, prefer a smaller rural church rather than the huge cathedral-like edifices. These small churches are a testimonial to those who established and worshiped in these little tiny Holy Places.

This is a work of fiction - based on the lives of one such small congregation set in the late 1930s and early 1940s. Churches, such as the one in this story, have a long-standing heritage that have survived a hundred or more years.

Many of the older generation will reminisce and remember these churches from their childhood, and perhaps their grandchildren will remember hearing similar stories from those who have gone before who were the pillars of small town society.

To that witness, this account was written to honor the thousands of small churches that made a tremendous impact... and an enormous difference in the settling and shaping of America.

Introduction: The Little Church on the Hill

In days gone by, old folks referred to services at the church as "Meetin's."

"Hey Joe, you gonna be at Meetin' Wednesday night?"

"Sally, did you see Susie's new baby, she had him at Meetin' last Sunday. Cute little fella."

"Howdy, Mr. and Mrs. Honea, we've been ah missing yor family at Sunday Meetin' – you folks over them bad colds? Been a cold winter, huh?"

This story will take you back to days gone by where you will find the Alrod family; their friends and neighbors.

You will see them as they come to church, and town, using various modes of transportation. The roads were mostly still unpaved, but there were paved sidewalks along the few establishments in town. While a more modern world flourished in the outside world, things were not as advanced in rural communities.

Church was important. They came by wagon, foot, automobile, and even a few came on bicycles. But they came. They came out of obligation and duty to be sure, but they usually came because of love. And besides... to avoid Meetin' would arouse a lot of speculation and sometimes gossip.

The story of the Alrod's will take you back to those days of more humble times in their little white clapboard church with wooden floors and benches. There was also a wooden bench altar down front where many souls got their hearts right with God.

While established by ancestors in 1850, this is the story about a church in the late 1930s and 1940s; but has flashbacks to many previous times. It is about the pastor and his family - and the families in the church. It is also about the people in the community that surrounded the church; and some of those from the outside.

Reading this saga, you will be swept away into another time and place. If this was your era, your memory will take you back to those times when you grew up.

If you are of the younger generation, you will see how it was that your ancestors lived, loved, and worshiped.

This story will take you on an emotional journey of joy, hope, and sorrow. Before you turn the last page in this book, you will feel that you became part and parcel of this long ago time. You will come to think of these characters as real people.

In these modern and progressive days, you will see principles that never grow old or out of date. You will identify with and cry with their losses. But at the same time as you turn the pages you will laugh with their hilarity and enjoy the humorous side of rural life.

This is a book of many genres. It is funny, serious, historical, scriptural, romantic, poetic, heart-wrenching, and political. *While set in pre-World War II, it parallels what the world is experiencing today.*

Five-year-old LeRoy will make you laugh. However, other episodes will make you cry. It is about love, redemption, war, sacrifice, trusting in God in all circumstances, and for you mystery lovers it also has mystery. It is delightful, amusing, tear-jerking, and heart touching. Each chapter could stand alone as a short story, but they all weave together to make the whole.

But it is mostly about a people who loved and worshiped God in the good times and the bad; so that makes it an instruction book, a book of devotion and a book of hope.

People had their work clothes and their "Sunday-go-to-Meetin' clothes." They also had their "Sunday-go-to Meetin' shoes" which when they would no longer fit... or were worn from so many hand-me-downs... they became somebody's "workin" clothes and shoes.

Everything was hard to come by, and nothing was ever wasted. They had strong morals, good character, and an abundance of love. But more than these, they had respect for their God, their families, their church and their country.

The Depression years of the 1920s and 1930s truly lived up to the name. Times were depressing. Many people in those days were depressed, physically and emotionally; especially those who lost everything. There were those who could not even feed their families. Those who had a strong faith in God, the church, and each other had victory; while others did not fare nearly as well.

As the story of the Alrod's begin, the decade of the thirties was finally passing away into the history books, and there was renewed hope in the hearts of the American people following the Great Depression.

The prayer of the heart and on the lips of everyone was that the 1940s would bring prosperity and peace with God and the world. That was not to be.

Unbeknown to most Americans, Hitler was making his plans, and his way, across Europe, enslaving some, alienating others in his march to dominate the world. He left behind a path of death and destruction as he marched across and conquered one nation after the other.

The world was awakening from their slumber of apathy and good times to the deafening sounds of German boots; as soldiers stripped them of their weapons, their belongings, and many times their lives.

The Japanese were planning, conniving, and training for their entrance onto the world's stage. Pearl Harbor lay just around the bend. But here in this little valley, times were uncomplicated... family life simple... and families had time for each other. They worked together, played together, ate together, and all of them went to bed when the last light of the sun faded, and they attended church together.

They rose at the crack of dawn when the rooster crowed, and they went to bed "with the chickens" in the evening. Entertainment was a special occasion and not a daily occurrence.

They were just plain good folks; not to say they didn't have weaknesses that befall all of God's creatures. They had to confront the same traits, habits and dispositions of all sinners. And like Pastor Alrod always reminded them, it was a balanced life that God wanted for His children.

Pastor Alrod preached a straightforward truth to an uncomplicated folk and used illustrations from nature much like Jesus did. He encouraged them to be like the ant in Proverbs 6:6 where it says, *"Go to the ant, thou sluggard; consider her ways, and be wise: which having no guide, overseer, or ruler, provides her meat in the summer, and gathers her food in the harvest."*

He felt it was his duty to preach salvation; but also righteous and productive living. He taught them they should work hard, be independent, and not look to the government for handouts. He warned them about becoming lazy and apathetic like the sluggard in that same chapter.

> *"How long wilt thou sleep, O sluggard? When will you arise out of your sleep? Yet a little sleep, a little slumber, a little folding of the hands to sleep: and so shall your poverty overtake you and will come upon you as an armed bandit."* Proverbs 6:9

He wanted them to know God and live for God. However, he did not want them to be so heavenly minded that they were no earthly good. He often reminded them though they were sinners by birth, and habit, they had received immunity as children of God. They had been made children of God, not because they were worthy or because of anything they had done - good or bad - but because of the finished work of Christ, His son, on the Cross.

He told them that gaining their salvation, and the promise of eternity, should be enough to spur them on to good works. He constantly reminded them that they are to love one another; for that is the will of God. And that God is love and without God, there would be no love. Most churches, like people, have their own personality, and this minuscule church was no exception.

The little church also had it own unique set of problems; more often as not the roof needed fixing, or payment on the organ came due with no way in sight to pay it. And, there was the occasional squabble about "who hit who over the head with a hoe handle." In times like these, they prayed hard and walked by faith and not by sight.

Often the needs of the church were met with bake-sales, carnivals, and other fund raisers. And the women gave generously of their egg and butter money.

Way back in the hills... and way back then... they did not have air conditioning like today.

It was so hot in the summer that they could hardly breathe. The windows and doors of the church were opened wide not only inviting the folks to come in but every flying insect as well.

To cool themselves, they had cardboard fans with beautifully printed scenes from the Bible. They were donated by the local funeral parlor. What would be a better place to advertize than when people's minds were on the hereafter?

If the handle became detached, they would take the cardboard part in their hand; fan it back and forth to cool themselves and sleeping babies. They were often used to shoo away flies that would buzz around them.

During the winter, inside the church could be drastically cold. The freezing, blowing wind would find every tiny crack to blow through. While the old wood stove would be roaring hot and would sweat those nearby, those in the back would often have to wrap themselves in their coats to stay warm. It was an incentive for some to get to the church on time.

The church was not an organization or a building, but a called-out group of people who came to learn the teachings of Christ. There were no entitlement programs to help them financially, and there were no 911 calls bringing help – most didn't even have a phone in their homes. The doctor was sometimes days away in some other community.

A number of them were still using kerosene lamps for light. Very few had indoor plumbing. Some had water pumped into the kitchen, but there were still those who drew their daily water from a well. Some women still washed their clothes in a black wash pot in the yard and hung them to dry on a clothesline.

They had many reasons for coming to church. While they came to church for spiritual teachings, they also came to support one another. The men would stand around afterward talking about the weather, the crops, and other things of interest to men.

The children would run around and play with one another while the women got down to some serious understandings of what was going on in the community... like who was sick and needed help... who was going to have another baby... who was headed for the altar for Holy Matrimony, who had something new... or just women talk.

This little country church was the bedrock of the community; and the glue that held the family together. The church was the town's social life. It was a place to worship together, to dedicate their babies, to marry their sweethearts and to bury their dead. Twice a year, they held revivals to remind themselves and others that Christians needed to be revived, every now and then, as well.

The church didn't have a lot of planned programs, events, distinguished speakers or seminars, but they had a message... a vital message of salvation and redemption. They learned from the preaching of Pastor Alrod how man and woman were to love and honor one another, and how to bring up good children - who loved and obeyed them and God.

Rain, shine, hot days or snow, you could find the faithful there every Sunday morning waiting to see and be seen, to hear and to learn, to worship and to be blessed. They were there to fill their spirits with the love of Christ just as they filled their bellies with the delicious home-cooked Sunday dinners that followed. A handshake made an agreement binding, but it was also a gesture to extend a welcome and friendship.

A man's word was his bond, and the congregation was bound to one another by honor, character and their covenant with each other and God.

Pastor Alrod's church was a simple place in an open field on a small hill where wild flowers grew in the spring and summer, and where the snow in winter covered the land like the white frosting on Mama's homemade coconut cakes.

The hot summers brought out the fun and frivolity of picnics, swimming holes, and fishing. The fall of the year meant harvest, and when it was done.... a day of Thanksgiving. These were times when neighbors enjoyed each other's company. Everyone seemed to know each other's business, and that was okay. As in the church and outside the church, they were all members of one family... the family of God.

The church was never more beautiful than when it was covered with snow. Like the scripture that says, *"Though our sins are like scarlet, they shall be white as snow."* The snow covered all the ugliness and the repairs that needed to be done on this little backwoods meeting-house. Even the wood pile out back looked like a little mountain of white sugar.

Spring, summer or fall was a time when families sat on their front porch as their reward for a long hard day's work. The men would usually be smoking their pipes, the women snapping beans or mending socks while they spoke of family and told stories of long ago. Each family had their own history and felt it important that the children knew it clearly.

Lack of paint on the inside and out of the church went unnoticed by the wreaths of holly and evergreens that adorned every corner at Christmas. The men cut the boughs and the women and children met for a day of "Laying out the green!" The very first Christmas and the telling of the birth of Christ were celebrated as the foundation and the beginning of their faith.

In winter, the grounds were covered with snow. At Christmas, the boughs of holly and cedar sprigs were placed in strategic places alongside the candles with their flickering lights. The scene would put one in mind of the Currier and Ives Christmas cards. Even in the cold of winter, this sight beckoned family and strangers alike.

In the spring, this little church shook off the coldness of winter as it burst into new life. The tulips that lined the path leading up to the doorway, split opened their buds; and brought forth an array of breathtakingly beautiful colors. The promise of that renewed life abounded as the dogwood trees bloomed.

There was a certain kind of happiness throughout the church as everyone dressed in their new Easter finery. Easter was a time for getting new spring clothes; which during that next year would be "Sunday Meetin' clothes."

The church in the spring was a place of dinners-on-the-ground, homecoming, and Easter egg hunts. But most of all Easter was the fulfillment of Christmas.

These families are fictitious. However, their stories are reminiscent of true families who lived during these times. Folks, who grew up during this time in history, will easily associate them with their own lives.

Someone was forever telling family stories and children learned their history not from a book; but from generations of folklore. Storytelling was also their entertainment. The message of this story is about love, hope, redemption, friendship, but above all, family.

They listened to sermons of redemption from God through Christ, and how love was to be metered out with tolerance for one another. This is a story of family ties, neighborly kindness, and strong leadership by men and women who believed in God. This is the story of how they raised their children to be the same.

This was a place in time where generations of ancestors were born, where they died, and were buried in the graveyard - awaiting others to join them on Resurrection Day. Their markers proved that they had lived and died.

The rains washed away the last footsteps of those gone before but could never wash away their strong work ethic, and the influence they left behind. Their influence would live forever in the lives of those who came after them.

Pastor Alrod often told them their life would leave behind a fragrance; one that would be a pleasing aroma or a stench in the nostrils of God. He once preached a sermon, "Are you a rose; or a skunk in the nostrils of God?"

The congregation was made up mostly of farmers, but there were a few shopkeepers, and a barber who cut hair and prepared the dead for burial until a new funeral parlor opened.

There was a smattering of those with a higher education like the school teacher, the doctor, and the judge. The bank was in the city. It was mostly for making and paying back loans. There were only a few who had a savings account. There was still a distrust of banks since their failure in the 1920s, and they preferred to keep what cash they had nearby to oversee it themselves.

However, for most families, cash was a limited commodity. More likely as not their bank would be a cookie jar or Mason canning jar. And there were a few practicing trades like blacksmithing, carpentry, and a few salesmen peddling farm supplies or insurance, but most were farmers.

None of the businesses were open on Sunday, not even their one-pump gas station.

The proprietor had a large sign that said, "Gas up on Saturday and go to church on Sunday!" They worked six days a week, and like the commandment said, they rested and worshiped God on Sunday.

The parents were eager for their children to have more in life than they received. But it was more important for them to be brought up in the nurture and admonition of the Lord. They were eager to love and swift to correct them.

They had two Biblical philosophies in raising their children. One was to bring up their children in the way they should go... and prayed that when they were older, they would not depart from it.

Another was that they did not believe in spoiling the child by sparing the rod when it was necessary to discipline them. Discipline brought respect not only for the parents and others, but prepared them for adulthood. Pastor Alrod had taught them the word discipline meant to disciple and to teach.

Character made of love, respect, and honor was what parents wanted to instill in their children. The Ten Commandments were not just words from an ancient old book, but a framework for life. Their understanding was simple... they lived by them, and they expected others to do the same. "If God said it, they believed it, and that settled it."

They understood God did not hand down the Ten Commandments for His own good; but for theirs. God is Holy and without sin. But God knew that men needed rules to live by in order to honor Him and each other.

"If I don't steal your stuff and you don't steal my stuff, then nobody's stuff gets stolen."

Chapter one: The Old Worn-out Church

"I don't care what you think, George. It has got to come down."

The real estate broker addressed George as if they were old friends using his first name; however, they had never officially met.

George Henry Alrod, Jr., was a history teacher at the local high school. Sammy, this man's son, was one of his students. It seems that this father was too busy working all the time and didn't have time to come to parent-teacher conferences.

Looking down at the business card that he was given, he read, "Richard S. Cunningham, Broker and Real Estate Developer for Stiffe, Bennington, and Cooper." He wanted to make sure he addressed the gentleman before him correctly.

"But Mr. Cunningham, do you know what that church has meant to this community for nearly 160 years? Do you know that it dates back to before the Civil War?"

"Yeah… well, it looks like it."

"It should be made into a historic landmark and not turned into a shopping mall," said George with deep emotion in his voice.

"Hey, George, old buddy, call me Richard or Rick. Do you mind if I call you George?"

He replied, "I think you already have. We are not in the classroom, so first names are okay with me! Somewhat laughing to break the ice, George said, "My folks always called me "Georgie" growing up to differentiate me from my father, George Henry Alrod, Sr."

Ignoring George's effort, Richard Cunningham continued, "George, we have been through this on the phone already, and the decision has been made. This old church has been abandoned now for more than a decade. I only came out here as a favor to you. My kid thinks a lot of you as his teacher and wants to make sure he stays in your good graces."

"Sammy is a good boy and a good student. He does not need to be in anyone's good graces. He does just fine on his own."

"But it is thanks to Sammy that I got word of what was going on out here. I overheard him telling some of the other students in the hall that your company had been hired to oversee the selling of the old Alrod farm."

"And of course, I was interested. I asked around and found out about the proposed notion of turning my folk's old farm land into a shopping mall. That is why I asked you out here today to see if there was anything could be done to prevent the church from being torn down."

Slinging his arms around in the air, Richard practically yelled, "The church has outlived its usefulness, you know that! Why, there is not one single member left. Just take a look at it... it is falling down!"

George answered back, "For sure, I was never a member here, this was before my time, but my grandfather used to be the pastor of this little ole church, and my Alrod family lived on this land for over a century. That should count for something."

Hatefully, Richard replied, "The only way it could count for anything is at the bank. You got enough money to buy it at the prime offer made by the investment group who intends to build the mall?"

"Richard, you know that teachers don't make that kind of money, but this church and graveyard are historical, not to mention sacred, that should count for something, huh?"

Richard speaking with an irritated voice, said, "Well, sorry... but it doesn't? The council said unless a bona fide member of the church can be found; the land will revert to the county."

"There has been a title search, and as far as we can tell this property was never legally transferred into the name of the church; so, therefore, it is technically still part of the Alrod farm."

"Well, it just might interest you to know that there are still people who are interested in this church!" replied George.

Missing George's emphasis on **this** church, Richard shot back at him attacking all churches.

"For those who still care about all that church and God stuff, this is the age of televised preaching; where people can cry on each other's shoulders, send their money to buy prayer handkerchiefs or religious doodads; without even leaving home," said the real estate broker.

"Richard, we all know that you are a hard businessman, but you are relatively a newcomer to this town. You just haven't been around here long enough to understand the significance of this little Holy Place."

"True, this old building has seen its share of unfavorable years; it is only a shell... the outside... of the church, if you will. The church was and is the people."

"They are the history... not the building. And sadly too many people think that the church has outlived its usefulness, but as a Bible believer, I know this is not true."

George was on a roll and hardly paused to catch his breath, "The church is the body of Christ, with or without a physical structure, but this old building has stood the test of time, and it should be restored."

"Perhaps the farmland is gone, but we should be able to work out something about leaving the little church on the hill alone."

"Holy, Moly, George, there just isn't any place for sentimentality when it comes to the need of this community to have a mall within driving distance."

"The people... as the church might survive... however; I doubt it... these old relics of the past won't."

"Look at it, George; do you really think that old falling down, worn-out, outdated, useless building means anything to anyone anymore?"

"The rumor is that even large active churches are on the way out because of lack of membership."

"Don't believe that, Richard! God will always have a witness in this world until the end of time?"

Trying another tactic, Richard came back with, "This building is coming down. They're building newer churches everywhere. But have you noticed? They "ain't" making no new dirt?"

"This land is needed for development that will earn tax money and revenues from those who will use the new mall. Modern civilization and progressive thinkers have just bypassed that old mantra about the church being the people."

"Yeah, well maybe that is what is wrong with modern civilization and why folks are going to the devil in a fast hurry!"

Then Richard tried to make a joke when he said, "This is just an old falling down building with no people inside. Remember the little game we used to play by lacing our fingers together? You know the one. Here's the church and here's the steeple; open the doors, and there are **NO** people?" He emphasized the **NO!**

"A group of people can call themselves a building if they want to, but it won't make it so."

George was becoming upset at the man standing before him. First-name basis or not he saw no point in being respectful to him any longer.

"Richard, ole boy, you just don't understand. And, by the way, other folks saying there ain't no God don't make it so, either! You can tell me that there is no wind either, but I know there is because I can feel it even if I can't see it. I can see the evidence of it as well. Did you ever see the evidence of the wind after a tornado strikes? Pretty powerful, huh?"

Richard still attempting to make his case replied, "You have to understand what a boon this would be to this community; a mall would mean jobs and easy shopping. For over a century, people have had to climb down off this mountain to shop, and when small businesses did move in, they were not capable of offering all that the outside world could."

"Well, Richard, maybe the folks liked it up here in these mountains away from all that worldly stuff? For generations, they lived here and took care of their own. What they needed they somehow provided from the land. This community and the church were carved out of a place that no Flatlander could ever understand." George said getting a little more emotional.

"Maybe so, but that is just hogwash when it comes to the economy; and what should be available to the younger folks who are moving in up here. They are building fine mountain-vacation homes. They want more than just a few general stores to do their shopping. They have money and aren't afraid of spreading it around."

"Let me get this clear," said George. "So what you are saying is that it does not matter what the folks who have their loved ones buried out

4

back of this little church think or feel. If city folks want what the city has to offer, let 'em stay in the city!" George was getting more and more upset with each response.

With a condescending attitude, Richard said, "Now I have already made it clear that the cemetery will not be touched. We will set aside a little of the land, make a park around it and put a nice brick wall around it. No one will even know it is there! But the church building, the structure, has to go!"

"Their descendants will know." George quipped.

"George, you are just an old mushy sentimentalist. You need to get on board and come on up in the world. Man, there is money to be made here. When the mall is completed, we will have to build a bigger bank, more grocery stores, and that will bring in more trades and professions."

"I hear tell there are still only two doctors on this whole mountain. Just think, in time, we could build a large hospital; even another school or two. For heaven's sake, George, this is the twenty-first century not the 1890s."

"To tell you the truth, Richard, sometimes I wish it was still the 1890s. People knew how to live in those days and didn't put a price tag on everything."

Then angrily Richard blurted out, "Sorry, George, but the property will be reverting to the community since there is not one living member left, and that will be that. I have it on good authority that the town council is more than ready to move on this."

"And just whose pockets will be lined with the proceeds?" George asked.

"Tell me if you don't mind, just how big is your cut out of all of this?"

Richard irritated and about to blow his top at that question, screamed out, "I don't keep up with these things. I was hired just to gather the facts and bring it before the council."

George could see that Richard was getting angrier and knew he had to change the tone of the conversation and said, "Keep your wits about you, man… don't be so hot under the collar. You don't have to bite my head off! We are two intelligent men here. We can work through this without all of this conflict. I asked you to come out here today to see this, not just as another land deal, but as the history of this town."

He saw Richard's face get bright red. He wondered if he had high-blood pressure. He surely didn't want to make him have a stroke or something. But his demeanor, rotten attitude, and snide remarks about the church got his dander up.

And before he knew it he responded in like-kind, "On second hand, anyone as heartless as you can't be too heated up, you've got ice water in your veins and dollar signs in your eyes." He thought to himself, "There I said what I was thinking but I shouldn't have!"

But he still was not finished. George was just about in a fit of rage himself and said, "Don't you know that one day you will be laying underground in some forgotten place; and then is when you will have to give an accounting of what you did; and didn't do while on this earth."

George responded in a way, most uncommon to his milder nature. He certainly knew that was no way to try and win a soul for Christ. While he was ashamed of the way he was acting, he just could not seem to help himself.

He was astonished that he had become so angry. He dealt with unruly students all day long and never lost his cool, but this was just too important to take lying down.

Richard came back with, "George, you sound more like a preacher every minute. Maybe you missed your calling by being a history teacher. Still got a little of that preacher Hell-fire and brimstone in your DNA, huh?"

Walking toward his car, Richard Cunningham said, "The matter is settled, I'm out of here, I have discussed this enough! This is a done deal... just a matter of time!"

Still angry, George's reply was, "We'll see about that! It won't be a done deal until God says it is a done deal!" Seeing that his nemesis was leaving, George fired back at him elevating his voice an octave or two saying, "And what if we were to find members still alive?"

Not waiting for a reply, he continued, "And what if they wanted it turned into a museum... ahh... maybe a museum to honor small churches in history?"

Only a few steps away, Richard turned to him and said, "George, you can't be serious? You can preach all the "pie in the sky' rhetoric you want to, but this old church is coming down... and soon... and God hasn't got a thing to say about it... if there is one!"

Taking a deep breath and extending his hand to Richard for a handshake, George said, "Okay, Richard, let's both cool off a little bit and take a walk up the hill and take a look out back. Have you ever been to the cemetery?"

Richard did not respond. He just stood there with both hands on his hips, looking down at the ground.

In a lower and calmer voice, George explained, "Each one of those graves has two dates; the day the deceased was born and the day they died. The spaces in between those dates represent something... their life. It stands for lives lived with joy, hard work; and troubles aplenty I'll bet."

"Dead people don't count!"

"They can't vote, and they had their turn and now it is time to move on and let the younger generation have their turn," Richard shot back.

George continued to plead the case and thought perhaps if Richard knew more about the church and its people, he might come around.

"These people may be gone, but they're not forgotten. Even if people don't remember them or even recognize their names, they were here, living on this mountain. Their blood, sweat, and tears are part and parcel of this land, this valley, and particularly this church. It was the first church that was ever built in these parts."

"These people should be written down in the history books! These are not just graves, but real people who had stories of life, death, and infinity. These people buried out back dug up every tree root to make the road, they cut down every tree to build this church, and they hauled every rock from the creek and from the foot of the mountains to lay the foundation."

"This church stands today, after all these years, as a testament not only to the people who built it; but to those who worshiped here for over a century."

"The building speaks for the strength it represents. It represents these very mountains from which the foundation was built. Buildings, churches or homes that are built on a strong foundation... last. They are not like a lot of new houses that are built today on shifting sands.

The mountains are still standing; and so is this little church. They have lasted. So should the heritage of the people who originally settled this valley because the foundation, they laid here, is more than rock or stone."

George had been standing like a minister preaching in the wildwood. He realized that he had been preaching a sermon that would have made his minister ancestors proud. Sitting down on a nearby rock wall, George motioned to Richard to come and take a seat as well.

Surprisingly, Richard walked up and sat down. Was it because he was tired, ill, or worn out from arguing, or was George getting through to him? George hoped it was the latter.

As he sat down, Richard said, "Look George, we are not going to accomplish anything here. We both know it is out of our hands. The powers that be want this land for a shopping mall, and that is what it will be."

In a much calmer voice, George, said, "I guess you could be right, but at least hear me out. While I believe that it could be out of our hands; it is not out of God's."

The history teacher in George began to shine through, and he realized that he actually had Richard's attention; for a while anyway.

He began to tell the story of the church, the people, and the community; stories he had heard all of his life.

He began at the beginning. "The earliest marker is dated in 1850, and that was even before the church building was being built. A family traveling in a covered wagon was passing through these hills on their way out west. Their infant daughter, Martha Sue, had taken ill and died just a few miles from here. She only lived a few days. The people were just in the early stages of clearing the land and were no graves out back when they pulled up in their wagon."

"The father asked to speak to the leader of the church. He had seen the smoke rising from where they were burning the brush to begin laying the foundation. My grandfather, Samuel Goodroe Alrod, seven generations back, was summoned to where the men were working on the church. They had to flag down his mules since he was plowing that acreage right over there... just below the rise in this little hill."

George motioned to the land a little further down to where the old barn was still standing. He continued, "After a discussion, Samuel Alrod and the leaders of the church voted. They decided they should let them bury their little girl here; rather than bury her somewhere out in the woods... where she would never be remembered... or have anyone to care for her grave."

Richard started to butt in, but George held up his hand to indicate he was not through speaking yet. "The traveler offered a five-dollar gold piece to the church if they would let them bury her here. Taking just one look at that grief-stricken mother, the leaders declined the offer of the gold coin, but rounded up folks from all around the fledgling town to attend a proper funeral and burial for her."

"They came and stood with this family as they buried their sweet little girl in the ground. One of the men had taken some of the newly hewn lumber they were using for the church, and made her a little coffin. Some say her spirit is always here."

Finally, Richard broke in and said, "George, Ole boy, you are a great storyteller. You must keep the kids at school spellbound with your tales, but that will not amount to a hill of beans regarding the rest of this property," countered Richard.

George was not about to hush and continued, "This little girl became a symbol for many generations to come. Born, but only living a few days and straight from the hand of God, some believed that she was a guardian angel sent here by the Lord to reign over their loved ones who would one day be buried here one by one."

"Now George, get real... that is just a bunch of nonsense. Modern day and smarter people have moved past those old ancient fallacies and fairy tales."

George continued speaking as if he had not heard a word Richard had said, "About twenty years later a young man came by and made arrangements with the church to erect an angel statue carved of pure marble in her memory."

"He placed a smaller marker at her grave and positioned the angel statue in the middle of the cemetery. That angel has stood there unharmed by war and weather for more than a hundred years with her wings outstretched as if she is protecting them all."

"Civil War soldiers camped all over this valley and they respected this church and cemetery as if it were their own. Not a blade of grass was harmed, and they were bivouacked all over this area. Only a few of the soldiers entered the church, and that was to pray."

"That man was her older brother who was only eight years old when she died. He had vowed to one day return, and place a marker on her grave to honor his parents and... those humble town folks who had accommodated them on that dreadful day when they had to leave her behind."

"That is a cute story, George, but won't cut it. The church still comes down." Richard saw a small window of opportunity and spoke quickly.

"As the years went by," George told him, "most people didn't pay any attention to the little angel statue; until the day came when they had to bury someone they loved there."

"Knowing that story made people feel better because they knew they did not have to move on and leave their loved one behind. They would always have a place to come back to in order to remember and honor those who had gone on before."

Maybe it was just to get George to stop talking, or perhaps remembering this was his son's history teacher, and grades would be coming out soon, Richard seem to calm down.

Or perhaps, he just wanted to hurry him along because of another pressing appointment. Richard stood up with both hands in his pockets and said, "I don't see any point in pacifying you, but I'll give you at least that much. And then I don't want to hear any more about it! Let's take a look out back."

The front door of the old church, which was always open to all who wanted to enter, was still standing; though closed. It was weather worn and cheerless looking.

Potential juvenile delinquents had thrown rocks through the windows, and the weather had taken its toll on the old structure. With its peeling paint, it had such a lost and forlorn look about it. If its walls could speak, you would know they would have many a story to tell.

George felt the story of the church would be best told by the lives of those who built it, cared for it, and worshiped in it. Their stories lay buried with them in the cemetery… or did they? Immediately after he heard of the possibility of the church being torn down, he began to check the public records at the courthouse. They were in such a mess.

There had been a fire in the original courthouse, and a lot of the files had either burned or been destroyed by water. He was told there had been some old cardboard boxes in the attic that had not been gone through in years. He intended to go through them. He even thought that would make a good project for some of his students who might like to earn extra credit learning about their county.

As they approached the church, George thought back to the last time he had walked through that old dilapidated structure. He recalled sitting there with his own Dad when he said, "Listen son; you can almost hear the singing of those old hymns, see those simple weddings, and hear the soft sobbing of those attending the funerals!"

George used to think he could. Some of those stories loomed vividly in his mind once again. His family had kept quite a history in journals, old Bibles, and there must be some deeds and other documents he could find. But the real history of the Alrod family had been handed down orally from generation to generation. He hoped to find something written down.

He could also visualize the many hundreds who had knelt at the little altar bench when they gave their souls and lives to Christ. George had never worshiped within these walls with a congregation. However, he had often walked down the old dusty dirt road and up the hill to the church with his Dad.

It was such a peaceful place, and he would sit for hours listening to the stories told to him by his Dad. He could also see the people who came before them as his father described them; not so much for the way they looked… but by the way they lived.

These stories were handed down from generation to generation; dating back to the original Alrod farmer, Samuel Goodroe Alrod, who came from New York with his wife Rachel, and their son, Henry in 1850.

George Henry Alrod, Jr., the history teacher, was the seventh generation from the original Alrod's. Three of the Alrod men had been pastors of the church. George, Jr. attempted to explain the genealogy of the Alrod family by saying. "The first pastor from the Alrod family was James Goodroe Alrod, who was my great-great grandfather.

James was the grandson of Samuel. And then later Herman James Alrod, son of James, followed in his father's footsteps. The last minister serving the little church on the hill was one of Herman's sons, George Peter Wilson Alrod, who was my grandfather."

There had not been any services held in the church for several decades. Since then, the aesthetic appearance was in a deplorable run-down condition. The church structure was practically the same as when it was built in 1850; with only a few changes. Over the decades, they had added indoor plumbing installed to replace the outhouses. Some forty or fifty years ago, they built on a little room at the back that was used as a fellowship hall and nursery.

But for the most part, the church had remained just like it was when it was first built. It still had hard wooden seats. There was the bench altar down front where many had humbled themselves in prayer for salvation, for healing, and for their country. Many a prayer was said within those walls for by those who lived through a Civil War, two World Wars; a well as the Korean and Vietnam Wars.

One by one, the charter members and their families were eulogized in front of that little homemade pulpit. Afterward, the friends and loved ones humbly passed their coffins to honor them and their lives on this earth. Their spirits were with God, but their bodies had been buried out back in the graveyard.

Family and friends had the assurance that one day there would be a glad reunion day at the time of Jesus' Second coming. George was sorry he had not looked into this situation before as he always intended, but the time was just never seemed right, and on a school teacher's salary there was never enough money to restore it.

Once when Georgie was a very small little boy, he was sitting in the deserted little church with his Dad, George, Sr. He envisioned Jesus coming back on a beautiful white cloud with angels all around. He thought about how all the folks buried there would one by one rise up; and have new bodies. They would fall down on their knees and worship the Savior, who made eternal life possible.

He looked up into his father's face and asked his father, "Daddy, when the people rise up to meet Jesus, will they know each other?"

His father thought about it for a moment and said, "Georgie, I don't rightly know all the details, but I think they will. There is a scripture in the Bible that says we shall know as we were known."

He reached into his shirt pocket and took out the little New Testament that he always carried with him, and flipped a few pages over to 1 Corinthians 13:12-13 and read,

"For now, we see through a glass, darkly, but then face to face: now I know in part; but then shall I know even as also I am known. And now abideth faith, hope, charity, these three; but the greatest of these is charity."

After reading the passage, his Dad looked down at little five-year-old Georgie, who was looking up at him with deep admiration because he thought his father knew everything. Little Georgie asked, "Daddy, what does chair-ity mean? His father answered as he tousled his hair and said, "Why Georgie that means love… just plain ole love."

Then his father said in a joking-like way, "Hey, wouldn't that be a sight to behold with everyone rising up and going around and hugging each other and shaking hands and discussing old times?"

With the giggling of a little boy, Georgie replied, "Yeah, it would Daddy, and then I would get to see all my grandpas and grandmas."

"Well, Georgie, that is one of the mysteries of God, and if people don't recognize one another in the cemetery, they surely will in heaven!"

George was so lost in those memories for a while, he nearly forgot about Richard standing there red faced from walking up the hill.

Few changes were ever made to the structure, but they came into a more modern world in some ways. That little church was built with huge oversized beams and framing of the strongest of oak cut from the very trees that once stood in the nearby forest. The joints and joist were dovetailed, notched and nailed with nails almost the size of railroad spikes.

The siding had withstood the worst of storms, but now in some places, it was falling down, and the hardwood floors had survived thousands of shuffling of feet. At some time in more modern days, the hardwood floors had been covered over with some kind of vinyl flooring. The church was surely in bad shape in some places. But the structure was as strong as the day it was built.

A furnace replaced the old pot bellied stove. However, there was never any air-conditioning. The cardboard fans from the funeral home had been replaced with four ceiling fans. They had long ago been ripped from the ceiling by thieves.

The Reverend Herman Alrod, George's great-grandfather, was the pastor during the Depression, World War II, the Korean War, and up to the beginning of the Vietnam War. He farmed the remaining 150 acres adjacent to the church as Samuel and James Alrod had in their time.

Henry was the son of Samuel Goodroe Alrod, and he was the father of James Goodroe Alrod. Henry never took to farming and left there as a young man. James was raised by his Grandfather Samuel.

George, Jr., felt he had grown up right in the middle of a history factory. No longer was history just a story about famous people in history books but was dynamic through the lives of those in his own family.

They had lived history. And... they were history.

These stories became all the more real when he associated them with the actual old pictures of his ancestors that were pasted in the family photo album. These people became real to him when he correlated them alongside the facts in the history books.

As a child, he would stare at those old photos, look into those faces, and remember their places in history. He sometimes felt they were looking back at him. Were they trying to tell him something?

Chapter two: Gone but not Forgotten

A group of immigrants came down from the other side of that mountain in a wagon train somewhere around 1850.

They could only bring with them what they could load onto a single covered wagon. Here on this land, where George, Jr., was standing, the Alrod's made their home, planted their fields, built a church and lived their lives in peace until the Civil War began in 1861.

Samuel Goodroe Alrod and his wife Rachel left New York and felt so blessed that they were finally able to have their own land. And to show their gratitude to God, they laid aside ten acres to build the little church on the hill.

It had been a long journey for Samuel coming across the Atlantic to New York from Northern Ireland in 1845. Finally, five years later, he was able to buy this land. There were many folks who came before, and after him, who were of the Scot-Irish descent and the Protestant faith. They had a tendency to settle in the mountain regions in America.

Most all the folks, who came in the wagon trains all across America, were immigrants; originally from places all around the globe. A church building was important to them. And so it was with those who came along with Samuel and Rachel.

Those immigrant farmers spent many hours cutting the wood and hewing out the huge timbers to erect the walls and roof of the church. They used axes and saws to fell the huge oak trees that grew on the Alrod land. They hauled rocks from the nearby creek to lay the foundation. All of the work done on the church was after the men had worked long hard hours on their own farms. They were skilled craftsmen.

They knew that God would send them a preacher when the time was right. However, it would be some time before they had a permanent pastor.

When it was finished, they met in the little church every Sunday for prayer and Bible reading with first one gentleman and then the other leading the service. Some of the women would sing, and they all would pray and worship God.

They met in the church even before the four walls were up and before the roof was attached. For several months, the roof was nothing more than several tarps from the covered wagons.

After a while, they were able to have real Sunday Meetin' services when the circuit-rider preacher came; which was normally twice a month. Sometimes, he could not come at all when the weather prohibited him from coming across the mountain on horseback.

He would arrive on Saturday evening and spend the night with one of the church families. Often it would be the Alrod family. He would preach both Sunday morning and Sunday evening services and spend the night again. He would then head back over the mountain at first light on Monday morning.

They planned weddings, christenings, and baptisms around the times when he would be there. They often had to bury their loved ones out back in the cemetery with a deacon or other church member officiating. That could not wait.

In the early days, there was never enough money to attract a full-time minister. That would involve building him a place to live and an income to care for his own family. They took up a collection on these two Sundays out of the month. What they collected, they paid the circuit-rider. On the other two Sundays, they used the tithes and offerings for the church's missions.

They had little or no money for the upkeep of the church, but the Lord's house never went lacking. The people who so lovingly built it – also lovingly cared for it. The men kept up the repairs, chopped the wood for the stove and the women cared for the inside; and the grounds around the church. Each family cared for the graves of their own loved ones buried in the cemetery which grew and grew over the years.

No grave ever went unrecognized on their annual Memorial Day when folks came from miles around to attend a special Sunday service to honor those who had died. Those who lived close enough came the Saturday before to make sure the cemetery was free of weeds and overgrowth. Many who had moved away made sure they would go back to the church on special occasions; if at all possible.

On Memorial Day Sunday, the family members placed wreaths on their loved one's graves, and afterward they had dinner on the grounds. They also made sure the cemetery was in tip-top shape before their annual Homecoming Day, which was held once every year in the late spring or early summer.

Graves, which no longer had a family member to honor them, were taken care of by the women of the church. They would make sure each one had freshly picked wildflowers on the graves.

Huffing and puffing all the way up the old overgrown drive, Richard, the real estate broker, walked briskly over the rubble and trash that had been dumped there by careless people. Someone had even dumped an old bed mattress there.

Half out of breath, he said, "Looks to me like a bunch of no-goods use this as a hangout for their parties and such. Just look at all the soda pop and beer bottles, the potato chip bags, and downright vulgar trash."

Catching his breath, he continued, "The sooner this place is cleared out, the better off the community will be!"

George, Jr., acknowledging the misuse of the property said, "Kids do hang out here. However, come Memorial Day, this place will look a whole lot different. Folks still come from all around to take care of their ancestors' last resting place. It is a tradition that has never changed; even if the world has."

George outpaced Richard, and while he was waiting for him to catch up, he stood quietly looking out across what once was vast cornfields, but now growing nothing but wild grasses and wildflowers.

He remembered standing there as a boy with his father and grandfather looking out over high fields of corn waving in the wind. For a moment, he was taken back to that time.

The house and the smaller out-buildings had long been demolished. However, standing as a keeper of the land was the old leaning barn. All the Alrod children had played in that old barn, and all across the fields.

Now the whole neglected area looked like a huge grave with the old barn standing as a marker for what once had been there.

George made a mental note to check the courthouse records to see who the current owner was. Someone must have been paying the taxes on it.

As they were approaching the building, Richard continued talking to himself, "Well, what is the big deal…get rid of the building…get rid of the kids – get rid of the trash and put up a brick wall around the graves. Solves all the problems, at once, huh?"

As they rounded the corner of the building, Richard was taken back somewhat. Everything all around had been overgrown for years, including the farmland where the Alrod's home and outbuildings once were.

Overgrown and rundown as everything was in the front of the church, the cemetery did not seem to be neglected. Richard was astonished to see there were fresh graves there as well. And even the older ones did not seem to be neglected. No sinking graves or busted up tombstones like he had seen in other abandoned graveyards.

He had actually seen trees growing up from graves in other old cemeteries; but not here. He was slightly impressed… but would never let George know it. Oddly enough, he felt a strange kind of peace when he looked at the statue of the guardian angel standing there in the center of the burial ground. She was covered with a green patina of algae and mold.

George explained how on cleanup day before Memorial Day, a group would come with brushes and a solution to clean off all the green gunk and bird droppings that had accumulated over the past year.

Richard thought to himself how he kinda liked it that way. Somehow, it stood for something he could not quite understand.

The first grave that George pointed out was that of little the infant child who was the very first one to be buried there. Her marker read:

Martha Sue Higgins Precious little Angel
Daughter of Joel and Martha Ann Higgins
"Budded on earth to bloom in Heaven"
Born 1850 – Died 1850

He could see the great pride on George's face as he pointed out his ancestors' graves.

George said, "Over here are some of the oldest Alrod graves. There are the graves of Samuel Goodroe Alrod and his wife, Rachel. They were my fourth great- grandparents."

He stopped for a second and jokingly said, "Hey, Richard, isn't your middle name Samuel? He might be kin to you."

Stomping through the overgrowth, Richard said, "Not likely, my folks came from a place so far from here I am sure they never knew it existed."

Being a city boy, he was looking everywhere he stepped for fear a snake would jump out and bite him. They had scared a rabbit off when they approached the building. There, it sat nibbling on the sweet grass growing beside the front stoop.

George continued, "Here are the graves of James Alrod and his wife, Sarah. He was the first of the Alrod's to serve as pastor. After coming back from the Great War, he felt the call to preach, and the congregation felt the call to let him. They were my great-great-grandparents."

George explained, "Later his son, Herman Alrod, would become the new minister. Herman... his wife, their children, spouses, and grandchildren are over there a little further. They were my great-grandparents."

"My grandfather, George Peter Wilson Alrod was the youngest of Herman's children. He and his family are buried here as well. He was the last minister to serve here at the church. He was my father's Papa."

"When my Dad was born they gave him George as part of his name; and then when I came along they named me after my father, George Henry Alrod; making him a senior and me the junior. My mother never liked it when people would call a child, "junior" as a name; so they started calling me, Georgie... and it stuck... at least in the family."

Richard, the real estate broker, was born in a big city. The people there were either cremated or buried in large city cemeteries. He had an odd sense of family as he walked past the many graves... graves of families who shared life together on this earth... and shared final resting places as well.

He shrugged off an intense feeling of family thinking to himself, "All of George's family and his 'God talk' must be rubbing off on me!"

George had not noticed. He kept right on talking, "Herman Alrod and his family, was the fourth generation to live on the farmland adjacent to the church. Several more generations would come after him. He was my great-grandfather."

George continued to point out the individual graves; as if he were taking a group of students on a guided tour through a historic cemetery.

His great-great-grandfather, James Goodroe Alrod, was the first Alrod to pastor the little church on the hill. He served from 1920 to 1931. There had been numerous pastors from 1850 to 1920; some of the early ones were circuit-riders.

None of them were Alrod's, and none of those preachers had lived on the land. However, all of them were men of God, and they had ministered to the people through the Civil War and the First World War.

James Goodroe Alrod was buried alongside his wife, Sarah. They were the parents of Herman James Alrod and his sister Pauline. Herman, James' son, would serve as pastor there for about 29 years from about 1931 to 1960.

George Peter Wilson Alrod was Herman's youngest son and the last Alrod to pastor the church. Wilson, as he was called, would farm the land and pastor through the late 1990s.

The 1980s had been troublesome times for American farmers when thousands of farmers were forced into bankruptcy. The value of their land dropped, and a huge increase in interest rates caused many farmers to fold and lose their farms. This was the worst disaster since the Depression.

The Alrod farm had survived that crisis; but barely. America began importing a lot of food from other countries, and small farmers could not compete with farming corporations. When old age and ill health, prevented Wilson from continuing on the land, he moved in with his son George Henry Alrod, Sr. and there he died a few years later. The church closed; the old farmhouse and outbuildings were torn down leaving only the barn and the church. George, Jr. (Georgie as he had been called) had not given a lot of thought to who owned the Alrod farm after then.

Georgie's own father George, Sr., had not enjoyed good health in the years following his own father's death. George, Jr. had spent many years away from the valley. He served a hitch in the Navy, and when he returned to the states, he made use of his GI bill and went to college. He had only recently returned to be with his father who was in poor health. He applied for and was accepted as the new history teacher in the very school he had attended before leaving for the Navy.

It never occurred to George, Jr., who would hold the land after his father's death. He never considered that the land might have fallen to his father after his Grandfather Wilson died. But if what Richard Cunningham was telling him was true, the land never appeared to have been deeded from son to son.

A lot of the records that far back were either lost in the courthouse fire or were lost when moving into the new one.

It was just the natural course of things since Samuel originally bought the land that it was handed down the line first to James, Herman and then to Wilson. It was a real concern now for George, Jr., that there were no apparent records showing that the land for the church had ever been deeded to the congregation. Somewhere in the back of his mind he recalled there had been a problem sometime in the past when Herman Alrod owned the land.

After coming back to the valley and getting settled into his new job at the school, he was preoccupied with caring for his aging father whose health had become progressively worse. His mother had passed away some years before.

Being relatively new to the community after his long absence, George had the responsibility of caring for his ailing father, and the old Alrod place had not crossed his mind. He assumed that someone had bought it.

Recently, it had become more important to him; especially when he heard one of his students saying that it was being considered as prime property for a mall to be built there. The rumor was that if the land deal went through, they were going to tear down the little church on the hill. That concerned him.

The membership at the church had dwindled to only a few between the time of Wilson's leaving and the new millennium. While a few still met for prayer and to oversee the cemetery, there was never another preacher or congregation there after Georgie's Grandfather George Peter Wilson Alrod had resigned.

Most members had died or had moved away. None of the younger generation was interested in the old church on the hill and by 2004, there was no one left. It was thought, at that time, there were a couple of members still alive, but living somewhere in nursing homes. But that had been almost ten years ago.

There were super highways where once there were only dirt roads, and most everyone in the mountains had a good running automobile. It took very little time anymore to drive into the city. The newer generation had little interest in the old country church.

They wanted larger everything; buildings with modern conveniences; and paved parking lots. They wanted more activities, more programs, and more entertainment. Wilson, Georgie's grandfather, always felt what they needed more of was God.

Georgie Alrod, Jr. thought the farm must have been sold many years before, but now it was important for him to find out because of the recent events.

After Grandfather Wilson had moved in with Georgie's folks, it was never again a producing farm after then. The land lay idle for years as there were no Alrod men left to plow, till, or dig out a living out from the soil. Most of the older generations had died out. Apparently, it had been of little concern to anyone as to who presently owned the land.

Could the bank have taken it over? No one had seemed to care, or be bothered enough, to find out until now. Georgie's concern was not for the land which may have been sold for back taxes – he didn't know. But he was concerned about having the little church on the hill torn down.

Nevertheless, the cemetery itself had received some minimal care. That led Georgie to think there must be some folks still around that cared. Sometimes when folks were doing the genealogy of their family lines, they would track down the old cemeteries and make tombstone rubbings to put into their albums, but when cameras came along – that was much easier.

Richard, the real estate broker, was only halfheartedly listening to George, Jr. He was preoccupied with something on his mind; as he was constantly looking at his watch. He kept reminding George that he had a meeting in town soon. George continued with his descriptions saying, "Then on over a little further are graves of soldiers who lost their lives in the Civil War."

He also pointed out where there were also graves with no actual bodies buried there. They represented soldiers who were buried in foreign lands like France, Korea, and Vietnam. Their families wanted a place so they could come and honor their fallen heroes.

George, Jr., had narrowly missed being caught up in the Gulf War in 1990. He was in college at the time. Georgie came home on few occasions during and after college. His childhood sweetheart, Samantha Jones, left the valley, where she was born and raised, to marry him when he came back from the Navy. They lived in a small apartment in another city during his college days.

George continued to point out the plots in the graveyard, saying, "Here in this first section was the place reserved for those charter members who actually built the church in the early 1850s."

The graves of the benefactors of the church, Samuel Goodroe and his wife Rachel had a prominent place in the center of the cemetery; since they had donated the land for the church in 1850.

Their grave plots were bordered by a small concrete frame around their graves with a marker in the center upon which was mounted a brass statue of a plowshare with a cross extended across it. The inscription read,

Dedicated to the memory of
Samuel and Rachel Alrod
Keepers of the faith - Sustainers of the land
"Well done, thy good and faithful servants"

Raising his hand and pointing in another direction, he said, "And over there scattered around are the hundreds who sustained the church through the many years that followed, including many of the old pastors and their families."

George went into a monologue of explanations by saying, "I am humbled, beyond words, to know the kind of people that my ancestors were."

Richard still out of breath and still not interested, kept looking at his watch; as he pretended to listen... just to pacify George. He reached into his pocket, to take out a cigarette; then had second thoughts and put it back.

George, Jr. had an epiphany. The thought, soft as a whisper, crept into his mind, and he found himself thinking for the first time, "Had it not been for them, I would not be here." That was the first time he had ever thought about that. He had this sudden perception that something extraordinary was being revealed to him.

Then he turned and spoke directly to Richard in a manner which was so deeply felt saying, "If it had not been for the settlers in this country, we would not have the magnificent and free country that we enjoy today. We rest on their laurels and are the recipients of their hard work, their devotion to God, family, and country. We only have today what they built in previous generations. Everything we have we owe to someone else who came before us!"

George walked up and stood before his grandparents' graves. He took his hat off. He bowed his head; and paid respects to his beloved grandparents; realizing for the first time just how much he owed them. George remembered what his Grandfather had said about the church when he was a small boy. He said, *"Sometimes the church had to be like cast iron and other times like eiderdown; soft to the touch. It couldn't be neither alone - but had to be both. The church had to be strong enough to stand against sin and those who would destroy it, and yet, it had to be loving, kind, forgiving, and accepting of all who entered her doors."*

George, Jr. was thinking to himself this might be the time for the church to be like cast iron. Then he remembered what his grandfather had told his father, George, Sr., when he lay dying. George Peter Wilson Alrod held George Sr.'s hand, and said, "Son, hand me my Bible and open it where the ribbon is and read to me what it says."

"I have underlined the passage there in Acts 20:28." George, Sr. read from his father's Bible, *"Take heed, therefore, unto yourselves, and to all the flock, over which the Holy Ghost hath made you overseers, to feed the church of God, which He hath purchased with His own blood."*

George, Sr., Georgie's father, asked his father, Wilson, "Papa, what does that mean?" He replied, "Son, God has blessed you with a little son, George, Jr., and one day perhaps he will have a son. That has been the plan of God since the creation of time that families be joined with a bond stronger than any other. He created them to be "blood kin."

"It is through the blood of our forebears that we have life on this earth, and it was through the blood of the Son of God that we might inherit eternal life. Then he said a profound thing to the ears of little Georgie, Jr. *"Just remember this one thing, families are forever, and no matter what - love remains."*

While standing there and looking down at his grandfather's grave, that scripture came back to him. It went through his mind like a flash that perhaps his grandfather was speaking to him from the grave that he should be strong as iron and take a stand for the little church on the hill. The epitaph on the double headstone read,

George Peter Wilson Alrod and Allyson MacIntyre Alrod
Joined together on earth by love and marriage
Forever together in heaven by faith

When Richard looked up, he saw tears running down the cheeks of George, Jr. and trying to get him distracted, said, "Hey, look at this grave over here. Must have been a pauper; for who would want to be buried in a place like this today?"

A short distance away from their graves was a newly dug grave. It was so new it was yet to have a marker. It was only a few steps from the graves of George's grandparents. And it was so fresh that the flowers had not completely wilted. Richard said almost mockingly, "Wonder, who **IS** buried there?" with emphasis on the **"IS."**

George did not respond but looked at him through tear stained eyes. He took off his heavy framed glasses and wiped them with his handkerchief; as the two men walked away. There was complete silence between the men as they walked away from the cemetery and back down the hill to their waiting automobiles.

Apparently, Richard was no longer paying attention, when George, Jr. turned and said, "My father!"

Richard said, "Your father, what?"

George, Jr., replied. "You asked who was buried in the new grave back there… and I said, "My father!"

With a cracking voice, he said, "It was his last request to be buried beside my mother, Martha Ann Simpkins Alrod; and his parents George Peter Wilson and Allyson MacIntyre Alrod. And some day I will be buried here alongside the other Alrod's who came before me; along with my wife, Samantha Jones Alrod."

He had never thought of that before as he and his wife had never discussed where they would be buried. But the roots of their ancestry grew deep in that little church, and he felt it only fitting that he should also be buried among the Alrod men who preceded him. Samantha was also a descendant of one of the early church members.

Richard was too stunned for words, but he did not let on. He felt embarrassed that he had asked in such a mimicking way.

George Alrod, Jr. left that day with a new determination to find out more about the church, the land, and the people who had owned it. The valley had been settled by the Alrod's, Simpkins', O'Brien's, Jones', Macintyre's, Ferguson's, and so many others. He could not let their legacies die.

Richard, the real estate broker, apparently was only somewhat moved by the day's events. He left there with the same determination to turn the land into a shopping mall. He could not let sentiment interfere with the large commission he would make when the land sold.

Chapter three: The Preacher's Wife

The year was 1939. America had not fully recovered from the Great Depression. But life had to go forward. Families continued to go about their daily routines trusting in God for the barest of necessities, and thanking Him for all that they did have rather than just bellyache about what they didn't have.

Mama had been rushing around all morning trying to put the finishing touches on Sunday dinner, getting little James dressed, and then herself. If there was one thing she didn't like, it was people coming into church late.

Some liked to make a spectacle of themselves parading in after everyone else was seated. Mama was a loving and kind woman; not apt to much gossip or criticism. Nevertheless, there were just some things that bothered her; mainly anything that was not honoring to the Lord or the little church on the hill.

As a pastor's wife, she had many duties other than just being a Mama. She and her husband, the Reverend Herman Alrod, had to make allowances not only for their large family; but also the family of God, who regularly attended services at the church.

It was not often that the women in the valley got anything new to wear, and when one did, the others took notice. Still it upset her when one of the women would get a new dress or hat - and then came traipsing into church late; just so they could be seen. Perhaps she was a little jealous. Perhaps she needed to talk to the Lord a little more about that.

Sometimes families would come in late with their babies and children. It would interrupt the meeting with all their noise and bustling around. It was important for her to be an example to other women and families by always being on time.

That put a lot of extra pressure on her. There was probably no other woman in the church that was scrutinized or criticized more than a preacher's wife. She had to be all things to all people, and sometimes she grew weary of that role. She often told Herman when something was bothering her, "I married a farmer - not a preacher – much less a farmer and a preacher!"

Mama loved the Lord, first and foremost. And she loved her husband, the farmer-preacher man. She had loved him from as far back as she could remember. She never wanted to embarrass him, or cause any undue attention brought to her.

Often, she asked him, "Do you reckon a preacher's wife should be called of the Lord just as a preacher is called?"

Then she would sometimes say, "Today, I just don't feel called!"

Herman would just grin at her and pull her over into his lap, or from across the bed, and say, "I know exactly how you feel, but you married me... the man – not the farmer and not the preacher –but the man. Besides, you could not hep yorself. I would never have given up on you until you said, "Yes."

Once, he said, "I could have easily been a shoe salesman."

"Squirming away from his tickling her, something she could not stand, she replied, "Sometimes I wish you were. At least we could get a discount on all the shoes that the children outgrow so quickly."

Sometimes he would say, "Well, I could have been a soldier." And she would say, "And, you would probably shoot yourself in the foot!" No matter what occupation he came up with, she always had an answer, and soon she would forget what she was bothered about.

When she got particularly stressed, she would ask, "Do you suppose the preacher's wife could resign without the preacher having to resign?"

He would only laugh at her and say something like, "But, Sweetie Pie, then the church would not get what they had bargained for... only one-half of me... since we are as one! Do you think the church would settle for half a preacher?"

Then she would say something like, "Herman James Alrod, you could never do anything half-way." And he would say, "Especially loving you!" When he said things like that, she was all gone.

Once, after a very trying meeting with the deacons about a difference of opinion, he came home and asked Mama if the preacher could resign and let the church just keep the preacher's wife? She popped him on the arm with her dishrag; because she knew when he was "ragging" her.

Still very much a beautiful woman in her mid-thirties, Herman adored her and loved her with every inch of his life. She would have never considered marrying anyone else. If he had not asked her, she would have probably just pined away and remained a spinster.

He had never been embarrassed about anything that Mama did. Herman depended on her in many ways with regards to the shepherding of the little flock; especially the women.

She was kind, loving, and always available to any of the women in the congregation that needed a helping hand, a bit of advice, or teaching. Then again, she did not bend her principles or her faith in God to be popular.

She was dutiful in all her ways at church and at home. She had learned well that which her mother had taught her growing up. She lost her mother when she, herself, was a young mother. Her mother had died in childbirth; and so did her baby sister. That was always a burden she carried; especially when she would be expecting a new baby.

God had been good to her. All of her children were born with no problems whatever. They all had been born at home… the first two were safely delivered by a local midwife that everyone called, "Granny Wilson." The others were born with the assistance of a doctor.

She was always thankful for the women God put into her life as mentors. She always wanted to follow in their footsteps, teaching the young women who came behind her.

After she and Herman were married, they moved into the house with Herman's folks on the Alrod farm. The farm consisted of one hundred fifty prime acres of bottom land, and for generations corn had been their major cash crop. Each year Herman rotated the corn crop and grew other produce where the previous year's corn had grown.

They had a small, but comfortable, house. The house was well built and tight against the weather. Samuel Goodroe Alrod, Herman's great-grandfather, had built the house some years after arriving in the valley in 1850.

It was built along about the same time as the little church on the hill. Samuel and his wife Rachel lived in their covered wagon for several months after arriving from New York. He later built them a little lean-to shack of a house where they lived several years; until they established their farm and crops.

Between clearing the land for the cornfields and for the church, Samuel worked as much, and as often, as he could building this home for his wife and son. He did not want to rush the process, but wanted to make it strong like the house in the Bible; built on solid rock, and not on shifting sands.

It had a solid rock foundation made from huge stones hauled a few at a time from the creek that ran through his property. The timber for the house, roof, and floors were made from hardwood cut from oak trees right there on the land.

Samuel built his barn before building the house since it was needed for farming the land and sheltering the farm animals. The other outbuildings consisted of a chicken coop, outhouse, smokehouse, and spring house next to the creek. Some years later he also took advantage of the drop-off in the creek to build a small grist mill for milling his corn.

Herman Alrod was the fourth generation to live on the land. Very few things had changed from the time his father, James Goodroe Alrod, had followed in the footsteps of his grandfather Samuel. The Alrod farmers skipped a generation as James' father, Henry, was born with wanderlust, and he hated living on the farm.

Henry left the farm as a young man and came back into the lives of Samuel and Rachel spasmodically; usually when he needed them for something. One of those times, he brought back a pregnant wife, and they would name the baby James Goodroe Alrod.

It was believed the reason they named him after Samuel was to get in his good graces. Soon after the birth of the baby, Henry and Rebecca left. They left in the middle of the night; leaving the baby behind. Samuel and Rachel raised James as if he were their own. And he inherited the land when they died.

Herman grew up thankful that his father, James, had such wonderful godly grandparents as Samuel and Rachel; but he often felt sad he never really knew his own grandfather, Henry.

Herman was also thankful for the care in which his great-grandfather, Samuel, had laid out the land for its best use and convenience. The barn and the house had stood the test of time. When Herman became the owner of the farm, he and Mama had to build a couple extra rooms on the front of the house for their growing family.

The back of the house was the main entrance for all of their comings and goings. The entry way came immediately off of the dirt road and up into their yard. A little further up the road past the house was the entry way to the little church on the hill just above their property.

There were huge oak trees on either side of the house that Samuel had planted many decades before. They were strong and had deep roots and kept the house cooler in the hot summer months, but they were a chore come fall when all those leaves had to be raked away.

There was no grass growing in the yard of the back entrance; but rather a sandy yard. The sand from the yard got tracked into the house, and the floors had to be swept often. The yard was almost as hard to keep as the house. It had to be raked often to clear it from falling debris.

The oak trees shed little tassel-like things called catkins, and the sweet gum trees shed little spiked-balls all over the yard, and there were plenty of leaves and pine needles to be raked up as well.

Papa always kept Mama and the kids a supply of brush brooms made from the strong, but fine branches, of oak trees. They were tied together with heavy twine or wire. They made crisscross tracks in the sand after it was swept clean from debris.

On the back of the house, there was a slanted roof that covered the back porch where many activities of the day took place. While it was really the back door to the house, it was always an "open door" for family, friends and strangers alike.

The porch was raised about four feet above the ground with wooden steps leading up to it. And you could almost always find "Snooper," their beagle hound sleeping underneath the porch.

There were plain wooden banisters on either side of the steps made from sturdy 2 by 4's. Instead of common rails around the top, there were shelves that rested above the balusters.

Mama used the shelves for many purposes. In warm weather, at the top of the steps, she had clay pots of red geraniums sitting on the shelves on either side of the entrance. She loved geraniums.

To the right side of the porch on the end was her utility space which she used every day. There she processed and prepared vegetables for cooking and canning. Above that stretch of shelves, was a clothes line where she hung towels, wash rags, and dish rags to dry; or any of the hand washing she had to do.

The screen door was aligned with the steps coming up to the porch. Against the wall to the right of the screen door, leading into the kitchen, was a shelf attached to the wall. Here sat a fresh bucket of water for drinking; along with a long handled dipper that was shared by everyone.

There was a small white enamel wash pan with a red rim that was used to wash dirty hands before coming into the house. Papa made corn shuck rugs so everyone could wipe as much sand from their feet as possible before entering the kitchen.

Beside the pan was a soap dish containing bar of Octagon soap for scrubbing those really dirty hands. Just above the shelf holding the wash pan, there was a small mirror and a towel rack that held a common towel for all to share.

Mama's voice could constantly be heard coming from behind the screen door from inside the kitchen saying, "Be sure to wash yor hands!" And likely as not, she would also say, "Be sure to wipe yor feet!" She kept old croker sacks near the door for wiping muddy feet. Shoes, that were especially muddy, would be taken off and left on the porch.

On the left side, of the porch; and to the left of the screen door, sat two oak rocking chairs. Just behind the rocking chairs next to the wall of the house there were a couple of mixed-matched straight-back chairs. On the far end of the porch to the left was a large porch swing hanging by sturdy chains.

James, who was a master carpenter, had made the two rocking chairs for himself and his wife Sarah many years before. He also made the swing. These showed his wonderful talent of woodworking. They all were made of the finest dried oak wood. All through the house, you could see the work of his skilled hands. He made most of the furniture for the woman he had loved all of his life, his beloved Sarah.

Sometimes Mama felt like an intruder living among the beautiful things that had belonged to other women, but she cherished each piece and took good care of them as they had, and she wanted them to be handed down to her daughters one day.

All the couples, whoever lived in the house at the time, sat in those rockers for many hours; looking out across the land and... beyond the low hills to the mountains. They could see the coming and going of all the seasons and the stars in the sky on a clear night. Sometimes, they would just sit and wait for someone to come home.

Sitting there, they watched as bad weather approached, or they would sit and pray that the little gray cloud way off in the distance was bringing a refreshing rain for the dry crops; and for their comfort on a hot day. Or, they would pray that the strong winds that made the corn wave back and forth would subside before they broke the stalks of the new budding corn.

The large barn was built by a true carpenter, Samuel. During the Civil War, it once housed a troop of soldiers passing through. Many new baby animals had been born inside. It had been used for other purposes as well – like playing hide-n-seek.

The beam, rafters and all of the support wood was made of solid oak using the mortise, or the tongue and groove method, for joining the wood together. The original roof was covered with thin wooden tiles; placed in an overlapping fashion that would allow the rain to run off quickly.

The original barn continually served the farm well for over a century. It never needed any additions or major changes; just modest repairs and upkeep. There were adequate stalls for the animals; when it was necessary for them to be inside. The hay was stored in the loft for feeding them. Inside the barn was a stair-type ladder for climbing up into the loft.

On the outside of the barn, high above the huge double doors was a window-like opening with doors that swung outward like shutters. Above the square opening in the barn, there was a pulley that was used to hoist the bales of hay up into the loft. Below, inside the barn near the back, there was a corn crib where the dried corn was stored.

In Samuel's day, and also in the early years when James was farming, the rich soil was turned by mules that pulled the plow for planting. In the 1920s, many farmers began using machinery to do the work, which was faster and more efficient.

During that time, James bought a second-hand tractor which Herman learned to drive at a young age. After Herman had taken over the farm, he kept it running by every means possible until finally one day it just lay down and gave up the ghost.

The Depression hit all of America hard, and there were few extra dollars for anything as extravagant as a new tractor. In 1938, Herman was between a rock and a hard place being unable to buy a new one, and without one, it would have been almost impossible for him to get his corn crop in the ground.

As with everything, Herman and Mama prayed and asked God to lead them toward a solution.

There was a member of his church who had purchased new a 1937 *John Deere AR* farm tractor. He, too, was between a rock and a hard place trying to keep the tractor and to save his land. He came to Herman, his minister, with a heavy heart for prayer and advice. The bank was just before taking the tractor. But for Herman, it was a God send.

Herman suggested that he turn over the soil for other farmers for the extra cash needed to pay his payments. Some of the farmers in the area were still using mules or horses to plow, and there were others who had lost their tractors back to the bank. It worked out well for him. Herman was his first customer.

Once or twice a year, Herman would hire him to plow up the soil prior to planting and then again in the fall to plow under all the leftover debris from that year's crop.

After the hard soil had been busted up in the spring, Herman had two old faithful mules to do the rest of the plowing at planting time. He had a corn planter that when pulled along by the mules would drop the corn seeds into the groove it made as it moved along.

Herman grew up understanding nature because he depended on it for his crops to grow and for the livelihood of his family. Planting the corn too early would cause the seeds to rot in the ground or to attract worms and insects that would destroy it.

The general rule of thumb for corn farmers was to wait until the leaves on the oak trees were as big as squirrel's ears. But Herman always waited a little longer than that. He knew the soil had to be warm in order for the seeds to germinate. Corn requires at least six hours of sun each day to develop and grow properly.

Mama and Herman had a slew of other animals around the farm both domesticated and wild. Along with the two mules, there was a couple of cows, a dog named "Snooper, several Calico cats, and a whole host of chickens. They raised a couple of hogs during the year for slaughter in the fall for the pork, which they would cure in the smokehouse.

Mama was suited to be a farm wife; mostly because that was all she ever knew. She grew up on her father's farm. From the time she could walk, she was like a little shadow following around behind her mother. She watched everything that her mother did.

By the time she married Herman, she was well-trained to be a mother and a farmer's wife. Sometimes she was not so sure about being a preacher's wife.

After the tragic loss of her own mother, she loved the companionship and friendship she found in Herman's mother, Sarah. They were women cut from the same cloth. Sarah was Mama's human strength when she lost her mother and then later her father. They named their first born daughter Sarah Louise in her honor; and after Herman's great-grandmother Rachel Louise.

And then far too early Sarah, her mother-in-law, died. James, her father-in-law, just seemed to go downhill after then. Mama had grieved for her as if she had been her own mother. She had taken care of Sarah through many weeks of the long good-bye as she saw her linger and suffer from the disease that overtook her body.

She realized it would be hard to follow in the footsteps of the women who came before her. But she was prepared as she took over a household consisting of her husband, her father-in-law, and her own children.

Mama learned well the needed skills of maintaining a home and providing the best she could for those God had placed into her life. Not only was she intelligent and industrious, but she was also wise. As far back as she could remember, her mother told her about the verse in Proverbs that said a wise woman could build up her house, but a foolish woman could tear it down with her own hands.

She didn't understand that when she was younger; but as she grew older she fully understood that nugget of truth her mother had taught her. She soon realized the difference in having knowledge and being wise. Knowledge came from books; wisdom from God.

She grew to love Herman's father, James, as if he were her own father, too. She lost her Papa in a farming accident only a couple of years after she had lost her mother. They both were buried in the cemetery behind the church.

Mama, blessed with a beautiful voice, often sang in church. But she did most of her singing while she did her work around the house and farm. No matter what she faced in life, she clung to the promise in songs. When things looked impossible, she would often sing, *"God will take care of you!"*

And when there seemed to be no solution at hand, but needed patience and fortitude to make it through, she would sing the lyrics to the song, *"Standing on the Promises!"* She would claim the promise of God as it was written in Hebrews 10:23. *"Let us hold fast the profession of our faith without wavering; for He is faithful that promised."*

Sometimes she just sang for her own enjoyment and the glory of God. Singing just seemed to make her work and her long days pass by faster. She never slacked in doing everything possible for her family. That is where she found her greatest joy and happiness. Nevertheless, she depended on God... and Herman... for she knew she could not make it all on her on.

⚜

Mama had many fine traits. She was a good cook, housekeeper, and nurturer. One of her best talents was as a seamstress. She had a good eye for designing as well. She could look at a picture of a dress and cut the pattern from old newspapers, sew the dress, and it would look just as nice as the one in the picture.

Rather than complaining about what she did not have, Mama took what God sent her way and turned them into things of value. She was also good at gardening and caring for plants. Herman often said she could poke a dead stick in the ground, and it would grow into a beautiful rose bush or something. She was a compulsive cleaner and keeper of her household.

Papa once teased her that heaven might not be clean enough for her; so when she died, he was going to put a mop and broom as her headstone. She always pretended to be annoyed, but she secretly loved the ways he had of telling her how much he appreciated her; and all that she did for him and their family. Not only did she love his ways, and the man he was, she just simply loved him.

Like the Proverbs 31 lady, she never ate the bread of idleness. She believed, and was taught, that idle hands were the devil's workshop. Mama didn't take the time to worry about all that she did, but often worried that she was not doing enough, and sometimes wished the days were longer.

Mama was frugal to a fault. She watched every penny; stretched every dollar. She was always looking for ways to save, and at the same time provide for her family.

Manufacturers had a good thing going because the women would buy their products to get the extras like the beautiful floral drinking glasses that came with peanut butter. Mama had collected over a dozen of those with the bright yellow daffodils painted on the sides. They were her company and Sunday drinking glasses. They drank mostly from mason jars and a few mix-matched drinking glasses for every day.

Sarah, her mother-in-law, left her a one-hundred piece matched flatware set that she had gotten as a young bride. She kept it in a walnut case with a red velvet lining. During the week, along with the mason jars, they used cheap spoons and forks, purchased at *Woolworth's 5 & 10 Cent Store*; known fondly as the "dime store."

Both her mother and Sarah had collected free dishes from the Depression years in the late 1920s when colored glassware was made by machine and produced rather cheaply. They got them for free at the movies; in flour sacks, soap boxes, and sometimes by mailing in coupons. You could also buy companion pieces in the dime stores. These cheap giveaways were used by manufacturers to get people to buy their products.

Mama's mother and mother-in-law had both collected the same pattern. As a result of their diligence, and swapping for like-pieces, Mama had a full set of luncheon plates, cups, and saucers in the delicate pink dogwood pattern from the two most important women in her life.

There was twelve of everything... plates, cups, and saucers. Also, in the collection, there was a set of salt and pepper shakers, a butter dish, and a couple of vegetable bowls. There was also her prized iced tea pitcher; which Herman had bought for her on their tenth-wedding anniversary. It wasn't the traditional crystal, but cheap glass. Nevertheless, it meant more to her than if it had been *Waterford Crystal* straight from the Emerald Isle of Ireland.

Mama had only used them once or twice when she had a small tea party for some of the women at church. Even though, they were inexpensive and sometimes free, they were priceless to her. She kept them safely behind the glass of a huge china cabinet that James had made for Sarah.

Sewing for a large family, Mama was especially thankful for the free cotton fabric she was able to obtain when they bought feed, seeds, flour, and sugar. She felt these feed sacks were truly a gift from God. She had also been able to get pretty bordered sacks; when emptied, they made beautiful pillow cases.

Mama used the printed sacks to make dresses for the girls and shirts for the boys. She reused everything, and nothing in her household went to waste. The scraps from sewing clothes went into a special box for her next quilt.

Items of clothing that were just too far gone for reuse were saved for making patches to sew on other clothing; or they were used as bandages or even strips to hold up her tomato plants. She was always careful to remove the buttons or trimmings that could later be reused.

When an adult piece of clothing was no longer wearable... she would cut it down and make clothes for the young ones. When the collars would become frayed on Herman's shirts, she would take them off, turn them, and sew them back on.

Once, she made matching jumpers for the twins from the suit Herman had worn when they got married. Mama's good cooking had rendered it too small for Papa, and the material was just too nice to go to waste.

They had little heart-shaped-bibs in the front and straps that crossed in the back. She embroidered a little row of flowers across the front. Those jumpers, along with their white flour sack blouses, made them look like the little girls in the Sears and Roebuck catalog.

She took great pride in the way her children looked and behaved; especially at church. Mama taught her children, from an early age, if they wanted the world to see them in a good light, then they had to be responsible for the way they looked and acted. She reminded them that their actions would reflect back on their family and Christ.

She told them that character and reputation were the greatest attributes they could ever have. She said, "Whatever you might get or accumulate in this world, you could always lose it."

She said that things could be lost through no fault of their own. A fine home could be lost to fire or tornado; a fine car could be wrecked or stolen, but a good reputation could only be ruined, or lost, by their own behavior and actions.

She repeatedly told them, "No matter where you go in this world, you will always take Jesus and the love of you mother with you, and you best not take them where they did not belong." She admonished them to remember that those were things that no one could take away from them, but could be squandered by their conduct.

Every opportunity she would say, *"Be of good character and reputation and don't squander your life with foolishness. Be honest and of good report and earn the trust of others, and you will go far in the world."*

Mama did her part to help her children look their best; especially when going to church. She felt that the way people dressed for Sunday, with their Sunday-go-to Meetin' clothes, was a reflection on their character, their family; and was pleasing to God. She always wore her little Sunday hat and gloves along with the best dress that she owned.

Hosiery was fairly inexpensive but did not hold up too long. She was able to buy them in Mr. Ferguson's store for twenty-five cents a pair. She would sometimes trade with him eggs for the stockings.

She was always careful to take them off as soon as she returned from church, a wedding, or a funeral. They would go immediately into the wash pan to "soak" clean rather than scrub them. Then she rolled them up in a towel to squeeze most of the water out.

She was always careful to make sure the seams in the back were straight even if it meant tying another knot in the elastic garter that held them up. She stuck her foot through the elastic hoop and brought it up to her thigh and then rolled the elastic down a little with the stockings; and then she would twist a knot into the elastic, and roll it down a little further and tuck it in.

However, as discreetly as she could, she would have to adjust them to sitting or standing as they would still slide down somewhat.

Mama had learned the basics of sewing from her Mama. On the other hand, Sarah, Herman's mother, had been a great seamstress, and she learned even more about sewing from her. When Sarah died, Mama inherited her treadle sewing machine, her sewing notions; and a lot of fabric.

Sometimes it would make her sad to use the things that her mother and Sarah had owned; knowing they had made such good use of them. Those things also served as a reminder that it was true that you took nothing from this world when you departed it.

Just about every fabric item in her house was once stitched together to hold sugar, flour, and agriculture seeds. The larger sacks held feed for the mules and the cows. They ate grass during warm weather, but their diets had to be supplemented with oats and barley in rainy, freezing or snowy weather. During the cold winter months, they ate mostly hay, oats, and barley.

Since Papa grew corn in his fields, he dried some of the corn and put it through a corn sheller that separated the corn from the cob for chicken feed. He gave the cobs to the pigs. He took the rest of the corn by the wagon load to the other side of the mountain to have the bulk of the dried corn milled into cornmeal that he sold to the mill for cash.

However, he also kept back some of the cornmeal for Mama to make her delicious cornbread and corn fritters. He also saved back some for any church folks who might need it. Mr. Ferguson, at the general store, bought all of his cornmeal from Herman as a jester to help out his pastor who was so underpaid at the church. He always bought Mama's eggs first… as well.

Before the Civil War, Samuel Alrod built a grist mill there on the property. It was just below the house where the creek had a drop-off and would turn the wheel and could grind the corn into meal. But with the advent of other more efficient and healthy ways of producing the ground corn meal, James, his son, later ceased using the mill there on the land.

When Herman was a young boy, he would help his father, James, mill the grain. After he took over the farm, it was better to take it to a grist mill just beyond the mountain. He could get all the corn ground and could sell it at the same time. That worked out well for Herman because he could get his corn ground much quicker, and more efficiently, without the extra labor it involved, and walk away with his profits for the year in his pocket.

In the early years, corn and other grains were stored in barrels or boxes, but was later stored in canvas bags that the farmer could bring back to have refilled. Then someone got the idea to use colored cotton sacks for feed once a double stitching machine had been invented that was strong enough to hold the bag shut. Later the idea of using reusable cotton prints for the ladies to use in their sewing caught on. Then most millers began putting just about everything in them.

The large-easy-to-match sacks would magically turn into dresses and blouses because of their pretty prints. A fifty-pound bag would measure about 24 by 38 inches and would be large enough for a small dress, boy's shirt, or an apron. A one-hundred pound bag would be about 39 by 46 inches; three of them would make a lady's dress. The scraps would be used to make smaller things and for quilting.

The smaller hard-to-match pieces would be turned into aprons, bonnets, or dishrags. The white flour sacks were used for the little girls' undergarments, and diapers for the babies; or handkerchiefs for men.

Mama would boil the white thinner sacks with a little bit of *No Boil* to get the print out. Sometimes all of the ink would not fade, and there would be some residue left. There was a time when Verna, one of the twins, was much smaller, and as she was stepping out of the big tin bathtub, Mama handed her a clean pair of new panties. She put them on and turned around to look at the back of them with the words *"General Mills"* still faintly seen.

She hugged her mother and said, "Mama, I love my new panties, thank you for putting my name on them." She skipped off. Mama smilingly thought. "Sometimes not being able to read was bliss."

Mama always insisted that on Sunday, or visitations, that Herman, the preacher, always carried a nice clean store bought handkerchief in his pocket. He never knew when he would have to offer it to some sobbing lady. Lady's handkerchiefs with fine embroidery work made nice gifts, and it was Mama's tradition to make each bride who got married in the church a special one with their names and wedding date embroidered on it with a fine crocheted edging done in blue.

But for wiping sweat… while working on the farm… the old rags were just fine for Herman, the farmer, to use. He also used them for various things around the barn that had to be greased or wiped down such as a mule or cow.

Mama worked all day and had to do her sewing mostly at night when the children were in bed. Sometimes her legs would already be aching from standing on them all day.

Even though she oiled the machine frequently and kept the belt nice and tight, it was still difficult to pedal back and forth and up and down on her old treadle sewing machine. It was also hard to keep the needle threaded, and the bobbin filled, with so little light. A couple of times she actually sewed through her finger.

If the machine had not been so heavy, she would ask Herman to set it out on the back porch so that during the day so she could sew more easily on dark fabrics. But she soon abandoned that idea. Herman had enough to do besides dragging that heavy machine in and out of the house.

Sarah's *"White"* treadle machine was manufactured in 1914 was twenty-five years old. Yet, the tiger wood-veneered cabinet still looked like new. She kept it polished to prevent the wood from drying out and cracking. On the front of the machine, there were little raised letters shaped like wooden logs that spelled out *"White,"* the name of the sewing machine company.

It had four drawers where Mama kept all of her sewing tools such as scissors, extra bobbins, spools of thread; both sewing and quilting needles. She had several Popsicle sticks that had been scrubbed clean to

42

use for turning things like collars, belt loops, and sashes. Mama treasured the things that Sarah had left behind and took excellent care of them.

Herman could not have chosen a better wife. He often compared her to the woman in the Book of Proverbs. But the attributes he saw and loved in her the most, beyond her striking beauty – was her ability to forgive and persevere no matter the situation.

When he would mess up, he was most thankful for that forgiving and thankful spirit of hers. She forgave others a multitude of trespasses against her; and tried to be thankful in all things.

She spent regular time in the scriptures and applied them to her life as a wife, mother, and churchwoman. She thanked God in the good times; as well as in the bad. And no matter what, she stood by her man... not the preacher man... but her man... the man God had ordained for her to love and marry from the beginning of time.

Mama's mother told her when she was a little girl that the boy she would one day marry was out there somewhere. She said that she often prayed for the man that boy would become. Little did she know then that God had already placed Herman in Mama's life; beginning on that first day of school.

Mama had kept that tradition as she prayed for the spouses that her own children would one day marry. She and Herman started out as school chums that developed into an abiding friendship. Everyone knew since they were in grammar school that they would one day marry.

When she reached her teen years, friendship developed into affection. Just to look into his bright green eyes sent chills up and down her spine. She once commented to someone how much they looked like green crystal cat-eye marbles, she had once seen... so clear and so green.

She could never remember the exact moment when she fell in love with that handsome, strong, strapping young man who carried her school books, pulled her pigtails and winked at her in school. Herman still winked at her.

She would see a twinkle in his eye and then a wink. It would make her heart flutter. That had been his signal at school to say that he loved her. And after they married with a houseful of kids and in-laws; she knew what that meant.

43

Even long after they married, his soft whispers to her when they were alone, made her feel like a goddess being worshiped; as the bride of Solomon in the Bible.

They were not just husband and wife. Their souls were so intertwined; it was difficult to know where one began, and the other ended. And they were friends.

Their personal relationship was nurtured by a strong mutual love for one another based on trust, admiration, and contentment with one another. They were attentive to each other's needs and nourished each other's self-image by kind, loving words, and deeds.

While some men teased their wives and made hurtful remarks; Herman never did. He once preached a sermon to the men, saying that marriage made a man and his wife as one. And they should never do or say anything to their wives they would not say to themselves or want said or done to themselves.

He said that some men might tease their wives about gaining weight by saying something like, "See you been putting on the feed bag a little heavy, there." He explained to them how deeply that would hurt them and damage their relationship. He encouraged the women to take care of themselves and to stay beautiful and healthy for their husbands.

He told them to take captive every word; for once they were spoken, they were like a bullet coming from the barrel of a gun. Once the trigger was pulled, and the bullet let loose, there was no calling it back. The damage would be done.

He told them rather than having to eat their words once spoken; it was better to swallow them before they were let loose. He told them of the tremendous power of words fitly spoken. Nations, as well as marriages, could rise and fall based on words.

The right words were like apples of gold and pictures of silver; very valuable. And as a side note, he reminded them of the adage; "You can catch more flies with honey than with vinegar." He jokingly said, "If yor wife has become bitter; perhaps it was because you have been feeding her too many bitter words."

Above all else, he admonished them that they would one day stand before God for the way they treated their wives. He added by saying,

"Men, you can make yor marriage heaven on earth, or Hell on earth, by the way, you treat yor wife."

He used two scriptures to make his point. He told them to read often Ephesians 5:25. *"Husbands love your wives, even as Christ also loved the church, and gave Himself for it."*

And in Colossians 3:19, " *Husbands, love your wives, and be not bitter against them."* He reminded them that Jesus loved the church so much that He died for it.

In that same sermon, Herman taught that the wife had an important role in the marriage as well. He said that in Proverbs, there were several descriptions of a wife who could ruin her marriage and relationship with her ways. He quoted them and expounded on them:

*"A continual dropping on a very rainy day and
a contentious woman are alike"*
*"Better is a dinner of herbs where love is, than
a stalled ox and hatred therewith."*
*"It is better to live in a corner of the housetop, than
in a house shared with a quarrelsome wife."*
*"It is better to live in a desert land than with a
quarrelsome and fretful woman."*

He told the men to love and honor their wives and to be kind and understanding for that is what a woman needed most.

As Herman was often apt to do, he gave illustrations that would make a visual connection in the minds of farm folks. He said that marriage is like being a part of a team. He said they were either like a matched or unmatched, team of mules; each with their own dispositions, and each wanting to go their own way.

But once they were harnessed together to pull a heavy load, they would discover it was better to work together than fighting against each other. When a man and a woman marry, they are bound together by their vows and God. As soon as they realize they should be of one accord, they can then work through anything that the ole devil sends their way.

He told them to picture a wagon with a mule on either end with them pulling in opposite directions and see how little progress they would make. But working side by side toward the same goal, the work could be finished in record time.

In order for them to be successful at pulling a heavy load, they each knew when to give or take; in order to stay on track together. He said that is the perfect example of a good marriage. But he also said the expression, "mule-headed' had meaning as well.

Mama was never bitter toward Herman... sometimes a little aggravated, but never bitter. She also knew there was scripture which said, "Be thankful in all things." She understood that did not mean you were thankful for all things that happened; especially if they were bad things, but to remain thankful in all things... or during those times. She would get frustrated if the rain messed up her freshly washed laundry hanging on the line, but she also knew the rain was needed for the fields.

⁕⁕⁕

It was not often that the women in the church were able to leave their own households to meet as a group. But several times a year Mama would teach the ladies a little Bible lesson. They would have a glass of lemonade and get away from their daily routines for a while.

Other times they got together to make quilts, to help at the church, or visit each other when there was sickness or a new baby. They had little projects they would work on to beautify the church, or to raise money for something special.

Mama heard that there was a pulpwood factory in the city that would pay for old rags and papers to be recycled into the making of new paper. So they started a drive to collect old newspapers and magazines for making money for the Ladies Missionary Society to send money to missionaries around the world who were sharing the Gospel.

There were few books in the Alrod home; and even fewer magazines. Herman would often pick up the day-old newspapers from Ferguson's store before he tossed them out. Magazines were swapped around among the ladies for new fashion and recipe ideas.

As usual, Herman was tired when he returned from visitation and after having already spent a long day working on the farm, he was just glad to be home. It was dark outside, so he just opened up the barn door, and put the papers and magazines down.

In a conversation at the table, Herman told her that there was bad weather looming. The man on the radio said they were in for a few days of heavy rain. Mama thought that would be a good time to go through the collection. She sent Billy Joe out to bring in the stacks since Papa had already gone to bed. When Billy Joe brought them in and plopped then down in the corner, she saw there were more magazines in that batch than newspapers.

Later, Mama would be thankful that Billy Joe had not stayed in the room. While the rain was pouring buckets outside, and everyone tucked into bed, Mama began sorting through the most recent ones published that year in 1939. She decided to put some of them aside for the family to read, and would later put them back in the barn for the next load to factory.

There were several copies of *Life Magazine,* which she thought Papa might like to read. They were mostly about people and news all around the world. There was one with a little girl on the front with a look-a-like doll; she thought the twins might enjoy looking at that one.

She took an interest in a ten-cent copy of *Better Homes and Gardens.* It had an adorable cover with a little boy reading a book while his dog was eating his candied apple. But when she flipped it open, she saw there was an ad for cigarettes, and she decided that was not such a good one for LeRoy to see… after all.

She was dividing the magazines into various stacks; one she thought she might like to read and another one for those her family might enjoy. However, some of the magazines had articles and ads that she did not want her family to see. They went into a stack where she would tear those pages out and use when starting a fire in the cook stove and fireplace. Then she came across a group that seemed to have come together from one place. There were several like-magazines stacked together.

Intrigued, she began to flip through the pages, and she could not believe her eyes. She never knew such material was available to families to see and read. Mr. Ferguson certainly didn't carry them in his store. She was startled at some of the magazines she came across.

These books were about pre-marital sex, illegitimacy, adultery, and other promiscuous behaviors. These were subjects that were taboo in a Christian home, and certainly were not a good influence on those who would read them.

And underneath them were crime and detective magazines that glorified death and killing. Mama was aghast at the pictures on the covers of half naked women, and women being killed and violated.

After her first initial shock at seeing them, she felt so sad in her heart because she knew that as a man thinketh in his heart... so he is. She was grieved in her heart that men would read such things, and perhaps one day act them out. She never gave any thought that women might be reading them as well.

She worried that some of the married men in the church might have been reading them. It bothered her because they were the spiritual leaders of their households.

She got down on her knees there in the kitchen and rested her elbows on the chair she was sitting in and cried out to the Lord. "Dear Lord, what is this world coming to? Lord, please don't let these magazines be lying around in the homes of our church people. Lord, keep them out of the hands and away from the eyes of young children and teens."

"Please give parents discernment in what they allow to touch the hearts and minds of their children. Lord, Yor Word reminds us of the seven most deadly sins. We know that these sins are those that harm us all; the innocent, as well as the guilty. Lord, please keep our nation from this because they could harm families." Amen

She thought how these magazines were true examples of what was written in Proverb 6:16-19 about the seven deadly sins that lead people to deadly and destructive lifestyles

Just as the ole devil had appealed to Eve through deception that brought sin into the world, Mama saw it being manifested in these magazines; haughty eyes, a lying tongue, and hands that shed innocent blood, a heart that devises wicked plans, feet that make haste to run to evil, a false witness who breathes out lies, and one who sows discord among others.

There were ads that led to temptation and glorified sin rather than condemn it. She knew how important books were when used to educate children and what powerful tools they were if they included pictures.

It distressed her to know that people were using books for the wrong kind of learning. She recalled that a picture was worth a thousand words. And the pictures in those magazines left nothing to the imagination. They spoke volumes about that which was an abomination to the Lord.

Mama had a hard time getting some of the images out of her own mind; which showed her how influential this type of visual material could be. She went for her Bible and turned to I John 2:16 and read:

"For all that is in the world, the lust of the flesh, and the lust of the eyes, and the pride of life is not of the Father - but is of the world."

Once again, she dropped to her knees there beside the kitchen table where upon lay the various stacks of magazines. She prayed that God would protect her children from the temptations of the world that would ultimately destroy their lives.

She prayed, "Lord, build a hedge of protection around my children and guard their eyes, hearts and footsteps that they would always honor You in everything they do. And Lord, I pray especially for the homes where these magazines came from. Lord, please protect them as well."

That was a lesson well taught, and well learned by Mama, because she began to see what even an innocent *Sears Catalog* could manifest in a person's life since it had always been an important book around the Alrod household.

It had become almost as valued as the Bible. She felt, while she could not protect her children from all the evil wiles of the devil, it was her duty to teach the principles of God's Word, and leave it up to the Holy Spirit to guide, lead, direct and protect them.

She, and everyone else old enough to turn the page could spend hours just looking at all the things in Sears' book to dream about and hopefully to own. That is why it was called "the dream book!"

Just recently she had seen a vacuum cleaner advertised for just $2.00 down and $3.00 a month. She "dreamed "of how useful it would be to keep up with all the sand that got tracked into the house. It could save her hours of sweeping.

The *Sears* book had beautiful factory-made dresses, and hats that she adored but could not afford. She realized she was lusting for them in her heart.

Papa didn't say much about it, but she noticed when it was his turn to dream, she saw where he had turned down the page that showed an *A. J. Aubrey* shotgun beginning at $13.85 and on up. He only once mentioned how he would like to have a new shotgun since he was still using the one his father had inherited from his great-grandfather.

Mama would often see a picture of something one of the children wanted since they circled it with a pencil and wrote their name beside it. This catalog was also sometimes called a "wish book." It made you wish for everything in it.

The few times when they able to order necessary things, it would be delivered to Mr. Ferguson's store, and they would redeem it there. The rest were just things they had coveted. She had often been guilty of saying, "It doesn't hurt to dream, and it don't cost anything."

Now she wondered. Sarah Louise had been complaining a lot recently about what other girls had at school; which she did not. LeRoy and the twins wanted every toy displayed inside.

Mama saw a Bible lesson coming for the children at church, and her own as well. She wanted to tell them the difference in lusting after things, rather than just working and saving to buy them. It was okay to want things and to have things, but it was not good to always put yor faith and self-esteem in things.

Somehow, she had to make it clear to her children that sometimes not having the things you dreamed about could cause discontentment since it seemed the more you got, the more you wanted. She told them that ole demon-greed would never be satisfied. She wanted them to realize their self-esteem and self-worth were not tied up with what they had or could buy.

The *Sears Catalog* also had a much greater use. When the new one came in, the old one went out... out to the outhouse. When it was outdated that meant that things might be out of stock or the prices had changed, or the company had gotten in new merchandise. Still everyone liked to look at them while in the outhouse waiting for nature's call. Then it served the most useful purpose of all... in the clean-up.

Several thicknesses of the pages were also useful to plug up those cold air holes where the wind came rushing in during cold weather. Suddenly, she realized why she would sometimes hear giggling from school boys in the church outhouse for men and boys.

Perhaps, she should take a better look at what was in those pages as well. Maybe, it would be that she needed to explain a few things that were in there. She never thought how Mama's could be looking at bloomers, and little boys could be sniggering about them.

Thinking about how they were used for cleanup in the outhouse, it gave her the idea on how to dispose of these deplorable magazines. Certainly not to put them in the outhouse to read, but to dump them in the pit; for that is where they belonged.

This burden was too big for her to handle... she would just have to take it to the Lord and leave it there. And it would be the subject of her next lesson taught at the Ladies Missionary Society.

Chapter four: A Woman's Work is Never Done

The weekdays just flew by, and it always seemed that Mama was doing something towards getting everyone back to church on Sundays.

On this particular Sunday morning, she was once again trying to get a head start on dinner. Everyone would usually be starved after church, and she never knew if they would be having guests for dinner. It turned out to be a harrowing morning for Mama, and most of the Alrod family.

Herman was big on asking folks over for dinner; not knowing if she had enough fixed to feed her own family. But she could not fault him any. He sometimes would see someone who looked lonely or down in spirit, and he would ask them to have Sunday dinner with them. On some of these occasions, when she had fried chicken, she would just not eat any herself. She could always put more water in the stew and cut the cornbread in smaller pieces.

Two whole chickens would give everyone in the family two pieces, but when company came, they all got one. Mama fried the whole bird, the wings, the drumsticks, the pulley bone, the breast, the thighs, liver, and gizzard. She even fried the neck... but she breaded it with an extra thick crust.

If she lacked enough to fill everyone up on those unexpected guest days, there was always lots of chicken gravy and biscuits. Green beans were almost always on the table come Sunday. She would also open up canned peaches or other vegetables that only needed to be heated.

Sometimes Papa would invite one of the deacons and their family, or someone else from church so they could fellowship together and then discuss some pressing church business. The women would clear up the dishes; the children would play outside, and the men would amble off somewhere to talk.

It was a long way for some folks to travel to church on Sundays, go home, turn around and then come back, and almost impossible to get with folks during the week. Most were farmers, and their wives had busy lives just like Mama. However, the majority of the congregation lived within a reasonable distance to the church.

On this particular Sunday, Mama had a run-in with Billy Joe, her eldest child, who was almost sixteen.

"Now Billy Joe, I done told you that you ain't gonna git out of goin' to church just because of no stumped toe," said Mama.

"You go out on that porch and pour a little bit... now mind you just a little bit...a drop or two of kerosene over that toe. And don't spill none on the porch either!" Mama was quite aggravated with him.

"But before that, git a clean rag out of the rag bag, and like I told you go out on the back porch and hold yor foot over the edge; then pour that kerosene over that toe."

"Mind you, don't spill it anywhere else. Then, take a rag, tear it into strips and wrap it tight about that toe. It will hurt a little bit; put yor sock over it and go ahead and shove it in the shoe. That will hep to put pressure on it to hep it not bleed anymore. You best wear them old shoes in case it does bleed some more."

"Make sure you git one of those clean rags... a white one that the sugar comes in... don't never put no colored rags on a sore ... the dye ain't good for it."

Billy Joe shoved a chair as he passed the breakfast table which was still laden down with the breakfast dishes. They rattled. He was supposed to clear the table on Sunday mornings.

Mama had the water boiling in the kettle on top of the wood stove and had already made room at the end of the table for two dish pans... one for washing and one for rinsing. She would do the washing, and it would be Sarah Louise's job to rinse, dry, and put them in the cupboard. Now she had to clear the table as well. Mama just couldn't deal with him right then.

Billy Joe passed Mama with a huff, and she saw that not only was he limping, but was also dripping blood drops on the kitchen floor. She was angry at him, to say the least. She didn't know it was still bleeding since he had cut his toe the day before. But she dismissed it from her mind since she was running late and didn't want to be showing up for church late. He came back up the hall dripping blood; as he had done going down the hall as he went for a rag for his foot.

As he passed by her, she gave him a little swipe across his backseat with her dishrag. She had been using it to lift the lid off of the pot to stir the deer stew; before moving it to the back of the stove. She paid no attention to what he had in his hand. She would have Papa handle him later.

It was getting close to Meetin' Time. The cornbread had been baked, and the tea made. She stopped for a minute to collect her thoughts; "Did I already put a pinch of baking soda in the tea?"

"Oh, well," she said out loud, "better safe than sorry... better not add anymore."

From experience, she had learned that a little bit of soda would keep the tea from tasting quite so bitter, and she would not have to use so much sugar, but too much baking soda would spoil it as well.

She stirred the sugar into the tea and then licked the spoon to see how it tasted. Nothing was better than good ole sweet iced tea, and nothing more bitter tasting when it has not steeped properly. She always had the iceman come around on Saturdays during warm weather so that they could have it for the tea on Sunday. During the week, they had water with their meals... or milk.

Sugar, she learned, should be added when the tea was still a little on the hot side, but not boiling. That way it would be melted with no grainy taste.

She had learned the hard way you should never pour hot boiling tea into a gallon glass jar. Once, when she did; it cracked, and the tea went all over the table and down onto the floor. Now, she would leave it sitting in the boiler for a while before pouring it into the jar. She had a special white enameled boiler for making the tea. Boiling it in a metal pan gave it a bitter taste.

She let the tea sit until it had cooled down some, and then poured it into the jar; and filled it to the top with fresh well water.

Mr. Ferguson, who owned the general store, saved big gallon pickle jars for the ladies. He sold the large dill pickles for three cents apiece and sold the jars to the ladies for a dime.

The jars had become so much in demand; he had to have the ladies sign up for the next jar; then sell them to the next lady on the list. After the tea cooled, Mama would screw the large lid back to keep the flies out of the tea. Flies just seemed to know when a Sunday dinner, picnic, or dinner on the grounds was happening.

When she got back home from church, all she would have to do was warm up the stew. It was rumored that Mama made the best deer stew of any woman in the county. It was her secret recipe. Women were funny about sharing their specialties; except from Mother to daughter. She put in lots of onions, carrots, potatoes, and her special blend of seasonings that turned the gravy a scrumptious medium brown color.

Papa always liked to tell her things like that to let her know how much he appreciated all of her hard work she did taking care of him and six children.

It was not long into her marriage, and with the children coming, she realized the truth in that old adage, "A man may work from sun to sun, but a woman's work is never done."

She called out to Billy Joe who was taking his own sweet time coming back into the kitchen. She had already cleared and washed the dishes. Sarah Louise had just about finished drying them. She thought that he was surely taking a long time fussing over that toe. He did not answer.

She sent Verna, one of the eight-year-old twins, out on the porch to tell him that his mother was calling him and he had better answer. He came limping into the kitchen with a scowl on his face. Mama looked around, and she was livid. He had grabbed a piece of white broadcloth she had just bought at the store to make Herman a new Sunday shirt. And… there were blood stains on it.

She felt the blood rushing to her face and unkind words rushing through her brain. She made every effort to not let them come rolling off her tongue. She just jerked the fabric from his hand. She felt he had done that on purpose. He had torn two long strips from the side.

Angrily, she told him, "Now that you are done with that get a real rag and clean up those blood drops off the linoleum runner in the hallway and here on the kitchen floor." She reminded him that she had just mopped it the day before.

She knew the kerosene would help to stop bleeding, and it would also help to prevent him from getting blood poisoning. But she was not too sure what it would take to correct his bad behavior. She decided to let Papa deal with that one.

It had become quite clear to her that Billy Joe had been trying to dodge church now for several weeks. He would make up some excuse, but it didn't hold water with Mama. His stories had too many holes in them. She wasn't so sure he was not overreacting with the toe business. She felt he might be using it as an excuse to stay home from church.

She knew her kids like the back of her hand, and she knew when they were lying, when they were sick, or when something was bothering them. It seemed for some time, Billy Joe had something in his craw that he just couldn't or wouldn't deal with; it was bothering him something fierce.

She always told her young'uns she could tell if they were lying, or not, by looking directly into their eyes. And she could.

While she was not magic, it often worked; because they either would not look her in the eyes or the expression on their faces would give them away.

Several times when they were telling the truth, they would put her powers to test by telling her, "I am telling the truth, Mama. Just look into my eyes." Sometimes it worked in their favor and sometimes not.

"When you are finished mopping up the floor, git on in yonder and git yor Sunday clothes on. I laid out yor fresh starched and ironed shirt, and it's lying on yor bed."

When he came back through the kitchen, she had cooled down some. She had already put the fabric in a wash pan with some ice… precious ice needed for dinner … and was making a paste of salt and baking soda to put on each stain. If that didn't work, she would later pour in a little *No Boil.*

She told him if the blood stains did not come out; she was going to make him earn the fifty cents she had paid for the fabric which she had paid for out of her egg money. Her mind was running ahead. She thought if the stains didn't come out then she would just dye the fabric and make something else out of it. But in any case, he was going to pay for what he had done.

Papa came in from feeding the animals to start getting dressed. It was almost eight o'clock and still a lot to be done. Sundays were also a day of rest for the Alrod's... if you could call what they did... resting.

On Sundays, Herman did no farming and only did the chores that had to be done. They honored the Sabbath as best as they could. Mama never washed on Sunday unless the "ox was in the ditch" like it said in the Old Testament. This morning it was, and she had to act fast to save the fabric. Papa only fed the animals and took care of things that just could not wait until Monday. Mama would not even sweep the back porch off on a Sunday. Papa and the boys never fished or hunted on Sundays either.

Papa had noticed a change in Billy Joe's mood as well; but understood what boys go through at that age; since he had been a boy; and Mama had not. He told Mama, "Oh, now Mama, he is just growing up and won't be long until he is a man. And besides, he likes to ruffle yor feathers now and again. Just be patient with him for a while until he works through what is botherin' him."

Mama said she would have none of that sass no matter how old he was or thought he was. Sure enough, he was almost sixteen. And soon he would be a man. But until that day, when he was a fully grown man, she intended to keep a tight rein on him. And dodging church was not going to become a habit.

Papa saw both sides of the situation and decided just to let it roll itself out. He knew that Billy Joe was in love; or at least thought he was. And he knew that boys went through various phases in their lives until they passed those up-and-down feelings during puberty. He remembered those confusing and exciting days, as a young man, when his own body and emotions began to change. It was a stage between being a boy, and becoming a man.

While Mama had no clue about such things; she knew the day was coming soon when twelve-year-old Sarah Louse would begin to question and wonder about things as well. She would soon be thirteen.

Mama felt she had just about all she could handle, having two teens to contend with; and then two identical eight-year-old little girls who were at that crying-discontented age. And then there was five-year-old LeRoy, who was always out there somewhere in the wild blue yonder with his head in the clouds or into something. Next was sweet Baby James. You hardly knew he was on the place... sweet little baby that hardly ever cried or clamored for attention. He was almost two.

Billy Joe and Mama had already had a sort of run in the week before when he tried to pull some excuse. She told him in no uncertain terms, "How would it look if the preacher's boy didn't show up for church. A man ain't got no right to stand and tell other Papas how to raise their young'uns; unless he's got a toehold on his own."

Billy Joe came limping back into the kitchen. His mother said in a tone not quite so angry, "Come here son and let me take a look at that toe."

He took his shoe and sock off and unwrapped it. The bleeding seemed to have stopped. Mama had not realized that the cut was so bad and so deep. There was a gaping cut right across the bottom of his big toe. It was bruised black and blue, and was swollen as well.

A rush of mother-love hit her heart, and she felt sorry for him. He went to the back of the house to finish getting ready for church.

But, she was still steaming mad about the fabric. She kept her fabric and feed sacks in special boxes in her bedroom. And the rag bag in a little closet off the hallway. She knew he knew that. And it made her boil all the more thinking he had done it on purpose.

Mama heard Billy Joe grumbling a little more, and she called out to him, "It won't kill you to hurt a little. Maybe next time when someone tells you somethin', you'll listen. You done been told about jumpin' off in that creek; especially barefoot."

Billy Joe mumbled underneath his breath, "You didn't expect me to jump in with my shoes, did you?" He knew Mama had not heard his reply. And he was very glad that Papa hadn't.

"What were you doing jumping off in that creek so early yesterday mornin' anyhow?"

Billy Joe had shut her out some minutes before, but not before he heard her say from down the hall, "There is nothing' I hate more than anything for folks to show up late for church, and make a spectacle out of themselves; especially the preacher's family."

Billy Joe mumbled underneath his breath, "Pride goeth before the fall."

And then he heard her praying as she continued working, "Lord, we ask a special blessing on Billy Joe's cut toe. We know that You've got all the healing power that man nor medicine don't possess. And we ask you to hep that worrisome cut to heal quickly." Sometimes Mama didn't bother to say "Amen" at the end of her prayers because to her they were ongoing.

In a louder voice, he said, "Awe, Ma... do I have to go to church this morning?" She just ignored him and decided again to leave him up to his Papa.

She turned her thoughts back to her Sunday dinner. It was always a special time at the Alrod home to have all the family sit around the table and eat together. She reached up into the cabinet and counted out the Sunday plates and put them on the table. She had already spread out her best tablecloth; going around to make sure it hung from the table exactly the same all the way around.

And under her breath, she said to no one in particular, "Pore fella, I know that toe must hurt heap bad. But sometimes you just gotta let them live and learn."

As Mama was often to do, she just broke out in prayer along with whatever else she was doing. "Lord, this is Billy Joe's Mama, again. Of course, You know we named him William Joseph Alrod, but we just call him Billy Joe. Lord, you know how it is with children they step on yor toes and tear at yor heart. but they are a gift from You, Lord!"

"You know I have told him a hundred times. Oh, excuse me Lord. at least a dozen times. Well, Lord, you know how many times I have warned him about jumping off into that creek barefoot; especially down on that low end with all them rocks."

"Well, now he done gone and cut his big toe on a sharp rock, and Lord it does look mighty bad. But next time, if I let him git away with this, it might be somethin' worse. If he don't listen in the little things; then he is not apt to listen in the big and important ones!"

"Lord, you give these young boys to us just for safe keeping so we can help make a man out of them. They ain't ours, but just for a little while; and then we have to give them back to you!"

"Lord, help us to make a good man out of Billy Joe. I ask You now to teach that boy a lesson about obedience and having to pay for his behavior. Lord, don't let that ole toe bother him too much in that tight ole shoe; just enough to make him understand that with choices come consequences. I am sure he is not too happy about wearing an old work shoe to church either."

"And Lord, I don't rightly know what is botherin' him and why he don't want to go to church anymore. But Lord, help me to understand more, and Lord, always keep yor hand on his shoulder; leading him in the right direction."

"And Lord, if You could see fit, give a little of that pain to me so's he don't have to bear it all alone. I'll be a thankin' ye, Lord."

Unaware to Mama, Billy Joe had been standing near the kitchen door and heard her praying for him. He felt a little twinge of guilt. Or was it a twinge of pain in that toe?

He walked back into the kitchen saying, "Okay, Mama, I got the shoe back on, but it shore does hurt."

"Well, just pray yor Daddy don't preach into overtime this morning, and you will be okay."

She then asked in a concerned tone, "Dip it in kerosene?" He nodded. "Wrap it good and tight in the white rag?" He nodded once again.

He nodded 'yes" to each question and was feeling mighty sorry he had done jumped off in that creek. The water was shallow in that end and filled with jagged rocks, but he just wanted to impress that certain young lady as she passed by on her way to town yesterday.

She had told him on Friday at school that she would be passing by his place at a certain time the next morning. And he had not exactly jumped off into the creek when she saw her coming. He was not paying attention, and his bare foot slipped in the soft mud on the bank, and he slid into the creek right on top of a sharp, jagged rock. She laughed at him as she walked past him. He held in the pain immediately and didn't respond right away to the jabbing pain in his foot that went all the way up his leg.

When she got out of earshot, he could see the water around his feet turning from a pinkish color to bright blood red color. When he was sure she was out of hearing, he let out a holler that scared the dog; and sent him howling toward the house.

Following Mama's example, Billy Joe prayed silently to himself, "Lord, this here is Billy Joe. I sure hate walking in this ole tight shoe with this busted up toe, and I guess I am ah gittin' what I deserve, but Lord, just for a few hours, could you just cut the feeling off in it for a little while?"

Sunday Meetin' Time

The path from their house to the church was rather a long one across the field. Often some of the folks would walk past on their way to church on a sunny, warm day. Papa would only drive the family across the field in his car if the weather was bad or the field was muddy.

Papa left early that morning to meet with the deacons about a church matter. He was gone by the time Billy Joe got his toe fixed and shoved it into the shoe.

Not only did Billy Joe's toe hurt, but he also had to help tote the baby for Mama down the path, and across the field, and up the little hill to the church. Baby James was growing bigger every day and at almost two years of age, he could walk pretty good, but if you put him down on his feet, he would just sit down and not get up. And if he fell down and got dirty, Mama would then be really mad.

They had to watch him close to keep him out of the fire, away from the wood cooking stove and when he was on the back porch to make sure he didn't fall off the high side.

His twelve-year-old sister, Sarah Louise, was walking not far behind holding onto the hand of LeRoy, who was almost five. She was holding on so tight he was squirming and yelling for her to let him go. If she did, the Good Lord only knew where he would scamper off to.

The eight-year-old twins, Velma and Verna, had skipped on ahead; holding and swinging hands as they merrily went their way.

The Sunday Morning Meetin' was the most important one of the day since some folks could not make it back in the evening. They always made sure there was a special time for the children to learn more about the Bible; and the ways of the Lord.

Church meetin' was a little less formal on Sunday nights, and there were fewer people in attendance. Sunday morning sermons were directed at everyone in general; with a special emphasis on the Gospel... and the way of Salvation and Godly living.

Sunday evenings were more for the home folks. They would dress more casually, and the women didn't wear their Sunday hats and gloves. The preaching would be more informal with more teaching, singing and testifying.

Each Sunday morning, Pastor Alrod would take his place behind the pulpit. He would then extend a great big welcome to everyone and asked if there were any visitors among them. He then asked if they would please stand to be recognized. He knew all the regular members, and he would set his eyes on any newcomers.

They were trapped when they had to stand and give out their names. Those around them would shake their hand and make them feel welcome. After the service, the women would single out the women, and the men would do the same for the men, making them feel personally welcome and invite them back.

This church was like a second home to Herman James Alrod. Before he became the pastor, he had sat for many years on the front pew listening to his own Papa preach.

First, he started out on his mother's lap and then only an arm's length from her on the pew. Herman also remembered, as a young boy, the many Sundays when he squirmed and grew restless sitting there. Often, he would fall asleep with his head on his mother's lap. Remembering his childhood made him tolerant of noisy, squirming, and sleepy little kids.

Herman's father, the Reverend James Alrod, had been the preacher there for over a decade. He had been greatly loved and respected by this faithful congregation... the younger ones could never remember when he was not the preacher.

The Reverend James Alrod served in the Great War and was sent overseas in 1917. He was wounded in the leg, and it had caused him considerable misery the rest of his life. All those years of farming the land, preaching the Gospel, and caring for those in the community, had finally taken its toll on him. With much regret, he stepped down and told the congregation they would have to find another pastor for their church.

The search committee looked for several months around in several other towns, but just could not seem to find the man they wanted as their shepherd. Herman James Alrod stepped in as a pulpit supply trying to help hold the congregation together, and to please his father.

On another Sunday morning, much like this one, but several years before, one of the deacons on the committee stood up and announced they had found a new preacher.

When Deacon Jones stood to his feet to make that announcement, there was a hush all across the room, and everyone listened intently to see who they were going to recommend.

Lately, former Pastor James Alrod's health had declined, and the doctor suspected he had suffered a light stroke. On the days he did not feel like walking across the field to church, he would sit on the front porch at home. And if the weather was good, he could hear the singing. He rested his open Bible on one knee even though his eyesight no longer allowed him to read it. But he knew sufficient scriptures to keep him in tune with the Lord.

In colder weather, James sat in the kitchen with his Bible on the table... along with his elbows... head in hands praying for his son as he filled in for him until a new pastor could be found. He prayed for Herman as he preached the Word to others in his place.

One of Billy Joe's earlier excuses had been when he unselfishly offered to stay home and "take care of Grandpa!" Mama saw through that like a clean jelly jar. Or so she thought.

But on a particular Sunday, eight years before, in 1931, Herman's father who had not been well for months was up and dressed before the rest of the family; so as not to slow them down. He did not want to miss this day for sure.

When Herman was asked by the deacons if they could make a report from the committee about their decision to hire a new pastor, he said, "By all means Deacon Jones, let us hear the report. We have been faithfully praying that God would lead just the right man here to be our shepherd."

Deacon Jones responded, "Well, Herman, I think we have. We looked high and low and up and down and all around. And then we came to the conclusion that was all in vain, and like the writer in the Good Book said in Ecclesiastes, "All was meaningless... just meaningless.""

The congregation sat motionless and held their breath until the deacon finished. "We done come to a conclusion as to why we should not be looking for what we already have?"

Turning to Herman, Deacon Jones said, "And like the Prophet Nathan told David in the Bible, "Herman, Thou art that man.""

Without exception, everyone stood to their feet and began to applaud a stunned Herman. He was standing there in the spot where once his father had stood. He looked down at his tired old Dad, who had managed to stand to his feet as well. Herman felt so honored; he didn't know what to say.

There were tears streaming down the face of both father and son. While totally unexpected of the asking, Herman had for weeks felt the work of the Holy Spirit in his life, and without hesitation, he said to the congregation, "In the name of the Father, the Son, and the Holy Ghost, I accept."

Most of the time, he would discuss such things with Mama, and they would talk about it, pray about it, do some soul searching; and come to an agreement on tough decisions. But not knowing for sure they would even ask him, he did not want to burden her. He did not want to cause her additional stress and worry; especially with another baby on the way. He had kept silent and allowed the Lord to work it out.

Soon, they would find it was not a single baby on the way, but two. God blessed them with the twin girls, Velma and Verna. He had already blessed them with Billy Joe and Sarah Louse, but their family was not to be complete; as then came Little LeRoy and Baby James.

Once, Mama had feared she would be barren and not have any children. God had granted the answer to her prayers and had sent her six.

Chapter five: God Will Take Care of You

Last Sunday had been a hard day for the Alrod family getting off to church and having to deal with Billy Joe's wound. This week had been easier.

Mama made sure most of the preparations were done on Saturday night before everyone went to bed. She had purchased new fabric and made Herman's new shirt during the week along with all the other things that took up her time from daylight to dark.

His old shirt was just too frayed to wear to church another Sunday. However, this Sunday Mama was worried. She knew that Grandpa was not feeling well at all. He did not eat breakfast and had little to say to anyone. He looked so very tired. She offered to have one of the children stay behind, but he would not hear of it.

James Alrod, also known as, "Grandpa" had attended as many of Herman's services as he was able after his son took over the pastorate. Mama suspected the doctor was right again, and perhaps he may have had another light stroke. She prayed that was not the case, but she suspected it just the same. He seemed to be having trouble buttoning his shirts, and he was not whittling as much as he had been.

By 1939, Herman was acclimated to his role on Sundays. He was a farmer on weekdays; and a preacher on Sundays. But he was a man of God seven days a week; as well as a husband, father, and friend.

He had taken over the farm, and the little church on the hill after his father could no longer manage either. He had been the minister since 1931. His family had grown in that time, and there were now six Alrod children, Mama, Papa, and Grandpa all living in the small farm house that had stood strong for eighty-nine years.

When Herman stepped behind that pulpit, something miraculous happened. He no longer was thinking about crops, unpaid bills or things of the world. He felt a peace come over him like nothing else he had ever experienced before becoming the pastor of this country church that was so vital to the community.

From the pulpit, his deep voice rang out all across the church. He had learned to preach over crying babies, fidgety kids, women who whispered during the service, and all those coughs and sneezes. He even dismissed a few "humph's" every now and then when someone disagreed with him. He came to do the Lord's bidding, and that was all that was on his mind.

ꙮ

Sunday Meetin' Time

"Welcome to all of you comin' out this morning. We've got a good service all lined up here and hope the Lord will bless you real good."

"Let's git these important announcements and prayer requests taken care of right away. If you were in prayer meetin' on Wednesday, you've done heard these, but it won't hurt none for you to be reminded. We always want to be keeping up with those who stand in the need of prayer."

He looked up just as Billy Joe took his seat in the last row at the back of the church. After depositing the baby in Mama's lap, he went out to the outhouse to loosen the bandage he had wound too tight on his cut toe.

The Papa in Herman overrode the Pastor in him for a moment. He saw the pain in the face of his son who was still dealing with a very sore and infected foot. Billy Joe's foot was throbbing something fierce, but since the preaching hadn't begun, he thought he might slip in unnoticed, but he was spotted right away.

It had been a week since the injury, and it had only slightly improved. It was still swollen and infected looking. Mama had paid close attention to it and had him soak his foot in *Epsom salts,* and that seemed to help for a little while.

She sent Papa to Ferguson's to buy some *Mercurochrome*. It had been around for a long time, since 1919, and was supposed to help cut down on infection and help the wound to heal. It seemed to work for a while and then it didn't. Billy Joe balked when she applied it because it burned so badly; he howled like a coyote each time.

Although, it bothered him a lot, he kept up with his schooling and his chores. He even managed to help Mr. Ferguson around the store and earned the money to pay Mama back for the soiled material. All of the blood did not come out; even with the *No Boil*. Mama was not about to be outdone. An idea came to her in the early morning hour just after the rooster crowed; and before she had to pull herself out of bed.

That afternoon, she cut flower shaped petals from some of the small scraps of printed fabric and then base-stitched them over the faded blood stains on the white broadcloth and added a button for the center. By appliquéing them around the edges and making two side pockets of the same print, she made a lovely Sunday apron to wear when they had company for dinner.

She had forgiven Billy Joe for misusing her fabric. She also had asked him to forgive her for not understanding the severity of his wound. She told him that she did not fully understanding the pain he was in as he hobbled around trying to take care of his foot. She told him she should have taken the time to stop and give him assistance. When she last looked at Billy Joe's wound, it had faint red streaks running across the top of his foot.

Coming into church late, Billy Joe glanced up at his father, already standing in the pulpit, and he knew he would not be happy to see him lagging in after the service started. He heard his father say, "I see young Billy Joe back there…"

He thought, "Well here it comes." But his father continued by saying, "He is on the last row still dragging his hurt toe in the door."

Perhaps his concern was genuinely for Billy Joe as a father; but it might have been also that he felt he owed the congregation and explanation as to why Billy Joe was interrupting the service by coming in late.

"But we are proud that he made it to church this morning hurt toe and all. You know many folks will use less than a cut toe to stay away from the Lord's house. Life is full of pain and sometimes you just have to grin and bear it."

Billy Joe was not grinning. The Alrod children were used to being used as examples in their father's sermons...well mostly.

Billy Joe felt like making a silly grinning face at his father, but only for a split second. He knew while his father was a moderate man with discipline, he also knew not to push him too far. But several times when he was younger, he had stuck his tongue out at him behind his back – but not in church; too many eyes to see. Besides, today he was sitting next to Mary O'Brien.

The Pastor, getting back to the prayer requests said, "We serve a good God, and He cares just as much about busted toes as he does busted lives. While we remember these here in prayer, remember that old sore split toe of Billy Joe's. It don't seem to be healing as it should."

"If you don't mind, ask the good Lord to heal it lickety-split." He smiled at his son to let him know he understood. Billy Joe was glad he had not made a face.

If Billy Joe had not been used to his Papa using them as examples in church, he would have been embarrassed, but he had been doing that all of his life.

"We got a number of folks who are down with the miseries, a new baby in the Johnson household, and that sizable loan we have here on the organ. Lord knows this time of year not many of us made a dollar this past week, but if anyone has an extra dime – it will surely go to the organ payment."

"Let's us bow our heads, and lift our hearts on high as we approach the King of Kings and the Lord of Lord's with our requests this morning."

"Lord bless this service, bless the sick and afflicted, bless the shut-ins, and those that have a heap of worries on their mind. Bless those what are here and those what ain't here. Bless those who can give and those who can't, and bless those who are hurting in ways of the mind as well as ways in the body."

"And Lord, we ask a special blessing on Billy Joe's wounded toe. We know that you've got all the healing power that man nor medicine don't possess. And we ask that you help that worrisome cut to heal quickly. Amen"

"And oh yeah, Lord, let the folks know that the payment on the organ is past due! Amen, again!" He repeated himself just to make sure both God and the congregation had heard him.

"Now moving on with the service here, let's sit back and listen real good to Sister Alice Faye Jones as she brings our story for the week. Now come on up here Miss Jones - the folks are awaitin' to hear what you got to say."

Alice left her seat in the middle of the sanctuary and stood in front of the children who were all sitting in the first couple of rows. She asked, "How many of you know how important it is what you think; and what you say?" Several of the older ones raised their hands.

She said, "I want to tell you a story about a little boy who thought it okay to mumble behind his mother's back thinking that she would never know."

She began her story. "His family had not lived on their new farm for long, and he had not fully explored all the land. His mother had told her son to do something. He dawdled and did not obey."

"While the task, she had asked him to do, was not all that urgent or important, he had still disobeyed. And she knew that if he were to get by with the little things in life, he would just move on to the bigger ones."

"After completing the task, he ran outside the house; still very angry at her. He ran across the field near the creek. Unbeknown to him there was a deep ravine on the other side of the creek bed. To get even with his mother, he shouted out across the ravine, "I hate you, I hate you, I hate you!"

"Then this huge billowing voice came back at him so loud he stepped backward; and fell down right there in the dirt. The looming voice that said, 'I hate you, I hate you, I hate you,' was the angriest, loudest voice he had ever heard."

"Jumping to his feet, he ran as fast as he could back to the house, ran into the house with the door slamming behind him. He ran into his mother's arms so fast and hard he nearly knocked her down."

"After catching his breath, he said, "There is a mean old man who lives on the other side of the creek, and he is going to get me!"

"His mother asked, 'Why do you think he is going to get you?' The little boy answered with a shaking voice, 'Because he said he hated me, he hated me; he hated me!'"

"His mother held him close for a minute or two and then took him by the hand. She walked him back down to where he had heard the mean ole man."

"She knew about the echoes across the ravine, but she only told him that she was going to find out why that mean old man hated her sweet little boy."

"The little boy was terrified and hid behind her skirts as she walked near the edge of the creek. She tenderly and gently called out, 'I love you. I love you. I love you!'"

"To the little boy's surprise, a kind and gentle voice repeated, 'I love you, I love you. I love you.'"

Miss Jones looked at the children and questioned, "Now what did we learn from this story?" Several hands went up in the air, and Miss Jones pointed to one little girl so eager to answer.

She said, "I learnt not to holler across no creek, especially if yor by yorself!" The rest of the kids giggled.

Another raised his hand and said, "That weren't no man - it were the echo!"

And then Miss Jones asked him, "What will an echo do?" And he said, "It always says the same thing that you do; only more times."

She told him that he was correct. Then she asked them what would they do if people were like that? Would they want to have the same mean words shouted back at them that they had shouted to someone else? They shook their heads, "No."

Then Miss Jones looked up away from the children and out to the congregation where the parents had been intently listening as well. She said, "There is a lesson here for us adults as well."

"When our children disobey and frustrate us or even anger us, we are sometimes apt to be angry with them and say brash things to them."

"But we should remember just as our children can impact our behavior, so can we impact them with ours. If our children have a hissy-fit, it does not mean that we have to have one."

"By responding with kindness and good cheer, you can usually turn around a child's tantrum, and maintain your own sanity at the same time."

"Preacher Alrod is faithful to teach us straight from the Bible every week, and we have often heard him read these scriptures."

"Soft words turns away wrath and words fitly spoken are like apples of gold in pictures of silver. And where there is no fuel, the fire goes out."

"Now you Mamas and Papas out there remember the Lord expects us to be the patterns by which our children will use as they cut out the fabric of their lives."

"Thank you, Brother Alrod - that is all for this morning."

"Thank you, Miss Jones," said Pastor Alrod as he resumed his place behind the pulpit.

Pastor Alrod said, "Sometimes in life we just have to learn the hard way about things and no amount of others telling us what to do matters none."

"And that brings me to the scripture for this morning. Sometimes learning the hard way is the only way, but often the surest way."

"Okay now, knock a little dust off them Bibles and turn in the New Testament to Hebrews 12:1."

"Wherefore seeing we also are compassed about with so great a cloud of witnesses, let us lay aside every weight, and the sin which doth so easily beset us, and let us run with patience the race that is set before us."

"Now let's try not to chew off the whole thing at once, and swallow it all at one time...but let's digest it a little bit at a time."

"What do you think that big word 'compassed' means?"

"Well, to my way of thinking we are told that we are surrounded by those who came before us who know exactly what we are going through. And we all know from experience that it helps us when others understand."

"Here, God is telling us that He knows when we are carrying heavy weights on our shoulders. He knows that sometimes we feel the weights are just too heavy for us to carry. But we ain't alone."

"Now He ain't talking about lifting no wagon wheel or plowshare... but the kind of weights that you can't see except in yor head and heart. We are to lay that aside."

"When we lay something aside for a while, it means we turn loose of it, and go to something else."

"God goes on further to remind us that we have sin in our lives that besets us. But we ain't to complain, but to keep on keeping on like we were in a race; one that is set before us whether we chose it or not."

"We just can't sit down in the middle of the road and expect to win the race. Remember the story of the tortoise and the hare?"

"Now when you are running a race to win, you go all out and don't get hindered to the left or the right, but you keep yor sights on that finish line."

"Paul tells us that we are to do what we have to do with patience. Miracles do happen, but most of the time they don't happen instantly. Now there are times when they do, but most of the time God uses things in our lives that teach us what He wants us to know and do."

"Now to 'beset' is just another word that means something that overwhelms us. And we all have had a bit of that in our lives; now don't we with this here Depression still going on?"

"Can I have an "Amen!" Several of the farmers complied with a hearty "Amen."

"Now take a closer look here. Now, if you don't have a Bible, look on with someone who does."

A few in the congregation moved their Bible over a little bit where the one next to them could look on as Pastor Alrod continued reading.

Billy Joe looked kinda startled when Mary O'Brien scooted a little closer down the bench and shared her Bible with him. He got a lump in his throat when she pointed to the place where his father had left off. Her little pointer finger was so pink and dainty. She looked up at him and mouthed the words, "I'm sorry I laughed at you!"

He could not even begin to read or hear what his Papa was saying? His heart was beating so hard it had closed up his ears.

Pastor Alrod resumed reading from Hebrews 12:11, *"Now no chastening for the present seemeth to be joyous, but grievous: nevertheless afterward it yieldeth the peaceable fruit of righteousness unto them which are exercised thereby."*

"Now we have to digest this with a little bit of some spiritual *Pepto Bismol* to understand this rightly. Now none of us likes to be disciplined. Now ask anyone of yor kids if they like it when they get punished; disciplined. They ain't likely to say that they do."

"And they ain't no different from the rest of us. It just seems to go against our nature not burl up when someone tries to tell us what to do."

Several of the women looked sternly at their husbands.

"But just as we discipline our children for their own good; and to help them keep on the straight and narrow, God does the same for us."

"Just as we discipline our young'uns to help them have a better life and to have peace in their life, that is what God does for us."

"Now the way I see this is… when things happen, it is like a teacher or parent training us for something; except in our case, it is God who is doing the teaching."

"It might not set too tight with us at first, but if we remain patient, we will come to the end of it and we will rake in peace… and understand it better by and by. Now granted, we may never fully know what God's plan and purpose is for our life, but that is where faith comes in."

"Now folks I want to start off my message this morning with another story. The story of a little boy who at age eight years old was told by his Pappy that he wuz old enough to work and pay for his own clothes and shoes. So at that young and tender age, that boy learned lessons that would take him far in life."

"Now little James Cash would grow up to have many jobs and work in many places. One particular place where he worked helped him to buy his own butcher shop. Now this was his livelihood, and he depended on selling meat; and meat only."

"And his best customer was the hotel across the street. This big hotel was the biggest buyer of meats in town. Now… Ole James Cash depended on that account to keep his business running."

"One day, he went to see the hotel chef to get his regular order and he was met with an ultimatum. Have you ever been met with an ultimatum? You know… right there in yor face? And you had to make up yor mind right then?"

"Well, this happened to James Cash. This here chef up and gave him an ultimatum. He asked James Cash to bring him two bottles of likker every time he came for the order, or there would be no order."

"Now James Cash, being raised by a minister-father knew it was wrong. However, he was sorely tempted. But he knew in his heart that would be wrong; so he told the chef, "No!""

"And he lost the hotel's business."

"Now the jewel of this story is that James Cash lost his butcher shop. Now at first glance it don't look like a jewel from the Lord; does it?"

"Now here comes the jewel! That forced ole James Cash to find himself another line of work, and he went into the dry-good business. He worked for a man and then ended up buying the man's stores. Oddly enough, they wuz called, "The Golden Rule Stores.""

"When James Cash started buying up these stores for his own, they flourished, he bought more of them."

"From the meager earnings of an eight-year-old, and lessons and discipline of learning the hard way, James Cash eventually opened up a big chain of department stores. He gave them his name, but rather than call them the James Cash Penney Stores, they became known as the J. C. Penney Stores."

"While we ain't got no J.C. Penney Store here in the valley, we know there is a big one over the mountain in the city."

"Now here is the real jewel - a lot of butcher shops went out of business with the big supermarkets. But here in 1939, only twenty-six years after the first J. C. Penney store was opened in 1913, there are more than 1,000 stores all across the country."

"James Cash Penney is a godly man – a man who calls Jesus, his Savior. He runs his business in a Christ-like manner, and God causes them to flourish to this very day."

"It might not be today or tomorrow, but God will make it right. Ole James Cash had a lot more lessons to learn, and when this big Depression hit, he nearly lost everything. He borrowed on his insurance policies to make the payroll for his employees."

"He was right partial to his employees and wanted them to all be good family folks. He didn't like them smokin' and drinkin'. He always paid close attention to the wives of his employees because he felt a good home life would just up and overflow into the business."

"His health suffered from that great economic blow to his business, he took mighty sickly and had to go away. And just seven years ago, he had to go into the hospital for a while. While he was there, he heard some people singing that great old hymn, *"God Will Take Care of You."*

"And right then and there, he truly gave his heart to Christ and became a real born agin' Christian. He took his burdens to the Lord and left them there."

"But it wasn't just the song that did it. It was those teachings he had all his life beginning when he was just eight years old; The Depression and that song, just brung it to a head."

"Folks, when times come hard, and you got worry on yor mind - and you don't know where nothing is coming from - just remember that old hymn written way back in 1904 by Civilla and Walter Martin."

"They had written that song just two years after James Cash bought his first Golden Rule Store in 1902. Little did they know he would hear it in 1932; and give his life totally to Christ. Now ain't that just like the Lord?"

"Now you stop and think about it... the Lord took care of yor Salvation many-a-year before yor oldest remembered ancestor was born."

"But what the Lord did back then, is new and ready for you here today. Do I hear any Amen's?" Herman, himself, said, "Amen, and Amen."

There were men's voices coming from all over the little church echoing the Amen's. "Amen, Amen, and Amen." They sounded like the echo in the ravine.

"Now before we end this Sunday Meetin' is there anyone who wants to take the floor?"

"Anyone?"

He waited for a few seconds and then he heard a familiar voice coming from the back.

"I do, Brother Alrod."

A young man rose and said, "This here is Billy Joe, and I have this here dime left over from when I swept and cleaned up some at Mr. Ferguson's store. Well, actually he paid me sixty cents, but I owed fifty cents to someone else. He looked at the back of Mama's head, but she did not turn around. But she was smiling just the same.

"I know it ain't much, but I just felt like the Lord was calling me to do this, and I just can't sit back here no longer without doing it."

"I want to give it to the church for paying on the organ."

If Brother Alrod's chest stuck out any further with pride, it would have surely burst the buttons off his new shirt. He was just barely able to say, "God bless you, son!"

"Now you folks sit back and listen as Miss Parrish comes and gives us her rendition of *"God Will Take Care of You."* And He will you know."

While most of the congregation was listening to Miss Parrish, Mama was thinking how proud she was of the way Papa had preached that morning, and she was proud of the way her son had acted.

Mama turned her attention fully toward Miss Parrish and soaked in the words that she was singing. She quietly thanked God for the lessons she had learned that morning, and for her son giving his last dime to the church.

She felt convicted in her heart at the harsh way she had spoken to Billy Joe about his injured foot. She knew she had handled it in the wrong way. She knew she had to ask him to forgive her.

"Be not dismayed whate'er betide, God will take care of you;
Beneath His wings of love abide, God will take care of you.

Refrain: God will take care of you, through every day, o'er all the way;
He will take care of you, God will take care of you.

Through days of toil when heart doth fail, God will take care of you;
When dangers fierce your path assail, God will take care of you.

All you may need He will provide, God will take care of you;
Nothing you ask will be denied, God will take care of you.

No matter what may be a test, God will take care of you;
Lean, weary one, upon His breast, God will take care of you."

During the song, Herman looked down at his wife and knew that God had spoken to her heart. As he rose to pronounce the benediction he said, "Let's be reminded that while the Lord Jesus disciplines those He loves, He also prays for them since He is sitting at the right hand of God. We must teach… live by example… and pray for our children."

He said, 'I want to leave you with something that a famous man once said about his mother's prayers."

"He said, 'All that I am or hope to be I owe to my angel mother. I remember my mother's PRAYERS and they have always followed me. They have clung to me all my life.' These words were spoken by Abraham Lincoln."

As was his custom every week, Pastor Alrod asked the congregation to rise for the blessing of the benediction, taken from Numbers 6:24–26.

"*The Lord bless thee, and keep thee: The Lord make His face shine upon thee, and be gracious unto thee: The Lord lift up his countenance upon thee, and give thee peace.* Amen"

Now there will be those who would say that Billy Joe gave his dime after hearing about the wealth of J.C. Penney by doing the right thing. Some might say he did it to impress Mary O'Brien who was sitting next to him, and still others might say he wanted to pacify his parents. But Mama and Papa knew their son.

After the service, a neighbor lady came up to Mama and said, "Take that chile home and fill that wound with table salt; pack it on there real good. Let it stay on there for about ten minutes, and then lightly brush it off."

She said, "Do this once a day. If that don't heal that boy's foot, you ought to git him to the doctor right away." Mama did what she said… and it did.

Chapter six: Mama, Do You Think I Am Purdy?

Mama and Sarah Louise were working in the kitchen together, and as they often did, they chatted while doing the cooking and the chores.

They had been talking about various things for a while when Sarah Louise had this far away look in her eyes and asked, "Mama, do you think I am purdy?"

"Sarah Louise, why do you ask that?"

"I don't know, Mama. It just seems all the boys at school like Thelma Ruth more than they do me!"

"What difference does it make what boys at school like or do? What they do ain't none of yor business. Besides, God made you who you are, and He made Thelma Ruth, who she is. We don't need to be questioning what the Lord does. Why it would drive us crazy trying to be like everyone else. We just need to consider who we are and what purpose God made us for!"

"Now you can't be ah hepping what other folks look at - especially boys. It's just a matter of what you look at... that is yor business. Keeping yor eyes on the right track will keep yor mind on the right track."

"Mama, do you think her family is more richer than us? She is always gittin' new stuff to wear to school."

"Sarah Louise, you know full well that the measure of a person is not what they got and ain't got... it's what is in their hearts. Luke and Matthew both say in the writing of the scriptures that we are more than what we eat and what we wear."

"Our bodies are more than what we stuff in them at the dinner table, and our bodies are also more than what we put on our backs."

Mama continued while she had Sarah Louise's attention and said, "Yor Grandmother Sarah, yor namesake, told me one time that you can take an old mean lady and dress her up in the finest of clothing, and she will still be a mean old lady."

"Sweetness, God don't give the same things to everyone. But, I am sure that you have some things that He has given you that are better than what Thelma Ruth has. But we are not to compare ourselves to what other folks are… doing… eating… or wearing. It ain't always what you got but who you are. It don't matter what is on the outside of a person; but what is on the inside."

As Mama was often to do, she would quote scripture as a matter of fact and not preaching. Mama said matter-of-factly, *"Man looks on the outward appearance, but God looks on the heart."*

"Don't you remember that Sunday School lesson a little while back that used the Bible verse to say what God does? As I recall, you were memorizing that scripture. It's right to memorize scripture. For in the time you need it, God will remind you of it. But we must do more than just memorize scripture to quote. We must hide it in our hearts and live by it. We are to hide God's Word in our heart so that we might not sin against Him."

Sarah Louise, who would you rather please, some boys at school or God?"

"I know Mama, but people don't look at yor insides… they look at yor outsides."

"Sarah Louise, you know full well that you are a purdy girl. That don't mean a hill of beans when it comes to who you are. The most purdiest people in the world ain't always the happiest or the most successful in what they are doing. You better learn to live in and like the skin you come in because that is the only skin yor apt to have."

"Some young girls get the idea that if they pile on enough lipstick and powder that makes them better than who they are! Well, it don't and in some cases makes them look cheap and easy."

"What does easy mean, Mama?"

"Never you mind, you will understand that when you get a little older; but it ain't nice. And besides the Good Book says that pride goes before the fall."

"I know Mama, but I think I would be more happy if I wuz purdy like Thelma Ruth. She has purdy hair. It is all curly like, and mine is so straight," she said, flipping out the ends of her long tresses.

"It ain't only that she's got a purdy face and curly hair and new dresses; she's got all the boys, too."

"Sarah Louise, shame on you! Ain't you heard a single word I've been telling you? What does a girl need with more than one beau? She can't marry them all, and that will leave the rest to find another girl. When the time comes, they'll be enough to go around. Besides you are too young to be thinkin' about no beaus."

"Why yor Daddy would take to his shotgun if he thought any squirrelly boys wuz hanging around after you with you only twelve-years-old."

"I'll soon be thirteen, Mama."

"Be that as it may you won't be until you are... and then that don't make you grown, yet."

"I know Mama, but at least I wish God would've give me curly hair instead of this ole mop."

"Well, if that is the onlinest thing in this world that is keeping you from being happy, not having curls... well, we can fix that."

"How, Mama?"

"Now you finish up peelin' them taters. It ain't tater salit with no taters. Tomorrow is Homecoming at the church, and you know how everyone sets store by my tater salit."

"If I'm peeling the taters, Mama, won't that make it 'my' tater salit?"

"Now Sarah Louise you just git on with it. Don't you know there is more to tater salit than just peelin' the taters? It takes my secret recipe to make it just right. If you are a good girl and do like I say, both you and the tater salit will be a big hit."

"Mama, bragging about yor tater salit, ain't that like having too much pride? Why is it that all the women of the church try to outdo one another at the church with their cooking?"

"Now child, there is two kinds of pride. There is taking pride in who you are and what you do when it is yor best. And there is false pride thinkin' yor somethin' you ain't or being somethin' you ain't, or like in thinking you are better than someone else. But just so's you don't git it in

80

yor head that making tater salit and curls can make you a good person, they can't."

"Purdy is… as purdy does. Sometimes boys like flashy girls because they's boys. But when they git to be a man… they want someone who is more purdy inside than outside when they git marrying on their mind. Sarah Louise, a person's looks can change; either with age, sickness or even an accident."

"You remember how cousin Maybelle got her face burned when that ember popped up out of the fire when she was a child? Well, maybe you don't. You weren't born yet. But anyhow, she wore that scar on her face the rest of her life. God rest her soul. There wasn't no prettier woman in all this county than Maybelle."

"She had a loving heart, a good reputation, and character. That was worth far more than gold or rubies or a purdy face. She was loved for who she was; and not for what her face looked like. When she died, the whole county came to her funeral. There wasn't an extra seat in a single pew. They had to bring in folks' kitchen chairs just so the old folks and Mama's with nursing babies could sit down."

"If a purdy face was all she had her live long days, when she got old and them wrinkles begin to set in, her beauty would have just up and left her."

"But it was that light shining from her soul all her live long days what won the admiration of everyone she knew. Beauty like that don't fade with scars or old age."

"Now wipe the tater juice off yor hands and go out to the barn and bring me a couple of grandpa's old *Prince Albert* pipe tobacco cans. Look in that old barrel, next to the wall, where he throws them. Now go on and hurry back."

Sarah Louise jumped up and ran toward the door and stopped for a second, turned around and asked, "Mama, what do you put into yor tater salit that makes it so good? Yors IS the best!"

Mama wiped her hands on her apron and smiled and said, "Love."

As Sarah Louise passed Grandpa on the front porch, she asked, "Grandpa why do you save that big ole barrel full of *Prince Albert* tobacco cans when you don't even smoke a pipe?"

Grandpa who was kinda startled being asked such a question out of the blue replied, "Well, Baby Girl, they are useful for a lot of things. They are made out of good tin that can be used for a lot of things when you cut them up. Since they have a tight lid on them, they can hold a heap of things like nails and such. Why do you ask gal?"

"Oh, I was just wondering," she replied.

That Saturday evening after everyone had drawn up the water and heated it for their baths, Mama and Sarah Louise took a big pair of scissors and cut those *Prince Albert* cans into tiny metal strips. They wrapped them with strips of brown paper sack which covered the sharp edges. Then they wound each strand of Sarah Louise's just shampooed hair around the strips. By bending the edges forward, they would hold each curl in place.

Come Sunday-go-to Meetin' time, Sarah looked lovely with her abundance of bouncing curls. She wore Mama's lace collar over her old Sunday-go-to Meetin' dress which made it look almost new.

❦

Sunday Meetin' Time

Pastor Alrod began the service by saying, "Being today is Homecoming, and we have so many mothers here with their children, I think it is only fittin' that we recognize the hard work they done put into that dinner out there on them tables. But most especially the love they put in their homes."

"Brother Seagraves, why don't you start the meetin' off with a prayer of thanksgiving to the Lord for all these women who do so much for all of us; and pray especially for us men folk; while most of the time, we appreciate them, we don't always say so."

"Lord, this here is Charlie Seagraves. We are beholding to you for such a fine day. Bless them what is here and them that ain't. Lord you know if it be a good reason they ain't here. Lord, you also know if they just be spending the day with the devil when they could be here spending it with You."

"Lord, it is plumb good to see so many folks here today. Wouldn't it be nice if we had this crowd every Sunday? Lord, it must be that good ole fried chicken and them chocolate pies what brung everyone here today." Everyone knew he was teasing.

"But Lord, it don't matter what brung them, we are glad that they are here! Thank You, Lord for the big donation made in secret by the one that ain't no secret to You... for the organ payment. We are truly blessed, and we know that You will take care of blessing them, too!"

"Oh Lord, every time we hear Sister Maggie pump them peddles and mash them keys, we are lifted in our spirits when all that beautiful music comes out. And it shore makes it nice to hear when a bride comes down the aisle to be married. But Lord, it shore can make us sad when we hear it at them funerals."

Herman cleared his throat as if to say to Mr. Seagraves, "Get on with it, we ain't got all day!"

"Lord, the pastor has done asked me to say a little prayer for all the women here in this little church. Lord, I just can't think what we would do without 'em. They take on a passel, and a heap, in keeping up with all the rest of us. And for each and everyone, we are most thankful."

"Lord, if we ever had to iron a shirt, sew on a button or nuss a crying baby, we would be at a complete loss. Lord, I guess it be Yor plan that men do the work of the men and women do the work of the women. Lord, you shore made us different."

Herman cleared his throat a little louder this time.

"Oh, excuse me, Lord for gettin' off track," said Brother Seagraves.

They thought he was at last about to say, "Amen," when he said, "Oh yes, Lord, that fried chicken shore does smell good. And we thank You for it, too. And for the women folk who killed the chicken, took off the feathers and cooked up them birds. They ain't nothin' I hate more than biting into a nice piece of fried chicken and finding a feather in my mouth."

With that, the whole congregation said in unison – "AMEN!"

The congregation always got a little humor from Brother Seagraves's prayers. He went straight to the point and usually prayed much longer, but the smell of the fried chicken must have gotten to him. And most of them suspected he was the "big" donor for the payment on the organ. He owned the feed and grain store and done right good.

Everyone loved the old deacon no matter how long he prayed, but some got kinda perturbed with those who prayed the same rote prayer, time after time, when it was their turn to pray. But they never heard a boring prayer come out of the mouth, and from the heart, of Brother Seagraves.

Pastor Alrod rose to his feet and once again took his place to begin his Sunday morning discourse.

"Brother and sisters, I feel the Lord is asking me to teach you what is a good and sound church – so we will know how to live up to it."

"The church is made of up of people. As sinful as we are, we each have a role in life, in our homes and in the church."

"This here sermon is taken right out of the pages of the Bible in a letter that the Apostle Paul wrote to Titus. It tells us plainly here that in order for the church to be right... the homes and families got to be right. We can't change the world, but we can be obedient to God in our own lives and households."

He held his time-worn and well-read Bible opened over his left hand. The covers flopped on either side, and he used his right hand to hold his place.

However, by the time he delivered his sermons on Sunday, he pretty much knew the scripture by heart. He knew what he was going to say; unless the Lord moved him in a different direction.

He read the scriptures late at night after working on the farm all day, and prayed night and day that God would teach him... so in turn he could teach others. He always arrived at church before anyone else and knelt down at the little altar praying for his delivery and the reception by those who attended.

He practiced his sermons while working in the fields, riding down the road, or sitting on the front porch at night watching the sun go down. He always felt an intense pulling in his heart that he was to rightly divide the Word of God, and not put too much of Herman in it.

Some weeks, he came away feeling that the spirit of the Lord was truly in that place through his preaching, the singing, and praying. However, from time to time, he felt discouraged and felt he might as well have stayed home himself.

This morning, he read, *"But as for you, speak the things which are proper for sound doctrine: that the older men be sober, reverent, temperate, sound in faith, in love, in patience..."*

"Are you listening men? Do you hear? Paul is saying here that we ought to be aware of what we say and how it affects people. We ain't to go around saying the Bible says this or that when it didn't. And when he talks about the older men, I think he means the men who have reached adulthood and who have responsibilities upon their shoulders."

"Now it is common knowledge that some of you men like to take a sip every now and then. That is between you and God. However, it says here that a man needs to have a clear head, and not all likkered up so as he ain't ah thinking right. And as some of you know, it don't take much of that ole demon drink to make yor head swim, and you can't think without a sober mind."

He said to them, *"Be aware that the Bible says that wine is a mocker, and those, who are fooled by it, are not wise."* He added, "The mistake many people make is turning to some form of likker rather than to God. And you know that likker does not drown yor problems it only makes them float, and when you sober up, up they pop again."

"As I said, you'd best take that up with the Lord. However, this word "sober" also means just to be clear-headed and able to think clearly; even if you ain't likkered up."

"That word, 'grave' don't mean a place like in the back of the church, but it means to be serious like and to see things as being important."

"Now the next word, temperate, is one busy word. It has a lot of meanings. Here let me take a look at what I copied out of the dictionary." He unfolded the little piece of paper he had tucked in his Bible.

"It means to be restrained in the things we do. In other words, don't go overboard. It means being pleasant when our ears are burning with anger and trying to be pleasant when we don't feel like it. And this one is a real knee-slapper... being calm in un-calm situations."

"It seems when you are not temperate; yor blood just doesn't make it to yor brain with good intentions."

"We've all been there; finding ourselves in a situation that calls for a clear head and quick action. But instead we run around like a chicken with its head cut off. And this is a time when we are most apt to throw something; like when that old tire iron won't loosen them nuts on a flat tire."

Herman liked to interject a little humor, when he could, in order to bring their attention back to his sermon.

He went on saying, "There once was a man who hit a huge pothole in the street and had a flat tire right smack dab in front of an insane asylum. He cussed up a blue streak, and that didn't change a thing; and especially not his flat tire."

"A group of inmates wuz standing behind the iron gate watching his every move. This angry man was kinda prickly about being watched. That ticked him off as much as the flat tire. And we need to remember that God sees our every action and hears our every word."

Continuing his story, Pastor Alrod said, "As he was taking the nuts off the bolts on the tire, one of them inmates said, 'Better tie them "screw on things" in your handkerchief; so they don't roll away and get lost."

The man thought to himself, "What does an insane, nutty person know about such things?" He was so mad; he didn't pay any attention to what he was doing when he removed the nuts from the bolts; he just laid them inside the wheel cap.

"Sure enough, when the man stepped back to take the tire off and get the spare from the boot, he kicked over the wheel cap and the 'screw on things' went through the grate and into the storm drain."

"He let out another stream of cuss words and stomped around and cussed some more saying, 'Now what am I going to do - now what am I going to do?'

"The same inmate spoke up and said, 'Why don't you take one each of them "screw off things" from the other three tires to hold your tire on until you can get to the gas station?"

"The man knew that was a good idea and probably his only hope. He turned to the inmate and said, 'Man, you are smarter than I thought. What have they got you in there for? Why are you locked up like that?'

"The inmate replied, 'I'm just crazy; not dumb and stupid.'"

Those who got the joke laughed; but those who didn't just looked confused.

"Many times things just don't have nothin' to do with how smart we are - or how much education we got – but just who we are inside."

"Now this word is mighty tricky. When a man or woman is temperate, it does not mean they have a bad temper and fly off the handle at the least little thing. It is actually just the opposite."

"Now here is where the wheels rut the road. Now you men folk… sometimes it is just plain hard not to raise yor voice and scream and holler a little when things ain't going too well; like when you mash yor finger with a hammer. But God expects us to do the best we can, and you need to watch what you say in front of the women and children."

"Often what comes from the mouth got started in the heart."

"Now this sounds like a tall order here, but while we may not be perfect… we are to strive to be. I looked that word up in the Webster's, and that is what it said. "Are you listening, men?""

"Now this next one is really important that we be sound in faith. Now 'sound in faith' means to be firm, secure, and reverent. Now how many of you, both men and women, know what reverent means? Let me see a show of hands."

A few raised their hands, and looked around them, and quickly put their hands back down again which seemed to indicate they were not quite sure.

Herman took a quick look and went on. "It sounds kinda like what some of you folks call me - but it's two different words that mean almost the same. I am not the 'Reverent' Herman Alrod but the 'Reverend' Herman Alrod, but most of you just call me Preacher."

"However, I pray that I try to be reverent every day in every way." Some of them had a kind of puzzled look on their faces because some of them called him that indeed.

"When one is reverent it means to be filled with respect, worship, and sometimes pure awe at the Lord." he further explained.

"To have faith means that you hang on to the promises of God whether you can see the answers yet or not. The Bible says in Hebrews, *"Now faith is the substance of things hoped for, the evidence of things not seen."*

"Like us farmers know all the time, we have to live by faith that the rain will come to water our crops; even if there ain't one single baby cloud in the sky. We cannot make it rain, or order up a shipment of rain, but we know that it will be coming sooner or later."

"And sometimes the rain don't come for a long time, and we lose our crops; like has been happening during this here Depression."

"Sometimes other things, we pray and hope for, don't come around either. That is when faith really has to take hold… when we just don't see no way. But we must always remind ourselves that God has a purpose."

"And we have to trust His reasons. Faith is not a single thing that we conjure up when we need something, but faith is the way we worship and honor God at all times. Faith is not in the substance of things - what things are made up of - but is trusting in God no matter what. Faith simply believes in God."

"In Ephesians, it tells us that faith is a gift of God and not something that we deserve. *"For by grace are ye saved through faith; and that not of yourselves: it is the gift of God."*

"And in Mark we find these words, *"And Jesus said unto him, Go thy way; thy faith hath made thee whole. And immediately he received his sight and followed Jesus in the way."*

"Remember the woman who felt if she could just touch the hem of His garment and she would be healed. "And he said unto her, *"Daughter, be of good comfort; thy faith hath made thee whole; go in peace."*

"Now her faith was not in the magic of the cloth in His clothing, but in Him. Apparently she had seen the miracles He had performed and knew He could do it. Now don't you go falling for them preachers on the radio who says for a dollar, they will send you a prayer cloth. They will tell you that by holding it in yor hands and praying, you will be healed. That would be putting yor faith in a piece of cloth and not in God."

"Strong faith must be based on the Word of God. It must fall in line with what God has promised. Faith does not mean we will receive everything we ask for in our own way. At the end of the Lord's Prayer, don't we say, *'Thy will be done?"*

"It means that we can have victory through the faith we have in God; even if our prayers are not answered like we want them to be. Faith means putting yor trust in God no matter what. It is sometimes hard to understand why God seems to answer the prayers of others and not answer ours."

"Misplaced faith can destroy a person's relationship with God if they do not understand this principle. Our faith is not in the substance of what we ask for - the outcome - but faith in God that He will prevail and keep His promises."

"Remember faith is not something we mix up or conjure up in our own minds, but living according to the measure of faith given us by God to accept whatever the answer might be. Sometimes God answers with a 'yes,' right away. Sometimes He answers with a 'no' right away, and then sometimes He says 'just wait a while."

"We often hear people say, but I prayed in faith, and God did not answer. And only God knows why we sometimes git what we ask for and sometimes we don't. But we must not lose sight of the fact that our faith is not in what we ask for; but in the One who is able to do what we cannot."

"Since God knows what is coming down the road, and we ain't got no idée, that is when we just have to have faith in faith."

"Now the rest of this is just plain simple and none of you should have any problem understanding the rest of these... sound in charity and sound in patience."

"If you tie up yor dog sound with a rope around a tree... he will be secure and won't run away. If your health is sound, it means that you are in purdy good shape. If you are right with God, you will be sound and be able to walk-the-walk and not just talk-the-talk. When we are secure in our faith, which is God, then we will be sound, and we won't run away either."

"Now charity here don't mean stuff that you give away. Sometimes the stuff we give away we didn't need anyway. Charity is what motivates us to give and to serve, and to bestow things on others. Sometimes we need to give until it hurts a little to help us understand the ways of others who are in need."

"Charity means to be sound in love; love to all people."

Herman could relate the whole chapters without even turning to them. Before he shared the verses, he reminded them that the word charity here means love. He said, *"And though I bestow all my goods to feed the poor, and though I give my body to be burned, and have not charity, it profiteth me nothing."*

"Love means that suffering might be long. Love means that there is kindness and not envy. Love also does not throw itself at others, and it does not swell a person up with themselves."

"Love does not behave in bad ways. Love does not seek attention for oneself. Love does not lose control easily. Love does not think about evil things. Love does not love wickedness, but Love rejoices at the truth."

"Love is constant and not wishy, washy. It is not hot one minute and cold the next!"

"Love, Beareth all things, believeth all things, hopeth all things, endureth all things. Love never faileth: but whether there be prophecies, they shall fail; whether there be tongues, they shall cease; whether there be knowledge, it shall vanish away."

"Love ain't like tracks in the snow that melt away; but like words engraved in stone."

"A lot of things in this old world will fail and change, but love never will. Children become grownups, and they no longer think like kids. They will put away the childish things they loved as children and will come face to face with who they really are, and they also understand that others will truly know them as well."

"And now abideth faith, hope, charity, these three; but the greatest of these is charity."

"The greatest words ever spoke about love are these, *"For God so loved the world that He gave His only begotten Son."*

"Now this last word came in at just the right place. Don't be impatient, that chicken will still be there, and I am almost to the end of this lesson."

"And last of all, we see, "sound in patience." Fathers, what you do today and how you speak to yor children will go with them the rest of their lives; especially them boys. Sometimes it is just plain hard to feel love toward a wayward child, but remember those who deserve our love the least need it the most."

"And you hollering and screaming and getting' out the barber's strap might make impressions on their mind and bodies, but it will surely make the wrong impressions on their souls. Remember what this here book says about love in I Corinthians 13. Look it up and live by it."

"Now with every eye closed and no one looking around... God will see you... don't none of you even look up here at me."

"I want every man here this morning, who has heard the Word of God, to raise their hand if this is the kind of man, husband, father, church member and neighbor you want to be. You have been given the responsibility of yor family; some of you as fathers and some of you as sons. There is no doubt that it wuz God's plan for the man to be the head of the family. Sadly, so many in today's world just don't understand this."

"Dear Lord, hear us when we pray. Lord, you know the hearts of man, and you know the actions of man and You provided a way that all men can come to you for Salvation, repentance, and right standing with You. Amen."

There was stillness in the room that was almost deafening. Herman remained silent for a few seconds and then he continued.

"God created man to be the head of the household and to be the leader, and protector of his family, but he also created women to be his helpmate. While Eve was taken from the rib of Adam, that did not mean he has dominion over her."

"Whether God put Adam to sleep in order to cut out one of his ribs, only He knows. Adam was asleep, and only God was there. It just might be His way of telling us how close God wanted man and wife to be. It might be representative of His intentions. God designed both male and female. Out of man comes the seed that reproduces mankind; and from out of woman comes new life. It takes them both according to God's design."

"We don't know how He actually made man, but He did. We don't know how He actually made woman, but He did. I think this means that God made the woman a part of man so that they would be as one... two in one... like in marriage. The word woman means "taken out of man." If a man regards his wife as part of himself, he will look at her differently."

"Adam understood that Eve was a part of him as it says in Genesis when he said, "This is now bone of my bones, and flesh of my flesh: she shall be called *Woman,* because she was taken out of *Man.*"

The Reverend Alrod said, "There was a man by the name of Matthew Henry, who lived many centuries ago. He was a Bible scholar, and he had this to say, *"Eve was not taken out of Adam's head to top him, neither out of his feet to be trampled on by him, but out of his side to be equal with him, under his arm to be protected by him, and near his heart to be loved by him."*

"God never did anything without a purpose. We, as followers of Christ, should also have a purpose while we are on this earth. A man or woman without a purpose is like a piece of driftwood floating in the ocean... never accomplishing anything, never knowing where it is going and of no earthly good to anyone else."

"God has a purpose for everyone on this earth; including the women and children."

"Men, this is where most women put us to shame. By nature, they are more gentle and loving. God created men to be the hunters, providers, and the protectors while he created women to be nurturers, the home-fire keepers; as well as the encouragement and strength behind the man and children. God created both men and women, and He blesses them in their own roles where each has only the burden of their part, but united together in harmony for the greater good of both of them and for their offspring. God created the family first.

Then he continued... "Now, ladies, I guess you done thought you'd get off easy this morning since the Lord led me to speak to the men this morning. Well, hold on to yor bonnets."

Continuing from the Book of Titus, Preacher Alrod read,

"The aged women likewise, that they be in behaviour as becometh holiness, not false accusers, not given to much wine, teachers of good things; that they may teach the young women to be sober, to love their husbands, to love their children, to be discreet, chaste, keepers at home, good, obedient to their own husbands, that the word of God be not blasphemed."

He went on to explain that "aged" did not mean the elderly, but the "older" women were to be reverent in their behavior and not to slander others and to be teachers of good things. They are to teach the younger women to love their husbands and to love their children, and to be discreet, chaste, homemakers, and to be good to them.

He explained that to be obedient to their husbands did not mean they were his servants and had no authority in the family. Women were to act like Paul says here - mostly to honor God and not anyone else; so that God's Word would not be blasphemed.

Looking in the direction of Mama, Herman said, "It is amazing what a good woman can do in the life of a man." She smiled at him with such love in her expression and her face he nearly lost his place in his sermon.

Herman went on to explain each word for the women as he had for the men. But these dedicated women, in the community and church, lived by these words... for the most part. They needed little more than a reminder to be aware of their awesome responsibility that God had entrusted to them.

Wives had to have good behavior in order to be an example to their children, or what they said would have no impact. They were to guard their tongues and language for the same reason. By deed and actions, they were to be teachers of what is good and right.

Women were not to be examples of blasphemy against God. They were to love their families; they were to use good manners. They were to keep themselves pure and only for their husbands and to keep their homes well.

They were to be compliant with their husband who has the responsibility before God for the entire family. Not that they couldn't offer their thoughts and opinions; but that the final responsibility rested with the man that God holds responsible.

Women were to be lovers of God and their home. They were not to be wildly seeking fulfillment in a worldly manner of amusement and entertainment for themselves that was sinful and harmful, and thus neglect their families.

He stopped for a second to get his breath and then continued, "Now you young folks. Paul does not leave you out by any means."

He commenced reading, *"Young men likewise exhort to be sober minded. In all things shewing thyself a pattern of good works: in doctrine shewing uncorruptness, gravity, sincerity, sound speech, that cannot be condemned; that he that is of the contrary part may be ashamed, having no evil thing to say of you."*

93

Being a father as well as a minister of the Gospel, Herman often took the time to talk with the young people of his church and warned them about the dangers of living lives unpleasing to God and the consequences of that kind of choice.

This morning he encouraged the young people to be the example and not followers in a crowd. He encouraged them to live like the scripture said by leading good clean lives... lives that they would not be ashamed of and would not open themselves up to have anything bad said about them.

In the next verses, Paul dealt with the relationship between slave and master which were part of the culture in his time. Herman felt it important to speak about that as well. While the Civil War had ended forced slavery in America, it did not mend the hearts and minds of those who fought it.

Their Preacher continued explaining, "Paul is telling the slaves or servants in Ephesians and I Timothy that it was to their benefit to obey their masters, but he was not condoning the act of slavery itself. He went on to explain the different types of slavery and the commitment a slave had to their master."

Herman read the scripture and then went on to explain by saying, "There were two types of slaves – those who had been captured and forced into slavery and those who sold themselves voluntarily into slavery. They were known as "bondservants."

"They entered into a contract or "bond" with someone to work for them. Often parents would bond their children out to others to help support the family. Later in America, this type of arrangement was known as being apprentices or indentured servants."

He further explained, "There were folks who signed on to be indentured servants in exchange for their passage to America." He went on to say, "Many of the original colonists who came to America were indentured servants."

"I hear tell the story about a Negro man by the name of Anthony Johnson, who was brought to America in the sixteen hundreds. He served many years as a faithful servant to his master on a tobacco farm. He was later given his freedom. He put what he had learned from working on his master's tobacco farm to work for himself. He became a successful tobacco farmer and businessman."

Herman then reminded them about how his great-grandfather, Samuel Goodroe Alrod, came to America as a young man from Ireland. He was penniless. Herman said with great pride, "He worked hard, and was able to buy not only his farm, but also the very land that this church is sitting upon. His legacy, hard work, and determination lives on today for those who came behind him."

Pastor Alrod surmised that in Paul's day and time, because of the culture of the people, he spoke to those who were slaves saying they should be obedient to their masters for their own benefit. It was a fact of life during Paul's days; much like it once was in America, that slaves were the property owned by their masters.

Paul spoke frankly about slavery over in Galatians when he said, *"There is neither Jew nor Greek, there is neither bond nor free, there is neither male nor female: for ye are all one in Christ Jesus."* And he added, *"In Christ all people are free!"*

"There were still people in the world who were slaves to others and that was not part of God's plan; but the evil of mankind. Today there are far more people who are slaves to sin no matter their skin color or race," explained their minister.

Pastor Alrod went further by saying, "Slavery here in America must have been a stench in the nostrils of God, and we all know about that awful war that was fought to free those in bondage."

He said. "While slaves were owned by people on both sides before the Civil War, this valley was cleared, settled, and farmed since 1850 without one single bit of slave labor." He went on to say, "White folks and colored folks have always gotten on purdy good up here in the mountains. Regardless of a man's color or position in life, we must treat all of our neighbors with respect and honor."

Preacher Alrod continued, "But in some places, especially in the big cities, there is a lot of wrong and bad treatment of colored folks and people of all ethnic backgrounds and races. While slavery has been abolished, the effects of those years are still felt by people everywhere here in 1939.

There are those who were slaves and others whose lives were ruined by the war even though they were not slave owners."

"There is still a lot of tension and bitterness between some people. It is as if they are still fighting that war with the north and south against each other."

"There are those who try to use the Bible against itself saying that it condones slavery. Atheists say that is one reason they do not believe in the Bible or in God because they condone slavery. The Bible speaks about thieves but does not condone stealing."

He told his attentive audience, "Today, that same principle could be applied here in the year of 1939, but in a different way. This scripture is good advice for the employer and employee relationship."

He went on to say: "While most of the folks here in the valley work for themselves on their farms, there are those who work for other folks. And, just about everyone in the city works for somebody else."

He said, "In a sense, we all work for someone else and employees need to realize that the employer is the boss man. When you work for someone else, you should work as though you are working for yourselves." Also, this here Bible says, *"Whatsoever you do – do it as unto the Lord."* It also says that if you don't work, you don' eat. And it also says that employers should treat their workers fairly. Holding up his Bible, He said, *"A man is worthy of his hire."*

He didn't have to remind them that there were a lot of men out of work. He added that most of them would jump at the chance of a job so they would be able to feed their families. Herman stopped and took a sip of water from the glass that was always there on his pulpit and said, "There is honor in that."

Taking another big swallow, he continued, "God tells us that any man, who don't take care of his family, is worse than an infidel. An infidel is one who does not or will not believe in God and is destined to spend eternity in Hell." However, once a man takes a job, they need to honor and respect the rules of the man who hired him."

He expounded a little more on the subject by saying, "If you work for a man, your reward is your wages. If either is displeased with the other, the relationship can be terminated. That was not true of slavery.

A slave was owned by his master, and had to do what he said or face the consequences."

Peering above his glasses, Herman added. "According to God's Word, both are responsible to God for the way they treat each other."

"Slavery to sin is no different. When a person is a slave to sin, they must also face the consequences." He explained, "But the wages of sin is death."

"As Christians, we have the joy and satisfaction of knowing that our wages for sin was paid for in full by Christ, and we have been set free." The relationship between a true believer in God, through Christ, will never be broken. And we never have to fear our Master; for those He sets free... are free indeed."

Pastor Alrod went on to say, "But that was not the case in most Biblical situations and certainly not in the case where people were kidnapped and brought to America against their will. God does not force us or make us. But it is of our own free will that we choose to be like Paul when he said, "I am a prisoner of Jesus Christ and righteousness."

"Sadly, today here in 1939, there are still forms of slavery in our nation for men and women of all races. Many are in bondage to unscrupulous employers who abuse and cheat them in sweat shops, cotton mills, and factories."

"We see in the Bible where the Hebrew children were forced slaves to Pharaoh. However, as Christians we are not forced into slavery. We are, of our own free will, more like indentured servants to Christ. We are not required to spend seven or even more years, but lovingly we serve a lifetime."

"Jesus Christ, Himself, was our true example of being a servant unto righteousness when He washed the feet of his disciples and died on that cruel ole cross."

"He was called, "Master" by his followers which more often means, "Teacher." His followers were obedient to Him unto death because they loved Him... and not because He forced them."

Herman said, "Take a look over here in the New Testament and see what it says, in Romans 6:17 and 18."

"*But thanks be to God that though you were slaves of sin, you became obedient from the heart to that form of teaching to which you were committed, and having been freed from sin, you became slaves of righteousness.*"

"So brothers and sisters here on this day set aside for Homecoming let us look forward to another Homecoming Day when the Lord gives us all He has promised; including Salvation unto eternal life."

"*This is the day of the Lord hath made, let us rejoice and be glad in it.*" And if you want to make sure yor salvation, today is the acceptable time. For God in no wise will cast out those with a good and true heart. Because we know, "*That man looks on the outward appearance, but God looks on the heart.*"

The preacher and father had just confirmed what Mama had told Sarah Louise only the day before. And he had no idea about their previous conversation. God is like that.

Mama turned and looked at her daughter who had an array of springy curls which outlined her beautiful face. Her daughter looked back at her with a smile of love that made Mama's heart glow.

Mama knew that one day Sarah Louise would find the man that God had created for her. And, she would be the wife God created her to be.

That morning after the sermon, the women in the church felt a glowing sense of pride in who they were, and what God had created them to be. Because when you love yor family, as God loves the church, it was easy.

Photo album reminiscent

of the times and era

of Sunday Meetin' Time

Intended as a walk down memory lane

and

Not intended to be representative

of the actual characters and story.

You have the joy of imagining those for yourself.

Acts 16:5
And so were the churches established in the
faith, and increased in number daily.

Acts 20:28
Take heed therefore unto yourselves, and to all the flock, over
which the Holy Ghost hath made you overseers, to feed
the church of God, which He hath purchased with His own blood.

Ephesians 3:21
Unto Him be glory in the church by Christ Jesus
throughout all ages, world without end. Amen.

Revelation 2:29
He that hath an ear, let him hear what the
Spirit saith unto the churches.

"The old worn out church!"

Martha Sue Higgins
Precious Little angel
Daughter of
Joel and Martha Ann Higgins
Budded on earth to bloom in heaven
Born 1850 - Died 1850

"The Little Cemetery on the Hill"

"Mama's Stuff"

"Papa's Stuff"

"Country Vittles"

"Pets and Animals on the Farm"

106

"Down on the Farm"

"Busy Hands Needlework!"

"About the Church"

Photography Credits
Cover designed by

Patricia McCullough Walston
Writer for
Atlanta Faith and Family Examiner http://www.examiner.
com/faith-and-family-in-atlanta/patricia-walston

Facebook page: Patricia McCullough Walston

Photography of cover painting and collages by
Rene Bidez Photography
103 Glynn St S, Fayetteville, GA 30214
(770) 461-4410

Photo Contributors

Special thanks to:

Hopeful Primitive Baptist Church
Restoration Committee

Antique Irish Quilts – Roselind Shaw of Northern Ireland

Art Hamill
Barbara Chapo
Cindy Biddy
Debra Griggs
Dewey Lee, University of Georgia
Drew, Lisa, Adam Walston

Gary Long
Ginger Moore
Jane Harkins
Lee Welborn
Lita Fannin
Lynda Warf

Dean Breest Photography of Fayetteville Georgia
600 North Glenn Street 404-915-1414
Hayden Bartlett Photography of Fayetteville, Georgia
Tony Tolbert Photography of Roopville Georgia

Chapter seven: Fishing, Lies, and Pennies

"Papa, why did God put fish in the water," soon to be five-year-old little LeRoy asked?" while he squirmed around on the creek bank.

"Cause, He wanted to, I guess LeRoy."

"But Papa; puttin' them in the water makes them too hard to ketch."

"Well, son, chickens are just as hard to ketch, but we like fried chicken don't we?"

"Papa is it true that you can ketch a bird if you slip up on it and put salt on its tail?"

"Dunno... son, I never tried it... but I wouldn't be ah wastin' no salt to find out either."

"Papa, why do you suppose it's just dogs and cats what's so easy to ketch? Ole "Snooper" never runs away. Most times he just tries to knock me down."

"Maybe it is because he thinks you gonna give him a handout. Why that worthless, flop-eared old hound, he don't even earn his keep by barking when a stranger comes up into the yard," said his father with a grin.

"Papa, are we done fishin' yet?"

"Well, LeRoy we ain't done much more than wet the hook. Don't you want some nice catfish fer supper?"

"Naw, Papa, I don't like catfish; if I gotta ketch them first."

"Don't you think Mama would be disappointed if we didn't bring her home a nice mess of fish... what are we gonna tell her?"

"What if everyone felt that way about working for dinner? Who would provide for them? And if we didn't work for our food, who would feed us?"

Ignoring the latter, LeRoy said, "Well, we could tell her a bear came and ate up all the fish."

"Why LeRoy, don't you know that would be lying? Son, do you know when the truth is the truth, and a lie is a lie?"

"Well, kinda," he answered.

"The troof is when you tell somethin' that really happened, and a lie is when you tell somethin' you just wish had happened."

"Pa....pa?" LeRoy said, kinda drawing out the word to make it a question.

"Yes, son?"

Hesitating a little and changing the subject, LeRoy said, "Papa, are we really made out of dirt?"

Chuckling, he replied, "LeRoy, sometimes I think you just might be from the looks of yor bath water on Saturday night. When I throw it out the kitchen door, I have to look back and see if some of you is missing... because the water is so full of dirt."

Trying to keep his restless little son's attention, Papa asked, "Son, you got yor birthday comin' up this week. You got yor pennies for the birthday jar at church?"

"Well, mostly!"

"How many you got?"

"I still got me four of them."

"But LeRoy, you will be five-years-old, and you earned five pennies – why do you only have four now?"

"Well, I got to thinking that there wuz lots of pennies in that jar at church for the missionaries, and I only needed one for a piece of candy at Mr. Ferguson's store. That ain't stealing is it, Papa. It's my money. I raked out the hen house, so that makes it mine... don't it?"

"Well, in a sense, it is, but you promised yor Mama that it was for the birthday jar at church, and now what you gonna tell her when you only have four pennies?"

"I won't tell her. I'll just pretend to put all of them in there... she won't ever know, will she Papa?"

"LeRoy, if there wuz ever a lie you could see right through, son, it would be in that glass Mason jar."

"And, LeRoy, you will know. Won't that make you feel ashamed for lying to yor Mama?"

"Not if she don't know... cause then she can't whup me... you won't tell her will you, Papa?"

"No, I won't… but don't you think YOU should?" said Papa with a strong emphasis on the YOU.

Changing the subject again, LeRoy said, "Papa, do you think the moon is really made out of cheese? Papa, where did they git so many cows to make so much cheese?"

"LeRoy, how is it that a boy as young as you can have so many questions rolling out of him?"

"I dunno… my head just makes 'em up."

"Son, it seems to me that yor head done made up a lie. Do you know that you can never get away with telling a lie… someone always knows the truth?"

"Who, Papa, you said you wouldn't tell, and I promise I won't!"

"But LeRoy, someone else knows besides you and me?"

"Who, Papa I didn't tell nobody!"

"Well, for one Mr. Ferguson will know because he is not only the grocer, but he is also the treasurer for the church. He knows you are five years old. When he counts the money you drop in the jar, he will know that you only had four. And, since he is the storekeeper, he will know what you did with the other penny, won't he?"

"I never thought about that Papa… but maybe he won't tell either."

"But son, someone else will know, too."

"Who Papa, there wuzn't nobody in the store, but him and me."

LeRoy sat silent for a bit, lowered his head, and started playing with the button on his shirt. Then slowly said without looking up, "Jesus will know won't He, Papa?"

"Yes, He will LeRoy. And you and I will know won't we? You told yor Mama them pennies wuz for the birthday jar; then you stole one of the pennies. Then you want to lie to yor Mama and the whole church about the number of pennies you put in the jar while they stand singing "Happy Birthday" to you. How will that make you feel, son?"

"Well…..not rightly good I guess."

"Well, what do you think you should do about it?"

"Tell, Mama, I guess."

"I think that is a good idea, son. The next time you tell me something that you want me to believe, do you think I might just not believe you?"

"Son, a man is only as good as his word. If he don't keep his word and isn't honest, then no one will trust him and believe in him. Once you think you get by with one lie, the ole devil will lead you on down the road into further lying; and then will come cheating and then stealing. It is kinda like us fishin' here for them catfish," said Papa pointing at the rapidly moving creek water beneath them.

"We put the hook in the water with a worm on it, and that looks good to the fish… so he jumps on it and ends up with a hook in his mouth and on the dinner table. Now ole satan, he plays many games to trick us. One of them is to hook you while you are young, and then he will have you on his stringer for life. The more a person lies, the less he will realize the truth himself."

"LeRoy, my father, yor Grandpa James, once told me when I was a lad about yor age that lying will lead to stealing, and sometimes that stealing will lead to killing. When people get conditioned to lying, they are capable of anything."

"Criminals, of the worst kind, usually start out by lying. Did you know that the very first sin in the Bible was a lie?"

"That ole serpent, satan, lied to Eve, and then she lied to Adam, and then they both lied to God."

"God made them leave the beautiful garden He had created for them, and sometime later when they had two sons, one of them ended up killing the other. Remember what Grandpa said; and what I am going to say. A man is only as reliable as his word… his truthful word."

"Now you run up to the house and tell yor Mama, about that penny!"

LeRoy, who was always scampering around like a whirlwind, rose slowly from his seat next to his Papa on the creek bank. Slowly, he headed up the hill toward the house.

◆◆◆

Sunday Meetin' Time

That next Sunday, Preacher Alrod stood to his feet and welcomed the little congregation to the Sunday Meetin'.

"Give the Lord a handclap 'cause you were able to be here rather than stove up in some sick bed." The small group acknowledged their good health with a robust hand clap.

"Lord, hear us as we pray."

They all knew that was Pastor Alrod's way of calling them to worship. It was a way of acknowledging God in their midst.

"Thank You, Lord, for all You've done for us, and all that You done provided for us, and all that You are gonna do for us in the future."

"Lord, this here year of 1939, has surely started off with a heap of trouble, as we are sure You already know about. This Depression has brought hard times for so many. Some have lost their crops, their farms, their homes, and many others are still out of work. Lord we ask Yor special blessings on those who have worked so hard to make a living off of the land, and now they have nothing to show for it."

"Folks just don't seem to be too happy with the government right now because of the bank closings, and folks are starving all over the country. And, Lord, that man Hitler just keeps taking over one country after the other. Lord, some think that before long we might be staring another world war right in the face."

"But Lord, we do humbly ask Yor blessings on the folks here who are having such a hard time what with this Depression still lingering here in our land. Families are having a rough go of things, and so many people starving who just can't do no better; no matter how hard they try."

"Lord. We know You own the cattle on a thousand hills, and You done said that none of Yor righteous folks will ever be seen beggin' for bread. Sometimes we just don't rightly know what is on Yor mind, and what we should rightly do about things that seem to be out of our control."

"Lord, according to the newspapers, there are people standing in bread lines all across America waiting for a hand-out. The unemployment lines grow longer every day. Lord, we share in their grief by the power of prayer asking that You bless all these people."

"Lord, we are so grateful to you for heppin' us get the crops in and fer givin' us the strength and might to get it done. Lord, you give us a whole dollar, and You only ask for one dime back."

116

"Lord, we know that it is hard for some to give that dime out of a dollar when times are so hard. Lord, we know that You love a cheerful giver; if it is a dime or a penny. For when we give out of love, You can use it and multiply it beyond our comprehension."

"Lord, don't let us be like Ananias and Sapphira, who owned a piece of land that was truly theirs, and they did not have to sell it, but they promised the proceeds to You; but then they kept back a portion for themselves."

"Lord, we don't know if you punished them for lying or stealing, but Lord you surely did punish them."

"Lord, bless them what are here and them that ain't. Lord, bless the sick and afflicted and all the shut-ins. Lord, bless this here service that Yor mighty Word will speak to the hearts of us all."

"Lord, hep us to all be good Christians and do our part and not be slack by depending on others for what we can do for ourselves."

"But, Lord for those around us who are truly in need, hep us to hep them; from what you have given to us."

"Lord, if you can see fit, please hep our country to stay out of the war. Lord, bless those who have fell on hard times and help us to be mindful of yor daily blessings toward us by sharing what we can. Amen"

Pastor Alrod never preached from sermon notes. He read his Bible all week long and asked God to lead and direct him to the scripture he was to share and to give him the words to help his people understand God's message for them to live by.

He arrived at the little church an hour before the congregation and knelt down at the little altar bench that was down front. He poured his heart out before God. He first asked God to forgive him of his own sins and to make him a humble servant.

He prayed for the members of his little church, the community, and the country, and more recently the oppressed people in Europe; as one nation after the other had fell underneath the heel of Adolph Hitler.

At the end of his prayer, it was customary for them to sing a hymn. The song leader, George Simpkins, motioned for them to rise to their feet. He then led them in a verse that they sing each week as a call to worship.

"Praise God, from Whom all blessings flow;
Praise Him, all creatures here below;
Praise Him above, ye heavenly host;
Praise Father, Son, and Holy Ghost."

After they were seated, Pastor Alrod said, "Our Sunday School lesson for the kids will be shared this morning by Sister Alrod… my sweet wife. Come on up here, honey, and let them hear yor sweet voice."

"Well, thank you, Brother Alrod," Mama said coyly. She referred to him as "Brother since he had called her, "Sister Alrod."

While she had her back to the congregation walking toward the podium, she flashed that playful smile of hers in his direction. That smile of hers never failed to warm his heart, and without any pretense, he smiled back at her.

As she passed by him, Mama turned and faced the congregation and said, "Ladies, you see what compliments you git when you keep them biscuits comin?" She playfully patted him on his plump round belly as she passed by him on the way to the pulpit.

One of the prudish ladies, sitting up near the front, whispered to the other, "Well, I never!"

Mama faced the little children and teens sitting in the first few rows and asked a question.

"Does it matter to God if we tell the truth?"

Little LeRoy slid a little further down in his seat as she began her story.

"Once upon a time, there was a school teacher who stood tight by the truth. She loved her students and wanted them to learn more than the ABC's. She wanted them to develop character."

"There came a time when four of her boys showed up late for school with their pant legs wet. They had missed the pledge to the flag, the saying of the Lord's Prayer and the singing of "My Country 'Tis of Thee!"

"They had also missed their arithmetic test on fractions. She asked why they were late and they all four said at the same time, "The wheel come off the wagon."

"They explained they had to get out and fix it before they could come on to school. She told them they had missed their arithmetic test, and they would get zeros for the day. They protested that she was not fair because it was not their fault the wagon wheel fell off."

"Wanting her students to know that she was fair to all her students, she said, "Okay, I will give you another chance.""

Mama injected, "She must have been a godly person like Jesus; always willing to give a second chance."

She glanced up at LeRoy as he slid a little further back up in his seat. She knew he remembered the talk they had about the missing penny.

Mama continued, "The boys thought they were fixin' to take their test when she gave each of them a paper and pencil. But then she sent each one of them to a different corner of the room."

When they settled in their places, she said, 'Now I want each one of you to write down on paper exactly which wheel it was that fell off that wagon. If all four of you have the same answer, you will get to take yor test at recess... if you don't, you will all get a zero, and a note sent home to yor parents."

"Now each one of them young'uns wuz ah afraid of being the one to make a mistake; so they all wrote nothing on their paper, and admitted they had lied, and had been fishin'.""

Mama said, "The thing we need to take outta this story is that there ain't no substitute for tellin' the truth. We sometimes think if we only tell a little white lie, we really aren't hurting anybody."

"Well, that is a lie telling a lie... right there."

"We are hurting ourselves when we take what we call a white lie and mix it with all the black lies that we tell. Then, we end up with gray lies. Gray lies makes it hard for us to ever know the real truth of what's right and wrong. When we lie, we always hurt ourselves; as well as others!"

She opened up her little prayer book and read from Proverbs 12:22 *"Lying lips are abomination to the LORD: but they that deal truly are His delight."*

"So you see boys and girls, God loves us even when we do wrong and lie; if we admit that we lied; and ask Him to forgive us, but it pleases Him much more when we tell the truth from the start."

119

"When we lie, we deceive ourselves as well as others and sometimes they are not as forgiving as God is. It causes them to not believe or trust us anymore. It is like the little boy who cried wolf, but we will hear that story another time."

Mama just stood there for a second to let the truth sink in, and then she returned to her seat on the front row where she always sat.

"Thank you, honey… uh… Sister Alrod. That story today comes mighty close to home," he said as he looked at a little five-year-old boy squirming in his seat.

"Well…" said Pastor Alrod scratching the back of his neck with his pointer finger, waiting a second to collect his thoughts.

Then he said, "The Lord works in mysterious ways and has many ways to confirm the message He sends to us preachers."

"Well, Lord, me and You talked about lying this week as the topic for my sermon, and Mama must have overheard our conversation; as she just about stole the thunder right out from under of my message today,"

They all laughed, and he began.

"One of the commandments says that we are not to bear false witness against our neighbor and that we are to love our neighbor as ourselves. If we lie to ourselves, we will lie to our neighbor and then our reputation for telling the truth is no longer a good one."

"Now you take Mr. Lewis Jackson back there on the last row." Everyone turned around to see that he was sitting there indeed.

"We all know that Mr. Jackson runs the bank in the city."

He nodded toward the banker and said, "We are always honored, Mr. Jackson, when you can come and share the Lord's Day with us."

Mr. Jackson nodded his head in response to him being recognized.

The Preacher continued, "And, there in the fourth row is Mr. Ferguson, who owns the grocery store."

They all turned around and acknowledged him as well. Mr. Ferguson ran the general merchandise store and the one-pump gas station. He was a faithful member of the church as well as its treasurer.

"Their businesses are run on the fact that they have to believe that the rest of us are telling the truth."

He waited a second of two before saying, "Either of them would be hard pressed to loan us money or to allow us to put groceries on account; if they knew that we were known liars when we say we will pay them back!"

The Preacher looked up and asked, "What would become of society if everyone lied and no one could believe anything that anyone said? Pity our nation if that ever happens." He waited awhile again as if to let the question sink in.

"How would we feel if we could not believe anyone because lying became so rampant, and everyone lied; including the president, the governor, and all those folks that are supposed to be taking care of the rest of us?"

"Wouldn't that be a terrible thing if everyone lied to everyone else and no one told the truth? Here in this community, we rely on each other, and we have to rely on the words of each other. We have often heard it said, 'A man's word is his bond.'"

"That means we can take what he says without having him to sign a pledge. And we can always depend on him to tell the truth. Telling the truth is a matter of respect to those we associate with, and honor for ourselves. When we lose those, we don't have much left."

"Now take the Judge Hendrix over there."

"Nice to see the judge down here from the city today – hope all goes well for you here tomorrow in court."

"How much justice can a court hand down unless it can be reasonably sure that the witnesses are telling the truth? That is why they have them swear on the Bible and say, 'So help me, God!'"

"Just as there is a penalty for lying in court, there are penalties for lying to and before God. One of the advantages of telling the truth is that you don't have to remember anything you've said."

A few members in the congregation shook their head up and down; while a few of the women fanned themselves a little harder.

He began his sermon, "Today, the Lord has up and done laid on my heart this passage of scripture: It is found in the first chapter of Mark, beginning in the fourteenth verse."

"John, the Baptist, had just been put into prison for preaching; and now here comes Jesus preaching the same Gospel. You know that the

121

word 'Gospel' means the 'good-news;' not to be confused with gossip. That means toting "bad news."

"Jesus was at the point where he was beckoning people to follow him. So he began calling the disciples; one by one. Some folks have pondered as to why Jesus just chose twelve men to follow Him as his disciples rather than a whole host of men."

"As you read the Bible for yorself, you will always be amazed at the way Jesus and God do things. There may have been a lot of reasons why Jesus chose the ones He did. I think He saw that among these men that they could be trusted, and He could depend on them."

"So often God uses the little things to show the world how much He can do with a little when it was dedicated to Him; with good and clean hearts."

"Sometimes, the ole devil will tell you that you ain't worth much; that you ain't got much; and you can't be used by the Lord. That is another one of them lies you have to look out for because the ole devil is the father of lies. Don't you go believing what he says; but what God says about you."

"God says in Jeremiah, *"The LORD appeared to him from afar, saying, "I have loved you with an everlasting love; Therefore I have drawn you with loving-kindness."*

"No one will ever love you like Jesus."

"Sometimes God shows His power in the storms and sometimes in the little things of this world. Remember them loaves and fishes?"

"On over in the Bible, it tells how those twelve men turned the whole world upside down."

"Jesus said in verse fifteen, here in Mark, that the time was fulfilled. He meant that the time was right in God's plan to call those men who were chosen to become companions and disciples of Jesus."

He begins by telling them that they need first to repent and believe in the Gospel themselves." Pastor Alrod reads to them from Mark 1:15, *"The time is fulfilled, and the kingdom of God is at hand: repent ye, and believe the gospel"* He went on to explain, "It was the designated time that Jesus began to reveal Himself as the Son of God."

"We see Jesus walking by the Sea of Galilee. Now why do you suppose He went to the shores of the sea? It was because He was looking for fishermen. What better place to find them, huh?"

"Jesus comes to us where we are. Every day he is looking for carpenters, roofers, shopkeepers, homemakers, bankers, and every person who will answer His call."

"As Jesus was walking along, He came upon two brothers, Simon and Andrew, who were casting their nets out into the water to ketch fish. People had to eat in them days too, and fish was a staple in their diet. Men made a living by catching fish to sell to others. They were skilled at their work and knew the process of how to ketch them."

"Their families depended on what they caught and sold. So they might have been confused when Jesus told them, "Come ye after me, and I will make you fishers-of-men.""

"That might have seemed a little odd to them. They may have asked themselves, what Jesus meant by that. How could Jesus expect them to use their nets to cast around men rather than fish? But apparently they knew what He meant."

"Jesus may have already laid out the work before them as believers. We don't read all the details here, but we do know that they left what they were doing: and went directly and followed Jesus."

"Remember John the Baptist had been preaching about the coming of the Lord, and perhaps they were just waiting for Him to come along as the deliverer. But John was now in prison."

"And we see that a little further on down He approached another set of brothers, James and John. They had been mending their nets. When you go fishin' you have to be prepared; and when you go fishin' for men you have to be also. And sometimes before the Lord can use us, we have to mend our ways to conform to His ways!"

"They left their father, Zebedee, along with the hired hands. They dropped what they were doing, and they also followed Jesus."

"The time has come," He said. "The kingdom of God is near. Repent and believe the good news!"

"Apparently, they knew what Jesus meant about the time had come."

Pastor Alrod explained, "Sometimes Jesus calls us to pick up stakes and follow Him to China or somewhere, but one thing is certain He calls us all to be fishers-of-men wherever we are; on the fishin' bank with a wee boy, or on a mighty boat out in the world; or in the belly of a whale."

"What God wants... is to ketch OUR hearts first. Then He wants us to reel in other sinners to be saved by His Grace. The illustration used here in Mark meant something to these men because many of them were fishermen. God knew these men before they were born while still in their mother's womb. He knew exactly who to call to be Jesus' first disciples."

"Just as most of us here in this area are farmers, by trade, many were fishermen by trade in the days of the Bible. God knew these men would be able to reach other men like themselves."

"However, fishermen were not the only people He called. He still calls men and women today doing all sorts of jobs and in many different occupations. Maybe, if Jesus had come in our time, he would have called a bunch of farmers. However, that is exactly what He is doing today. He is calling folks from all walks of life to share His sweet message of love, forgiveness, and redemption."

"These men here were the first men to follow Jesus in His earthly ministry. Jesus said, "Come follow me... and they did!""

"They were not all highly educated men, but ordinary men just like me some of you men sitting out there under the sound of my voice." Pastor Alrod said that as he waved his hand across the room.

Several of the men nodding their heads in agreement said, "Amen!"

"They worked to feed their families just like we do. They had families and problems just like we do. Their life was hard living under the rule of the existing government control like so many of us find today."

"Jesus chose men who had a longing in their heart for bigger and better things. They wanted to follow a true leader; an earthly leader they hoped would overthrow the government and become their long awaited Messiah."

He went on, "Men and women are looking for the same thing today. Sadly, the world is still looking for a charismatic leader who is strong on promises and speaks with a glib and persuasive tongue, telling them what they want to hear and to solve all their problems. But we need to keep our eyes upon Jesus."

"We hear more and more about that man Hitler over there in Germany who came presenting himself as a new kind of messiah. And now the real villain is coming through as he intends to conquer the whole world for his own pleasure and satisfaction."

"Millions of men will one day rue the day that they followed Hitler, but I'll say nary a one of the disciples ever thought they had made a bad decision by following Jesus; even though, like Jesus, it cost them their lives."

"There might come a day when following Jesus might cost us our lives. Just because we live in America, the land of the free, it don't mean that we always will be free. Many governments before ours have come and gone."

"God has blessed America because America believes in God!"

"Jesus told them when they had caught no fish; they were to let down their nets on the other side of the boat. And they did. When they lifted them up out of the water, they had so many fishes their nets broke. When you follow Jesus, He will meet yor needs."

"God don't ask for what He don't first give. Now I feel that there might be someone here this morning that is feeling Jesus tugging at their net and asking, 'Come follow me!' You can be one of millions who have answered the call of Jesus when He said, 'Come follow me!' But there is always room for one more at the foot of the cross."

"God's Word says that we are to become like little children who are obedient to their earthly father as we step forth to be obedient to our Heavenly Father."

Closing his Bible and placing it on the pulpit, he said, "Now, I want Mama to come up here once again and get the children ready for the little song they have rehearsed."

The youngest children rose from their seats from all across the little church and filed down front to sing what they had learned; a little song about fishing; and also to do the motions that went along with it.

"I will make you fishers of men, fishers of men, fishers of men; I will make you fishers of men, if YOU"LL follow ME."

They pretended to throw out a fishing line, reel it in and sang, *"I will make you fishers of men, fishers of men, fishers of men..."*

When they sang that last phrase and made a motion of reeling in a fish, a couple of cut-up clowns in the choir struggled as if they were catching "the big one!"

Although, it was hard for their parents to keep a straight face, they were smiling inside.

The kids continued. They would throw out their imaginary fishing line when they sang, *"Fishers of men,"* pointed to the folks when they sang, "you" or "you'll," and pointed toward heaven when they sang, "follow Me"... which was for Jesus.

"I will make you fishers of men if you'll follow me, follow me." When they sang, *"If you follow me,"* they turned around and motioned with their thumbs for the congregation to follow them.

A thought came into the Pastor's mind about how some people were just like the fish those clownish kids were portraying. Sometimes you have to struggle to bring some folks to Christ while they are fighting you all the way... but he knew the struggle was worth it when they gave their hearts and lives to Christ.

If parental pride came with a light, there would have been enough pride in that room to light up the sky on a moonless night!

Papa then called for anyone who had a birthday that week and asked them to come forward. Several adults and children came forward and deposited their coins in the missionary jar that Mr. Ferguson was holding.

LeRoy did not move.

They sang "Happy Birthday" to those standing there and then they took their seats.

Papa gave LeRoy a stern look. LeRoy knew what he meant. Papa was not happy with him. LeRoy stood up and started down front. Then he hesitated, and then sat back down.

He finally made up his mind and slowly walked up to the podium. Looking straight up at his Father, he said, "Papa, it was my birthday this week, and I got a cake and everything... a chocolate one just like I like. I got a new spinning top from Grandpa, a new bag of marbles, a new hat, and a bolo-paddle."

Patiently listening, Papa knew how hard it was for Little LeRoy to be in the fix he was in, he asked, "And just how old were you this week, LeRoy?"

He replied quite emphatically, "Papa, you know I am five-years-old," holding up five fingers.

And then the words came tumbling out so fast they were nearly overtaking each other. "But Papa, I only got four pennies to put in the birthday jar 'cause I ate one of them. The crowd gasped.

Without missing a beat in rapid fire, he continued, "I ate it 'cause I wanted a piece of candy more than I wanted to help the missionaries. And that candy... it's done gone ... and I only got these four pennies left."

And then he asked sincerely, "Do you think Jesus will let me owe Him one penny?"

Holding back tears, Brother Alrod managed to say, "Yes sir. I think He will. It's a heap more we all be ah owing Jesus than one penny."

While poking his little hand into his tight-fitting pocket to pull out his pennies, he walked up to the birthday jar, and began dropping them in one by one: clink, clink, clink, and clink. The congregation sang "Happy Birthday," once again!

When he passed by, Papa ruffled up the hair on his head; as he often did when one of his children made him proud. LeRoy started back to his seat when he heard one clink, two clink, three clink, four clink. And then clink, clink, clink, clink, clink, and clink as the deacons of the church stood behind him with their hands coming out of their pockets.

It was on that day that the missionaries got fourteen pennies instead of five. Pastor Alrod said to the congregation, "You just can't out give God!"

He took the podium again to finish his sermon. He said, "Once there was a father who took his ten-year-old son fishing. It was a time when this father not only spent quality time with him that bright and sunny day, but he also taught him a lesson that would go with him forever."

"Let this be a lesson to you fathers. Children will learn more from what they see you do than from what they hear you say."

He continued his story illustration by saying, "It was not quite time for the finishing tournament to begin; everyone had to sign up and get a number. The tournament would officially begin at the first shot of the pistol."

"They would have four hours to fish until the second shot signaled the tournament was over. The one with the largest fish would win the $25.00 cash prize and the trophy to hold until the next year."

"This father and son went to the river bank early in order for the father to show his young son casting techniques; his tried and true method of successful fishin'."

"On the first try, this young man caught the biggest bass either of them had ever seen. The son reeled it in. His father's face showed his immense pride in the skill in which his son had fought the fish and won."

"So excited, the boy jumped up and down and said, 'Daddy, I know this will win, I know it will win, won't it?"

"After congratulating his son on the fight, he said, 'But son you know we will have to throw him back!'"

"At first the boy thought he was kidding, but then the look on his face showed that was not what his father was thinking, and he asked, 'Why, Daddy, why?'"

"Well son, it is almost two hours before the official opening of the fishin' tournament, and we just caught him too soon. We will have to throw him back? The boy began to whine and made every effort to talk his father into letting him keep the big fish; but to no avail."

"Finally, and reluctantly, he took him off the hook and with a great effort threw the big fish back into the water; making a huge splash while saying, 'But Daddy no one would ever know!'"

"The wise father said, 'We would!'"

"Many years later, when that young boy became a highly successful businessman making deals every day reeling in the sales, he was so often tempted to cut corners, but what his father said on the creek bank many years before would resonate in his mind, 'We would know!' He learned a life-time lesson that day on a fishin' bank with his father that the 'We,' meant that his father, himself, and his Heavenly Father would know."

"Somehow he always felt that even though his father had departed this life decades before, both his earthly father and Heavenly Father would know if he did not deal fairly with people. Most of all, he knew that God had abundantly blessed his business because of the principles upon which he had built it."

Pastor Alrod ended with, "Now in closing this Sunday Meetin' time, folks I want to remind you that we are to *'Train up a child in the way he should go, and when he is old, he will not depart from it.'* You can look it up fer yorself. It can be found in Proverbs 22:6."

"But one thing, I want to make perfectly clear this morning is that the Bible ain't just for kids for it also says in Mark 8:36, *"For what shall it profit a man if he shall gain the whole world, and lose his own soul?"*

He said, "I want to end this sermon with this, and then you can be dismissed."

"You will struggle the rest of yor life like a huge fish that does not want to be caught if you fight the leadership of the Holy Spirit when you are wooed. Don't put off today what you might not have a chance to do tomorrow!"

"If you want to discuss anything today, or you need special prayer, some of the deacons will be down front. And after I finish shaking hands at the door, I will be here also for a while."

"Remember today is the acceptable day to come to the Lord.

Chapter eight: Until the Storm Passes By

It had been raining all week, and the Alrod farm was standing in several inches of water. Mama had spent the whole week scrubbing out socks on her little rubbing board she used in a small tin tub in the kitchen.

No matter how much she insisted, it appeared that every one of the children found every mud hole on the way home from school. She made them each carry a clean, dry pair of socks in their book satchel in case their socks were wet. But what they just could not understand was how dreadful water was on their leather shoes. In order to get them dry by the next day she had to line them up by the stove; and the heat made the leather draw up and sometimes crack.

Shoes were practically a luxury they could not afford most of the time. In the past, she tried to buy galoshes for them to wear over their shoes to keep them dry, but they outgrew them as well. And that was like having to buy two pair of shoes when money was hard to come by just to buy one pair for each child.

She feared they would catch their death of cold if they went too long with wet socks at school. Of course, they would be muddy as well. That meant two pairs of socks for the four oldest ones every day. So to make sure they had clean ones for the next day, and so that stains did not set in until washday, she scrubbed them each night and hung them by the wood stove in the kitchen to dry.

The socks and the wet diapers hanging around made the room feel somewhat damp, and she had to keep turning things to help them get dry quicker. Papa said when a long rainy spell kicked in; Mama's kitchen looked more like a Chinese laundry

Papa had not been able to work out in the cornfield for days, but according to the Farmer's Almanac, there were sunny days coming. The rain had been steady, and he hoped that it would not turn into a storm with high winds that could destroy his corn crop.

Papa was an old hand at farming and at reading the signs of the weather. But it didn't hurt to check with the almanac; as well as listen to the weather reports as they came over their old radio.

Sometimes when the weather was bad, it was almost impossible to pick up the station and hear the report because of all the static. He also wanted to listen to the farm reports each day to get an idea of how crops were selling, and at what price.

He kept pacing back and forth to the window to make sure the rain was not beating down too hard... like there was anything he could do if it were. He thanked God over and over for the rain because there had been a dry spell over the last few weeks, and his corn was looking a little droopy. However, he asked God to protect his crops from extremely heavy rain and hail; which could destroy the corn in the field

He kept fiddling with the knob on the old *Philco* radio. It had seen better days. Mama, already at her wits end, said, "Herman, sweetie, the weather has not changed in the last five minutes since you heard the report. All that static noise is driving me to distraction."

When the weather was nice and clear, the radio worked just fine, but when the weather was bad, it just would not stay on the station. Papa wished he could buy a new one for Mama since he knew how much Mama liked listening to the soap operas as she did the baking, cooking, and ironing. And he had to admit he enjoyed listening to *"Amos 'n Andy,"* and they were all becoming fond of the new *"Henry Aldrich"* program.

Papa bought one of those dual sockets to screw into the light socket hanging from the middle of the kitchen ceiling. That way, Mama could use the light bulb, the iron, and listen to the radio at the same time.

One of Mama's favorite programs was *"Ma Perkins."* It came on at three o'clock every day. That was an inconvenient time; what with the children coming in from school. But on warm, sunny days, she would shoo them out the door to play while she listened to her story. Not so easily done, when the heavens were opening up and pouring down rain, hail, or snow.

Sometimes she would send them into the bedrooms to do their homework or to read. Mama was big on the children reading. She did her indoor housework around the time her soap opera came on so that she could be ironing, snapping beans, or shelling peas. Not one to be idle, Mama was just not going to be like the old saying she grew up hearing, *"Idle hands are the devil's workshop."*

Mama didn't know what it was to sit down... to just sit down and rest. Papa used to tell her to sit down sometimes, but she would usually remind him that Mama's didn't have that luxury and that there was no rest for the weary. He was not too fond of her other maxim *"A man works from sun to sun, but a woman's work is never done!"*

She would not feel guilty about wasting her valuable time if she could listen to the radio and do something else at the same time.

And it gave her some time during the day to get off of her feet for a while. So she would save other chores, like folding diapers, for the time when *"Ma Perkins"* came on.

She just couldn't miss the antics of the family and had to see what Ma's three children, Evey, John, and Fay were up to next. And each episode left you hanging so as you didn't want to miss the next one. Other women in the church listened to *Ma Perkins* as well. If anyone missed an episode, they could catch each other up.

She liked some of the others like *"Stella Dallas, Pepper Young's Family,"* and *"One Man's family,"* but she still liked the clever information that Ma Perkins was always sharing about family life.

On this rainy day, Papa could not get a good clear reception so he got himself another cup of coffee and decided he would just spend the time with Mama. He often spoke to her about concerns of the farm, the children, and the church. He admired her wit, her intelligence, and her keen observation of what was going on around the church. He often discussed church matters and sermons with her.

"Mama, what do you think about having an old-fashioned 'testifying meetin' come this Sunday?"

"You know, Herman, it has been quite a while since we did that. It always seems to be good for body and soul every now and then to just to stand up and tell the world what God has done in yor life."

"There's been a heap of complaining going around recently... if it ain't one thing it's another. Some folks just need to stop and think of somethin' other than themselves; and their own passel of troubles."

Mama reminded him, "Since we didn't have church last Sunday evening with that torrential downpour, thunder, and lightning... and what with the creek overflowing and washing out the road... there ought to be a good turnout at church this Sunday. That would mean more folks will get a chance to say what is on their hearts and minds."

"But you know Mama, there are some that just don't know when to shut up once they get started and before you know it, they done took up the whole meetin' time."

Mama replied, "Yeah, I remember the last time when Florence Clifton stood, almost forever, talking about how she couldn't find no scraps to make a new quilt. She told about how she had to take good money to buy new material... when she knew full well that there wuz some folks who had scraps, they could lend her. She went on to say that it was their Christian duty to lend them to her." Mama sounded just like her, and Papa smiled and told her so.

Then she added, "Why, she ain't never paid back nothin' what she's done borried. And she won't be the first in line to give another soul a crust of bread, God bless her. May God forgive me, but He knows it's the truth."

"Well, Mama, I will think of somethin'... so everybody will have a chance to share what is on their heart!"

‿‿‿✧✧‿‿‿

Sunday Meetin' Time

"Okay, folks, find yor seat. LeRoy, you take that hat off"en yor head... you are in the Lord's house! Them five-year-olds," he said, shaking his head. But you can't give up on 'em; you just have to keep in after 'em, until they learn.

"Now you young folks put yor mind on the Lord, this morning and not on each other! The church done voted on giving you kids the privilege of sittin' together back there. Live up to their confidence in you; unless you want to go back to sitting with yor folks!"

"Well, it is mighty good to see so many of you here this morning. That sure was a storm last Sunday nite, wasn't it? We thought the thunder would take the whole roof off this here ole church... and the lightning danced around the room like huge flashes of daylight."

"Me and Mama didn't know if anyone would make it or not, but we just decided to come on over just in case. We brung buckets to catch the rain dripping from the holes in the roof. With it raining so hard, it kept us both purdy busy keeping them emptied out."

"We had a fine old time just the two of us. We left the young'uns at home. We put on our old mud boots and slickers and trekked on over here to light a fire in the stove just in case someone was determined to make it."

"We sat right here on this front pew and we sang some of the old hymns from memory... and no organ music. Then the lights went out. We didn't even bother to light the coal oil lamp... we just used a couple of Mama's homemade candles. The lightening made it heap bright in here. We prayed for those of you who were ailing, and suffering in some kinda way... and we felt the power of the Lord in this place."

"We bowed our heads to pray and then we felt so humbled and filled with praise, we got right down on our knees and prayed some more. Why, me and Mama just about had revival right here by ourselves with the Lord."

"But the good Lord, He hears our prayers no matter if we are standing, sitting or kneeling...but sometimes when yor heart needs a little extra care... there is just something about being humble enough to git down on yor knees."

"I heard tell once when a little sister got the news her little brother might not make it through the night with the croup... she wanted God to know how sincere her prayers were so she got down on her knees in the outhouse."

"And you know what? That little brother got well. It mighten' not had a thing to do with where she prayed, but it was shorely the way she prayed with humbleness."

"It's a shame that some folks think they're too big for their britches and won't humble themselves and pray fer what their heart's aching for... but they'll git down on those knees to shoot craps, play mumbly peg, pitch pennies, or shoot marbles."

"They'll be so stubborn; they don't want no one tellin' them what to do. They don't want to be controlled by no one – and yet they live their lives controlled by the devil... doing everything he tells them to do... including drinking demon rum. They want life their way and not what the Lord's wants, and oh, how sorely they reap what they sow."

"This morning, I want to talk about prayin... done that I reckon. And then "testifying.""

"Me and Mama thought it had been a long time since we had an old fashioned testifying meeting. For any of you who don't know what that is, it is where people rise to their feet one by one and tell the rest of us what God has done for them. Sometimes we are so busy praying and asking that we don't remember that we also need to do a whole lot of thanking God for His blessings, as well."

"Now we gonna bide by some rules tonight. You git yore thoughts together before you stand up – and I am expecting every one of you to stand up... and put what you want to say in one sentence." They looked at each other like as to say, "What is Brother Alrod, up to now?"

"Now while the organ plays and we take up the collection, you think on what you gonna say. You come back here brother, Jim. They ain't gonna be no sneaking out early here this morning."

"Lord, as we ask you to bless this offering and to bless the gift and the giver, help these kind folks to know that we done got enough money to pay for the organ, the only thing they don't know it is still in their pockets! Amen."

"Now, let's have each one of you pop up like popcorn in the fireplace. "As soon as one is hushed, another one stand up and give yor say. If you just want to praise the Lord, then that will be good; but if there is something sticking in your craw that keeps you on the opposite side of a good disposition, let's hear that too."

Those in the congregation who had never been to a testifying meeting, looked around at each other wondering what he meant by that.

Surely, he wasn't asking folks to air their dirty laundry right there in church. Or was he?

"What we want to do here this morning is to share our blessings and answered prayers but also a word or two that would be encouraging to all of us."

"Remember the ABC's of testifying. A... Audible. Make sure folks can hear you. B... Be brief and to the point. C... Make sure it is Christ-centered."

"We don't need a blow by blow account of how you got yor prize pig out of the mud hole, for example. We want to praise the Lord that he got out."

"Let's use this time to encourage one another with words of wisdom to help them along the way." The Reverend Alrod continued standing to acknowledge each one as they stood.

"We'll start with Brother Ferguson and run around this church until everyone has their say... even the young folks."

Brother Ferguson stood to his feet and said, *"Don't let yor problems drive you crazy. Remember Moses was a basket case!"*

Some of the people chuckled. The folks seemed to be expecting a good time. It was good to be in the house of the Lord.

Mr. Ferguson made the motion to sit down, and before his bottom hit the pew, he stood back up. He said with a more serious tone, *"I am so blessed to live in this valley and to have such good caring friends like all of you. You make my work at the store a pure pleasure just waiting on you all."*

Then one by one the people began to stand up and take their turn; and rose quickly as each one before them sat back down. The next one said, *"Some folks come into the church with a smile on their face until we see their other side...when they realize that someone is sitting in their place in the pew."*

Before recognizing the next one, Herman replied, *"Instead of sitting there with a scowl on yor face, smile and be happy to see them, and hep to turn that frown upside down by praying for them."*

"Remember the mother of the two disciples who wanted Jesus to promise that her sons would sit on His right and left when He came into His kingdom. He told her she didn't have no clue what she was asking of Him. Remember who was on His right and left when He was crucified."

Mrs. O'Brien spoke up and said, *"Lord, I thank you that you are smarter than us. Some folks want to do things for the Lord, but mostly they want to tell Him what to do."*

Reverend Alrod began to see what was going on. Apparently, they had read the same old copies of the Farmer's Almanac that he did. Most of these folks had the same reading materials that the Alrod's had; the Family Bible, the Farmer's Almanac, and the Sears and Roebuck catalog.

Each had their own use; but especially the Family Bible. It was to teach them how to live righteously and would be handed down from generation to generation with all the births, marriages, and deaths recorded in it for history.

The Farmer's Almanac was used for predicting the weather, advice on when and how to plant, great recipes, famous quotes, and the daily advice column often wise, but humorous. He saw a lot of that being reflected this morning.

And then there was the Sears Roebuck catalog. They were a necessity in more than one way; useful for ordering items not available locally, but they were also very useful in the outhouse.

Little girls loved cutting out the pictures as paper dolls. They were also useful for school projects. And, sometimes they were stacked in a kitchen chair so little folks would be able to reach the table.

Another stood and said, *"I am thankful that we got us a faithful preacher who don't hold back on the Word of God. But as far as the rest of us, we need to be a living sermon so that others can see Jesus in us. I heard tell someone hit the nail on the head when they said, "I would rather see a sermon than hear one!"*

Sarah Louise chimed in by saying, *"The good Lord didn't create anything without a purpose even them chiggers, I guess! But I am thankful for kerosene that can help take the sting out."*

And then she added. *"God, also, taught somebody at the Cutex Company how to invent clear fingernail polish to kill 'em. And, I'll be glad when I am old enough to wear bright red. But right now I am glad Mama keeps a bottle just for smothern' them chiggers to death and stopping the runs in her stockings."*

A few giggles followed from the other young girls. But for some, just the thought of chiggers made them want to scratch. Mama wanted to slide down in her seat, or hold her hands over her face. She knew that would not be the last of that.

Papa said jokingly, "If God wanted you to have fiery red fingernails, he would have made them that color, too."

Sweet Miss Parrish said, *"Remember that God is always with us and will never forsake us nor leave us, and He is our guide down the road of life. When you think you can't travel on down the road, take hope, God will be there before you."*

That seemed to resonate with the congregation as they thoughtfully nodded their heads up and down. When good Ole Deacon Seagraves stood to have his turn, folks got ready for a long spiel and explanation, but they were pleasantly surprised.

"A good chance may come and knock on yor door kinda easy like, but old satan and his temptations will just stand there and bang on and on...until you let him in or shoo him away with God's Word."

"Amen's" rang out everywhere. Some because of what he said; but most because he said it quickly.

Mr. Simpkins said, *"I want to praise God for all these blessings He gives me, my farm, my family, and even this rain that I shorely thought was going to wipe out my crops, but they are still standing tall. I am also thankful to you folks for letting me lead the singing."*

Applause rang out through the church. They made him feel appreciated. Precious little else he ever received for his time and dedication to the music and singing at the church.

Mama said, *"I am thankful for those what come before us and built this here church... most of them buried out back... and how because of them we have this church building, today."*

Lem O'Brien stood up hardly able to keep from laughing even before he said anything, but then sheepishly and with a grin said, *"If you go around making fun of the church; and saying, it ain't a perfect church, be grateful that it ain't... for if it wuz, they wouldn't let most of us belong here."*

The only ones laughing were the young people in the back. Would that be strike one; for them no longer being able to sit together in a group?

Another stood up and said, *"I just want to praise the Lord for Brother Alrod and his family and all that they do to put up with us. And if you ever think about gittin' another preacher, you might just consider praying for the one you got."*

Judge Hendrix stood up and took his usual pose with his hands in his vest pockets; and said, *"In the Kingdom of God, we're called to be witnesses, not to be lawyers or judges."*

Several folks looked in the direction of Florence Clifton. However, she paid no never mind. It just went completely over her head. Then the judge stood back up and said, *"God doesn't judge a man's reputation and ways until he is dead. So why should we?"* It seemed he just could not pass up an opportunity to talk about "judging."

"Friendships can start with a smile," said sweet little eight-year-old Velma Alrod, with that innocent smile of hers." Reverend Alrod injected, "Out of the mouths of babes!"

"Sometimes folks git mad at the church and they move their letter around like it was the mail. I guess they are just looking for the perfect church that suits their notions. But I don't know why some people change churches; what difference does it make which one you stay home from?"

"That's a good one, brother!" said the preacher.

And stunning to everyone, Old Jim added, *"I am thankful for the many folks who take Christian life to heart, and they do unto others. A lot of folks stand, and wholeheartedly sing 'Standing on the Promises' while all the time, they are just sitting on the premises."* That was odd for he was not one to sit on the premises for very long.

The others began to get in the spirit of this interactive sermon today and began jumping up eager to share what they wanted to say.

"We ain't to judge a body's life, and we ain't to pass judgment on their past, and we don't have to tell them to clean up their lives before coming to Jesus."

"Jesus tells us to be fishers of men. I reckon if we can catch them for the Lord, the Lord can clean them up just fine," said Clem, the fisherman in the bunch

Chubby little Mable, who was wearing her crushed straw hat that she wore every Sunday, pushed herself up from the pew. She astounded everyone when she said, *"At school, teacher told us that if we ever stood too close to the fireplace and ketched on fire, we are to stop, drop, and roll."*

Then she added, "My Mama says *'Stop, Drop, and Roll' won't work in Hell. For nothing is gonna put that fire out down there,"* and she pointed toward the floor.

Everyone knew where that was coming from because when she was a much younger child, she stood too close to the fireplace one cold winter morning, and her gown tail caught on fire. Her mother threw her to the floor and rolled her up in the rug that was in front of the hearth, and put out the fire. Her leg was barely singed and didn't even leave a scar. But it had made Hell real to Mable. And she sure didn't want to go there.

Florence Clifton turned and whispered to her neighbor, "Did you hear the language that young girl just used? You'd think her mother would teach her better than to say that "cuss" word." Mable heard what she had said and hung her head and almost cried. Mama sitting close by heard what was said and quickly rose to her feet and said, *"Hallelujah, Mable, we need to get that fire insurance ahead of time don't we sweetie pie?"*

One of the local school teachers, Clarice MacIntyre, rose and meekly said, *"Don't put a question mark where God put a period."*

"Now leave that one up to a teacher, with them question marks and periods," replied Herman in good humor. Then the local funeral director spoke and said how he mourned along with the people at the loss of a loved one; but particularly one who did not know Jesus. He started to sit back down and then continued, *"Don't wait for six strong men to take you into church."*

"We all know how important the fruit of our labor is to our families, but we must be aware of the dangers of forbidden fruit. Forbidden fruit can get you into a lot of jams!" said Mama.

Lemuel stood up again after his previous performance and trying to keep a straight face once again said, *"I know for a fact that God loves and forgives everyone, but He probably prefers 'fruits of the spirit' over 'religious nuts!"*

Preacher Alrod responded, *"The Will of God never takes you to where the Grace of God will not protect you."* You keep on studyin', son... yor gonna make a preacher, yet." He liked to say that to all the boys especially when they were cutting up.

And to everyone's amazement, Brother Jenkins, the beekeeper, stood up and said, *"A lot of folks wants to change what is writ in the Bible, but when we read it, it changes us!"*

For a moment, the room was silent, not knowing how to respond for he had struck a chord in their hearts. However, he felt he had said something wrong and then added, "Well, I read that somewhere anyway!"

And then the Reverend Alrod looked square into the face of Mama and said, "Most of the young'uns understand this one. Life isn't about waiting for the storm… to pass. Living is more about learning to dance and play in the rain!"

"Oh!" Putting her hand over her mouth in surprise, Florence Clifton said as she whispered to her neighbor, "Do you think they were dancing in the church last Sunday night?"

Her neighbor waved her hand at her as if she needed to hush. Brother Alrod ended the "testifying" with, *"When we pray we ain't supposed to give God instructions, but to have a two-way conversation with Him. We most likely have our say, and then we say, 'Amen.' And then we don't wait around for God to have His say."*

And then he said, "Let's end this wonderful time in the Lord as we sing, *"What a Friend We Have in Jesus."* For most folks in attendance, a hymnal was not needed for these folks were almost born knowing the words to this time proven hymn.

"What a friend we have in Jesus, all our sins and griefs to bear!
What a privilege to carry everything to God in prayer!
Oh, what peace we often forfeit, oh, what needless pain we bear,
All because we do not carry everything to God in prayer!

Have we trials and temptations? Is there trouble anywhere?
We should never be discouraged—Take it to the Lord in prayer

Can we find a friend so faithful, Who will all our sorrows share?
Jesus knows our every weakness; take it to the Lord in prayer.
Are we weak and heavy-laden, cumbered with a load of care?
Precious Savior, still our refuge—take it to the Lord in prayer.

Do thy friends despise, forsake thee? Take it to the Lord in prayer!
In His arms He'll take and shield thee, thou wilt find a solace there.

Blessed Savior, Thou hast promised Thou wilt all our burdens bear;
May we ever, Lord, be bringing all to Thee in earnest prayer.
Soon in glory bright, unclouded, there will be no need for prayer—
Rapture, praise, and endless worship will be our sweet portion there."

When they finished singing, Pastor Alrod raised his hands and said, "As you leave this place of worship, may you go in peace. *"Now may the God of hope fill you with all joy and peace in believing, so that ye may abound in hope, through the power of the Holy Ghost."* Romans 15:13

Chapter nine: Mama, Where Do Babies Come From?

Perhaps it was the heat or just having worked so hard all morning, but Mama's legs began to wobble before getting to town. She had taken quite a large basket of eggs to sell and picked up the few things she needed.

On the long walk, returning from the store, she actually felt like lying down on the road for a while, but she knew she could not do that.

Home at last, she felt extremely tired, and it was only mid-afternoon. She still had to prepare for Sunday dinner the next day.

Mama wiped her sweating forehead a couple of times with her apron while twelve-year-old Sarah Louise sat at the table, making a pitiful attempt at stirring the cake batter. "Forty-one... forty-two... forty-three..." slowly she counted each stir.

Mama told her it had to be stirred one hundred times for it to rise to the top of the pan.

Sarah Louise sat at the table with her left elbow resting on the table with her chin propped on her left hand; she was using her right hand to slowly stir. She looked as if she were millions of miles away.

When her mother spoke... it startled her, and she jumped back like she was doing something she should not have been doing.

"Sarah Louise, you gonna take all day stirring that cake? The fire is roaring, and the oven is just right... get a move on girl... what's got into you? You, ailing? You been moping around here like you wuz mourning the dead all day. Now, git a move on."

Continuing to stir slowly, she asked out of the blue, "Mama, where do babies come from? This new girl at school said she knew where they come from, and she wasn't gonna tell us. Her Mama said she had better not. Mama, why is some folks so mean? If she wasn't gonna tell nobody, why did she have to say anything at all?"

"Mama, where DO babies come from?" She just continued stirring and asking a string of questions. "While we were at recess, us girls went up to the edge of the woods and sat on that old tree that done fell down in last year's storm, and we got to talkin' about having babies."

"You did what?" asked her mother, who was somewhat alarmed.

"You know, we all told what we knew about babies gittin' born."

Mama asked again? "You did what? And just what did they have to say?"

"Justine's Mama told her that she had found her in the cabbage patch, and Susan said her Mama told her the elves brought the baby in the night and left it in behind the nearest tree stump. Mama, what if it rained or got cold before the Mama found it?"

"And what did you say Sarah Louise?" "Well, I told them I wasn't sure, but I thought Dr. McPherson delivered them in that big black bag of his."

"Why did you say that?"

"Well, when Baby James was born, I saw the doctor drive up and go into the house, and he was carrying nothin' but a big black bag. Then we got sent to the neighbor's house, and when we came back the next mornin', the doctor was gone, and the baby was here. I didn't see no other way he coulda got here."

Letting her have her say, Mama waited to see what else she would come up with.

"But Mama, what Sue Ann said kinda scared me. She said we best not let no boy kiss us. For, if'n we did; we'd wake up the next morning with a baby in the bed with us, and there wouldn't be nothin' what could be done about it."

Mama gulped as she asked, "You ain't never kissed no boy have you, Sarah Louise?"

"Oh no, Mama!" That is yuck. Ain't no boy gonna kiss me! Why, I'd knock his block off."

"That's good, Sarah Louise... you do just that."

"But you can't pay no attention to what Sue Ann says 'cause she don't always tell the truth. One time she said that Mrs. O'Brien done up and lost one of her babies. She said she heard some of the women at church talking about taking some food to her house."

"But then the next Sunday morning there sat Mrs. O'Brien with that string of kids, and we counted them and there wasn't a single one missing."

"Mama, do you think Lemuel O'Brien is kinda cute?" Her Mother ignored that last question completely.

"Mama, you know Sue Ann's so nosy. She one time told Mary Alice that she was a second-hand baby 'cause her parents got her from the orphanage. Is that true, Mama?"

"Shame on you, Sarah Louise, you know full well that God don't make no second-hand children! All of God's children are special from the time that tiny seed is planted. Each child is created with a purpose in life... and in the image of God Himself."

"What seed, Mama? Do babies grow in the garden?" She giggled knowing the answer to that one. She had pulled too many weeds in the garden, and never a sign of a baby.

"Of course not, silly girl?"

"Here give me that cake batter; you gonna take all day jawing and not stirring." Mama cracked three eggs and added them to the batter.

Taking the bowl back from Mama, Sarah Louise said, "What seed Mama?"

"The seed makes the egg in a Mama's belly grow. Then when it is fully growed... with nothing but time and patience... the baby is born...just like when Ole Molly had her calf."

Sitting straight up in her chair, she asked, "Mama, you mean I growed in yor belly just like that calf growed in Ole Molly's belly? Or did you lay an egg like the hens do?"

Sarah Louise was feeling kinda silly, but mostly uncomfortable because they were talking about things she had wondered about, but knew nothing about.

Struggling not to laugh, Mama said, "No sweet child, babies are born alive, just like the offspring of other animals; they are not hatched."

"But Mama, how did the seed get planted, did you swallow it?" This time she was serious. That seemed logical to her.

"No chile... you don't swallow it. It is a precious gift from God... just as God made heaven and earth, and He made all the people of the earth in His own image. He made you special because there is no other little girl in all the world just like you... not even if her name should happen to be Sarah Louise Alrod as well."

"Mama, how did God know that you wanted a baby? Did you pray and ask Him to plant the seed? Mama, if God put my seed in yor belly that would make you my Mother. But how did He make Papa my Father?"

At first Mama started to say... because he was married to me, but she did not want her to get the idea that only married women could have babies.

"Well, it all began when me and Daddy got married, and we decided that we wanted a big family with lots of children. God would put a glint in Daddy's eye that meant he loved me, and I would smile back and that meant that I loved him, too. And when that love between a man and woman comes together then God plants the seed, and nine months later that love makes a baby."

"Mama, we done got six kids in our family so I guess Daddy's done got a lot of glints in his eyes, huh?"

"I guess you could say that," was Mama's answer with a smile.

"Mama, do you think Daddy will get any more glints in his eyes?"

And before Mama could answer, Sarah Louise added, "If so, Mama, I wish you would not smile back – we got enough babies and wet diapers to wash around here already."

◦◦◦

Sunday Meetin' Time

Preacher Alrod stood to his feet after the organist struck the last chord on the almost paid for organ. He nodded her way and thanked her for playing. He walked up to the pulpit and opened up his Bible and said, "Let us bow our heads before the Almighty with a prayer of praise and thanksgiving."

"Lord, we praise You for all You are... our maker, our creator, our healer and our friend. We praise you for all the wonderment you put in the world for us to enjoy and see."

"We thank You Lord for life itself... a wonderment at how You created the earth and all the folks in it... but God that be Yor business... it just is ours to wonder and enjoy."

"We are thankful for each person who fills a seat here this evening in this little ole church… for if it wuz empty… we would sorely miss their presence. And Lord, we know that each one is special in Yor eyes."

"Lord we come to the asking part of praying. Lord, bless this here service and make us all aware of Yor presence among us where Yor seat of honor is never empty. And, Lord, we all know that You get here before any of us do. Please guide, lead, and direct us. Help us to be what we ought to be. And may we never leave You here alone; waiting for yor children to show up. Amen"

"Welcome friends to Sunday Meetin'. This evening our text comes from the very first book in the Bible and the very first chapter. That ought to be easy for them of you who ain't used to finding the books in the Bible yet. Don't worry you will get the hang of it… the more you read it."

"It says in verse 27: *"So God created man in His own image, in the image of God created He him, male and female created He them."* Do you git the idea that God did a lot of creating in this verse? Why, He says so three times."

"There is a sentence I hear tell was written right in the Declaration of Independence. It was put there by Ole President Thomas Jefferson himself."

Putting his glasses to his eyes, Preacher Alrod began to read, "We hold these truths to be self-evident that all men are created equal."

Now, that don't tell what man done…when he done things that wuz wrong…but Ole Jefferson wrote that God created all folks equal. But the important part is that He actually created all people."

We are apt to believe the things other folks say about God. Sometimes they are telling the truth and sometimes they are not; but because of who they are… we believe them."

"However, there are some people today who'd dispute God's Word. I know that it is hard to believe… but they are actually standing up and saying they ain't no God. They must be blind and deaf at the same time, or they certainly don't live in these beautiful mountains."

"But now Thomas Jefferson and his cohorts didn't have one speck of trouble in believing that God is who He said He was… right here in this Bible. If we believe what he says, shouldn't we believe all the more what

147

God says? Some folks think the Bible is just a book to drag around to church every now and agin to make themselves look holy."

"Once, an old time preacher went to visit some new neighbors to invite them to church. They had a little girl about the age of my twins there; who are eight. When the preacher asked her if she knew what was in the Bible, she said that she did."

"Upon quizzing her further about what was in the Bible, she said, "Well, there is a pressed rose from Grandpa's funeral and a picture of Grandma before she died."

Amused, the preacher asked her if there was anything else in there, and she said, "Mama and Papa's insurance papers is in there, too. And Mama writes down every time a new baby is born, or someone dies... and oh, yes if someone gets married."

"He then asked her if she knew anything about James, John, and Peter being in the Bible. She quickly said, "Naw, they ain't in there. They are all buried back home in the cemetery. They be my uncles."

"The old preacher went away from that house with a prayer on his lips and challenge in his heart to help that family know that the Bible is not a keepsake place for flowers, a photo album, or a filing cabinet for important papers."

Then Pastor Alrod said as he raised his Bible in the air, "And then some are saying that Jefferson didn't believe the entire Bible as being a true fact. But one thing's for sure, he surely believed God created every mother's son and daughter of us. He said so right in the Declaration."

"Now the pure bone truth cannot be changed no matter how many people don't believe it. The truth is that God created you, and there just ain't no way of getting around that."

"Everything, that was created, was created by God. God put that down in the very first chapter in the Bible. He wanted folks to know from the beginning... see it says in the beginning that He is God!"

"You are created in the image of God ... and not only that... He created you for a reason and for a purpose here on this here earth. Whether you are a man or woman, He puts great store in you and has put within yor heart the desire to know Him."

"It is just there, folks. You can't ignore it. You can't say it ain't true. But one thing's for sure the truth never lies, and Jesus is truth. Now folks, I'm standing here right now telling you the truth. There ain't enough money in the entire world to pay me to lie, and send my immortal soul to Hell."

"Don't let those who doubt discourage you from believing what many of our founding fathers accepted without question. God did make you. You are valuable to Him and "endowed with inalienable rights.""

"Even better than the life, liberty and the pursuit of happiness that Jefferson wrote about… this here Word of God offers you something even better…eternal life."

Herman liked to use humor sometimes in his sermons to bring home a point, and often he told stories handed down from his Irish background. He said, "There once was a man who lived a terrible life by ignoring God. He often got drunk and preached to everyone in the pub that they just wuz'nt no God."

"As it is for all people, the day came when he died. There were few mourners at his wake, but a couple of folks stood there looking down at his lifeless body all dressed up in a fine suit of clothes. One of them said, 'You know he didn't believe in God?' The other one said, "Much is the pity, he is all dressed up with no place to go.""

"After them folks in the Garden of Eden messed up and separated us from God, He sent His Son Jesus to die on the cross a death that we cannot imagine. Now the truth of the matter is why would God have done that if He didn't love you? You have got to know that God loves you. He so loved you that He allowed His Son, Jesus, to die in order that you might believe and be saved."

"You ponder on that when you think about how God created us in the first book of the Bible and then in the new part of the Bible, he had John write these words found in John 3:16."

"For God so loved the world that He gave His only begotten Son, and whosoever believes in Him shall not perish but have everlasting life."

"Now if that ain't love... you just try and tell me what is. I stand here and look back yonder and see my little LeRoy. There just ain't anything inside of me that can deny how much I love him... even if he does snitch a penny every now and then. There ain't no way I would let him die for a bunch of scoundrels like us."

"Now if God loved us enough to create us; and Jesus loved us enough to die for us, ought we not to love ourselves, our families and our neighbors? And yes, like Ole Jefferson, we ought to also love our country."

"Nobody knows where all that turmoil will end up in Europe. We might be called upon to send our boys to their death to defend this country. My Papa went during the Great War. That was supposed to be a war to end all wars. But folks, I believe war is hovering over us today. We need to prepare and be ready!"

"God gave Moses the Ten Commandments for us to learn to live for Him and with our fellow man. But Jesus rolled them all into one when He said, "The greatest of these is that we love one another."

"You think on these things this week. Ask yorself if you live like a person God should love. Lord, knows we ain't worthy, but He does. Then ask yorself if you love others... like God wants you to love them."

"How can anyone even say they are in love with their spouse or sweetheart... and not believe in God? God is love, and He is the creator of love? And without God, there is no love."

"Now turn in yor hymn books and see just what God's love can do. I ain't gonna stand here and beg you to come to the Lord. You can only come when the Holy Spirit speaks to yor heart, and you can only receive salvation when you understand the concept of God's love."

"If you feel you want to accept this love of God, or if you already have and want to become a member of this here church, step out on the first verse and come forward."

The song leader, George Simpkins, stepped up to the podium while Herman stepped down to meet any who should come.

George had loved music since he was a young boy. He became the song leader of the church when he was but sixteen years old. He spent many hours with James Alrod, Herman's father, when he was the former pastor.

George did not only lead songs, but he wrote many of his own. He always liked to give credit to the ones who wrote the wonderful words to the hymns and a little background when possible. He felt to sing these wonderful old hymns and not give thought as to how they came about, and who wrote them, was not the Christian thing to do.

He said, "Open up yor hymnals to page 356 and sing this like you mean it. Even though this hymn was written twenty-seven years ago in the year of our Lord in 1912, we should do honor to the man who wrote it, James Rowe." He then made a motion for them to stand. They stood to their feet and began singing,

Love Lifted Me!

"I was sinking deep in sin, far from the peaceful shore,
Very deeply stained within, sinking to rise no more,
But the Master of the sea heard my despairing cry,
From the waters lifted me, now safe am I.

Refrain:

Love lifted me!Love lifted me!
When nothing else could help,

Love lifted me!

All my heart to Him I give, ever to Him I'll cling,
In His blessed presence live, ever His praises sing,
Love so mighty and so true, merits my soul's best songs,
Faithful, loving service, too, to Him belongs.

Souls in danger, look above, Jesus completely saves,
He will lift you by His love, out of the angry waves.
He's the Master of the sea, billows His will obey,
He your Savior wants to be, be saved today."

A young child and an old man came forward to receive Jesus, and Herman thought to himself, it is never too early and never too late.

After the benediction and blessing upon the crowd was pronounced, Herman said, "And one thing more before you folks leave tonight, I want to make another announcement. Come on up here Mama.

He waited until Mama joined him down front. He put his arm around her and looked deeply into her eyes; then he proceeded to say, "Not only did God create us all... we want to announce that the Alrod family is gonna have another blessed event. For right now He is creating another Alrod for us all to love."

While the congregation stood and clapped, Sarah Louise nearly jumped to her feet to beg Mama not to smile back... but it was too late... she smiled right back into Papa's eyes.

Sarah Louise slumped back in her seat and thought, "Well, I guess there ain't nothing can be done now...she done smiled back at him ... and kissed him.

Chapter ten: Mama's Episode

The kitchen was hot from the heat both inside and out. The old wood stove had a red glow on the side where the wood was burning rapidly. Mama hoped that one day she would have one of those new stoves that did not require having a fire in it all day.

Spring 1939 had been hotter than usual, and early summer already seemed hotter than usual; at least Mama thought so. The days were growing longer, and the heat outside in the middle of the day was just about too much to bear.

She had allowed the twins to go down to the creek to splash and cool off as long as they stayed together. She reminded them to stay in the shallow end; which was only about two feet deep. She warned them about the other end; where the jagged rocks were. As always, she cautioned them about snakes.

Copperheads loved being in the tall grass; where it was cool on a hot day. But the deadly water moccasin slithered along in the water and could sneak up on you without you knowing it. Both were not kindly toward man or child.

Papa once said after seeing a man bitten by a snake; it was no wonder why the Bible referred to satan as a snake or serpent. Like the snakes, satan, seeks out who to victimize, and is always sneaky about it.

Children living on a farm in what seemed like the middle of nowhere had to learn early about the dangers of predators of all kinds. Papa had thought it more prudent not to teach the twins about the different kinds of snakes at their age for fear they would get too close to one to try and figure out what kind it was. He just told them to watch, and get out of the way of all snakes.

Mama had grown weary of the twins constant bickering. Verna wanted to play dolls, and play-like, but Velma didn't. Velma wanted to play jump rope, but Verna didn't.

She put them on the front porch shelling peas and discovered that they were shelling a few, and then throwing a few that was unshelled into the pile of hulls. The whole time they had been sitting there, they had not shelled enough peas to cook for supper.

She made them sit there and separate the good peas from the hulls; and then finish shelling them. She hoped that would teach them a lesson about being dishonest. She told them after they dumped the hulls in the slop bucket for the pig pen; they could go down to the creek to cool off and to wash the pea scum off of themselves.

Inside the hull of these peas, there was a substance that made your fingers feel numb, and they stained your fingers and hands purple. Mama would often make a game out of the chores she assigned them like having a pea shelling contest, but not when it was for discipline. She just left them to their own agony. Today, the twins were not allowed to talk during the pea shelling, but had to sit next to each other to do it.

While discipline should never be harsh or physically abusive, it should not be fun either. Purple fingers would remind them for the rest of the day why their fingers were purple. Mama was trying to get everything lined up for dinner and had begun shelling the peas herself, but then she saw how the peas could get shelled, and two little angry sisters could learn to get along without bickering.

The stains would not have lasted long on Mama's hands since she had her hands in soapy water all day long for one reason or the other. And today of all days, being so tired, she needed all the help she could get... so because of their bickering; she saw an opportunity to "kill two birds with one stone."

Her nausea was mostly past now. It usually lasted for only a few hours in the morning. This pregnancy seemed to be very different somehow. She was tired when she woke up in the morning and even more tired when she went to bed. She was flat out exhausted.

Saturday was a day when Mama had so much to do to get her brood all ready for church the next morning. She had been busy since before daylight when the rooster first crowed at the rising sun; welcoming a new day. She still had not gathered her eggs for the day.

Her short walk to Mr. Ferguson's store to sell the extra eggs was usually a time for her to walk alone. Rarely did she take anyone with her. It was her time, and she guarded it intensely.

It was her time to get away from things, and to get a little break from all the work and chaos at the house. With eight people in their small farm home, it got pretty tight some of the time. Saturdays and Sundays were always her busiest days.

She looked forward to her Saturday walks to town for the walk itself, the alone time, and being able to see people in town. It gave her the opportunity to invite people to church as well. She sometimes hungered for time just to talk and visit with other women. She missed her mother and her mother-in-law; now both in the arms of Jesus.

But mostly she needed the time to clear her mind of all the cobwebs, and just enjoy being by herself. There was no place like that on the farm where she could hide except in the outhouse. Even with all her scrubbing, summer was not a time when you wanted to spend any more time than necessary in there.

Bad smells were not something she needed in her delicate condition. But even when it was necessary for her to be in there, she would have to answer a million questions through the door. There was just no peace to be found except for her cherished walks to town.

As much as she hated it, it seemed this morning that Herman would have to take her eggs to Mr. Ferguson. She was just not up to it. Papa and Billy Joe went out to the fields at daybreak to get some work done before the noonday sun got so hot. Papa or Billy Joe would always come closer to the house to work around the barn while Mama went on her walk. Although Sarah Louise was competent in caring for Baby James; the others could be more than a handful.

In bad weather, Papa would drive her to town, and the two of them would have time to talk about grown-up things; without LeRoy chiming in every minute.

Mama rarely had time to think; much less waste her time thinking about herself. Sometimes when asked what her name was, she hesitated before simply saying, "Mama!"

She loved all of her children dearly, but some days she felt she would scream just to hear another one holler out "Mama," again. And now there would be another little voice crying for "Mama," soon.

She was in her mid-thirties. Time was going by so fast; she dreaded seeing the clock of time turn over when she would be forty. To her, forty was old. And this morning she felt old. She was no longer the young "lassie" like her father used to call her.

During her long days, she didn't have time to think; even less time to ponder on things. But nonetheless, she had recently noticed the little graying in her hair, the hairline wrinkles around her eyes; she felt that the "change" was not far behind. And speaking of behinds, she rarely did.

Growing up, she would often overhear her mother and other women talking about the "change." As a child, she just couldn't wait to see what, or who, they were going to "change" into after it happened. But now she understood that life continues to change, and no one stays sixteen forever.

While she was not vain about her appearance, she could certainly tell the years were beginning to add up on her body. For months, she had figured she was going through the change what with all the fatigue, sweating, and uneasy nights. She thought it was probably just another one of nature's dirty tricks that was played on women.

It had kinda made her feel sad to think there would be no more Alrod babies in the house. So it caught her by surprise to know that she was pregnant again. She thought that missing her cycle was just all part of the change-of-life. She was much further along than she realized.

She remembered with a smile how she had feared she would never have a child when she and Herman first married. She read about women in the Bible, like Sarah and Elizabeth, who were well into old age when they had their first child; so Mama never gave up hope.

But after Billy Joe was born, they just seemed to be blessed with more and more children. It was not unusual for some farm women to have as many as a dozen children in their lifetime.

With mixed emotions about this pregnancy, she tried not to dwell on the added expense and work another baby would bring. She felt every child was a special gift from God. Each deserved to be wanted and loved.

This baby, still being formed in her womb, would be as welcome as the other six had been.

While she tried not to worry about it, there always seemed to be a nagging thought in the back of her mind about how Herman would manage if anything happened to her before the children were grown and able to take care of themselves.

Her mother had died in childbirth, and that loomed increasingly in her mind now that she was pregnant for the sixth time; with her seventh child.

She felt assured that God knew what He was doing by sending Billy Joe and Sarah Louise first. They were sorely needed to help take care of the other children. After the first two, then came the twins that meant double everything; and then along came LeRoy, who had been the challenge of their lives.

Later came Baby James, he was their dream baby. He rarely cried; was always so pleasant. He would sit for hours in Grandpa Alrod's arms without making a fuss as Grandpa rocked him in Grandma's old rocking chair on the front porch.

He must have been the special blessing to make up for LeRoy's rambunctiousness. Sometimes LeRoy would get on her last nerve, and then he would do or say something that made her laugh. Or, she would admire his straight forth manner, and his courage to attempt almost anything. Truly, that little five-year-old would go where angels feared to tread. She didn't know where he would go in life, but she was sure it would be at break-neck speed.

Mama could only wonder about this new baby. Boy or girl did not matter. She prayed it would not be twins again… and that it would have Baby James' disposition. But mostly she prayed that she would have an easy delivery and that the baby would be born healthy.

After Grandma Sarah went to be with Jesus, Grandpa James seemed to slow down and wither a little bit more each year. Wounded in the Great War, James Alrod had continued to farm his land and pastor the small church adjacent to his land as long as he could. And then came the day when he could no longer do either. He had been the first Alrod to pastor the church. There had been many ministers before him. His son, Herman, had followed in his footsteps with the blessing of the congregation.

Grandpa had been a tremendous blessing to Mama by helping around the house, and entertaining the children. He and LeRoy were particularly close because he listened to LeRoy rattle on and would answer as many of his questions as possible. Mama often said, "Thank goodness for grandparents!"

After James' decline, Herman had inherited both the work of the farm; and the church. It seemed to happen overnight.

When Mama was in her worry mode, she would also wonder how Herman could ever take care of his father along with the children. How would he run a farm, raise children, and pastor the church alone? It took both him and Mama working hard all day long just to keep up. While they worked separately during the day to get their individual work done, they were always united in decisions that had to be made concerning the family. If not at first, they would work on it.

At night when the house was quiet, and all the children and Grandpa were asleep, they would lie awake and discuss the day, the decisions to be made; and then as in their wedding vows they became one. God had blessed their union and like in the Bible when God said, "Go forth and be fruitful," they had been.

Although these scary thoughts came rushing into the forefront of her mind, she could not help but wonder things like, "Would Herman ever remarry? Would he ever bring another wife into his heart, home, and bed?"

That would make cold chills of fear go up her spine just thinking about that... but then she knew Herman. If he ever did remarry, it would be someone he loved, and not just someone to be a housekeeper or companion.

She thought about all the women who had lived in the old house on the Alrod farm before her. There was Rachel, Samuel's wife, the one the house had been built for originally, and then there was Sarah, James' wife, and now her. She thought about how every child in the Alrod family had been conceived in that house except Henry. He was born in New York, but came to the farm as a small boy.

She wondered if not being born on the land had anything to do with his the lack of concern for it. He liked living in the city much more. Henry did not live in the house as an adult for very long. And Rebecca, his wife, had only been there as a visitor.

All the Alrod men had loved only one woman in their lifetime, and she knew whatever Herman decided, it would be right, and with God's blessings. But these thoughts would make her feel jealous of someone who was only a figment of her imagination; which she knew was not of God. She knew that should Herman ever remarry, he would have the right to do so, but she wondered if he ever would.

God was always faithful to remind her of His Word that she had hidden in her heart. God knew just when to bring the right scripture to her mind. While she could not quote chapter and verse, she knew that God's Word had the right answer to all of her quandaries.

In times like these, she remembered this admonition from the Lord that the children of God were to cast down all vain imaginations and everything that put itself against the knowledge of God. She knew she was to take captive every thought that might lead to disobedience to Jesus.

She just had to shake off those thoughts, and come back to what was now, and leave the rest up to God.

Mama seemed to be feeling worse by the minute, and that meant she was going to miss her leisurely stroll along the road toward the store today. On previous trips, she often looked up at the glorious blue sky and listened to the birds chirping at each other.

She looked at the weeds that grew alongside the road and thought God must have created them for a reason. But this Saturday, she would have to leave the trip up to Herman. She was just too tired and had so much to do still. And she was so hot.

Often she would see some of God's creatures either slithering across the road or flying up out of the brush as she walked past. On a warm day, like today, she would have enjoyed a gentle breeze blowing across her face. It was going to be another hot summer.

Sometimes during windy seasons, the wind would blow hard enough to ruffle the hem of her dress, and a couple of times it blew so hard it nearly blew the skirt over her head. Modest as she was after that happened, she would make sure on blustery days that she wore dresses with straighter skirts. Mama had a nice figure and could wear just about any style dress or skirt.

Mama had a natural curl to her hair. Unlike most ladies of her day, she did not have to suffer through those *Toni Home Permanents*. However, at only $1.00 for a perm, it was a good bargain considering they did not have a beauty parlor in town. And perms were costly at $5.50 for a professional one in the city, and often they burned your hair as well.

You could always tell when one of the church ladies had a new permanent. Because, even days afterward, they would stink up the whole church. It was not unusual for folks to get up and move in church when they would be sitting down draft from a new hairdo; especially in hot weather.

In the 1930s, the more modern women wore their hair in finger waves close to the scalp. Many of the older women still wore their long hair pinned up on their head.

Not Mama, she wore her hair short, loose, and fluffy. When she did heavy cleaning in the house, she sometimes wrapped a rag around her head. When gardening, she wore a large straw hat to keep the sun off her hair and her complexion. With her natural curl, a good shampoo on Saturday night with *Ivory* soap and a few pin curls with her *Bobby* pins... she was set for most of the week.

On her walks into town, she loved it when a gentle, soft breeze would sometimes flow through her loose curls. She loved the feel of the wind blowing across her face and through her hair. Once after a quite blustery day, she happened to get a glimpse of herself in Mr. Ferguson's store mirror.

She had tried some of that new setting lotion on her hair when she rolled it up in the pin curls. That Saturday when she went into Mr. Ferguson's store, she got a glimpse of herself in the store mirror, and she was between being horrified and breaking out into laughter. Her hair was sticking up in every direction. She later told Herman she looked like a porcupine.

Even though extravagant that day, she spent twenty-five cents for a small compact and a five-cent comb to bring along with her on her trips to town. She did not bring a pocketbook along with her on these trips because it would just be something else to carry. And besides she had her egg basket; both coming and going. It was easy to tuck the little compact and lipstick inside the egg basket along with her little change purse.

The compact was a little flat case shaped like a little frying pan that snapped shut with a flip-up mirror with light face powder in the bottom half. And in the handle part there was a small tube of light colored lipstick.

She never used the pancake make-up like so many of the other women wore. It made her skin feel heavy and closed up. She had beautiful skin and really didn't need it. Just a light touch of face powder and she was ready to meet the world.

Every night before going to bed, she religiously used her *Ponds Cold Cream*, to keep away wrinkles and to keep her skin soft and not dried out. Only occasionally did she pluck her eyebrows; since she had a natural arch to them; and only had a few strays every now and then. The women before her time used chicken fat as a moisturizer.

Since she had dark eyelashes and brows, there was no need for pencils or *Maybelline*. Mascara came in a little plastic rectangular case no more than two inches by one inch. Inside the case, there was a tiny black bristled flat brush that resembled a tiny toothbrush.

You would have to wet the brush with water and wipe it across the top of the dry mascara before applying it to your eyelashes. It made them look thicker. Mama tried it once, and since she cried a lot, she didn't like those black streaks running down her face.

She often shed tears in church both of joy and sorrow. She would often cry when she was praying and laying her soul before the Lord. When God touched her soul, the tears would flow. And Mama was often known to cry with other women over their sorrows.

Some of the women used an eyebrow pencil to accentuate their brows, and Mama thought some of them looked like clowns in the circus, but who was she to judge?

She was born with dark hair, dark lashes and a natural brow that surrounded those sparkling emerald-green eyes. While *Maybelline* had become quite the thing for many of the women to use, she just really never needed it. But if it made the other women feel good about their appearance, who was she to judge? There were certainly a lot worse things.

These early Saturday morning walks rejuvenated her; and got her blood to flowing. It made her feel good about just being alive. But this morning, she felt that she was barely alive. She felt faint. She pulled a chair out from underneath the table and called for Sarah Louise to come and take the baby out of the kitchen. He had been playing quietly while sitting on the floor.

She sat there for awhile with her head on her crossed arms resting on the table. She was confused and could not figure out what was happening.

As the weakness began to overtake her, the room started to spin around. That awful thought came prancing through her mind once again, "Oh, Lord help me!" she said. "Lord, please don't call me to heaven before these children are older. Please Lord protect this little one that is soon to be here."

Trying to feel better, she just pushed that thought aside. She was so hot and felt like she was smothering. She felt that she needed to get outside and get some fresh air.

She picked up a clean washrag and took it out onto the porch with her. She poured a dipper full of water from the bucket into the enamel wash pan that was kept there for washing up before coming into the house. She put the rag in the water to wipe off her face, and reached to get a second dipper of water to drink.

She took a few sips. The water was lukewarm. It had a rancid, metal-like taste since it had been sitting there in the pail so long. She was overcome with nausea and had to lean over the back rail of the porch to throw-up.

Sarah Louise heard her and came running outside to check on her. She put Baby James down on the porch and tucked the tail of his gown underneath the heavy churn to keep him from crawling off. He began to cry. He felt that something was just not right in his world. She helped Mama to Grandma's old rocking chair.

Sarah Louise ran out to the well to draw up a bucket of cool fresh water. She usually held her hand across the windlass to control the speed with which the weighted bucket would fall into the well. But since this was urgent – she just dropped the weighted well-bucket over the side; and stepped back and let the handle fly.

Papa had taught her how to draw water when she was much smaller, and he warned her about that iron handle and her height. He told her children had been killed when hit in the head with that spinning iron handle.

Then as quickly as she could, she began to draw the rope up through the pulley and back around the windlass as she turned the iron handle. Each turn wrapped the rope around the windlass and brought the bucket closer to the top. She reached over and caught hold of the rope and pulled the bucket toward her.

She held it up a few inches while she slid the wooden top across the opening. It was heavy, but she was a strong little girl. When in a stressful situation, you can do more than you ever thought possible.

She sat the bucket on top of it. Then she realized she had not brought the water pail from the porch. She ran back up on the porch. She stepped over a squalling Baby James, with both his arms reaching up for her to take him. Ignoring him, she picked up the bucket and ran back down the steps and poured the old tepid water on the ground.

Mama was pale as a ghost and barely able to hold herself up in the rocking chair.

Scared to death, and while running back to the well, twelve-year-old Sarah Louise said out loud, "I ain't never gonna git married and let no man git no glint in his eye at me."

Running back to the house and splashing most of the water all over her legs from the bucket, she looked again at Mama and knew that she needed help.

Papa and Billy Joe were some distance out in the fields. She had already lost track of LeRoy, and the twins were down playing in the creek. She took a small metal rod hanging from a rope over the iron triangle to be used in an emergency to call Papa in from the fields. She stood on her tiptoes and rang it with all the strength she could muster.

163

LeRoy came out of the kitchen with peanut butter and jelly all over his face, clothes, hair, and hands. Sarah Louise turned around and screamed at him, "LeRoy, sit down on the porch and don't you move." He knew she meant business and did as he was told.

Grandpa had still been in bed. He came running out in his pajamas and asked, "What is going on?" He took one look at Mama and went to her immediately.

At that moment, Mama grew limp and passed out. Grandpa reached over and lifted her from the chair down to the floor of the porch. He brought her legs up and rested them on the seat of the rocking chair. He had seen men pass out during the war, and the medic had always told them to get their feet higher than their head.

He began washing her face with the cool well water, and loudly calling out to her. She opened her eyes and looked into that kind, sweet, face of his; and said, "God, you are so good!" Did she mistake Grandpa to be God?

While half-conscious and half not, she just helplessly lay there on the porch until Herman ran up on the porch bypassing Sarah Louise, stepping over Baby James, and pushing Grandpa aside. He hollered out to Billy Joe to start up the car and to drive it up close to the porch.

Sarah Louise cleared a pathway by removing both LeRoy and James out of the way. Herman knelt down and picked Mama up, and practically ran with her down the steps toward the car. Billy Joe had been driving since he was fourteen on the back roads, but this would be a true test of his driving skills. Papa got in the back seat with Mama and said to Billy Joe, "Get to town quick."

Sarah stood on the porch watching as they sped out of the driveway and onto the road. Her heart sank. She bounced the baby up and down in an effort to calm him. She wished she had someone who could do the same for her.

Grandpa knelt down on his bad knees and began praying out loud.

"Dear Lord, please dear Lord, hep us all. Lord, hep the sweet, sweet Mama of this family to be okay; hep Herman to be calm and in control, and especially hep Billy Joe, who is doing the emergency driving. Keep the roads clear of traffic, don't let anything happen to that old car... and Lord... above all else... please Lord... let the doctor be there. Amen"

Fear struck in his heart as he had flashbacks of losing his mother and his wife, Sarah. He pulled himself up while steadying himself with the arms on the rocking chair. He turned around ...and sat down in the rocking chair exhausted. He asked Sarah Louise to bring him a dipper of water. With Baby James still on her hip, she still managed to get Grandpa, a cool drink of water.

By this time, the twins had come up into the yard after hearing the triangle alarm. They were wide-eyed and frightened at seeing their Papa carrying their Mama from the porch to the car. They wrapped their arms around each other and began to cry.

Sarah Louise was still standing up with Baby James on her hip. He was screaming in her ear. And she didn't know what to do next. Grandpa was struggling to get up from the chair, and it nearly toppled over. She turned around to look at LeRoy still frozen on the spot. She felt like smacking him for getting into the peanut butter and jelly.

She knew that the twins were terrified because they thought their Mama was dead. She called for them to come up on the porch to help Grandpa back into the house.

Chapter eleven: Mama's Restoration

A full two months had passed since the episode with Mama. God had answered all of Grandpa's prayers. He had blessed Mama that day; the doctor was in town. Since it was so early in the day, he had not yet started making his house calls. God had also protected the baby.

Papa told everyone how proud he was of Billy Joe for keeping the car on the road and for not killing them all while driving at such a high speed. He was also thankful they did not run over anyone when they were speeding through town; on such as a busy day as Saturday.

He praised Sarah Louise for her heroic efforts to help Mama and for ringing the alarm. He told her a grown woman could have done no better. Sarah Louise had indeed saved the day.

After the car had left taking Mama to town, she had made LeRoy strip and get into a cold tub of water out on the porch. She didn't have time to warm it up, and the water from the deep well was cool even in the summertime. Besides, she said he deserved it when she poured the water from the well over his head. He howled.

As it turned out, Mama had an episode of low-blood pressure along with extreme anemia caused by insufficient amounts of iron in the blood.

After he had made sure she was no longer in shock, Dr. McPherson called the hospital in the city. They sent an ambulance to the valley for her. She stayed in the hospital for two days and was sent home with cautions. She was to be on complete bed rest, and she was to take one tablespoon of Lydia E. Pinkham's vegetable compound formula twice each day... morning and night.

She was to have a lot of lean beef... even the broth... and to eat lots of fruits and leafy green vegetables. She was to eat lots of calves' liver any way she could get it down.

She was to go into town every three weeks where Dr. McPherson was to give her Vitamin B-12 shots. It was never known, for sure, which of these helped to give Mama back her energy. If she had known the Pinkham's had contained alcohol, she would never have taken it. She had heard that any amount of alcohol could be harmful to an unborn baby. She was also to get a lot of exercise. Both she and Papa laughed at that one.

Over those first four weeks, she followed the doctor's orders to do everything he said. Since he said for her to get a lot of exercise, she resumed her light daily work within two weeks. Slowly, at first, then like LeRoy full speed ahead by the eighth week."

Papa had been driving her to town to sell her eggs and to get the shots. But this Saturday morning, she awoke feeling chipper and with a bad case of cabin fever. She announced that she was going to walk to town as she had done in the past. Papa protested a little at first, but he knew there was no arguing with her about this.

She needed to do this. It had been hard for her to stay down...or to "stay put"... as Grandpa would tell her when she tried to get up to do things before she was actually able. But she finally felt she was able and "up to" the trek into town.

The trip would be her proving ground where she would satisfy herself that she was well, and strong enough to do it. The birth of the baby would be coming soon, and she not only had to build up her stamina for the birthing, but also for the strength she would need to care for a newborn. She said, "Time and housework waits for no one!"

She knew the short walk down the old country road would be good for her. Because she enjoyed it, it made her senses keener and helped to clear her mind. She loved all the seasons of the year. Even in the heat of summer, there seemed to be a breeze blowing down from the mountains.

In the spring on the way back, she would stop and pick a handful of wildflowers to adorn her kitchen table. She put the flowers in a mason jar filled with water. In the fall, she often picked an array of fall colored leaves or picked up pine cones. She often arrived home with her recently emptied egg basket filled with things of God's creation.

Summer would soon be turning into fall. She could feel a hint of fall in the air... ahhh...the fresh air. It filled her lungs, but it also gave her a carefree jubilant feeling of pleasure. She loved being out in the open without four walls to close her in like they did back at the house.

Sometimes when she wasn't pregnant, she would find herself skipping just like she did when she was a child. She always hoped no one was looking, or some of the ladies would have a field day gossiping and making fun of her. When she was walking, there was no one but her and God.

Determined, she felt sure the walk would be far greater for her than all the medicines in the world. These were the times when she felt the closest to God and nature. There were no ceilings or roof tops to hinder her prayers and little talks with God.

Often she would stop by the spot where the first church service was held back in 1850 before the little church on the hill had been built. Under a little stand of trees, there once were crude benches made with pieces of lumber extended from one tree stump to the other. The trees were cut down to stumps of the same height. This place had been their first little church in the wildwood.

Knowing how much Sarah, his wife, loved that spot, James made a little wooden bench similar to the one in the church for her to sit on when she used to take those walks to town. Sarah, Herman's mother, planted rose bushes nearby and other naturally returning plants. Mama always felt so close to God, to the early settlers, and to Sarah when she stopped halfway to rest and pray.

Mama loved the things that God created and often brought things from the outdoors into her home. She just had a knack for placing small pieces of wood, pine cones, little shiny rocks, or brightly colored blooms in the center of her big kitchen table.

She took great pride in how her table looked for it was where her family met for food and nourishment. It was also a time for her to have all of her family around her together at the same time. And it was a time to talk about the things of God.

Often she used natural things to teach her children about God, and the life He wanted for all of His children. As her children grew and noticed her practice, they began to bring all sorts of things for her centerpiece.

Once, LeRoy brought her a turtle. She hugged him and thanked him and made a place for the baby turtle to live on the porch in an old pan.

She got outside with her children as much as possible and often used the time to be with her children enjoying and exploring nature… the world that God made.

Sometimes she would sit in a thick bed of clover that grew along side of the house under an enormous oak tree. She taught them how to make daisy chains by linking the clover blooms together while teaching them Bible stories.

She would have them look for four-leaf clovers because they were to bring good luck. She did not believe in omens, but she did believe that God created everything for a purpose. If you believed that good things could come your way, then that was having faith.

She used the three-leaf clover to explain how God could be three-in-one… the Trinity. She said, "Just even though the leaf had three separate parts, it was still just one leaf. And that was a good and simple way to show that God was "Three-in-One… Father, Son, and Holy Spirit."

She would use God's creations to teach them about the Creator God.

They would watch the ants coming back and forth from their mound, and she would tell them about the scripture that honored them for their being so busy and not sluggardly.

"Mama, what does "sluggery" mean?" asked the ever inquisitive LeRoy.

Mama explained that it meant lazy. Velma popped him on his arm and said, "Like you, LeRoy!" He hit her back. Mama warned them; she had seen that; and did not like what she had seen.

Their Mother picked up where she had left off, "In the book of Proverbs, it says that while ants were so small and had little strength, they stored up their own food for the winter and did not depend on others. She said that was a lesson for everyone."

"Like we do, Mama?" asked, LeRoy?" "What do you mean, we?" asked Velma.

LeRoy had his feelings hurt. He had begun to whine as he turned that sweet cherub-like face to his Mother and asked, "I hep too, don't I, Mama?"

Mama replied, "Yes, you do, LeRoy! You run and git diapers for Mama when she needs to change Baby James. You clean out the chicken coop, and you keep Mama company while she is cooking, and that is heping a lot."

Then she scolded Velma by telling her to stop picking on LeRoy. And even before she finished her sentence, Velma started to speak, but Mama beat her to it and said, "Velma, if you find that you cannot be kind to yor brothers and sisters, then you may retreat back into the house and sweep the kitchen."

She told them that everyone in the world had a special job to do, and when they didn't do their part, it made it harder on everyone else. She had them to watch the trail of ants to see how they traveled in a straight line just like soldiers.

She said, "Ants have no school teacher or army sergeant to tell them how to do what was right; they just knew it by nature." She told them, "People were like that too. They were born with the knowledge of right and wrong, but it was their free will that they use to make choices."

LeRoy always had an answer for everything and said, "And they sure do bite you, and it hurts!" Velma poked him again and said, "And it ought to teach you to leave them alone." She got up and moved over before he could poke her back. He started for her, but Mama snapped her fingers and pointed for him to sit back down. He did.

"The actions of the ants," she said, "shows us that every living creature has its place in the scheme of God's plans." And before LeRoy could say anything she explained that "scheme" meant the reason and method by which God did things.

She said, "LeRoy, God made ants be ants, and people to be people, and trees to be trees; because that is what He wanted to do. And maybe, God gave them those stingin' bites to protect them from their enemies."

Mama reminded him how God also gave them turpentine, kerosene, and baking soda to put on the stings, and they all came from things that God had made as well.

"Mama, tell Velma to stop poking me!"

"Velma, stop poking LeRoy!"

"But Mama, he keeps erupting yor story, and I love to hear you tell them!"

"Velma, the word is "interrupting" and LeRoy, sometimes we all need a little poking to keep us straight!"

"And Velma, I expect the kitchen to be swept clean by the time we get back in the house."

Chapter twelve: Eggs, Chickens, Jars, and Vittles

Preparing for her trip to town, the first one since her "spell," Mama gathered her eggs early that morning. She was proud of her hens this past week as they had cooperated and helped her to add some extra money to her "nest egg." This money was spent for things the children needed; that they otherwise would not have. School would be starting up soon, and they would need so many things.

LeRoy and Billy Joe Bob were always running out of overalls. Many times she would find herself patching the patches. When their shirt collars got frayed, she would detach them and turn the worn side over and sew it back on just like she did on Herman's work shirts.

Boys were so much harder on clothes than the girls. It was little or nothing to make them a dress from a couple of feed sacks. They came in such a variety of pretty prints.

Papa had a cast-iron shoe anvil that he used to repair shoes. He could repair them, but he could not make them. It was hard to keep up with their ever-growing feet. He bought the anvil early on from the *Sears Roebuck Catalog* when Billy Joe and Sarah Louise were just starting school. Seeing how it cost as much as fifty cents to half-sole a shoe, he could replace them and the heels for only a few pennies a pair.

The kids went barefoot most of the year, and sometimes they had enough wear left in their shoes to hand down to someone else. During the Depression, Papa found himself mending not only the shoes for his family but for others in his little church as well. They saved money, and he made a little extra.

Going barefoot had its drawbacks. There was always a piece of glass or a splinter to be extracted from somebody's foot and then there were those stumped toes. It seemed that once you stumped your toe in the summer; you would keep on stumping it all summer long. Mama always kept clean white strips of cloth and lots of turpentine and kerosene for such occasions. Mercurochrome was one thing that would start the kids hopping. It burned.

Folks in the country had to deal with all sorts of things on their own since there was often no doctor around. Mama kept a bar of *Neko* soap handy. That was about the only germicidal treatment that was effective against impetigo. It contained Mercury and could not be used often.

The egg money helped to buy many things they needed for the family; that they could not grow. Mama had been raising chickens from as far back as she could remember. She had her own little flock when she was but a girl back at home with her parents.

She had learned very early they were a lot of trouble, but she had also learned the value of having them. She learned there was a profit to be made from the eggs, and she always seemed to have a little "nest egg" hidden somewhere.

She kept them fed, watered, and made sure no wild animals had access to them... even egg sucking dogs. Often a fox or other animal would try to gain access to her little chicken coop, but her father kept a shotgun close by the back door. One blast from it would send the intruder running for the woods, and the chickens running all around the coop squawking and clucking with feathers flying in all directions.

As a young bride, she learned to wield her own shotgun.

Mama knew a lot about chickens. She had learned by trial and error which chickens were the best for meat, and the ones best for egg production. She chose a variety to satisfy the needs of her family and to have extra eggs to sell. Sometimes she would also sell baby chicks or one of her good laying hens every now and then. An over abundance of roosters would end up in the cooking pot.

She had a nice brood of the White Plymouth Rocks ... they were best for their meat, and her bunch sure liked fried chicken.

There were times when she was able to get beef for her family; but not so often since the Depression. Many dairy and cattle farms had gone under.

Beef was harder to come by, and it was expensive. Most of their food was free from the cost of cash money. But it still came at a high cost because of the back-breaking work it required to grow it.

Beef had gone up to twenty-five cents a pound. And for a family of eight, a roast could cost as much as two or three dollars. That would have bought both the twins a new pair of shoes.

Chickens were still the best thing they had going. She had become artful at catching the hens and wringing their necks. The kids never got tired of watching a chicken run all over the yard while Mama still held its head in her hand. She gave that to the Calico. They never lacked for understanding when she would tell one of them that they were running all over the place like "a chicken with its head cut off."

Often LeRoy would beg, "Mama, make the chicken wave good-bye!" After cutting the feet off the chicken, Mama could pull one of the tendons, and the claws would open and close as if it was waving good-bye. When he learned to do that... he would chase the twins all around the yard as if he were playing a game of tag. They would scream much to his delight. He chased Velma especially hard.

When the chicken would finally flop over, Mama would tie their legs over the clothes line with twine for the blood to drain out. Afterward, she would plop them down in a pot of boiling water outside. Then she sat down and plucked them clean. She saved the feathers to make feather pillows and to stuff cushions just like her mother and grandmother had done.

She and Papa kept a couple of milk cows, and they had to be kept fresh in order for the children to have milk, butter, and cheese. She made the children take turns churning the butter... if they complained they went a week without butter or buttermilk, but they still had to take their turn at churning.

And since that fresh butter tasted so good on Mama's hot biscuits, they learned to do other things while they churned. Billy Joe would usually churn with one hand and hold a book to read in the other. Sarah Louise would sometimes sing. She was going to have a nice voice like Mama.

The twins would team up and cut their churning time in half switching back and forth after so many "ups and downs" of the paddle for each. They would be busy counting. Churning not only produced the great tasting butter, but it made their arms stronger for the doing of it.

Sarah Louise was the biggest help on laundry day. She was finally tall enough to help hang the clothes on the line. Billy Joe helped Herman with chores around the farm.

When a new calf was born, they sold it to Mr. Ferguson to buy clothes for the children at school time. It was difficult for the children not to become attached to the baby animals that were born on the farm. But they grew up knowing they were not pets. They had "Snooper" their Beagle Hound and a number of old Tabby and Calico cats for that.

The Alrod's were dirt farmers, not dairy farmers. Occasionally some of the families would get together and buy one of Mr. Salem's steers, and they would share the portions. That meant that Papa had to stoke up the smokehouse to dry out what meat they could not eat right away.

They always had a few pigs they would raise from piglets. There was a huge tin bucket out near the barn for all the scraps from the dinner table to be put into what was called the slop bucket. That was not to be confused with the slop jar that was used inside in place of the outhouse for use during the night and in bad weather.

Once when everyone was sitting around the radio waiting for the *"Amos 'n' Andy"* radio program to come on, Papa asked, "Billy Joe did you take the slop bucket down to feed the pigs?" He said he had, but then he jumped up and said, 'I'll be right back, I forgot to bring the slop jar in from the outhouse when I took it out this morning."

LeRoy spoke up and asked why they called it a "slop jar" when it didn't look like a jar. Mama, who was sitting in her rocking chair knitting a pair of booties for the new baby, spoke up agreeing with him that the big white enameled bucket-like container didn't much look like a jar. She thought that would pacify him.

She had bought the matching set from Mr. Ferguson's store. In the set, she got the two-gallon slop jar, a large dish pan, two wash pans, and a water dipper all for $5.00. There were all white enamel and had a red rim about the edge. She had paid him a dollar down and a dollar a month until it was paid in full.

The ones they had been using needed replacing long before. She was so excited when she brought them home for her family's use. It was not often that she had things that matched. The white enamel helped her to know when the utensils were really clean.

It still bothered LeRoy why it was called a "slop jar," or was he just trying to get the whole family's attention while sitting on the floor in front of the radio? He was persistent in wanting to know why they called it a jar.

Sarah Louise, tired of his interruptions, quickly got down the dictionary and looked up the word during the *Campbell Soup Company's* commercial; thinking it would shut him up. She said, "LeRoy, the closest thing I can find is that it comes from this big long word… j-a-r-d-i-n-i-e-r-e. I can't say it, but it means a fancy flower pot. Now are you satisfied?" she said hatefully.

Papa gave her a stern look which indicated he did not approve of her last words.

Just as the radio program began, *"Amos and Andy"* were trying to figure out their next move when Billy Joe came running back inside with the slop jar in his hand, out of breath asking, "Did I miss anything?" They all told him to shush….

The last episode had left Amos Brown and Andy Jones in a pickle once again by falling for another of the Kingfish's schemes along with his wife, Sapphire. Everyone leaned a little closer to the radio to hear better… and then LeRoy, looking puzzled, tried to say the word, "jardines."

Everyone hushed him, but he was not about to be outdone. Papa was sitting in the big stuffed chair with LeRoy sitting on the floor next to him. LeRoy yanked on Papa's pant leg and said, "Papa, that word sounds like sardines don't it. I don't like sardines… they smell bad!" Is it called a slop jar because it smells bad?"

Papa, who was reading the paper, halfway listening to *"Amos 'n' Andy"* said, "Pot, LeRoy, it is a pot, okay?"

Then LeRoy asked why they would call it a pot when they had to "go" in it, and then call it a pot when Mama had to "cook" in it. The quick fifteen minute radio show was off, and the family was disgusted at LeRoy for interrupting at the best part, and they didn't get to hear how it ended.

Sarah Louise, crossly spoke up and said in a harsh voice said, "LeRoy pots are used for a lot of different things... like when we plant marigolds in clay flower pots." She got up and left the room; so did the twins.

Then LeRoy asked, "Then why do we call the stove in the church, a pot-bellied stove?" Then he began to snigger and said, "Some of the boys at church said that Judge Hendrix has a pot belly."

Papa said, "That will be enough, LeRoy!" But he was not to be outdone and asked, "But Papa, if the judge has a pot belly, which pot did he get it from the one he uses to "go" in or the one his Mama cooks in?"

Before Papa could answer that the judge had a wife and not a Mama to do his cooking, LeRoy began to tear up as if he were afraid, crawled up in Papa's lap and said, "Papa, I don't want to get no pot-belly. I don't want the boys at school laughing at me. I ain't gonna use the slop jar anymore."

It was all Papa could do was not laugh out loud. But he knew that LeRoy was confused, so he told him, "Don't you worry LeRoy, only old men git pot bellies, and it is from standing over the kitchen stove eating too much deer stew from out of the pot! You don't have anything to worry about."

"LeRoy said, "Oh!"

And then LeRoy asked, "But Papa, why do we call that big black wash pot that Mama washes clothes in a pot, she don't plant flowers in it?"

For a long time around the house, the kids kept torturing LeRoy about pots. They asked him had he heard about the pot at the end of the rainbow where he could find a lot of gold. He asked them how he could find the end of the rainbow, and Billy Joe feared he might get lost in the woods looking for the end of it when they had another rainbow. He said, "They are just kidding, LeRoy, there ain't no pot of gold at the end of the rainbow!"

LeRoy said, "Oh!"

Another time, LeRoy overheard Papa say he had to clean out the barn because it was just going to pot. LeRoy looked into the barn and then up at Papa, and said, "Papa you'd better git a big pot if yor gonna put all of this stuff in it."

Papa just tousled his hair and said, "Don't you worry, son, we will make do."

Mama and Papa decided that before the next *"Amos 'n' Andy"* radio program came on, they were going to make sure LeRoy was in the bed fast asleep.

The hog bucket, the garbage pail, the slop bucket or whatever it was called mattered little to the hogs; as they would eat anything that was put in it. Mama would often tease her bunch about eating her "out of house and home" like a bunch of hungry hogs.

The Alrod's ole sow produced enough piglets during the year that enabled them to sell some of them and still have several to keep for themselves.

As soon as the weather was cold enough in the late fall, they would butcher several of the hogs they had fattened up all year long. Papa would put them in a pen by themselves and feed them only corn and feed for about a month before they were to be butchered. He was told that when you ate a hog, you would be eating the last thing that the hog ate. He had actually seen them eat rats, and that was enough for him.

After the arduous process of getting the meat prepared, Papa would hang the pork in the smokehouse for curing. Papa would hire one of the colored ladies, and sometimes two, from down the road to come and help out during the hog killings and other busy times during harvest. They worked for portions of the bounty.

Their husbands would also come to help when it was time to harvest the corn.

There was just no better smell than when the smoke house billowed out a waft of smoke that floated across the farm... nothing like the smell of bacon and ham being smoked. They made use of just about every part of the hog. They even ate the brains scrambled with eggs for breakfast.

Mama cleaned the pigs' feet carefully to make sure there was no mud or refuse left in between the toes. She pickled them in her finest homemade vinegar. These were a treat to go with her dried butter beans.

Mama would make fried meat skins and cracklings. The kids enjoyed watching her put the meat skins over in the hot boiling grease in the black wash pot and waited for them to rise to the top. She would then scoop them up and put them on a platter covered with a tea towel. She gave the entrails to the women who helped at harvest time for them to make "chitlins" out of them.

By adding sage, peppers, and other herbs right from her garden, Mama used the leftover pork to make delicious breakfast sausage. She would fry it up in her big iron skillet and then use the grease to make thicken gravy to drizzle over her hot homemade biscuits.

They used the rest of the hog meat to render down to make lard and cracklings. After the fat from the hog had been rendered down, there would be little bits of hard pieces left behind. These could be collected when the lard grease was strained through a piece of cheesecloth. These were called "cracklings."

On a cold winter's night, Mama would add them to the cornbread batter, and when added to a cold glass of buttermilk... they would make very fittin' vittles.

Lard was important in frying chicken, pork chops; as well as vegetables like fried potatoes, okra, and green tomatoes. Mama kept her lard in the ice box and then sometimes out on the back porch after the weather was freezing outside. But it would last for a long time at room temperature.

Mama had a grease crock near the stove with a strainer on top. She would pour the grease through the strainer to collect it when she fried bacon and sausage. She used this grease for frying foods. But to make Mama's big fluffy biscuits, she needed lard.

However, by late spring, early summer, they would usually run out of pork. Then it would be back to assorted chicken meals, baked, roasted, or fried. Fried chicken was the family favorite.

They did not always have meat at every meal; especially during the week. Mama cooked special meals for Sunday dinner, when company came, on birthdays and holidays. They had desserts only on Sundays.

During the week, they sometimes had meatless meals and enjoyed the fresh produce from the garden or home-canned vegetables from their previous garden. Often they would have freshly made cornbread, buttermilk, fried fatback or streak o' lean along with sliced tomatoes and spring onions pulled right from the ground.

She could stretch the pork and beef by using small amounts in stews and soups. When they got really low on meat, Papa would go hunting for wild game. They often had fresh fried catfish caught right in their own creek.

Corn was Papa's main crop. He depended on it totally for the expenses of running the farm. Everything else that he grew was for his family and for feeding the animals.

Fresh corn is ready to be harvested when you pierce a kernel with your thumbnail, and it squirts a white milk-like substance. Fresh corn is harvested for immediate enjoyment on the table for eating; and for canning. The corn that was left on the stalks to dry would be ground into cornmeal or saved to feed the chickens.

Dating back centuries, the Indians had farmed the land. They grew what was called maize. They celebrated the harvest each year with a corn dance. The pioneers that came after them celebrated the harvest by having corn-shucking parties and dances.

When the fresh corn was ready to be harvested, Herman hired extra hands to help with the picking of the ripe ears of corn, and paid them both in what money he could spare; and with as much corn as they could take home with them.

At corn harvesting time, everyone got involved, and the ladies filled long tables with all sorts of good home-cooked foods, including many corn dishes, meats, vegetables, and desserts. These men would also come back and help when it was time to harvest the dried corn.

Even the cows and pigs got in on the celebration when they got the shucks to eat and then in turn for their thankfulness; Herman had a lot of manure to fertilize the ground putting back what the crops had taken out. Such was the cycle of life and use. The manure would be stacked in high piles and turned often until it was dried out and was then spread on the fields.

Herman needed a good crop to meet the needs of his ever increasing family. A good crop depended on many things; not the least being the weather. A hail storm, when the corn was barely rising out of the ground, meant that the corn would have to be planted all over again.

However, when it was approaching maturity, sometimes it would be totally wiped out. Too much rain or not enough rain would also spell disaster for his crops. Also, infestation of corn worms left untreated could wipe out the whole crop of corn.

Herman often thought, when doing his Bible study, how little he needed reminding just how much farmers had to recognize and depend upon God.

There were a few times when food got so low that Papa had to resort to hunting up on the mountain for deer, raccoons, squirrels, or turkeys. But he always went up there just before Thanksgiving to search for a turkey to grace their dinner table.

Old Mr. and Mrs. Wilson, who lived in a little cabin up on top of the mountain, always invited him up to hunt on their land. They had no children and were always happy to oblige their preacher. They kept an eye out for where the turkeys would be roosting, and Herman would have little trouble bagging a couple of them… one for his family and one for them. Last year Mr. Wilson went to be with the Lord, and she was left up there alone. But she said she was never truly alone because Jesus was always with her.

Sometimes meat came at a premium. The last time Mama bought a roast at the butcher's she felt guilty to have spent twenty-five cents a pound for it. Since she had to buy a large one, it had cut sharply into her profits from the egg money.

But it was Papa's birthday, and she wanted to make him something special. On the other hand, she sure knew how to get her money's worth. First she boiled it with the bone in and the fat on. She saved the broth from it to make homemade vegetable soup. Then she baked it a little longer nested in an arrangement of carrots, potatoes, and onions in her large cast iron Dutch oven with the lid.

Everyone sat around the table in great expectations as Papa gently sliced each one a piece of roast; being careful to give portions according to the size of the appetites. There was never any waste.

Even as lazy as he was, their ole Beagle, "Snooper," got in on the celebration dinner; when he finally got the bone. He would gnaw on it for a while and then trot out and bury it somewhere. He got the name

"Snooper" because of his uncanny way of sniffing the air and tracking a rabbit.

The family enjoyed the delicious meal for Papa's birthday. They had beef roast with carrots, potatoes, and onions, alongside the fresh stewed corn and green string beans fresh from the garden.

They also had sliced tomatoes, cucumbers, and onions. Mama made plenty of cornbread in her cast iron skillet. There were always plenty of jams, jellies and relishes right from Mama's own pantry. But the best part of the birthday meal was one of Mama's famous chocolate cakes.

Mama ground up the small pieces of beef in her sausage grinder for Little James since his tiny teeth had a hard time chewing. Then after dinner, she would carefully take the leftovers and put them in her icebox. The next morning for breakfast, they had chipped beef and gravy over her homemade biscuits. The hogs did not get a chance at any spoiled leftovers.

Ice tea was often the only beverage they had beside nice cool water from the well. They had water most of the time because sugar and ice for the tea was a luxury. But sometimes, Mama would take her ice pick and chip off a sizable chunk of ice and put it in the dishpan; and then chip it into smaller pieces to fit into the ice tea pitcher to cool the tea all at once. That way there was no loss due to the ice melting in individual glasses.

Mama saved the sugar for her pies and cakes. Mr. Jenkins, over the way, kept bees and Mama was able to trade sometimes for delicious jars of honey; which she also used in baking; and "sweetin." Mama traded fresh vegetables, eggs, or sometimes even live chickens for the honey.

There was another fella, who lived on the other side of the mountain who grew sorghum cane. Several times a year, he would bring jars of sorghum syrup from his farm and sell them to Mr. Ferguson. Then Mr. Ferguson would in turn either sell or trade them with the other folks in the valley. It was always a treat when Papa would bring home a couple of long canes for the children to break open and suck the sugar out.

While Mama was busy raising a crop of kids, Papa was battling the elements to raise a crop in the cornfield.

Their children had an ample supply of both milk and buttermilk to drink. They also had plenty of butter, cream, and cheese.

181

Sometimes when Mr. Ferguson got in fresh lemons, Mama would trade eggs for lemons and the kids got a special treat when Mama turned them into lemonade or a lemon meringue pie. Her eggs made the meringue rise nice, high, and fluffy.

The iceman came but once a week during mild weather, but twice a week when it was hot. He didn't come at all during the winter. Those huge blocks of ice in the ice box had to last them in order to keep their food safe, but often Mama would still allow herself to chip some off to put into tea or lemonade.

Coffee was a staple in the household. Papa once said. "God knew what it would take to keep a farmer going sixteen hours a day and therefore He 'invented' coffee." Sometimes Mama allowed the children to have a cup on cold winter days along with lots of milk and just a hint of sugar or honey. Mama also used the honey to mix with lemon juice for bad coughs.

Once, when croup hit the family, and everyone was coughing, Papa had to go for the doctor. He gave Mama some hard rock candy and a small medicine bottle of whiskey. He told her to put a piece of candy in a spoon and pour a little of the whiskey over it until it melted. And then she was to give it to the coughing child.

Mama was nice and polite, but as soon as he left she went to the back porch and poured it over the rail and out into the back yard. Papa only smiled at her. He approved.

She turned to him and said, "I won't ever be the one to lift spirits to the tongue of my children!" In years to come, many medicines would contain alcohol. But Mama did not believe it was the right thing to have a bottle of likker in her house to have before her children.

She turned to Papa and in unison they said, *"Woe unto him that giveth his neighbor drink, that puttest thy bottle to him and makest him drunk!"* That scripture came from Habakkuk.

She was raised with a theory that if you never took that first drink… you would never become a drunk. She, for one, was not going to be the one to give her children that first "drink!"

Even though in another place, the scripture said that Paul told Timothy to take a little wine for his stomach's sake. Mama said, "That was a suggestion; not a commandment!"

After the doctor had left, she made up a poultice of mustard seed, flour, and lard.

It helped them to breathe better. As she applied the poultice on the chest of each child, she prayed and asked God to do the healing. He did. She quoted from Jeremiah, *"Heal me oh, Lord, and I shall be healed!"*

Each year before Papa harvested the mustard greens, he would cut the seeds from the top of the plants after they appeared. He gave Mama the seeds for making yellow mustard for eating; and mustard for poultices, and also to keep the wind from blowing the seed all across the fields. Mustard seeds reproduced themselves. They could easily take over a farm if they were allowed to spread. The Alrod's ate the mustard greens boiled along with turnip greens and the turnips.

Mama separated the seeds, put them up to dry out, and then kept them in glass jars for such an occasion. She put a little jar of the seeds on the medicine shelf along with the bicarbonate of soda and camphor. She also gave a lot of them to other women in the church for making their own condiments and poultices.

Mama used other herbs and roots to help them through illnesses. Sometimes the doctor would be available and sometimes he was not. She kept a nice clean container of kerosene and turpentine also for cuts and other medicinal uses. She saved the clean white rags left from old pillow cases and sheets to tear into strips for bandages as needed.

She learned a lot from Granny Wilson, who had served as a midwife for years before poor eyesight and age prevented her from doing so. Often she and Mama would trek through the woods above her cabin on the mountain, and they would collect herbs and roots to be used for various illnesses. Granny knew which ones were good for each malady. Mama learned from her as well.

The mixture for a mustard plaster had to be precise so as not to burn the skin. Mama knew from her mother just how to make it. She often thought of her mother at such times and the scripture that said the older women were to teach the younger women. She prayed every day that she would be as faithful doing that as her mother had been. All three of her girls were learning to cook, knit, sew, crochet, quilt, and how to run a household.

The use of the mustard seed plaster was centuries old and often the treatment was worse than the malady. In times before Mama's, folks used to mix the ground powdered mustard seed with flour and a little water. Then it was applied it directly to the chest or painful area.

The heat from the seed would indeed draw the blood to the affected area, but was sure to blister the skin. Mama's grandmother had told her that when President Lincoln was shot, and for lack of knowing what else to do, the doctors applied mustard plasters... but of course to no avail.

Mama made hers up by mixing the powdered mustard seed and the white of an egg, adding just enough flour to make a plaster. She placed the mixture between two pieces of muslin or flannel so as not to put the concoction directly next to the skin.

Again, she felt blessed to have such loyal laying hens, and a mother who taught her how to be a good mother by example. Once, when everyone in the household had come down with the croup, there were no eggs for Mr. Ferguson's store that week.

Mama knew that the white of the egg served not only to protect the yolk and nourish a chick before it hatches; it was also used for a variety of other home remedies such as an ointment after a minor burn or a facial to dry up oils on the face which caused pimples.

Mama had a variety of chickens; as some were better layers while others were better for the meat they produced. Her layers were Leghorns, Rhode Island Reds, and Bantams. They produced both white and brown eggs as well as double-yokes. The eggs had to be collected early in morning before the sun got too hot; or before they froze in the wintertime.

If Mama had any worries about the freshness of the eggs, she would place them in a bowl of cold water. If they floated, they were bad. To make sure they were not fertile and didn't have a chick inside, she would hold them up to a candle so she could see through the egg. Cracked or bad eggs were given to the pigs.

Once she commented that she wished people could be like that by holding themselves up to the light in order to see what was on the inside.

Then she stopped for a moment and said, "I guess that is what the Bible means where it says that Jesus is the light of the world. For when we hold ourselves up against Him we can see what kind of person we are."

She also told her children that it must be where the adage of a person being a good egg or a bad egg came from. She was never quite sure how a person, who had faulty wisdom, would be called an "egghead!"

Pork was mostly eaten at breakfast time; while fish, chicken, pork, and sometimes beef were the mainstay for Sunday dinner. Weekday suppers would be a variety of vegetables and bread, and on some occasions; there was meat, even if it was only in the stew or soup.

When Mama was low on pork for breakfast, she made heaping platters of flapjacks. She would also make corn fritters to go along with the fried fish for dinner.

Eggs were vital in their everyday diet. Mama made them scrambled for breakfast. She made egg custards for desserts, and she used them in potato salad, and always put them generously in her cornbread and dressing. She often made what others called "deviled eggs," but she would have nothing named after the devil in her house. She preferred to call them "angel eggs."

Chapter thirteen: A Death in the Family

"LeRoy, son… Mama done told you to git out from underneath my feet. You're gonna git yorself burnt if you don't watch out… this here jelly is hot comin' out of the pot. Now git that top and go spin it somewhere's else!"

"Awe, Mama."

"There you go agin LeRoy, awing ME! I done told you that ain't respectful to yor Mama. Now when I speak, you listen and keep yor bee's wax to yourself. Now git on out of here!"

Mama had not been feeling well. Her patience with LeRoy had grown thin. She had so many things she wanted to accomplish before the new baby came, and she was hot, tired, and pushed to get the berries turned into jelly and jam for the coming winter.

"But Mama, I'm bored, I ain't got nothin' to do. I want to go fishin', but Daddy said we couldn't go today… he had to do the stupid plowing."

"LeRoy Alrod, you're aiming for a switching just as shore as you wuz born. I dare you call stupid what yor hardworking Daddy is doing to feed yor hungry belly. Where do you think them beans, peas and greens come from? They don't grow on trees; that's fer sure. And they don't grow at all unless they git planted."

"Mama, how do those little bitty ole seeds turn into beans and peas?"

"LeRoy, are you stalling me?"

"No, Mama, I ain't! I just don't understand how you can put one little ole seed in the ground, and it makes a whole lot more beans out of it. How does it do that Mama?"

Calming down, Mama said, "Well, LeRoy git on the other side of the table and out of my way, and I'll see if I can tell you. First of all, it is one of God's secrets on how things came to be since the creation. It is just

186

the way God made things to be. "But Mama, how can we plant seeds on different kinds of ground when we only got one farm?"

Laughing, she said, "LeRoy, the Bible talks about seeds being planted in different ways. It tells us that we can't plant seeds on hard ground, they just won't grow. And if we plant the seeds where the birds can see them, they will come and eat them up. But in order to get yor crops to grow, you have to work the soil, get all the rocks and roots out to make the dirt nice and soft.

The Bible tells us about the different kinds of ground that seeds get planted in and that is why yor Daddy is plowing up that field to make it just right for the seeds he wants to plant for a winter crop.

"Mama, you still didn't say how the seed grows into so many beans."

"Well, LeRoy, after the soil is right, and after we plant the seeds, then only God can make it grow. He sends the rain, and the sunshine and the little seeds die."

"Dies? Dies? How can a seed grow if it dies?"

"LeRoy that is part of the mystery. Before it grows, it has to die first and from that tiny seed grows the plant, and from the plant grows many more beans. Do you understand that?

"Naw, Mama, I don't."

"That is kinda like our hearts. When we git a soft heart for God, He plants a seed into our hearts through His Good Book or another good soul. And then He allows both good and bad things to happen to make us grow crops of good deeds in our hearts. Then that goodness grows and reaches out and feeds the souls of others."

"You will understand that someday. Now git out on the back porch and check on yor Granddaddy. Go and keep him company."

"Awe, Mama!" "Oops I'm sorry, but I don't want to go and sit with Grandpa he don't do nothin' but sit on the porch and whittle with his knife. He don't talk to nobody and when he does, he don't make no sense. He just wants to talk about when he was a little boy and when he was in the war."

"Mama, you said that the Bible says, "If you don't work, you don't eat. That's what you tell me when I have to feed the chickens. Chickens don't work, and they eat."

"LeRoy where do you suppose them eggs come from?"

"Well, Grandpa don't lay no eggs, and he don't work, and he eats."

"LeRoy you got a heap of learning to do, but for a five-year-old, you do pretty good."

"Did you know that Grandpa's family was born all the way across the ocean in another country? They were pore, and they didn't have a farm of their own. They worked for someone else who took away mostly what they growed in their garden. Then there came a great famine in the land."

"What is a famanin, Mama?'

"It is when there is no food to eat, and people starve to death."

"Well, I hope no famanin comes over here, don't you Mama, 'cause I like to eat!"

"I sure hope it don't either, LeRoy. And you are right; you really do like to eat!"

She didn't have the heart to tell him about all the people in America who was starving since the big Dust Bowl event and the crashing of the stock market along with so many bank closings. He was just too young to understand, and children should not have to bear the burdens of grown-ups.

Pointing her finger toward the back porch, she said, "Back to Grandpa."

"I'm gonna go outside and play," he said.

"No, you won't young man; you will do as you are told. Git out there and talk to yor Grandpa. He's been feeling porely for the past few days, and his eatin's been way off."

LeRoy picked up his little spinning top to go outside, and he took a good look at it and said, "Grandpa made me this top didn't he, Mama?"

"Yes, he did son. And he did a whole lot more."

He ran out onto back porch slamming the screen door behind him; as usual. There sat Grandpa on the end of the porch in the same old chair he sat in every day; just sitting and whittling and never having much to say.

"Hey, Grandpa, what you doin'?"

"Whittlin'."

"Why?"

"Just cause,"

"What you makin' this time?"

"A bird."

"What you making another bird for, Grandpa? You have a whole box full of 'em?"

"Cause I just like to make 'em."

"Grandpa, how come you don't work?"

"Well, LeRoy, it ain't that I don't want to, but you see this old game leg of mine just played out, and I just can't stand on it like I used to."

"Why don't you tell Mama to rub some kerosene on it and maybe it will work better?"

"Well, it's a mite past that, son."

"Grandpa, were you ever a little boy like me?" LeRoy knew he had been but if he could get him to talking, he might have a way of escape into the yard.

"Well, LeRoy, I was a little boy; but not like you. They ain't nobody like you."

"They ain't, Grandpa?"

"No, LeRoy you see little boys are kinda like these here birds I carve. Some of them are made of hardwood and some soft and some from one grain and then another. In all the years, I been whittlin' birds; I ain't never been able to make any two exactly alike."

"Why, Grandpa?"

"Well, because LeRoy, it seems that God just didn't allow no two things to be exactly alike, and that makes each one special."

"You mean I'm special, Grandpa?"

"Yes, son you are very special and very different."

Laying down his whittling and his knife, he rubbed the top of LeRoy's head tousling his hair, and said, "And LeRoy, in yor case one of you is about all we could stand."

"LeRoy, did I ever tell you the story of my folks who came here from a far off land a long way across the sea?"

"Where is the sea Grandpa, I ain't never see'd the sea, is it like the ocean?"

"Mama said that God created everything including the ocean, but I ain't never see'd it. How can you believe in somethin' that you ain't never see'd before, Grandpa?"

189

"Well, LeRoy, you can't see the wind, but it is there, and you know it is there because of what it does. That is the way it is with God. While we cannot see Him; we can see what He does."

"We can't see the wind, but we can hear it when it comes whistling around the house on a cold winter's night! And we can't feel God with our hands, but we can feel Him in our hearts just like we can feel the wind blowing on our faces, can't we?"

"I don't know about all that stuff, Grandpa, 'cause I guess I am too little."

"LeRoy, you look up here in these tired old eyes of yor Grandpa and listen to me and you listen to me, good!"

Using his two fingers, he made a motion with them to his eyes and said, "LeRoy, eyes up here!"

LeRoy reluctantly stood up and went closer to his Grandpa and said, "Okay, is this close enough?"

Grandpa had to giggle a little bit because LeRoy had put his nose right up to Grandpa's nose, and they both started to laugh. Grandpa tilted back in his rocking chair a mite too much, and almost turned over because he was laughing so hard.

Mama heard them in the kitchen and came to the door to see what was going on. She wiped her hands on her apron while staring out at them from behind the screen door. She smiled and went back in the kitchen. She was grateful for the times when Grandpa occupied LeRoy. Taking care of the chores, and Baby James kept her trotting all the time. LeRoy thought he was taking care of Grandpa.

LeRoy hoped Grandpa would forget about telling him about his war stories and the time when his mother and father lived in this very same house when he was a little boy like him.

Grandpa James had inherited the land directly from his Grandfather Samuel Goodroe Alrod. His parents named him after this grandfather and from James in the Bible, one of Jesus' disciples.

The land would normally have been passed on to James' parents, Henry and Rebecca. But, Henry was a wanderer and didn't seem to be able to settle down anywhere or be still for long at a time. Perhaps, that is where LeRoy got his impulsive wandering from… skipping from one thing to the other. It was just that way with some folks.

When Grandpa James became disabled, he passed the land on to Herman and Mama. Herman had one sister, Pauline, and she had no love for the mountains and the land like Herman. She felt perfectly okay with him keeping it in the family. When she married, she moved away with her husband to the city.

James Goodroe Alrod had been the only grandson of Samuel Goodroe Alrod. So when his father, Henry, showed no interest in the land, Samuel left it to James.

⁂

Samuel originally came from Ireland. He arrived in New York, where he met and married his wife, Rachel. He lovingly called her "Rach."

They worked hard and saved every penny until they could come to this valley which was nestled in the foothills of a larger mountain range.

The year was 1850; they built a home, a farm, and a church. They spent the rest of their lives together seeing the good times and the bad.

Henry, their only child, was born in New York, and he was but a little tyke when they moved into the valley. It would become a farm that would see many generations come and go. Samuel would leave the farm to James, his grandson, since his son Henry had no inclination toward the farming life. James had now handed the land, house, farm and church over to Herman, his only son.

Almost immediately, Samuel dedicated his 150 acres of land to God and then set aside a portion for a church and graveyard.

Grandpa continued to tell LeRoy the story of his family; while LeRoy could care less. He was already off into another world spinning his top off the end of the porch, jumping off and retrieving it. Each time he left the porch; Grandpa would call him back foiling his plan of escape.

He kept doing it again and again. Grandpa didn't seem to notice that he was not listening.

He told LeRoy about growing up on the land there in the valley, and then how hard it was to leave during the Great War to defend it against the Kaiser.

That word caught LeRoy's attention and asked, "What's a kaezer?"

Grandpa went on to tell him about the evil in some men's hearts and the greed within their souls; how they wanted to conquer the world.

"What does "konker" mean Grandpa?"

"It means to move in and take a man's land away from him," he replied.

LeRoy jumped to his feet and said, "Ain't nobody ever better try that here cuz my Papa's got a double barrel shotgun, and he will shoot 'em!"

"Well LeRoy, you just about described what war is all about; men having to shoot other men to protect their lands."

"Oh, I know all about that Grandpa. One time, we went to town to see a cowboy movie with Roy Rogers in it. It was 'bout these ole mean cowboys who wanted to steal their land. Roy Rogers shot them too!"

"But he didn't shoot them dead. Roy Rogers just shot the guns out of their hands. He put them in the hoosegow." Grandpa, what is a hoosegow?" Before Grandpa could answer, LeRoy went on, "And... he didn't have no shotgun, but two six-shooters. I wish I had me some six shooters, Grandpa."

"Did you have a horse too, Grandpa?"

"Grandpa, did you want to go to war; or did someone make you go?"

"Well, it was both, LeRoy. I had to go because they were drafting all the young men once the United States declared war, but I wanted to go ahead and join so that I could be in a special unit hoping to go to Ireland. We left America for France on a big transport ship!" He waited to see if LeRoy was going to ask what a transport ship was, but he didn't.

Then he said, "I had hoped to be attached to a unit in Ireland, but my hopes were dashed, and that didn't happen."

He laughed a little and said the people over there referred to them as "Dough Boys." There were different stories on how that name came about. Some thought it was because they were green and ill-trained and had not "risen" to their full potential.

He thought that would attract LeRoy's attention, but it didn't. Apparently LeRoy had tuned him out.

He continued with his story like it was urgent that he tell someone. Mama was still making jelly, and she was listening to every word he said.

"LeRoy I went along with all those other young men so the enemy could be stopped over there before they came over here. And I didn't want them to come over here to take our land."

He continued with his story "And another reason was to help our friends in Europe who needed help in defeating them. It took a lot of men shooting from trenches to push them back,"

That peaked LeRoy's interest, and he asked, "Grandpa did you shoot people dead or did you just shoot their guns out of their hands?"

LeRoy's question didn't seem to resonate with Grandpa. Or perhaps he just didn't want to answer. Or perhaps he didn't want to acknowledge the answer to LeRoy.

He sat quietly for a while and without saying anything, he continued to reminisce about those times so long, long ago when he traveled to fight in a war and had to kill other men.

Most of these young men were still wet behind the ears; extracted from their homeland and sent to a foreign country; to live in wet trenches; to be shot at by enemy soldiers; many even younger than him. All of them were suffering from homesickness; many still suffering the aftermath of being seasick.

The food was terrible and when it rained in the trenches; they would nearly drown.

James had no trouble handling a rifle… he had been hunting since he was a very young boy on his grandfather's farm. But he had trouble aiming his weapon against another human being.

James was in such a trench near Bathelemont, France when they were attacked in the early morning hours. James quickly knew it was shoot or be shot. He, along with the others, began returning a hail of bullets against a formidable foe.

Afterward, three men lay dead and many wounded; among the wounded was James Goodroe Alrod. He was taken to a hospital in England where he remained for many weeks. He received the Victory Medal for his injury and was honorably discharged.

LeRoy's question kept lingering in his mind…"How many men had he killed?" "How many had he just shot their guns out of their hands by wounding them?"

He never really knew. But the screams of wounded men all around him both Americans and the enemy haunted him the rest of his life.

He loved America and did not want to see her become war-torn as Ireland had been. Also, he felt it his duty to defend Ireland, his grandfather's homeland. His grandfather, Samuel, was proud to see him go off to war.

Samuel often spoke about his ancestral home and the constant warring and conflicts the people of Northern Ireland had to endure. They were such a tiny country and if England fell; so would they.

As so often these days, Grandpa's mind would come and go, and he would be talking and then get that faraway look in his eyes, and would seem to drift off into another world.

He never really talked about the particulars of the war itself; and what happened while he was in the battle. But he often thought about it. For years after he came home, he had nightmares and would awaken to the screams of men dying. He would sit up in bed, sweating, and have a panicked look on his face.

Sarah would light a lamp and get him a cold washrag to wash his face. Sometimes he woke up Herman and Pauline, but Sarah would tell them everything was okay and shoo them back off to bed.

Before he joined up and sailed across the Atlantic Ocean to France, he had little concern about things going on in the outside world. His life was there on the Alrod farm with his grandparents. He had just married Sarah and started a family when Herman was born.

The only news that the Alrod's received in those days, prior to the Great War was word of mouth, and old newspapers. When the US went to war against Germany, it became illegal for private citizens to own a radio. Most knew that they would likely end up in the war, but hoped against hope that they could somehow avoid it.

On Sundays, before and after church, the men would stand around and talk about events, and especially the prospect of America becoming involved. Most of the people in the valley didn't have any idea where Germany was and could not understand why they were attacking innocent American people. The men didn't talk in front of their families in order to protect their wives and children.

A series of events took place that finally forced Congress to convene and declare war against the German Empire.

Germany had repeatedly been warned about sinking passenger ships and merchant ships, but the Germans paid no heed. The Lusitania, a passenger ship, had left the port of New York headed to Europe. Before she could return to America, she was fired upon and sunk on May 7, 1915.

The Germans claimed that the passenger ship was transporting weapons. Many more ships were sunk thereafter. Germany still paid no heed to previous agreements and continued sinking non-military ships.

Then there was another event that really got America roused up and angry. The British had intercepted a telegram intended for Mexico from the Germans making promises to the Mexican government of returned lands in America if they would attack the United States.

Two years had gone by since the sinking of the Lusitania when enemy torpedoes sank the SS California just off the coast of Ireland. That was "the straw that broke the camel's back" for America.

The ships being attacked by Germany were not military ships, but passenger and cargo ships; and those who lost their lives were not in the military, but were civilians.

President Wilson felt it was time to act and called for a joint session of both the Senate and House to meet. When they convened, they voted to declare war against Germany on April 6, 1917. James volunteered and signed up that year.

While Ireland tried to implement a draft, it was not successful; since Ireland was already divided because the Catholics were against the war. When the draft was proposed in 1918, it led to a huge campaign of civil disobedience.

However, by this time, the United States had already entered the war and implemented a draft. The first one took place on June 5, 1917, and every eligible young man between the ages of twenty-one and thirty-one was required to register.

By September of 1918, those between the ages of eighteen and forty-five were required to register. As America became more and more involved in the war, they had to increase the number of soldiers being recruited, so the government increased the age gap; making others eligible for the draft.

James Goodroe Alrod felt it his duty to join other people from America and to stand against Germany for Ireland. So he left his wife, Sarah, young Herman and his newly-born baby sister, Pauline, to sail across the ocean to help stem the tide of aggression by the Germans.

He came back wounded, but not defeated. Some of his neighbors and friends asked, "How are you going to continue farming with a crippled leg?"

He replied, "With the help of God." And he would add; "Besides it is my duty to feed and clothe my family. It is none others' duty; but mine."

When assisting a fellow farmer with a barn raising, a sick horse, or the loan of a few dollars, he only said that it was his duty.

The war had changed James dramatically, and when he returned he felt the call of God upon his life. At first, he thought it might be his imagination and his conscience plaguing him about those he had killed in the war.

Some years later, the last called preacher at the little church on the hill had died, and the little flock of sheep was left without a shepherd.

So James Goodroe Alrod, their neighbor, friend, and a true man of God took over the pastorate and became their minister too.

Grandpa realized that LeRoy was not all over him, making a noise, or asking a question. He looked down at his feet and there laid LeRoy and "Snooper," huddled up against one another fast asleep. LeRoy ran full speed ahead most of the time, but when he slowed down, he would drop off in a minute.

❧

Grandpa's thoughts traveled back in time when his grandfather, Samuel, would tell him stories about his youth. He told him about the time when he came from the other side of the ocean to America.

The English began to drive the Irish out of Ireland in the mid 1800s, and during that time, cholera and starvation killed many others. Samuel had to beg the owner of the plantation for two small patches of earth to bury his parents; who had died from the disease. There all alone, he stood over their paltry graves and made them a promise that he would find his way to America; and become the man they had taught him to be, and the man God created him to be.

The potato blight had destroyed most of the potato crops in southern Ireland. Many of the Irish had died from starvation and disease. After the death of his parents, the overseer of the manor threw Samuel out of the cottage where he had lived all of his life.

He said he needed a family living there that would do a hard day's work in exchange for the property. Samuel, without success, tried to tell him that he could do the work of both his parents, but the overseer was to hear none of it and pitched him out.

He was sent to work in the poor house. There, he slept on the cold stone floor with only one bowl of corn mush each day to keep him alive. The corn, sent from American to a starving Ireland, was not part of their regular diet.

Unlike rye, wheat, and barley, corn was hard to digest, and they had to try many ways to cook it for it to be palatable. It was hard dried corn, and it often caused him to have stomach upsets.

Soon he was able to convince another manor overseer that he was strong enough to work in their fields. He was able to sleep in the barn with the horses, and was able to have somewhat better food to eat. His love for horses grew. His love and respect grew for all hard working farm animals.

By the time he was twenty-five, he had saved up enough money for his passage to America. He received a modest pay for his field hand work and earned a few extra coins by feeding the horses, spreading out the hay, and mucking out the stalls.

During hunting season, he also picked up a few extra coins caring for the hounds that belonged to all the genteel folks who came and stayed several days for the hunt. He saved every coin.

At night, he would lay low out of sight and listen to the many stories the visitors to the manor brought with them. He learned about faraway places. Although hidden away, he had a front row seat in the best of schools; as he picked up everything he heard. He would lay awake many a night on a fresh bed of hay and dreamed of all the things he would one day do.

Upon arrival to America, he had yet another dream. He dreamed of not only owning his own farm, but also one with lots of horses and other animals. He realized one dream fully by owning the farm, but was never able to have a lot of horses – he grew corn.

James Goodroe, Herman's father, had so often listened while his Grandfather, Samuel told stories of Ireland, England, and New York and how he came to America, and finally ended up in the valley.

Just as LeRoy and the other children often sat on the back porch and listened to Grandpa's stories, he had at one time sat on that very same front porch at night watching his grandfather, Samuel, whittling another small animal from a chunk of wood. James listened to Samuel's stories and wanted to hand them down to his grandchildren.

James continued whittling the little bird he had been working on, and as his shavings fell to the porch floor, he could see in his mind's eye that same scene between his Grandfather Samuel and himself.

Samuel's sharp knife cut away at the wood, and the chip, chip, chip of the shavings falling to the floor caught James' imagination as well. He had often attentively watched his Grandfather Samuel as he turned a chunk of wood into an image.

James hung on to his grandfather's every word. That was also when he became interested in taking a piece of wood himself, look at for a while, and decide what was hiding inside of it. He learned to take his own knife and begin to dig out a bird or some other image. However, birds were his favorite thing to carve.

Samuel was more than a grandfather to him. He was the only real father he had ever known. They spent hours on that porch talking about the farm, the weather, the church, and life in general. James could feel his grandfather's spirit all around him even more keenly when sitting on the porch whittling. In his aging years, he felt close to his grandfather and would often think about him or talk about him to anyone who would listen.

James Goodroe knew his grandfather's life stories by heart. He remembered being told that immediately upon arriving in New York; Samuel knew that city life was not for him. And after James traveled and saw big cities like Paris, London, and Belfast, he too decided that the farm was the best place for him as well.

Samuel worked to get to America, and then he worked to own a part of it. He often remembered his Da, Joseph Alrod, telling him about when he was a small boy back in Ireland, and how he loved the land even if he did not own it. He said of the city, "Too many people and not enough land!" That love for the land was handed down from Joshua Alrod in the old country to his son Samuel, and then skipping a generation to James and then Herman.

Samuel saw the same poverty on the streets of New York he had seen back in Ireland, and yearned to be out in the country. In those early days in New York, the only animals he saw were stray hungry dogs and cats and a couple of horses; one belonging to Officer O'Malley; and the other to a taxi driver named Pete.

Every chance he would get – he would quietly walk up beside one of the horses and would pat it on the neck and gently whisper something into its tall pointed ear. The horse would immediately swoosh its tail and turn its massive head toward his face. The horses would respond to him by curving their long necks around him as if to give him a hug. Samuel was so lonely even a hug from a horse was better than no hug at all. He sure missed the hugs that his mother used to give him. Sometimes he could actually feel them.

He continued to ask around the city if anyone knew of a farm that might be looking for a hand, but none had. That kind of work was hard to find.

Grandpa James took another look down at his little sleeping grandson, LeRoy. He thought how much he loved and missed his own Grandfather, Samuel, remembering had he not ventured across the ocean, and worked his way to owning this land, neither the land nor he would be there.

Seeing LeRoy sleeping there so peaceful, he thought about how that little boy was made up of so many wonderful ancestors that came before him who had lived, loved, and worked hard all of their lives. He said a prayer that God would also use LeRoy, and all of that energy he had, for a good and upright purpose. He prayed that somehow the land would always remain in the stewardship of future Alrods.

He prayed that the little church on the hill would grow and be a symbol of hope to all who came to her door. He prayed that if it was God's will that it would still be standing when Jesus returned.

In the year of 1845, Samuel Goodroe Alrod came to New York by way of a schooner from England. He traveled many miles on foot to reach Belfast, Ireland. There, he left the quay for London, where he booked passage on the "Lilly Belle' bound for America.

He was a third-class passenger and spent most of the time crossing the Atlantic in the steerage section of the ship. That was the cheapest fare. The passengers had little comforts with limited toilet use, no privacy, and low-quality food. Working on the farms in Ireland, he finally saved enough to pay his fare, and after docking in America, he had only a few coins left. His hope was to find a job immediately.

He was near penniless when he found a job working in a tavern near the docks. Many shopkeepers and businessmen turned the scruffy looking lad away simply because he was Irish.

Many establishments had signs in their windows saying, "We don't hire any Irish!" There was no escaping that this lad, fresh off the boat, was indeed Irish. If the accent didn't give him away; that bushy red hair... not cut in months... would have. And then there were those reddish-brown freckles sprinkled around his face. The hair and the freckles set off those intelligent green eyes.

Once it was said, the way to person's soul was through their eyes, and that tavern keeper looked into that young man's soul; and saw a lot of goodness in him.

He was hired to wash up the spittoons and sweep the floor. He ran errands and was always deeply respectful. The tavern owner had decided to watch him for a while, and that he did. Never once did he see any impropriety in him. He had bigger ideas for him working in the tavern.

Sometimes in the beginning, when he would be carrying out his duties, Samuel would be pushed around and made fun of by some of the intoxicated customers. Samuel never fought back. He was not a coward but respected the establishment of his employer... and his job.

The tavern owner put an immediate stop to that right away. The word soon got around if anyone sought to harm the lad, they would be banned from the tavern forever. They would have the long arm of the law reaching out for them. Besides, the tavern owner was Irish, too.

Samuel was always on time and never left until his chores were finished and always asked if there was anything else before he left. He was an impressive young lad, but God had a plan for his life that would not include the tavern business – but God's business.

Samuel Goodroe was mid-twenties when he arrived in New York. He slept in the alley behind the tavern. He made himself a little hide-a-way with some old wooden crates covered with a discarded piece of canvas sail. Once it was a mighty sail blowing in the wind propelling the ship forward, but now it was serving a place just as noble, by providing protection for him against the harsh driving cold wind of winter.

He had never had much to call his own while living in Ireland, but he had learned to make do with what he had. And at the knee of his mother, he had learned to be thankful in all things. He had been raised in a strong Presbyterian home until his parents died in the cholera epidemic.

Those last months he spent in New York were bitter cold, and he almost froze to death several times. He worked by day in the tavern. And in the evening, he continued to find other discarded items to shore up his home.

Then one night, he awoke with warm kisses on his face. He had been dreaming that his Mama was planting gentle kisses all over his face as she had done so often to awaken him when he was a wee lad. They had lived in a very modest cottage on the edge of a huge plantation. They worked for those who lived in the manor house, but owned nothing of their own.

Suddenly, he got fully awake when he heard a sound that was not his dear departed mother's voice. He had heard a distinctive "meow." He opened his eyes wide and lay there staring eyeball to eyeball with a huge Calico cat.

At first he was afraid that it would claw his eyes out. He had never seen such a huge domestic cat. However, he had seen some wharf rats in the alley almost as large.

Samuel gently and carefully lifted his arms from underneath his tattered old blanket and reached out to rub the head of this monster-sized cat. The huge Calico wormed its way underneath the blanket and lay close to him as if she was used to sleeping with a human.

The warmth of that big old furry fat cat felt so warm next to him. It reminded Samuel of the warming pans his mother used to heat his bed at night. Just like the heating pans – the cat made him feel toasty warm. She rested her big old cat head in the crook of his elbow and looked straight into his eyes as if to say she trusted him also.

Early the next morning after he had drifted back off to sleep, cuddled next to the Calico, he was awakened for the second time to the sound of a young woman's voice. "Felicia! Felicia! Here kitty, kitty, kitty. Here kitty, come, come..!"

He raised the flap of his homemade tent and peeked underneath for a better look. There, he saw what must have been an angel straight from God. He shook his hands to see if he had frozen to death during the night.

Swallowing hard, he finally got up enough gumption to call out to the young lady asking her if the cat, she was looking, for was a huge Calico. Somewhat startled by the voice coming from underneath a shabby piece of ships sail, she stepped back a few steps.

"Why...why... Yes, she is! Have you seen her?" was her skittish reply. With almost as much trepidation, he answered back, "I think so lassie as I have a big cuss sleeping right here next to me."

He lifted the canvas up a little, and she leaned down a little closer. Somehow she was not afraid of that scruffy-looking young Irishman lying there on the ground. He peeled the old blanket back, and she saw her cat cuddled next to him still fast asleep.

"Oh, thank you, sir. Thank you so very much. I feared that I should have to leave her behind for we must return to the farm no later than today. She squatted down and lifted that big old cat with some difficulty. While holding her close and stroking her fur, she also chided her in gentle tones for running away. "You naughty kitty, you had me worried, and it nearly time for your litter."

While standing on his nearly frozen feet, Samuel thought to himself, "Oh! That is why she is so fat!"

Samuel shuffled those cold feet back and forth; not so much from the cold now, but from dreaded fear of speaking to such a lovely young lady. He immediately felt embarrassed because of his dirty appearance and decided not to extend his hand to her as he said, "Hello, my name is Samuel Goodroe Alrod. I am from Ireland.

Breaking into his sentence with a slight giggle, she replied, "Who would have ever thought?"

Puzzled at her answer, he pushed his freckled hand through his mop of red hair hoping to push it down a little.

She curtsied and extended her gloved hand and said, "My name is Rachel Louise Cunningham. I thank you so much Mr. Alrod for rescuing my beloved, but naughty, cat."

With a sheepish grin on his face, he said, "Well miss, it seems to be the other way around, she rightly rescued me, she did."

Trying to keep the conversation going, he continued, "Well, perhaps we rescued each other that we did!"

It seemed that Rachel and her father had come into the city to sell their winter vegetables at the city market. Her father had sold the entire load of kale, broccoli and carrots to the chefs in the restaurants and hotels.

She had begged her father to let her bring her cat, Felicia, seeing she was so close to giving birth to her kittens. But he had refused. Never wanting to disappoint this only child, he explained that it would be better for the Calico to remain in the barn since her birthing time was so near. He rarely ever demanded things of her and was more apt than not to overlook her disobedience.

Rachel had wished she had listened to her father. When it came time for them to leave the farm for the city, she put the Calico in a box on the back of the wagon to be driven by the hired man.

Once they arrived at the market, the noise in the mobbed streets spooked the cat, and she jumped out of the box and ran away.

Rachel was afraid her kitty might be lost forever, but now she would be forever thankful that she had disobeyed her father this one time; for more reasons than one.

Because of that fateful day, Rachel met Samuel, and he went to work for her father on his farm. And in years to come, the love between the two grew until one day Samuel felt worthy enough to ask her father for Rachel's hand in marriage. Rachel had been educated in a fine school in New York and was bright and funny, and fell deeply in love with Samuel.

Her father was not a rich man. But because of having Samuel there on the farm, the crops increased abundantly, and he paid him well. Just as Samuel had always done, he worked hard, spent little, and saved a lot.

And then came the day when he and Rachel would marry, and they would later have a son named Henry. And when he was still very small, they moved a long way from New York to their own farm; this one nestled among the rolling hills in the greenest of all valleys.

Samuel always teased her about being like the Rachel in the Bible where Jacob worked for her father to win her hand in marriage, and she would always reply, "Well, I am just thankful I didn't have an older sister, named Leah. And I am glad it took you only five years rather than seven."

※ ❦ ※

LeRoy and Ole Snooper were still fast asleep on the porch, and Mama had finished pouring the jelly into the jars. It was time for Baby James' nap, and she felt like she needed to lie down for a while herself. She didn't recall having been this tired with the other babies she carried. While the jelly cooled, and Little James napped, and while Grandpa had a reign on LeRoy, she felt it would be a good time for her to get some rest like Dr. McPherson had suggested.

James felt the quietness all around him; which was most unusual in that noisy household with so much activity going on all around him on a daily basis. He couldn't remember when it had been so quiet. In moments like this, his mind always drifted toward God and how thankful he was for all the blessings that God had given him in his lifetime.

He thanked God for bringing his grandfather to America and for finding Rachel, his grandmother, to be his wife. He thanked God for his wife Sarah and the two children she had given him, Herman and Pauline. He thanked God that Herman had found a godly wife and for all the children He had given them. He prayed for the little one on the way that God would use that baby also for His honor and glory.

But most of all he thanked God for His Son, Jesus, who came and lived on earth to tell the world about God and then give His life for the ransom of many to all who would accept Him. He thanked God that

Samuel and Rachel had raised him to love Christ and for instilling in him the desire to please God in all things.

He thanked God for allowing him to be the leader of the little church on the hill though he often felt inadequate to stand behind the pulpit. He thanked God for bringing him back from the war to the family and land that he loved.

Peace like he had never felt before flowed over him, and he realized that his pain was gone. He felt lifted up and euphoric. One of his favorite hymns came to his mind, and he began to hum the tune as he thought of the words,

"When peace like a river attendeth my way, when sorrows like sea billows roll; whatever my lot, thou hast taught me to say, "It is well, it is well with my soul."

James traveled across the sea during the Great War. He defended his country and was able to make a trip to Ireland and lay flowers on the graves of his own great-grandparents. He somehow felt that it was the least he could do for his grandfather... a grandfather who had done so much for him.

When James arrived in Ireland, he went immediately to the manor home. He knew exactly where to go, based on his grandfather's stories. Those stories made him want to visit Ireland and see the land of his ancestors. After leaving the hospital in England and before heading back to America, he crossed the Irish Sea to look for the burial place of his great-grandparents.

He found the manor house and went to the door, and asked if they could direct him to the burial place of Joseph and Earlene Alrod. He explained they had died during the 1832 cholera epidemic and had been buried somewhere on that property. He explained that they were his great-grandparents.

Seeing that he was wearing an American uniform, the servant went immediately and fetched the landlord of the manor. The proprietor himself walked James down near a creek near a stand of Alder trees.

The area was overgrown and nearly impossible to walk through. James asked the owner if it would be possible for him to acquire a scythe to clear the land. It was plain to see with his crutches and his leg wound; he would not be capable of strenuous labor.

What seemed like minutes later, a group of farm hands came down and cleared the small, wooded area. James felt such sorrow seeing just a couple of plain rock headstones marking their graves that were exactly where his grandfather said he had buried them; when he was but twelve years old.

He asked the owner if it would be possible to erect a small engraved headstone to honor his ancestors. He only had a few more days to be in Ireland, and would have to leave the country forever. That idea was reminiscence of the angel statue that stood in the center of the little church on the hill back home.

James was staying in a small nearby inn and was awakened early the next morning by a knock on the door. Summoned back to the spot, he was surprised to see an engraved marker which read,

Final resting place of Earlene and Joseph Alrod
Beloved Citizens of Ireland.
Victims of 1832 Cholera Epidemic

All that James knew about his great-great grandparents was their names. He did not know their birth-dates, but knew they both had died in 1832. Oh how, he wished he had known them, but in a way he did. They were forever pressed into his mind from all the stories his grandfather Samuel had told him.

He said they were god-fearing, humble tenant farmers. They attended the local Presbyterian Church and were good neighbors always helping anyone they could even though they had so little to offer. They honored God and taught Samuel to be thankful and to pray every day. In his twelve short years, they had prepared Samuel for what lay ahead of him in life.

The manor owner decided to make it a memorial to all who had died during that epidemic. James knew his kindnesses had a lot to do with the war effort there by the Americans.

It was a surreal moment in James' life as he stood there looking down at those long ago forgotten people who had been bone of his bone, flesh of his flesh, and then feeling their blood pulsating through his veins. His heart was pounding, and he felt as if he had personally known them. And he had, through their son, Samuel. He wept as though they had just died.

He could visualize his grandfather, Samuel, standing there as a young twelve-year-old saying a final good-bye to his parents. It broke his heart.

And to his great surprise, many of the Ulster citizens showed up with flowers for their graves. Many of them had ancestors who died during the time of that epidemic; which swept across Ireland and Europe taking the lives of so many. There was a lovely young lassie who sang *"Amazing Grace,"* and a minister who read Psalms 23. Then he prayed a blessing over all the ancestors of those who had died.

A little-red-faced lady, with a scarf on her head, approached James and gave him a beautiful handmade wreath made from the native wildflowers that grew in the county. He placed it with great pride and joy there to honor those who had come and gone before him. When James returned to America, his grandfather, Samuel, wept with joy to know what he had done for him and his parents.

❧❀❧

The organ was playing softly; everyone had found their seat when the Alrod family came slowly walking down the aisle toward the coffin.

LeRoy came in first. He proceeded to lay a wreath, which Mama and Sarah Louise had made, on the coffin of his beloved Grandpa James. Just at the same time a big old fat Calico cat swiped around his little chubby legs. The family had been unaware that she had followed them inside the church.

Mama, Billy Joe, Sarah Louise, Velma and Verna had followed LeRoy down the aisle taking their seats on the front pew. Some of the church ladies were back at the house preparing the food and taking care of Baby James. He would grow up never remembering the godly man he was named after. But to be sure, he would hear the stories that his grandfather had told about his life to the other family members.

Their Papa, the Reverend Alrod, had already taken his place in the pulpit.

Billy Joe jumped up and scooped up the Calico to take her outside. As he walked toward the door, he stroked her fur and whispered, "I know you will miss him as much as we will, won't you?" When he bent down to release the Calico outside, there on the stoop of the church laid, "Snooper." Never before had he followed them to the church.

When Rachel and Samuel came to the valley, she brought her Calico cat, named Felicia, with them. Over the years, she had many babies, and then her babies had babies just like the Alrod's had since 1850.

There was much sorrow in the Alrod family. People came from miles around for Grandpa's funeral. He had truly been a much-loved neighbor, friend, and minister. But more importantly he had been a loving grandson, husband, father, and Grandpa. And only God knew what a devoted grandson he had been to Samuel and Rachel.

The Reverend Herman Alrod took his place behind the pulpit as Mama, and all the Alrod children sat in their seats on the front row. While the older Alrod children were all softly crying. Little LeRoy sat stoic, completely unemotional. Everyone figured he didn't understand. Like in other times, they had often heard him say "I guess I'm just too little."

Choking back tears the Reverend said, "When the old preacher of this little church died, and there was no one to fill this pulpit. My father, James Goodroe Alrod began preaching the Word of God at Sunday Meetin' Time."

"He simply stated that it was his duty. He didn't hold any college degrees, but he was an educated man. He knew God's Word. He served his country in a time of war. He had traveled the world."

"He lived the life of an honest, truthful, law-abiding man, never asking anyone for anything, but giving all he had. He took care of his family under difficult circumstances and grieved at the loss of his beloved wife, Sarah. He saw to it that his children had all he could afford, and saw that they received a high school education."

"He never turned anyone down in need. Now you older folks know that is the truth, and none can deny it."

"We ain't saying good-bye to James Goodroe Alrod today. He said his good-byes by the way he lived his hellos. We have come to show our respect for this old body of his what used to house his spirit and soul."

"They both departed him when he slumped over on the back porch three days ago. You see, his spirit and soul was holding up that old, sick and time worn body. When they left, it was just like stepping out of an old pair of long-johns leaving them behind."

"He had been talkin' to LeRoy and telling him about the early settlers on this land; Samuel and Rachel Alrod. LeRoy was asleep at his feet on the front porch, and Mama had just returned to the kitchen to check on her jelly. She heard Grandpa talkin' or prayin' when in mid-sentence, he stopped talkin', and she heard the thump of the little wooden bird he was carving; as it hit the porch floor."

"She rushed outside and found that Grandpa had departed this life. She rang the triangle, and me and Billy Joe came running in from the field... too late to say our last good-byes."

Stumbling for his composure, Herman continued, "My Dad... he was... he was... a man of honor. And if he gave you his word, you best take it; because he would never go back on it."

"We have to believe with Paul when he says that to be absent in the body is to be present with the Lord."

"If Heaven is real... and it is... my father is no longer in pain and is reunited with his beloved wife, Sarah, my mother! He is getting to meet once again with his father and mother, Henry and Rebecca. There must have been bells ringing in heaven when he was once again embraced by his Grandfather Samuel and his Grandmother Rachel. And for the first time, he has now met his great-grandparents, Joseph and Earlene, who died in Ireland many years before he was born."

"He is relishing in the fact that once again he can feel the arms of his beloved Grandfather, Samuel Goodroe, wrapping tightly around him; like he did the day he returned home from the war saying, "Welcome, home James. We have missed you. We are glad you are safely home!""

"He is not gone. He is just gone before. Just as he came to this earth first and prepared the land and a home for us here, he went on before to do the same in Glory Land."

"He was young and then he was old but the heart that beat in that man was as young in spirit and feelings as our young LeRoy sitting there. He had the bravery of a soldier, the heart of a preacher, and the love of a husband, father, and grandfather. That legacy... he leaves behind to all those who came after him."

With that, Preacher Alrod set his eyes on Little LeRoy to gain his composure. He was sitting there motionless which was a great feat for LeRoy.

The Reverend Alrod said, "Now reading from the Holy Bible: in I Thessalonians 4: 13 through 18."

"But I would not have you to be ignorant, brethren, concerning them which are asleep, that ye sorrow not, even as others that have no hope.

For if we believe that Jesus died and rose again, even so them also which sleep in Jesus will God bring with him.

For this, we say unto you by the word of the Lord, that we which are alive and remain unto the coming of the Lord shall not prevent them which are asleep.

For the Lord himself shall descend from heaven with a shout, with the voice of the archangel, and with the trump of God: and the dead in Christ shall rise first:

Then we which are alive and remain shall be caught up together with them in the clouds, to meet the Lord in the air: and so shall we ever be with the Lord.

Wherefore comfort one another with these words."

As the large congregation filed slowly out of the door to the graveyard behind the church, Little LeRoy was heard to say, while clutching his mother's hand, "Mama when they put Grandpa in the ground will he grow more Grandpas like the beans? I sure hope they do 'cause one Grandpa like him ain't enough."

All Mama could do was just squeeze his little hand. She was speechless.

The enormous crowd huddled close around the freshly dug grave of James Goodroe Alrod which was now next to that of his wife, Sarah. As they lowered his father into the grave, they were surprised when Herman broke out in a hymn.

They listened to a song coming from the heart, and not just from the voice of Preacher Herman Alrod. It didn't matter that Herman was not a gifted singer; he sang from a place so deep inside of his soul that one by one the congregation entered into the song.

"Sing the wondrous love of Jesus; sing His mercy and His grace;
In the mansions bright and blessed, He'll prepare for us a place.
When we all get to heaven, what a day of rejoicing that will be!
When we all see Jesus, we'll sing and shout the victory."

You could hear the sincere tones of the song drifting toward the mountain and into the sky above toward heaven. The angels must have bowed their heads and cried.

One by one, the folks filed by shaking his hand, hugging his shoulders extending their heartfelt sympathy to him. Mama just stood quietly by her man… not the farmer… not the preacher… but her husband.

They came one by one, by couples of two, or whole families. Folks of all ages came to extend their condolences to Herman, the man who was their friend.

With Mama by his side, it gave him the strength to stand there. Little did he know that she was holding on to him in order to remain standing, as she held tightly onto his arm. The child within her moved around and caused her to feel nauseated. She had not fully recovered from the episode that had recently landed her in the hospital.

Many old members had moved away years before, but the little valley remained close to their hearts because some of them had family buried there in the little church graveyard as well. They came to pay their respects to a man they highly admired and adored… a man who had followed in the footsteps of his ancestors and helped grow the church and the community. He now had followed in the footsteps of Jesus.

After paying their respects to Preacher Alrod, some of them wandered around the yard looking for the final resting places of those they had lost as well. Finally, when Herman had shaken the last hand and received the last hug, Mama held him in her arms for a long time. She knew he was putting on a good front, but she knew the struggle it had been to preach his own father's funeral.

She also knew that family and friends would be arriving at their house, and she needed to be there to see about the massive amount of food that had been brought to their home. The men had earlier set up sawhorses with planks across them for makeshift tables. The ladies of the church had taken care of the details as well as taking care of Baby James.

She reached up and kissed him tenderly on the lips. She didn't care if God and the whole world saw her do it. She held him close for a few minutes and then walked away without saying a word.

She could finally let go of the hot tears she had been holding back. She stopped by the outhouse and squalled her eyes out. She threw up her breakfast and felt some better. She did not want her children, or Herman, to see her grieving for a man she had loved like a father. She thought about how only a short while before, he had helped her when she passed out on the porch.

Sometimes words between Mama and Herman were not necessary. This was one of those times... this was one of those times.

Herman had officiated at many funerals in his time as pastor of the little church on the hill, but being the minister to officiate at his father's funeral was different. It had been difficult. For the first time, he realized what his father had gone through when they buried his mother when he had preached her funeral.

He kept reminding himself of the promise God made that He would never leave nor forsake him. He felt God's presence all around him. But he also felt the emotions of a grieving son whose heart was about to break.

He removed his black Fedora hat he had donned when he left the church. He went down on one knee, holding his head in his hands, and sobbed as if he were no more than five years old like LeRoy.

Herman's heart was divided into so many pieces as he knelt over his father's grave. While filled with love, joy, admiration and honor for his

212

father, it also felt like there was a huge empty hole in the center of his chest where his heart was supposed to be. The pressure in his chest pushed every other emotion aside as reality hit him.

That was HIS Daddy laying there in that freshly dug grave... and not that of someone else.

But he was wrong for standing a few paces behind him was his sister, Pauline.

Unaware that she was standing there for a few minutes, he caught a glimpse of her out of the corner of his eye. He could say nothing, but reached out his hand and motioned for her to come forward. He walked toward her, and they embraced for a long time. They just stood sharing grief as only two siblings could who had just lost their one remaining parent.

They were not aware that Little LeRoy was standing off to the side, behind a tall monument near an adjacent grave. This sad little boy just looked puzzled and afraid. He was wondering how his Grandpa was going to breathe in that box, and underneath all that dirt.

Chapter fourteen: There is a Thief Among Us

"Herman, what was all that ruckus out near the hen house last night? You'd think there was a fox nosing around out there; by the way those hens were clucking. By the time I got little James back down, I was so tired I just drifted off to sleep before you got back in."

"Ain't sure Mama, by the time I got my pants on and my suspenders up, they had quieted down. So dark, I couldn't see much anyway. I stayed out beside the barn out of the way with my shotgun, but never did see anything to shoot."

"Couldn't make a step for Ole Snooper trying to wrap himself around my feet. If there was never a no-good watchdog, "Ole Snooper" takes the cake," said Papa.

Mama laughed out loud saying, "I remember a time when my Papa went out in the middle of the night in his nightshirt to see if there was a fox in the hen house, and his ole hound sneaked up behind him and stuck his cold nose up Papa's nightshirt. It scared him so bad that he jumped, and the shotgun went off, and the hound went howling back to the barn." The next morning, he realized he had shot down a huge tree limb from an oak tree. At the time, he dared us to ever tell that story.

Pulling out his chair from the head of the table and sitting down as Mama poured him a cup of coffee; he decided to chide Mama a little by saying. "Maybe them old hens wuz having a disagreement with one another...you know how ole hens can be," he said as he playfully patted her round-baby-filled belly as she leaned across him.

He reached up to pull her toward his lap. She pulled away and said, "Ole hens, indeed," as she flipped the end of her dishrag in his direction.

She had been up for hours making big cat-head biscuits, fried a whole side of bacon and perked a huge pot of coffee. She was stirring a frying pan full of thickened gravy and was waiting for daylight to fetch the fresh eggs. It was Saturday with many chores to be done, but she let the children sleep a little later on Saturday - at least until daylight.

She snapped back at him playfully, "Well, it is the rooster's duty to keep law and order in the hen house, so why don't you just trot on out there and fill this here basket with eggs while I get the children up?"

Herman knew he had walked right into that one. It was usually Mama who collected the eggs. Along with all his other work, he tried to make it easier on Mama since her "spell." He did what he could to help her and saw to it that the kids did as well. He headed to the hen house. He wanted to check things out anyway.

Even with that large family still in the house, it seemed empty without Grandpa. He often got up early to have his cup of coffee with her before the others got up. Mama looked around at his place at the table and tears began to well up in her eyes.

She had tried several times to let the children collect the eggs, but they broke too many. And she depended on what they did not eat to sell at Mr. Ferguson's store. He paid her twenty-one cents a dozen and sold them for thirty-five.

Folks set store by her big brown double-yoked eggs. And they sold rapidly. With that money and her butter money, it kept the kids in things that had to be store bought. With today's extra eggs, and what she already had on account at the store, she should have just enough to buy some more diaper yardage to hem if she could get that old treadle machine working again.

Many a garment, quilt, and apron were made on that old 1914 *White* sewing machine. What with the new electric models on the market, it was getting harder and harder to get new belts to turn the wheel. It wouldn't even do any good to hint for a new sewing machine as she knew that Papa was doing the best he could. And with the depression only slightly behind them, there was just no money for such frivolous things.

With one still in diapers, little two-year-old James, and another one on the way, she would need more Birdseye cloth. Maybe all the sewing machine needed was a little more oil.

She was also hoping to have enough extra to get a box of *Argo* starch, a box of *Oxodol* washing powders, a bar of *Ivory* soap and some *Johnson's* baby oil. She guessed that would come to at least fifty cents; the *Oxodol* costing the most. She was preparing for the new baby to come, and the starch was good for baby bottoms.

She made her own starch for the laundry using flour and boiling water. She would dip the clothes into that and then squeeze them out and hang them on the line. Before she ironed them, she would have to sprinkle them down with water. She used an old *Coke* bottle and a sprinkler top with a cork that fit the top of the bottle for that purpose.

During the Depression, when there was no money for a lot of things, she often made a small amount of lye soap for cleaning stubborn dirt and grease stained clothing; especially Herman's "farming clothes." It was too harsh for bathing young-un's. Mama used *Ivory* when she bathed the babies. She kept a big bar of *Octagon* soap out on the porch for scrubbing grimy hands.

She tried to allot at least one bar of Ivory soap a month. Mr. Ferguson sold *Ivory* bar soap at three for twenty-five cents, but he often allowed her to buy only one cake at a time. The baby oil was also used to slick down the boy's hair after a clean shampoo with the *Ivory*, and the oil kept down that dreaded cradle cap which some babies got. But not Mama's babies!

She was cautious with the use of the soap, making sure they only used it on their washcloths and never let it float around in the water. She had heard it advertised on the radio, and the man said it was "99 and 44/100 percent pure" and that it floats. Other soaps sunk to the bottom and would waste away in the water.

Papa made his way to town for Mama and was greeted warmly by the storekeeper. "Howdy, preacher what can I do for you?" asked Mr. Ferguson as he stepped behind the counter. "I see you ain't got no basket of eggs this morning, did the Missus forget today is Saturday?"

"No, Brother Ferguson, she didn't. They wasn't no eggs in the hen house this morning."

"That's mighty odd," he replied. "I know how she was counting on that diapering cloth. I guess them kids of yors was a might hungrier this week."

"Wasn't that. Either the hens are on strike, or someone came in the middle of the night and took them all."

"Who do you think done it?"

"Couldn't rightly say… the gate was still closed. If it had been a fox or egg sucking dog, there would have been a mess of broken eggs and scattered feathers, but there wasn't none."

"Saw a couple of big boot prints in the dirt."

"Preacher, are you saying we've got a thief among us?"

"Well, it certainly looks that way."

"Heard of any other folks having problems… missing stuff? Seen any hobos around," inquired Mr. Ferguson?

"No, don't say that I have," Herman replied.

"Well, fill this here list of Mama's and add the cloth she needs to git started on them "hippins" for the new young'un. Just take it out of my salary at the end of the month when you do the church bookkeeping, and I'll pay for the stuff on the list."

Putting the items in the bag, Mr. Ferguson said, "That will be $1.47 cents; plus $2.50 for the diapering cloth; that comes to $3.97."

Then Herman said, "You might as well make it an even $4.00 and give me three cents worth of that penny candy from them jars over there. Don't care what kind. The kids will eat any kind in a quick hurry."

"But on second thought, make it peppermint sticks; they last longer. Them jawbreakers ain't good for LeRoy. Mama lets Little James lick on a peppermint stick every now and then."

While handing the bag over the counter, he said, "Preacher, do you think we got some stranger lurking around town stealing his way through?"

Looking very concerned, Papa replied, "Naw, Brother Ferguson, it wasn't no stranger."

"How do you know, preacher, do you know who it is?" "Well, let me tell you, I got my idee."

"Well… who then? Ain't we got a right to know who's slippin' around in the dead of night… stealing?"

"Well, no, not until I am sure."

"Will you call the sheriff when you are?"

"Well, let's don't count our chickens before they hatch, so to speak. Let's don't be hanging a man 'til we know fer sure he's guilty."

"Then you think it was a man?" The preacher turned to leave the store with his merchandise and said, "Well... almost."

On the way back to his farm, Herman stopped by the O'Brien farm. He had heard they were having a hard time what with Mrs. O'Brien losing the baby recently and Harry off looking for work. The depression had hit everyone hard, and while most had made it through the worst years, Harry O'Brien just could not seem to be able to get out of debt; much-less get ahead.

He got down in his back after that horse kicked him and then his crops didn't produce hardly enough to pay off his bill at the store, and it was rumored that he still owed the doc, the feed store, and the hardware store.

When Pastor Alrod walked up into the sandy front yard of the O'Brien place, he saw the distinctive boot marks leading to the house; but not away again.

"Howdy, Mrs. O'Brien," he said as he took off his hat and looked up at the life-worn women standing on the porch barely still in her thirties, but looking much older. She had one young'un hiding behind her skirts, another on her hip, and still another peeking out from the torn screen door.

"Howdy, preacher," she said, returning the greeting. "What you doin' out this way so early in the morning on a Satadity?"

"Well, just thought I would come by and speak to Lem... He about anywhere?"

"Lem... Oh, Lemuel!" she called out, looking down at the one behind her skirt, she said, "Go find Lem, and tell him the preacher wants him."

"No need hollering, Mama, here I am," said a big tall teenager who was half child and half man. Looking up at the preacher, he said, "I figured you'd be around, but I guess just not this soon."

"What you talkin' about, Lem," his mother asked puzzled?

"The preacher knows, Mama!"

"Knows, what?" she asked with deep concern on her face.

Papa didn't wait for Lem to reply when he spoke, "Well, I am not so sure what I know yet, Mrs. O'Brien, but I think me and Lem will take a stroll down by the creek for a spell."

Often times Reverend Alrod would find himself between a rock and a hard place as he ministered to his little flock. There was always the right and wrong of a thing, but often there was more to a situation than met the eye; at least at first glance.

And that was certainly the case here where a young man was desperate enough to steal in order to help his mother.

But he also knew he could not allow Lemuel to turn to a life of crime. After all, he broke the law. The O'Brien's had certainly had more than their share of troubles recently, and he didn't know the full details yet.

Lem admitted to stealing the eggs.

After a lot of prayer and discussing it with Mama, Herman decided it would best be left up to the judge to handle this situation.

Herman had grown up with Judge Hendrix, and he had many times sought his advice. He had a talk with the Judge before he turned Lem into the sheriff.

Mr. Ferguson's store was packed on the day of the hearing. Since this was a minor offense, it was held there rather than at the courthouse in town.

"You see, yor honor... yor judge, sir, it was like this... my brothers and sisters wuz hungry, and I saw Mrs. Alrod always taking them extry eggs to town each Satadity, and I figured she must have extry, or she wouldn't be toting 'em to town. And you see, yor honor, my Daddy, he, ain't got back with no job yet, and my Mama, she's been porely since she lost the last one, and I just didn't see too much harm in taking what seems extry."

Judge Hendrix sat a little taller in his chair from behind the counter, straighten his glasses and made a "humph" sound and said, "Lem, you mostly been a good boy. You got into some scrapes like most boys your age, but you did come in on your own, and that counts for something."

"Yes, sir, I did. But, I didn't remember that the Preacher had done give me his old boots last month, and I didn't pay no 'tention to the marks they left, but he shore did."

"Well, Lem, what does the Good Book say about stealing?"

Standing up straight and proud he knew, he said, "It says "Thou shalt not, Sir!"

"And Lem, what does the law say about stealing?"

"Well Sir, I guess it is like that new game of Monopoly we done played at school when you throw over that little card, that says: 'Go directly to jail!'"

"Lem, the law trusted me with this here black nightgown, and this here gavel, and I can't play no favorites. You understand that don't you, son? Now sneaking in the middle of the night on another man's property, and taking anything that belongs to him is a crime – even if it ain't nothing more than a tree limb. It belongs to him. Do you understand that, son?"

"Yes, sir, I knowed I done wrong, but the gnawing in my belly done overrun what was right and wrong, and I just can't stand to hear my Mama cry at night because they ain't no food in the house for the young'uns."

"But, I done a heap worse than that."

"What was that, son?"

"Well, yor honor, I lied to my Ma when I told her those old scrawny hens of ours had started layin' again. Yor honor, if you could have just seen the smile on her face and how much them young-uns enjoyed them scrambled eggs, you would understand! Why them big double-yoked eggs wuz so good, I could have eaten ten biscuits just sopping off the spoon she stirred 'em with."

"I understand that, son, but the law is the law, both in the Good Book and in this here law book," he said holding up a big thick book.

"God's Book says, 'If a man doesn't work; then he don't eat.' Son. What kind of world do you think this would turn into if what one man worked for and earned was taken away by a man who won't work?"

Lem just stood there with his eyes cast down at the floor and did not offer an answer at first. And then he straightened up his posture and looked the judge right in the eye and said, "I would work, yor Honor, if someone would just give me some chores to do."

"I would work every day after school, and on Saturday. Now Ma won't let me skip church, but I could work Sunday afternoons as well! I would do anything to help my Ma and my brother and sisters. I would work just for food if that is all they could pay me."

The judge continued, "Why, pretty soon the one that worked would say, what's the use to work so hard; when someone's just going to take it away from me? Son, do you understand that principle?"

"Yes, sir."

Judge Hendrix said, "I got myself a choice here. I can fine you or put you in jail for thirty days."

"Well, yor honor, I reckon it will be jail 'cause I ain't got no money for no fine; for if I did... I wouldn't done stole Mrs. Alrod's eggs."

"Well, that is it!" the judge said as he banged the gavel against the wooden podium, ten dollars or thirty days." Startled, Lem jumped back. Low murmuring could be heard from some of the women in attendance, and Mrs. O'Brien failed in her brave attempt not to cry.

Lem looked around at all the neighbors who had showed up for the hearing, and he heard his mother softly crying in the back. He turned and said, "I'm sorry Ma to embarrass you. And Mrs. Alrod, I'm sorry I done stole yor eggs." She was crying, too.

Lem put his wrists together and raised them toward the sheriff who was standing nearby with handcuffs in his hands. Lem was ready to take his punishment.

"Now hold on Lem, I ain't finished, son." said Judge Hendrix.

He got up and took his robe off and hung it on the rack in the corner of the room. He then picked up his summer straw hat that had been resting on a nearby table. Everyone thought he was leaving, and the trial was a done deal, and Lem was headed to the jail house.

But without any fanfare, Judge Hendrix reached into his pocket and took out a ten dollar bill; a scarce sight around there. He walked around in front of the podium where Lem was standing and said, "I hereby pay your fine for you, and then I hereby rescind the charge... marking it right off the books." He dropped the money into his new hat.

Lemuel O'Brien was just too stunned to say anything.

Then Judge Hendrix turned to look at those packed into the room and then he said, "I know some of you came out here this morning for reasons of your own... some to support the O'Brien family... and some just to gloat and rubber neck at another family's misfortune."

"Being what may, I hereby levy a fine of fifty cents on every family here in this courtroom for living in a town where a boy has to steal to eat." Handing his hat to the sheriff, he said, "Here Sheriff, collect the rest of the fine and give it to this boy."

Reaching back up across the bench, he banged the gavel on the wooden surface, saying, "Case dismissed." And with that he walked back up the aisle and left the room without his new hat.

The sheriff made his way to the exit door and as the folks passed by ... one by one... each head of the family dropped in their money. Some dropped in even a little bit more... a few some actual folding money. One thing you did not do in a small town was pass by a sheriff without doing what a judge told you to do.

Hardly a word was spoken as they passed by, but several of the men offered Lem some work about their farms, and he gratefully accepted.

It seems the preacher and the judge had gotten their heads together and made a bargain to teach Lem a lesson; but not saddle him with a criminal record.

Many had experienced hunger during those harsh depression years, and most had not fully recovered, but they had learned a good lesson right along with young Lem. But little did they know the lesson was yet to be fully taught.

⁓⊶⊷⁓

Sunday Meetin' Time

That next Sunday, Preacher Alrod rose in front of the congregation as he had Sunday after Sunday for many years.

He said, "Now that was some mighty good singing by the choir. You can tell they done been practicing. We praise the Lord for them what can sing and praise the Lord with their voices, and we praise the Lord for them what know they ain't got the calling."

We need all of you doin' what you do best. Just like there is the different parts on the body of a man, there are different parts of the body of the church. If you can't sing and you know you can't sing, then you just keep on looking, and the Lord will lead you to yor gift. And you can always sing while you are plowing the north forty... ain't that right, Brother Jones?"

"Now some of you may be asking why I am pickin' on Brother Jones today... have you heard him sing?" The congregation laughed.

"But have you seen him swing?"

"There ain't no better lumberman in these here parts. Week after week in the cold winter, we sit here warm and toasty from the roaring fire in that wood stove over yonder because he can swing a mean ax."

Pointing at Brother Jones, Pastor Alrod continued saying, "That man, Rufus Jones, can cut more stove wood in an hour than any man in this town!"

"Ever give any idee to where that wood comes from? Well, it comes from Brother Jones, and ever since I've taken my Daddy's place here in this little church, I have never seen that wood pile empty."

"We thank the Lord, Brother Jones that you ain't wastin' yor time trying to mosey into the choir. For if you had the voice of an angel, our feet would shorely be cold."

"And just because it's now mid-summer, it won't mean he will be idle. He makes it his business to help the church and the folks around here by looking for all the trees that fell during the winter and spring storms. He cuts them up for the church's firewood and don't charge a single person a single dime."

"But if you listen carefully, you can hear them golden dimes clinking in that heavenly bank account with the name of Brother Jones on it. Let Brother Jones know if you have a tree to donate to the church's wood pile. And let him know you are glad yor feet don't git cold in the wintertime."

"Them what has a Bible, I want you to open them to the scriptures as I give them to you and if someone next to you ain't got no Bible, kindly let them look on with you."

"Today, we are going to look at the condition of man. We are all sinners, and we know that, but in different states of our sinning. Some of us are sinners saved by God's Grace and some of us are still living in a state of sin."

"Now committing a particular sin and living in the state of sin is two different things. So this does not give any of us reason to gloat over anyone else when they are guilty of committing a sin. I've got news for you… they ain't no big sins and little sins in God's eyes. If you steal a penny, you might as well steal a million dollars."

"Anything that separates you from God is sin. And not being aware of yor sins, and living just lickety-split going on down the road 'cause you ain't robbed no bank, that don't make you a saint."

"Sin can sometimes be what you ain't doing. 'For him that knoweth to do good and then don't do it… then that is sin as well. It's right here in the Bible," he said as he held up his old time worn Bible.

"But, there is a cure for both, be it committing a single sin or living a life of sin. We will commit sins until the day we die; that is because we are sinful creatures. However, to deny Christ, and go our own way and to refuse to accept God's atonement for our sins, that means that we will miss out on heaven."

"And to point out the sins of others in order to make us feel better about our own sins won't cut it either."

"Remember Jesus said, "He who is without sin cast the first stone. Well, they won't be no stone throwing here today for I fear most of us would end up with a topknot on our heads."

"This week we saw a demonstration in real life of how we deserve to face the consequences of our individual sins; but how God, the judge of all of us, done come down from His high station in life and took off His royal robes and paid our debt just like we saw Ole Judge Hendrix do this week."

"Now I ain't holding Judge Hendrix up in any better light than the rest of us. He is a good man. But I went to school with him, when we were boys, out on the play yard he…"

However, before the preacher could finish his sentence of…. " well I will leave it there," the Judge spoke up with a louder than usual, "Amen."

His lawyering served him well in speaking up just in time; as he had been a real cutter before giving his life to Christ. The turnaround in him was like night and day.

As the loud "Amen" came from the lips of the judge sitting in the back pew, he uncrossed his legs where his finely woven straw Fedora hat was resting on his knees. When he shifted a little bit in his seat, he knocked his new hat onto the floor. As he bent over to collect it, he bumped his head on the back of the pew in front of him. Only a few days before, that new hat had served as a collection plate.

No one knows who, for sure, but someone sniggered about the hat or the fact he bumped his head; probably thinking that is what he gets for strutting around in his new hat.

Pastor Alrod stopped in mid-sentence looked out across the congregation, leaned over, and held his right hand up to his right ear as if to listen to see where the sniggering came from. There was no more sniggering. That was a message in motion rather than one in words.

The judge was a snappy dresser, and Mr. Ferguson had previously told some of the men, he had bought the hat from Dobbs Fifth Avenue, in New York City. He knew this because the judge opened the package while still standing in his General Merchandise Store.

Mr. Ferguson told everyone how he carefully opened it up, and put it on his head, and stood there before the store mirror cocking it to one side and the other. Even though, he lived in the city, the judge often ordered things through Mr. Ferguson. Some speculated that perhaps he didn't want his wife to know about his extravagance.

He told Mr. Ferguson he had chosen that particular one because of the sandy color of the straw, and because of the multi-colored blue band that surrounded the crown. Looking at himself a little closer in the mirror, he said, "My wife often tells me how the color blue sets off my blue eyes!" Mr. Ferguson just rolled his eyes a little but didn't dare say a word to the judge.

The judge, a stocky little man with a little paunch for a belly, who wore gold-rimmed glasses, was in his late forties and had come from little, but his father saw that he went to law school by the blood and sweat of his brow.

His father had died before he became a judge. But in a sense, the whole town was equally proud to have one of their own go so far in life. While many of the farmers wore nice starched and ironed overalls to church on Sundays, he wore expensive three-piece suits. Often the belly paunch was a little bit lower than his vest. Once, Herman spoke up in defense of him saying as a judge he had a certain reputation and stature in the county to uphold.

However, there was not a lot of resentment because men his same age were strong, muscled, and tanned; where the little judge was round and pale.

Judge Hendrix could quite afford such luxuries; just like he could afford to give the ten-dollar bill toward Lem's fine, but down deep he was a good man. He was a good and fair judge, and that is what mattered to most of the people.

He had left the valley to go to law school and stayed in the city after graduation. He was quite the dapper young man then and snagged the hand of a wealthy young lady. And he never returned to the valley to live, but would come there to preside over petty crimes several times a month; if the docket required it.

He always attended the little church on the hill when he was in town. He grew up listening to James Alrod preach the "Word of God" before his son, Herman.

Major crimes were seldom a problem there. But when something of a larger magnitude happened, the trial would be held in the courthouse in the city.

It was once debated if they should hold court in the church, but there was stern opposition for using God's house in such a manner. Not only did the citizens believe in the Bible, they also believed in the Constitution. They felt if they gave the government a foothold into their church, they would eventually move in and take over.

And since there was already a U.S. Post Office in the store, that made it more government official. So small claims court and minor misdemeanors were taken care of in Mr. Ferguson's store at lunch time when Mr. Ferguson was closed.

Judge Hendrix would not bend the law, but often in minor brushes with the law, he would use his discretion to restore an offender. He would use methods of restoration rather than incarceration. He believed if possible under the law, to give a person a second chance.

Pastor Alrod's voice wafted across the church room as he continued his sermon.

"Jesus didn't have to do it. Naw, He didn't. But He did. And because of what He did, our debts are forgiven, but it cost God His Son, and let me be the first to tell you right here, and now, no ten dollar bill could pay my sin debt… no sirree."

His wanted to bring back the attention of what had happened in the courtroom the previous week.

"It would take a heap more than that. But just like that thief that hung on the cross beside Jesus, I know that I have done wrong, and so does Jesus. But just the same, like He done told that thief, I've been forgiven."

"The difference in a man committing a sin and living a life of sin is that a Christian man will know that he sinned and will repent. Often a person living and wallowin' in sin; just plain don't know he's lost. Or worse, he don't seem to care!"

"Because I am forgiven, does that mean I would never sin again? Mercy, no! Don't believe me, just ask Mama over there. Wives are better at keeping records than anyone on the face of the earth. But them what loves; they also forgive."

He smiled at her, and she smiled back at him.

The ladies in the front wondered what Papa had done recently to evoke Mama's forgiveness. They always wanted to know other people's business.

"Now, I hate to break it to you, but you all done sinned and broke fellowship with God. And you know that, like me, you ain't no better off than that thief that hung beside Jesus."

"And like Jesus done told us as children of God, we are not to judge other people. But now that don't count for judges of the law which must keep the civil law, but it is up to us to keep God's laws. He just don't give us the right to go around sizing up folks and pointing out their faults. And without skipping a beat, he said "Ladies that includes gossip. I think some of you don't know it is a sin to gossip… and you men, too!"

"Well, it says so right here in the Bible."

"There are as many as fifteen verses that talks about different forms of gossip and nothing can tear up a church any quicker than gossip. Gossiping can mean backbiter, busybody, slanderer, secrets, talebearer, and whisperers."

227

Preacher Alrod looked up, and all he could see were the tops of the ladies' hats as they looked down at their laps. Then he said, "Well, that is another topic for another day."

"And as I said, it don't look like there will be no stone throwing here this morning or any mornings to come." He looked again, and the ladies were sitting with eyes front again."

"Now like I done said, them what have a Bible, I want you to open them to the scriptures as I give them to you and if someone next to you ain't got no Bible, kindly let them look on with you."

"Sharing good things makes God happy."

"Now Brother Jim, you sit back down, it ain't leaving time. You hang around here a little longer, and you're gonna hear a new rendition of "Just as I Am" that will make goose bumps roll down on yor arm and up yor back. That's right Brother Jim... you just sit back down and listen to the Word of the Lord."

"Flipping over here in the New Testament in the book of John let's take a good long look at John 3:16 to be specific as we read these words."

In unison, the congregation began to read: "*For God so loved the world that He gave His only begotten Son, that whosoever believeth in Him should not perish, but have everlasting life.*"

"Are you folks grasping what I am saying... what God's Word is saying? Most of you have heard these words preached to you either at home or church; but have you ever deeply considered what they mean... what they mean specifically to you?"

"Now this is a much deeper verse than what it appears to be. Now there is no doubt that God loved the world for He created it with all these here mountains, streams, and even the sun that makes the crops grow and the stars that light up the night. When he finished creating all this beauty, He stepped back and saw what He had done was good."

"Yessiree, God loves this beautiful world. He was satisfied with the work of His hands, but herein John 3:16 it is not specifically talking about the earth...but them what inhabit it."

"Here, go back and substitute yor name for "world." For me, it would read, *For God so loved Herman Alrod.*"

Now if you don't already be knowing it, God has a Son... and His name is Jesus. Most of you know that from the Christmas story."

"But we see in the next line that *"whosoever"* means anybody... anybody at all who believes in Him. This means believing that Jesus is who He says He is... *shall not perish*... which means not to die eternally... but will have eternal life. That simply means you will live forever."

"Are you with me here to this point?" Herman stopped and surveyed the audience, and those he was sure were Christians were nodding their heads up and down. But there were a couple who still looked a little bewildered. He made a mental note of who they were, so he could pray for them.

And he would just have to keep on praying for the light of day, or the light of God, to set up inside of Ole Jim for he had already slid down in his seat with his arms crossed over his chest, and was fast asleep.

"Now you might be thinking how could believing in a man, claiming to be the Son of God, keep you from dying and allowing you to live forever?"

"That is what this verse means and it is a powerful one because it wraps everything up in this one verse."

Pastor Alrod looked up again and saw little lights coming on in the heads of those who looked bewildered before. And to himself he said, 'Thank You, Lord for heping them to see the light."

He began again, "God made the world."

"He liked what He had made."

"Man messed up and lost his relationship with God because of sin."

"God sent His Son, Jesus, to teach the world about God and His love."

"And when it says, "gave" here... it means that God let His own Son die to pay for man messing up, and that put man back in the right relationship with God. God gave the Son, and the Son gave His life for ours. By rights, it should be us hanging up there on that cross...because we did the sinning... and Jesus never did."

"But God is not talking here about life on this earth which we all know comes to an end... for everyone born ...they have to die! That is just a fact, and there ain't no gittin' around it."

229

"However, here He is talking about a new life... after the earthly death... where those who believe that Jesus is the Son of God... and... accepts what He did on the cross... will have a transformed life from this one to the other one; where they will never die again!"

"God's Word also says that man is appointed to die only once. Ain't that wonderful to know that with death here on this earth, we won't never have to go through it again?" And, we won't never have to bury our loved ones in some other graveyard like what's out back here."

"Now you farmers will see the beauty of this when you think about the earth as being what God created. Man is the seed that messed up... so to speak. It gets dropped into the soil, and it dies in the earth, but from that seed sprouts new life. And so on and so on."

"The seed produces more seed, and that seed produces more seed. It is like the eternal life those who believe in Jesus will have. We will just keep going on and on forever. But also be aware that there are also bad seeds that get planted, and they too spread and multiply throughout the world."

"But if we skip on down a little bit to John 10:10, we will see that God didn't just send His Son to die in order to keep us from dying eternally, but He also sent His Son so that we might have a better life here on earth as well."

> *"The thief cometh not, but for to steal, and to kill,*
> *and to destroy: I am come that they might have life,*
> *and that they might have it more abundantly."*

"Now git a hold on this as Jesus is talking here, and He is saying, *"I came that they might have life and that they might have it abundantly!"* Now that means that Jesus didn't come just to give us a little bit of life, but a whole lot of it; counting time here on earth and the time that we shall have in the Promised Land of Heaven. Some will have a shorter time on this here earth, but we will all have the same promised time in Heaven...forever!"

"But now some of you might be thinking that you don't recall a time when you messed up with Jesus. But you would be mistaken. For in Romans 3:23, Paul, the Apostle of Christ, says, *"All have sinned and fall short of the glory of God!"*

"Now just what is sin and what is not? Remember there is a difference in committing a sin…and living a life of sin."

"Man was created to have the fellowship with God; but, because of his stubborn self-will, he chose to go his own independent way, and fellowship with God was broken. This self-will, characterized by an attitude of rebellion and indifference, is an evidence of what the Bible calls sin."

"You might say. So what if we sin, what difference does it make if we are going to die anyway? A little further over in the book of Romans, God, through Paul. warns *"The wages of sin is death – both on this earth and in the world to come."*

"But it also says, *"God demonstrates His own love toward us, in that while we were yet sinners, Christ died for us."* Notice, we didn't have to clean up our act first, but God accepts us just as we are."

"And a little further on over in I Corinthians 15: 3-6 we are told, *"Christ died for our sins... He was buried... He was raised on the third day, according to the Scriptures... He appeared to Peter, then to the twelve. After that, He appeared to more than five hundred..."*

"Now this happened to show us that God has the power over life and death."

"A lot of folks think they can live their life any way they want and then at the last breath…holler out to Jesus. We are always looking for ways to shirttail around things… have our cake and eat it too, so to speak. You can't have it both ways. God will know the difference."

Preacher Alrod continued reading, *"Jesus said to him, 'I am the way, and the truth and the life; no one comes to the Father, but through me."*

"And John continues with *"As many as received Him, to them He gave the right to become children of God, even to those who believe in His name."*

"By grace, you have been saved through faith, and that, not of yourselves, it is the gift of God; not, as a result, of works, that no one should boast."

"Now no matter how much wood a man cuts, or how he helps to save a young boy from crime, or how many pies you women might bake for the church bazaar..that don't get you to Heaven."

"Now back to the book of John, where he says, by receiving Christ we receive the new birth. Now some of you may be thinkin' how can a person be born twice...once they are already born once?"

"There is birth on this earth and a rebirth in mind, body,
and spirit which entitles us entry into Heaven."

"Here in the county, it is now law that when a baby is born, you have to register that baby in the courthouse. That is the first birth, but when you receive Christ and are born again... you receive a second birth by the forgiving of all yor sins."

"When we accept Jesus as Lord and Savior, you get a different kind of certificate, but more likely you get "certified" to enter heaven. Now I ask, are you sure you are "certified?"

"And yor certificate of the new birth is obtained by the death of Jesus on the Cross. How do you know if you are born again? Because, you will have an exchanged life, and yor life will reflect things of Christ and not man."

"Now all of you under the sound of my voice, I pray that tonight before you close yor eyes, and trust that you will wake up again tomorrow, that you hear these words in yor heart, *'Behold, I stand at the door and knock; if anyone hears My voice and opens the door, I will come in to him."*

Looking up from his Bible, Preacher Alrod said, "Now the question, "Is there anyone here who believes what this here Holy Book says and wants to be put back together with God ...no more separation...not here or in eternity?"

"Now if there is, you just step forward and we will pray with you, and accept yor commitment, baptize you into the membership of this little ole country church; but also into the family of God, which is a forever family. Once, you join this church, you will no longer just be a neighbor, stranger, or friend, but you will be brothers and sisters with all these good folks; for we are all the children of God, and He is the Father of us all."

"Now, you don't have to be baptized to be saved. That is just showing the world that you have decided to be on God's team. But if you are truly saved you will want to be baptized."

Now is an excellent time of the year to be baptized when the creek water is as warm as the hearts of those who fellowship here together. We will soon have another baptizing, along with dinner on the ground, and all day singing.

"Amen?" quizzed the preacher. He waited for that echo of "Amen's."

"There were several strong "Amen's" from the men folk."

The organist slowly began to play the invitational hymn as was the custom of this little church after such an invitation from Preacher Alrod. He invited any who wanted to come forward to have the opportunity to do so.

He waited down front beside the little wooden altar. After giving enough time for any to respond, he would then invite any down who just wanted to come and pray to do so.

The voices in the choir melded together in such a sweet song as Pastor Alrod read the first line, and the choir echoed it behind him. They continued to hum as he read the rest of the lyrics of this time honored old hymn.

He raised his hand with his open Bible in it and said, *"Just as I am without one plea, but that His blood was shed for me,"* the choir echoed his words.

Again, he said, *"That thou bids me come to thee, O Lamb of God, I come…I come to rid my soul of one dark blot; to thee, whose blood can cleanse each spot… though I am tossed about with many a conflict and many a doubt, fighting's and fears within and without,"*
"Though I am poor, wretched and blind; sight, riches, healing of the mind… Yea…all I need in thee to find."

And while the choir hummed the tune softy in the background, Preacher Alrod continued with the words,

"Just as I am, thou wilt received, wilt welcome, pardon, cleanse, relieve; because thy promise I believe, O Lamb of God, I come, I come."

The choir softly repeated, *"Because thy promise, I believe, O Lamb of God I come.*

While they softly continued to hum the tune, Pastor Alrod said, "Anyone...anyone want to come to Jesus today?"

There was a rustling noise coming from the back, and heads turned to see who was walking down the aisle.

Not slowly or timidly, there stood a tall, good looking... rather handsome sixteen-year-old young man that proudly walked down the aisle of that little church. He was wearing the same boots he wore when he stole the eggs, but with a new zeal in his steps.

He paused for a minute and glanced at Sarah Louise Alrod; and she blushed and turned her head away. And that young man accepted Christ that morning. And that was only the beginning of where Christ and those boots would lead him with a devoted wife beside him to places he had never even heard about.

"God bless you, son," said the preacher. Then he turned once again to the congregation and said, "Just like the thief on the cross, and all the Lem's and you and me, and all the preachers in this world, we will all be with Christ in Paradise. It won't be because of what anyone has done good or bad; but for what Jesus did on the Cross of Calvary!"

And looking at Lem, he added... "but not before we have completed God's work on this earth."

After praying with Lemuel O'Brien to accept Jesus as his Lord and Savior, Reverend Alrod turned to Lem and whispered, *"If you want to make footprints on the sands of time, you'd better wear work boots."*

Chapter fifteen: The Twins Velma and Verna

"Papa, did you ever want to be somebody else?"

Looking hard into her face, he said, "Well....uh....uh, Velma, I don't rightly recollect ever being unhappy with the way God made me; so I guess I wouldn't. Why do you ask?"

"Cause I want to be different, I don't like to be called, "One of the twins."

"I want to be just me and nobody else."

"Velma, are you and Verna fussing again?"

"No, Papa...well maybe... but not like when we are fighting over somethin'."

"Well, what then, don't you like being a twin?"

"What I don't like is... not being just me! I don't want to look like her. I just want to look like me."

"Well, sweet pea that is something to think about."

"Just like that Papa!"

"Like what, sweet pea?"

"I don't like to be called sweet pea!"

"Why not honey, that is what we have always called you, Velma."

"And Papa, I don't like to be called 'honey' either?"

"Well, Missy, what do you want to be called?"

"Not Missy, not sweet pea, and not honey."

Finally, Papa was beginning to get the picture says, "What else don't you like, Velma?"

That's just it Papa; I'm not Velma I'm Verna."

"I'm beginning to understand... because there are two of you that look exactly alike and talk alike and dress alike...that does not mean you are both exactly alike, is that it sweetie – uh Verna?"

Seeing a little sadness in her eyes, he continued, "And what else, Verna?"

"Papa, I'll bet God is mad at you?"

"Uh... mad at me, why, Verna?"

"Because, you did not tell the truth in church?"

"Didn't tell the truth, when did I not tell the truth?" Papa asked leaving off her name and all the nicknames.

"You said in the last Meetin' that God made everybody different and that there weren't no two things in all the world exactly alike not even snowflakes or leaves on a tree."

"Papa did you forget about me and Velma? We are exactly alike. We have the same color of hair and the same green eyes, and the same birthday... AND... the same clothes!"

"Well, Sweetie, uh Verna... that is what I said, but I can understand why you don't think that was the truth, but let me explain further."

"While you and Velma are very much alike in a lot of ways; you are still not exactly alike. You two are just as different from each other as the other children in this family. You all have the same color of hair and the same green eyes."

"Yeah, they don't have the same birthday, the same age, the same clothes, and when people don't know who you are, they call you sweet pea or something like that."

"I see," said Papa.

And then she chimed in, "And they don't have to share the same birthday cake."

"So that is what is bothering you. Yor eighth birthday is coming up, huh?"

"Verna, it is like this... we are all alike in many ways because we were created in the image of God."

"Papa, what is 'image'?

"Well, an image is something that looks like something else on the outside... like looking in the mirror or having yor picture taken."

"But the mirror or camera can only see the outside of a person. Like God's Word says, *"Man looks on the outward appearance, but God looks on the heart."*

"But Papa, how can we be made in the image of God when no one knows what He looks like?'

236

"That's just it, Verna... it is not the outside of us that is made in God's image; but the inside."

"But how do we know what God's insides look like, Papa?"

"Because the Good Book tells us what God is like by His actions. The way we think and act tells us how we are on the inside by the things we do and say."

"Papa, I don't always act like Velma, do I?"

"No, you don't, and she does not always act like you. None of you kids act just like the other, and that is a good thing! Why, Mama and I could not stand you all being nice at the same time; it might give the ole ticker a startle!"

"Papa, what is a ticker?"

Putting his pointer finger on her chest near her heart, Papa said, "That is just a name for that heart that grows deep inside of you that keeps you living. It is different from the heart that God wants us to give him. We have both a physical heart and a spiritual heart; God wants our spiritual heart."

"Oh," was her somewhat confused reply.

"Verna, does it bother Velma that you both look alike?"

"I don't think so, Papa, she ain't never said so, and you know Velma, she don't say much about nothing that's important!"

"Ah, ha!"

"See, while you like to talk about the things on yor mind that you think is important, Velma doesn't... don't that make you different?"

"And Papa, I like apples, but Velma don't."

"Now you see, while you look alike on the outside, you are still very different little girls. For whatever reason God decided to bless us with two little girls at the same time, He also created you to be two different and separate human beings."

"Let's think of other ways you are different. You like to read books, and Velma likes to climb trees, don't she?"

"Yes!"

"And I like to help Mama in the house, and Velma likes being with you, Papa, outside. She'd heap ruther help out in the vegetable garden than to help cook the vegetables in the house."

"Verna, will you do something' for yor Ole Papa?" "Will you get yor school tablet and pencil and start making two lists?"

"Label one of them "How I am like my sister" and the other "How I am not like my sister.""

"That's a good idea Papa; I like to write, but Velma don't.""

"Ahh…that can be the first difference on yor list. Velma likes to climb trees, and Verna likes to write.""

"I know Papa. I like to be quiet, and Velma likes to talk a lot, huh, Papa?""

"That can be yor second item on the list," her father said giving her a sideways hug.""

"But Papa, I don't want to look like Velma anymore.""

"Why, do you think Velma is ugly?""

"Oh, no Papa, I think Velma is purdy; just not me?""

"Not be as purdy as Velma… how could that be?""

"I just think she is purdier than me, that's why.""

"I think what you have got here is a good case of the jealousies, little lady. You are spending more time watching yor sister than watching yourself.""

"You think because you two look alike… that makes you less in some way, right?""

"But that is wrong – it makes you more.""

"How is that, Papa, everybody calls us 'the twins' and not by our names. Mama makes our dresses just alike and combs our hair the same. Everyone thinks we ARE the same.""

And everyone is always asking, "Now, which one are you?""

"Well, that… young lady, will be up to you to show them you are different, huh?""

"Just remember this one thing…people look on the outward appearance, but God looks on the heart.""

❧

Sunday Meetin' Time

"It is good to be back in the house of God once again. The weather has been good, and the crops have been good, and the harvest looks to be good. We got the hole in the roof fixed, and the wood pile is stacked high for the winter."

"Course, we still owe a few payments on the organ…but that will come when the church members bring in their crop. God is in His Heaven, and even on the heels of this Great Depression, we are doing better than most. We have truly been blessed."

"It is when we start looking at what we don't have instead of looking at what we do have and watching to see how our neighbor is faring is when we take our eyes off of God."

"Just when we think we have got it all tucked away, something comes along and makes us realize that someone might have a little more than we do. Envy is a strong feeling because it not only takes our attention away from the things of God, but it puts it right-smack-dab on ourselves."

"I had me a grand time this past week with one of the….with Verna, and she started me to thinking about the way WE think. And the way we think is sometimes the way WE act."

"This here Good Book says here that, "As a man thinketh in his heart, so he is.""

"And it also says we should not think more highly of ourselves than our neighbor."

"When we get all caught up in who we are, for our own satisfaction, we fail to satisfy God. In the long run, we cannot be satisfied no matter how much we have; for we always want more. It is like trying to fill a deep dark hole that never gets filled up. It just seems to get all swallowed up, and we can't see what we have got until we begin to realize that we are living in a deep dark hole."

"Just as we compare ourselves to others; don't it just naturally set us up to compare ourselves to God?"

"That was the same ole mistake satan made before he got kicked out of heaven. That was the way Adam and Eve thought before they got kicked out of the most beautiful garden ever created."

"Mind you, now… before they disobeyed God, they didn't have to turn a rock, or steady a plow, or drop a seed, or pray for rain, or put up a fence to keep the animals out."

"God provided all they needed, but then when that ole snake showed up, he convinced them that the only reason God did not want them to eat from that tree was because He was afraid of them becoming like Him. And that just tempted them all the more."

"Sometimes you and I may feel like we would not have made that mistake. We might even think that the world would be different today if it had not been for Adam and Eve disobeying God."

"We can just sit back and blame the first couple, and God, for the condition of the world when we don't lift a single finger today to make a difference."

"Now I want to talk to you Papa's a little bit here now. Some of you think the only thing you have to do is earn a living and put the food on the table, and that is required of a man to do right by his family; for sure."

"But sometimes us men folk can be so busy making a living that we forget to live and forget those little ones that are growin' up right under our noses that need only what a Papa can give."

"Until yor sons are old enough to figure things out, when they look at their earthly Papa, they are gittin' a picture of their heavenly Father, God."

"If you find a man who shakes his fist in the face of God, you can almost be mighty sure that his Papa here on earth has been shakin' his fist in his face."

"Papas set quite a bit of store in producing sons. They are for posterity because they will carry the family name for example and because they can help them run the farm someday."

"Somehow a man thinks he can live on through his sons. And frankly, most Papas just don't know what to do with little girls. But did you know, in those early years of life, you are but a dress rehearsal for their marriage someday?"

"It just seems natural that little girls will grow up and marry a man like their Papa ... good or bad."

"Some while back there was a man who only had one child... a little girl... but his wife died. He was so wrapped up in his loss; he forgot that little girl done lost her Mama as well."

"That is natural for a while, but as time went on, he cared for her needs. He worked, fed her and sent her to school. But she was desperate for his love and attention. Maybe he didn't know how to give her the love and affection she needed, but he didn't seem to try."

"Every time she would say, 'Papa, will you play with me?' He would continue reading his paper and smoking his pipe and tell her to run on outside to the street and play with the other children."

"Finally, she didn't ask anymore but grew up in the streets and later became a streetwalker. And to her dying day she continued to search the streets to find someone to give her that love and affection. She continued to look for someone to keep company with her and make her feel safe and loved."

"Neglect is one of the most devastating ways you can abuse yor child. Tell yor children that you love them. Yes, even yor boys!"

"Farming is hard work and long hours, but if you spend more time with yor animals than yor children, yor children are likely to grow up like animals."

"Little girls adore their Papa's and will listen to him when he gives her good advice. Now he ain't built to give her the same kinds of training a Mama can, but it don't mean a Papa don't have a part in her life."

"That little girl will look at men the rest of her life by the way you treat her, and she will know the difference in a good husband and a bad husband."

"One of the best things a man can do for his children is to love their mother; to show her respect, honor, and appreciation, as well as affection. The boys will have a good example of how to be a good husband. While at the same time, the girls will know the qualities that make for a good, honest husband for themselves."

"Some folks think that a Papa is the king of the house; well just let them keep on thinkin' that for as a man thinketh, so he is."

"When you begin to think highly of yourself, it will make you think more highly of others. For if you are the king, it makes yor whole family royalty… Mama, a Queen, and those little ones… Princes and Princesses."

"Now what they say is true, "Confession is good for the soul but bad for the reputation!"

"I gotta confess that I have fallen short many times as a Papa, but when you know that, it means you can do somethin' about it."

"This week, I realized what I have been doing wrong. It was to think that they are all the same, and they need the same things in their lives. I never realized while in many ways they are all alike... they are all different in many ways as well. They are all as different as snowflakes and leaves on a tree."

"But down inside those snowflakes and leaves, each is made up of the same elements. And they were all created by God."

"Papas, I want you to take this verse along with you this week as found in Proverbs 20: 7 *"The just man walketh in his integrity: his children are blessed after him."*

"Now you Papas think on these things this week. Now let us all pick up our hymn books and sing a hymn of invitation."

Sitting on the front row of this Sunday Meetin' were two little girls. One had on a pink dress with a pink bow in her curls. The other had a newly short-bobbed hairdo with no bow and a blue dress.

As the congregation passed out the door to go home, it was their practice to shake hands with Preacher Alrod. Brother Ferguson shook his hand extra hard and said, "Fine sermon, preacher. Guess you are looking for another boy soon, yeh?"

Papa looked down at a little girl standing next in line. She was wearing a blue dress, a new short bob, and no hair bow. He winked at her and said, "Not so Brother Ferguson, another little girl would be just fine; even two, if the Good Lord wills."

As Verna passed by, she reached up and gave the preacher such a big hug he almost fell over, and she whispered loud enough for the world to hear, "Thank you, Papa. I am now up to twenty-two differences, and thank you for telling Mama to cut my hair."

Chapter sixteen: The Election

Mama watched Billy Joe as he scratched his head with his yellow No. 2 pencil while resting his elbow on the kitchen table. He had just about whittled the pencil away; sharpening it with a kitchen knife. She watched him for quite some time while she was standing in front of the stove stirring the black-eyed peas.

Mama told him several times to sharpen his pencils with Papa's pocket knife and not dull down her kitchen knife. But she would not fuss at him for now. She sensed that something was already bothering him.

He would scribble something in his *"Big Chief"* writing tablet, but would stop. He shifted in his chair, moaned or grunted. She figured he was stumped trying to figure out a difficult arithmetic problem. It was clear that something was bothering him. He would write for a while and the tear out the page and wad it up.

She waited for him to say something, knowing that men and boys did not start conversations; they instigated them. They would humph... grunt... squirm... and make irritating noises until someone would say, "Is there something bothering you?" They initially will say, "Naw." But if you don't pursue the conversation, they will just keep making grunting noises until you ask again.

He flipped the cover over and started drawing eyeglasses on the eyes of the chief. He kept going over the circles making them darker and darker. He was bearing down so hard; he broke the point off of his pencil again. He reached over to pick up the paring knife and his Mother put her hand on top of his so he could not pick it up.

She cupped his face in her hand and asked, "Billy Joe, what is wrong with you... somethin' botherin' you son?"

First he replied, "Naw."

"Now don't "Naw" me son. Somethin' is eating at you, and it is plain to see somethin' is clearly botherin' you."

He pushed back in his chair, ran his fingers through that thick clump of hair, and began to open up to her in a typical male manner; talking about everything, but what was really at the root of his discomfort.

"Ah, Ma, I was just thinkin' 'bout not running for president of the 4-H Club," he said bouncing his pencil up and down on its eraser against the table.

Without looking up at her, he said, "With all the work to be done around here and with the new baby comin' soon, I figure I might be needed around here more."

"Well, what brought about this turn of events? Just last week, you boasted how you were going to beat that Robert's boy out in no time at all. Everybody knows that you done raised the biggest, fattest pig in the county, and you are shore to win a blue ribbon."

"Well, that is different Ma" He seldom ever called her, "Ma." But, every now and then he did. Papa said it was because he was growing up and didn't want to call her "Mama" for that sounded so juvenile.

"All I had to do is feed that dumb ole pig. She will eat just about anything including the corn cobs along with the shucks. She's so lazy... just living in the mud all day... with nothing to do... she's getting fatter every day."

"I ain't done nothin' special to take care of her. All I did was feed her the slop every day."

"Now, son, you ain't done gone and got partial to that old hawg have you? You knew from the start that you were raising that hawg for food and not as a pet."

"Bet you done went and named her didn't you after we told you not to?"

"Naw, Ma, I didn't name HER unless you count, "Move over you dumb ole pig."

"Well, raising a pig is one thing, but not running for the 4-H... now that is somethin' mighty different. What's done up and changed yor mind about being the president of the club? What does the president of that club do anyway?"

With a little anger rising in his voice, he said, "Ma, ain't you never listened to anything I been tellin' you for the past two years? The president is a mighty important person to the club. He tells everyone else what to do. He takes charge of the meetin's and calls the roll when the secretary ain't there, and she hardly ever is."

"Well, that couldn't be too hard of a job... calling the roll... how many members you got anyways... about four?"

A little more irritated he responded, "See there you go, Mama, not giving me credit for anything. I done got the membership up to ten, and some more promising they will join later when they see who the new president is gonna be?"

"Well, son, do they dislike you or somethin'? Did you trample on some toes or act too big for yor britches? How come the others are waitin' to see who gits elected before they join up?"

"Well, it ain't me; they are afraid of... it's him?"

"Him, who?"

"Mama don't you remember nothin'?" Irritated, he had slipped back into calling her, "Mama."

A voice coming from the back porch through the screen door loomed out at Billy Joe. "Now hold on boy that is yor Mother you are talkin' to, but more important that's my wife you are talkin' to like that."

With sternness in his voice, Papa said, "Now don't you be speakin' to her in that tone. And just because there was somethin' she didn't remember that you said, don't give you no call to disrespect her!"

Sullied up, Billy Joe did not respond.

"Do you hear me son? Do you understand what I am sayin' to you? Now, apologize to her and git down off yor high horse and go on with yor conversation!"

"Gee, Mama, I'm sorry, but you wouldn't understand anyhow."

He got up from the table where he had been attempting to do his homework and pushed his chair under the table with a little bit too much force. It slammed against the table with a thud. He picked up his pencil and tablet as he brushed the pencil shavings off onto the floor.

Papa came bursting in from the back porch, slamming the screen behind him. He just stood there for a second or two and then spoke in a milder tone saying, "I don't recall nobody tellin' you that you can duck out like that, son."

"You sit back down there until yor Mama says she is through talkin' to you. Now go on back to whatever you two were talkin' about."

Billy Joe just stood there for a while and then eased the chair back from underneath the table; just as Mama handed him the broom and motioned at the pencil shavings on the floor.

He tore a page out of his tablet and put it on the floor holding it tight to the floor between his feet. Using it for a dust pan, he swept up the shavings and wadded up the paper and threw it in the garbage pail.

Papa turned to his wife and said, "Mama, how long before supper is on the table? I am hungry enough to eat Billy Joe's pig; ears and all," he said poking fun to lighten the air.

"It will be ready direcky, but you gotta wait a spell until the cornbread is done."

Papa picked up his Farmer's Almanac and headed back out to sit on the porch while there was some daylight left. When the weather permitted, and he got in from the fields before dark, he tried to stay out of Mama's way until she finished supper.

The children knew they could not run around in the kitchen while Mama was cooking. They usually played out in the sandy front yard as long as it was still daylight. Sometimes the twins played Chinese handball, kick the can, or alphabet ball if they were the only ones there.

At other times, if there were more kids around, they would play games like Red Rover, Bum, Bum, Bum, and Kickball. During the summer when it was still daylight, they would trap a June bug, and tie a string around its leg. Then holding onto the string, they would let it fly around in circles.

Other times along about dark and after supper, Mama and Papa would sit on the front porch while the kids played hide-n-seek. Another fun activity along about dark was catching lightening bugs in a jar. Sarah Louise showed the twins how to pull off their tail and put it on their ring finger and pretend it was a precious jewel. Oddly enough, it would actually still glow.

However, on this particular evening Verna and Velma were in the back of the house playing Monopoly while waiting for Mama to get supper finished. Baby James was asleep. LeRoy was out in the yard playing fetch with "Snooper." Sarah Louise was sprawled out across her bed doing her homework and day dreaming.

On this particular evening, Papa was sitting on the back porch listening to the conversation between Mama and Billy Joe. He had scooted the rocking chair closer to the screen door so that he could hear them more clearly. It seemed that the conversation was upsetting Billy Joe, and Papa did not want it to get out of hand.

Billy Joe was a good kid, and he respected his parents; and never gave them any trouble, but as his father, Herman wanted to make sure he stayed that way.

There was a deafening silence for a while and then Mama spoke first. "Billy Boy," her pet name for him, "you are more important to me than anything in this whole world; you and yor brothers and sisters. If you hurt, I hurt, and if you get into trouble then, my heart is troubled. I think you had better finish what you started."

"Started what, Mama, are we still talking about this conversation or running for president of the 4-H Club?"

"Both, son."

"Both…but let's start with the why of it all."

"Why are you no longer interested in somethin' that was important to you just last week?"

"Papa leaned a little closer to the door so he could hear better."

"Well, Mama, John Roberts, you know he ain't from around here… he came to live with his grandparents while his folks went to Europe or somewhere, and he isn't like the rest of us kids."

"He has always got whatever he wanted; whenever he wanted it; and now he wants to be president of the 4-H. Mama, he ain't got a clue as to what 4-H is all about. He just wants to be a big shot and take away what ain't his and rub it in my face."

"He likes this girl at school and she used to kinda like me. He done bought her things, and promised her things, and now she kinda likes him more better than me."

"Oh, so this is about a girl, huh?"

"No, Mama… well, not exactly."

"Anyways… well maybe a little bit… but not all the way."

"I don't understand, son. If you got questions about the girls, maybe you had better be talkin' to yor Papa."

With that, Papa leaned over a might too far in his rockin' chair, and it tipped right over causing him to fall against the screen door. Just the thought of talking to his son, about the birds and bees, unsettled him greatly.

Mama didn't even raise her voice; as she knew what had happened. But she demurely asked, "Papa… you all right?"

"Yep, just kinda rocked too hard I guess."

Mama thought it was more like "listening" too hard.

Taking a longer look at her son, she thought how it seemed he grew up more and more every day; right before her eyes. Realizing that, it took her aback for a while before she returned to the conversation and to the business at hand.

"Son, are you jealous of this other young man?"

"No, Mama. It's not like that at all." "Well, he said some things."

"Said what, Son?"

"I don't know if I should say or not?"

"Well, Billy Boy, if it is botherin' you that much, I think it is high time you stop dancing around and git right down to the roots of the matter."

"Well, Mama, you know we have all been working toward the 4-H Fair. We all want to win. But we mostly just want someone to win from our district. But right in the middle of all that, it came time to elect new officers. We had already decided that we needed a new secretary; as ours couldn't always be at the meetin's because of her sick mother."

"But then this new kid shows up and he don't care anything about the same values and things we care about. In fact, he makes fun of us and calls us 'country bumpkins' and other such names. But he thinks he can just shove his way on in and ruin our club."

"Well, son, if none of the other kids want him as president, you should not have anything to worry about… should you?"

"That's just it Mama; no one likes him. He makes us all feel bad by making fun of us. He calls Harry, 'four eyes' because he wears glasses; he pulls Mary Alice's pigtails and makes her cry. The other day, George's button popped off his pants, and he said, "Fatty, fatty two by four can't get through the kitchen door!"

"What did the other kids say?"

"Nothin' really."

"If he acts that way, then so much the better; that means no one will vote for him."

"But they will, "Mama," because they are afraid."

"Afraid of what?"

"He told each person in the club that if they do not vote for him, they will be sorry; because he knows a secret about one of their parents; and if they don't vote for him, he will tell everyone in town."

"He said they would be disgraced and wouldn't be able to hold their heads up around decent folks anymore."

"They didn't know which parents he was talking about, and they were afraid it might be theirs. And besides he told them, he would give everyone a quarter who voted for him. But if everyone didn't vote for him one hundred percent; and he still won, they won't git the money."

"And the thing of it, he won't tell us what the secret is, but says that he can prove it all… it will make trouble for everyone. So, yesterday we took a vote to see who was going to vote for him, or not. Everybody raised their hands that they would… excepting me."

"He laughed and looked at me with a disgusting grin on his face and said, 'How'd you like them apples, sodbuster?"

"I don't mind so much not being president, but if I don't vote for him then all the other kids won't get their quarter, and they will blame me."

"Mama, do you think he knows something about you and Papa?"

Not waiting for an answer, he said, "No matter, I can't take the chance either; so I need to decide to be the only one who votes against him; or just pull out of the race and let him have it. I could just quit the 4-H and not enter Sylvester in the contest… ah… I mean… that stupid ole dumb pig."

They both looked around as Papa came in, letting the screen door slam behind him as he said, "Son, it seems you have a real man's job of deciding what to do. We are not afraid of anything he might say about us.

We know the people we are. But you must make this man-size decision for yourself; for it will be the first of many to come throughout yor lifetime."

Just remember when you are faced with hard decisions, you don't have to make them alone. There is always someone you can turn to for help."

"I know Papa; you and Mama have always stood beside me; even when I disobeyed and got into trouble; but…"

"No, son, I was not speaking about yor Mama and me."

"Oh, yeah, Papa… I know you are speaking about God. But what do I ask God?"

"You will figure it out son, and just remember you can never go wrong doing right."

As he walked by his chair, he placed his hand on Billy Joe's shoulder and gave him a gentle squeeze. Billy Joe turned around and looked up at him His father said; "And as far as you being a sodbuster, you come from a long line of the best of them."

⁓⁓⁓✦⁓⁓⁓

Sunday Meetin' Time

Mama always set up the communion table down front of the church. She carefully filled the tiny little glass tumblers with less than an ounce of grape juice and placed several fresh baked loaves of bread on the table wrapped in a towel.

Everything was covered with a white lace tablecloth that had belonged to Herman's mother, Sarah. It was the one that she had used so many years before when she tended to the preparation of the Lord's Supper. It was special and only used for those occasions.

In each generation, there had been a special lady assigned to overseeing the preparation of the Lord's Table. She had to be stalwart in her devotion to God, a woman of impeccable reputation, well liked and loved by everyone… a woman given to much prayer.

It was truly an honored place for the women to have in the church. Once when Herman's mother, Sarah Alrod, had that duty, her husband, the Rev. James Alrod, asked her if she was planning the upcoming observation of the Lord's Supper, and why she had not started baking the bread for the next day.

She replied, "I ain't going to do it this time!"

Somewhat astonished, James asked her, "Why, not?"

She said, "Well, it is like this, Sister Mildred and I have had words over the plans for the next homecoming dinner on the grounds. And neither of us would give in. I just could not abide her attitude and her pigheadedness."

"But, Sarah, what will we do for bread for the Lord's Supper?" asked James. "Well, I don't rightly know. But it won't be me baking it! It wouldn't be fittin' for me to bake the Holy Bread with such ill will against her in my heart."

"But, this is important, can't you just find it in yor heart to forgive her and move on?"

"No, I won't do that!"

"Why?"

"Because, I am not through being mad at her, yet!"

That story was often told about Grandma Sarah and Grandpa James, but they never told if she baked the bread or not. The secret died with both of them.

Brother Alrod, took his place standing in the pulpit above the white-covered table for Lord's Supper and said, "Glad to see all of you here today comin' to the House of the Lord to praise and worship Him. Today is the quarter Sunday, which means that we are going to break bread and drink from the Lord's cup."

"None of you should be taking of the bread and cup unworthily; which means that we are only worthy when we have been made right with God through His Son, Jesus Christ."

"If you have any doubt about yor salvation; wait until next time after you have talked with me privately. The Scripture plainly says, in First Corinthians that we should examine ourselves and not take of the elements with an unworthy heart."

"Now, you parents watch the children. If they are not of age and have not professed their faith in Jesus Christ, don't let them partake of this communion. They need to know the significance and the reason why we do this the first Sunday in every quarter."

"Now, you refresh this tired old mind, who was it that wrote the instructions explaining who could partake of the communion?"

No answer. Then he put his hand up to cup around his ear and leaned over waiting for a reply. Then several in the congregation meekly said, "Paul."

"Good," say the pastor.

In I Corinthians 11:27-29 we find these words, *"Wherefore whosoever shall eat this bread, and drink this cup of the Lord, unworthily, shall be guilty of the body and blood of the Lord. But let a man examine himself, and so let him eat of that bread, and drink of that cup. For he that eats and drinks unworthily; eats and drinks damnation to himself, not discerning the Lord's body.*

"Now what do you to think that means?"

He leans over cupping his ear again and heard one voice... that of Mama's.

She said, "Only those who are called by His name should take of the bread and the cup!"

And then Judge Hendrix chimed in with, "This is a sacrament to be taken by only by those who have accepted Jesus as their Savior."

Pastor Alrod then asked, "And what do the symbols of bread and wine stand for?"

Again he put his hand to his ear. Another voice rang out, "It stands for the blood and body of Jesus!"

Their minister then said, "In our own right, we could never be worthy... for there is nothin' we could ever do to merit the love and forgiveness of a righteous God, who is so Holy. He cannot look upon sin: but knowing our weaknesses, He provided a way. He sent His Son...His only Son... to bridge the gap between a Holy God and sinful man."

Holding his Bible up for everyone to see he continued, "Right here in this here Bible, it says that whosoever believes in Jesus will be saved. You might be asking saved from what?"

"Saved from the punishment that God had decreed thousands of years ago when sin broke the bond between Him and man, and God cannot tell a lie."

"It is in His character and nature to always tell the truth. He will never go back on His word."

"You see it is like this, man needed to be saved from himself."

"God needed to remain truthful, but a loving and forgiving God as well. Known only to Him is why He chose to send His Son to the world; a world that had turned its back on Him."

"Well, folks it is kinda like this. There once was a young boy that made a little sailing boat. He worked hard creating it so that it was just the right size, the right proportion of the mast to the hull; and with just the right kind of fabric for the sail."

"The day came when he launched his little boat at the nearby lake. It was a very windy day when he set his little boat over into the water."

"And along came an angry wind that just pulled that little boat away from the shore and out into the middle of the lake where it was the deepest and the swiftest."

"But as much as he had loved his little creation; he knew he had to let it go. He was one sad little boy."

"As much as God loved the people He created, He had to let them go."

"Some months later the little boy was walking through town. As he passed a pawn shop, he looked into the window and there to his surprise was his little boat...none the worse for wear."

"He went bounding into the shop and exclaimed, half out of breath, 'Hey, mister, that is my boat in the window, I lost it in the lake when a mean old wind took it away."

"That may be so, son, but I paid a goodly price for that boat, and the only way you can get it back is to buy it."

"The little boy went home rapidly, shook out his piggy bank and ran back to the store and counted out every penny until he had satisfied the cost of the boat."

"And he was heard to say as he left the shop, "Little boat, you are twice mine; once because I made you and twice because I bought you."

"You see folks... that is the way it is with God. He created us, but by giving us a free will, we are swept away by the first wind of temptation, and we are lost to Him; but He sent His Son to pay the sacrifice to buy us back. Now, how can anybody not understand a love like that?"

"Let me tell you; it is no sin to be tempted. We are all tempted; even Jesus was tempted; by the devil himself. However, this here Holy Book says that we can never be tempted so much that if we trust God, He won't make a way out for us."

"When Jesus was tempted, He knew what He was going to do even before He was tempted. He knew that He would do the right thing no matter what. With each temptation, the ole devil made his offer more appealing and more tempting."

But Jesus just told him, "Get thee behind me, satan."

"Don't wait until you are staring into bald-faced temptation to decide what you will and won't do. Make up yor mind in advance which side of the fence you're gonna be on, and then it will be harder to climb over that fence and turn that temptation into sin."

"Now take Brother Jackson, over there, that illustration won't mean a thing to him." They laughed as Brother Jackson stroked his long beard.

Often when Papa thought he was losing the congregation's attention, or some seemed to be daydreaming, he would throw in a little humor to get a laugh and to get their minds back on the sermon.

"Now there were men in the life of Jesus, who said they would never leave Him, nor deny him, but they did. Peter, his friend, denied him... not once, but three times. Judas betrayed him to the authorities, and he was so filled with remorse that he took his own life."

"Temptation will come. You can't keep it away from yor door no more than you can keep birds from flying over yor head. But, you can shore keep them from building a nest in yor hair."

He continued with his sermon by saying, "Just before Jesus faced that brutal cross to hang there for our sins, He was tempted once more in the Garden. He had already been tempted greatly once before when satan promised Him the world. That old reprobate satan tried to tempt Jesus into jumping off the mountain so that angels could come and ketch Him before He fell."

"Just remember folks; no matter how hard and how steep the road to righteousness, it will always be better than the road that looks pretty good along the way; but ends over the cliffs to destruction. The fall will be mighty far down."

"There comes a time in every man or boy's life, when he has to take a stand… hard though it may be. He must decide between good and evil." After saying that, He looked directly into the face of his son, Billy Joe.

"Jesus knew He was to bridge the gap between sinful man and Holy God. He could not yield to temptation."

"Jesus prayed so hard that He was sweatn' blood drops from his forehead. He said to God the Father, 'Lord, take this cup from me if possible; but nevertheless, not My will but Thine.'"

"So as the good sister plays the organ and the good deacons pass around the bread and the cup; remember why we do this. It is to remember the Body of Christ, which was broken for us, and the Cup which represents the blood that Jesus shed so that we might have remission of sin."

"After we truly accept the work of Jesus on the cross, we will be saved from the wrath and damnation that is to come for those who do not believe and accept."

"Amen, thank you, Jesus!"

"Now just sit quietly and bow yor head and make yor peace with God confessing all yor known sin and asking God to forgive you. With no one looking around, heads bowed, and no one stirring around as the organist plays softly, search yor own soul. Don't be concerned about what you neighbor is doing, but take this time to get straight with God."

The organist softly played a familiar strain of music as the members obeyed their pastor.

Communion was a solemn celebration. It was the realization that a blood sacrifice had to be made for the forgiveness of sins. But God's people no longer had to offer the sacrificial lamb on an altar for the remissions of their sins; because Jesus offered up Himself. When the Son of God has given His life as a sacrifice, what else could be offered?

After he blessed first the bread and then the cup, he read from Matthew 26:29 the Words of Jesus, *"But I say to you, I will not drink of this fruit of the vine from now on until that day when I drink it new with you in My Father's kingdom."*

Herman told them that after the disciples had partaken of the Last Supper with Jesus, they sang a hymn and went out to the Mount Olives.

There He was betrayed and taken before the authorities who condemned Him to die.

They thought they were getting rid of Him, but they only ushered Him back into the Kingdom of God where He sits at the right hand of God waiting for the day when He will return for the redeemed.

"Let us pray."

"Dear Lord in the name of Jesus we pray. No matter how dark, the night, how low the finances, no matter how defeated we might feel... there is nothing that can separate us from Yor Love.

And Lord, just as you created Jesus with a purpose, you also created each of us for a reason. Hep us always to steady the course, and to make the right decisions, and to have the courage to make the right moves that we might always stay in Yor good Graces.

Hep us Lord, to acknowledge You in all our ways, and then we will know that we are on the right path...a path that is directed by You. Amen."

Reverend Alrod looked out at the beaming faces of his family and friends and encouraged them with these words.

"God never told us that this journey will be easy, but He did promise that He would never leave us nor forsake us. He will never let go of yor hand. Have you let go of His? If so, tell him about it and ask Him to extend His hand in yor direction one more time. He will."

It was the tradition after a communion service that the congregation would sing a song of praise to commemorate the significance and importance of the taking the Lord's Supper. There were tubs of warm water waiting alongside the outside walls with towels stacked by each one.

Pastor Alrod said, "Now if any of you have the notion, and the humble spirit, to wash the feet of someone else who is here today, you may do so. You are not obligated, but it is an act of love and obedience to do anything for each other that Jesus did for His disciples."

Then the congregation rose to sing, "*Redeemed—how I love to proclaim it. Redeemed by the blood of the Lamb; Redeemed through His infinite mercy, His child, and forever, I am. Redeemed, Redeemed, Redeemed by the blood of the Lamb; Redeemed, redeemed, His child, and forever, I am!*"

Chapter seventeen: The Election, a Girlfriend, and a Hawg

Billy Joe had moped around all week long. Both Mama and Papa knew what was ailing him, but they had decided this was a decision he had to make for himself. This was Friday. And come Monday there would be the election at the 4-H meeting to decide on the new officers for the following year. That had been a coveted position for Billy Joe ever since he joined the 4-H Club.

He saw it as a position of leadership, and the other kids had looked up to him since becoming the president two years before. Their group was small, but they were serious about what they were learning.

There was a 4-H Fair held every year where they could show off their accomplishments. The girls had worked hard quilting, sewing, and crocheting, and they were anxious to see who would be the winner this year. Then there was another group of young ladies that had chosen to enter their jellies, jams, and pickled goods in the 'Taste -O-Rama.' They were also hoping to win a blue ribbon.

Each 4-H'er had decided on a project that involved something they enjoyed doing and something that they were good at and could do their best.

Most of the boys had tended an animal of some sort during the year, and Billy Joe was the favorite to win this one with that huge sow of his. He had actually lied to his mother the week before when she asked him if he had named the hawg. Saying "no," seemed like a technically to him since Sylvester was a "she." And, he called her by a "he" name.

But he knew in his heart, it was a lie all the same.

At first she was just "dumb, or stupid ole hawg" to him. But as he tended her, he grew fond of her while all the time; knowing he had been told not to get too attached. He was told not to name her because the winner of the "big fat pig" contest would be given twenty-five whole dollars, but the pig would belong to Mr. Ferguson to be butchered and sold for pork chops in his general store.

So he figured if he named her a boy's name that would keep him from actually naming "her." But still he knew in his heart that a lie was a lie. And it was playing heavily on his mind that he had lied to his mother.

Billy Joe had started out with the runt. Mr. Ferguson had a sow with ump-teen piglets, and he furnished a pig to each child who wanted to enter the contest with the understanding that the biggest pig would win the prize money. But the full grown pig would have to be surrendered to the butcher's knife in exchange.

There had been four boys to choose a pig. Tender-hearted Billy Joe chose the runt. For the hard work of the non-winners, they each would receive ten dollars for their work; along with a year's teaching from one of the best hawg raisers in the area. They also benefited from the knowledge they had acquired.

They learned to care for these pigs when they were small and to watch for any kind of sickness or weight loss. They would learn how to care for them until they were grown, and then at the end of the year, each family had the option of trading the pig back in for the ten dollars, if they did not win the top prize. Or they could pay five dollars to Mr. Ferguson for the original piglet, and the hawg would belong to their family.

Everyone knew for sure that Billy Joe had this contest sewed up. "Sylvester" had grown far beyond his, and everyone else's, expectations. She would make a good breeding sow, or would provide a lot of bacon for the store. An agreement had been made. Each boy understood the rules, and they knew the biggest hawg would go back to Mr. Ferguson.

Now, accounting time was coming on Monday. And Billy Joe was faced with keeping his word. He had been taught not only by his father, the man; but also the preacher, that a man was only as good as his word. Whether a man kept his word or not signified what kind of man he was… or in Billy Joe's case …what kind of man he was becoming.

With that already on his mind, and the fact that John Roberts was moving in on his girl, he knew this city slicker wanted his position as president of the 4-H club as well. He was now also faced with having to give up Sylvester to the butcher's knife. He just could not bear the thought of her being slaughtered.

Billy Joe could not figure out which would be worse…losing his girlfriend, his pig, or his position. It seemed like a tall order for a boy; not quite a man.

Then there was that sermon that his Papa had done gone and preached; the one about Ananias and Sapphira where they fell down dead by lying to the disciples; and not keeping the pledge they had made to God. With all the verses in the Bible, why had his Papa done gone and picked that story… and at this particular time?

He wondered if in 1939 if God would do the same thing He did back in the Bible days. Would He actually strike somebody down dead for lying to Him? Well, that is one contest he did not want to enter.

He sure wished he knew what his Papa was going to preach on this Sunday just one day before the election. He was fearful of what was to come before the 4-H Fair. He was fearful that he might have to surrender Sylvester to the butcher's knife; possibly his girlfriend to John Roberts; and lose his position as president of the club.

The next Sunday evening after the meetin' time, each young person running for election had to stand before the congregation and give a speech as to why they should be elected to the four offices in the 4-H club.

It had been narrowed down to two candidates in each category… president, vice-president, secretary and treasurer. Billy Joe knew he would have to give a good speech if he hoped to change the minds of the kids; who were already spending their quarter promised to them by John Roberts. If John Roberts didn't win 100% of the vote, they would all lose the promised quarter, and he would tell some dreadful secret about one of the families.

Then Billy Joe thought that perhaps he should just give a bad speech, but that would surely disappoint his parents and his teacher. But just maybe… if he gave a bad speech, and he didn't win… then he wouldn't be president… and somehow he could save "Sylvester's" bacon.

And as far as his girlfriend was concerned, he had about decided if she was that fickle, then maybe he didn't want her as a girlfriend… after all. He just could not imagine his Mama treating his Papa that way.

They worked together like a good team of horses... each pulling their own weight, and not pulling in a different direction, making it hard on the other... both going in the same direction, sharing the load; and not making the other stumble and fall.

He certainly didn't want to end up with someone like the old banty hen and rooster in the yard. She was always clucking at the top of her clucker, and he was always crowing his head off at her. Those two were just like oil and vinegar or matches and kerosene.

When he married, he wanted a wife like his Mother. His parents went together just like turnip greens and cornbread.

⁓⊰⊱⁓

Sunday Meetin' Time

"We want to thank all of you for coming out tonight to share together the joy of praising and worshiping our living Savior, Jesus Christ." said Brother Ferguson.

"Preacher Alrod, ever in rare form, presented us with a true and good rendition of the scriptures; the choir sang to the wonderful playin' of our dedicated organist. If you were blessed by being in the meetin' here tonight and enjoyed sharing with one another, praying for each other and listening to the Word of God, then stand to yor feet and say "Amen."

He continued, "Please remain standing to stretch yor legs for a while, and we will then proceed with tonight's speeches from our 4-H'ers!"

"You know how hard these kids have worked all year and now is the time to give them some recognition. All rise and say, "Amen."

The little packed-out church rose to their feet and let out in unison a hearty, "Amen!" There were a few "Thank You Lord's" thrown in for good measure.

The folks stood, stretched their legs and turned around and began talking to their friends and neighbors as the excitement began to build in anticipation of the speeches made by their children.

The parents, above all, knew how hard their children had worked on their projects, and how hard it was for them to keep up and do what was right. There were no organized football games or other sports in this little country town. The 4-H Fair was a time for coming together to support their children's endeavors and to reward them for jobs well done.

They resumed their sitting positions and listened intently as their children came to the front and told what 4-H had meant to them, what their project had been, and why they were running for a particular office in the 4-H.

One by one, they came to the podium starting in reverse order of the offices; beginning with the office of treasurer. Two very bright youngsters told of their love for math; as well as their honesty that qualified them to handle the treasury collected.

The next two came forth in turn, two young girls, explaining their hopes of business school one day and their qualifications to serve as 4-H secretary.

And then came the two running for vice president. Each participant was warmly encouraged by the rounds of applause given by everyone; even though each parent was secretly pulling for their own just a little bit more.

Brother Ferguson, who was the 4-H sponsor for the town, said, "Now we come to the highlight of this program with the two young men vying for the office of President. They are Billy Joe Alrod and John Roberts."

"The president of this club has the responsibility of holding the group together and making sure all the national rules are carried out as well as the local ones. They are in charge of discipline and decorum as well. The order of speaking was decided by the drawing of straws. John Roberts drew the longest one... so he will go first."

There was an enthusiastic applause with most of the kids jumping up and clapping hard as they could; seeing that quarter in their hands already. They had polled their club once again before the meeting. Everyone was in accord, and the cry was, "Vote for John Roberts."

They approached this election not for what the candidates could contribute to the club and the community but for what John Roberts had promised to contribute to them personally. He had made other promises to them as well... as well as the threat.

John Roberts, wearing a new store bought suit and tie, approached the podium with surly confidence. He made a flowery speech about how he was going to change the way things were done in the club, how he was going to offer the club more entertainment and fun.

He said that he would put more emphasis on picnics, ball games, and make the club more exciting with less work for everyone. With each promise, the kids clapped all the harder. But the parents sat there in dismay as they turned to first look at their children and then at each other questioningly as if to say, "Where did this boy come from? What do we know about him? And what in the world does he think he's doing?"

Having finished his speech, John Roberts all but took a bow to the arousing applause of the other kids. He triumphantly walked from the podium with his arms held high in the air like a prize fighter who had just won a fight.

After the applause had died down, there was a kind of hush that fell over the congregation. Children looked up at their parents and saw their reaction by the expressions on their faces realizing that they had not approved.

Billy Joe, wearing his freshly ironed and starched overalls, slowly and even a little timidly, took his place behind the podium. He placed on the dais a paper with his notes.

He cleared his throat, looked out across the congregation and for a moment felt sick to his stomach. It had been a hard week. He had thought his brain out, prayed his heart out, and now here before all these people; his legs were shaking. He felt like he was about to pass out. He knew this was it. No backing down. He realized what he said could make a difference in whether or not he could continue to be president of the 4-H Club.

He cleared his throat again and said "Preacher Alrod, parents, and students, I come before you with no promises of anything other than serving this club as I have in the past. I bring honesty, integrity, and appreciation for the work of 4-H. I hope to bring back to the forefront the importance of 4-H; and what it teaches us about work and life."

"The 4-H Club was established in 1911 with the desire to help young'uns all across America; to educate them in ways to make farming and agriculture, not just for fun, but to be productive and meaningful. The premise of the club was to give young folks the opportunity to learn about new and innovative ways to increase farm production and to apply new ideas to rural life."

"Our club, though small by the standards of others, has contributed much to our town. Many new things have been learned by way of growing crops, caring for animals, and even safer ways to preserve and can the food we grow. The plan of 4-H is to grow people and not just crops. It is also to help us grow us into people who will contribute to our society and not merely figure out ways to take from it."

"I would like to remind you of what 4-H stands for and what it means not only to this little town, but to towns all across America. First of all, I would like for all the members of 4-H in every age group to stand and repeat our pledge which explains what the 4-H's mean to us."

All the kids eagerly stood ready to say their pledge and show out a little in front of their parents. With eyes forward they said in unison:

"I Pledge my Head to clearer thinking,
my Heart to greater loyalty,
my Hands to larger service,
and my Health to better living,
for my club, my community, my country, and my world."

The kids began their recitation with vigor but by the time they had said the first line, "My Head for clearer thinking... they began to think. And then that word "loyalty" stuck out at them like eyeballs on a toothpick. Hands to larger service made each of them glance down at their hands, and by the time they had said... health to better living, there was a noticeable lag in their excitement. Having finished their pledge, they plopped down in their seats.

Billy Joe said he would end his speech with a reminder of their motto, *"To Make the Best Better."*

He also reminded them that their challenge was *"Learning by doing."*

"I have put before you the purpose of 4-H, and the challenge before you to live up to these standards. And if that is not yor purpose for being a part of this club, then I will gladly step aside and resign not only from the election, but from the club as well; for it will have lost its purpose. And that is all I have to say about that, but I would like to add one other thing on another matter."

"Mr. Ferguson, I know that I stand a good chance of winning in the hawg raising contest for this year, and I am fully aware of the rules and promises that I made regarding the surrender of 'Sylvester'.

"And yes, Mama, I lied."

"I did name that ole stupid, dumb ole hawg like you done told me not too. I'm sorry that I fudged on the truth… but fudging is lying all the same. And because of that, perhaps I do not deserve to be the president of the club. But I do confess, repent, and ask forgiveness."

Mama smiled her forgiveness with that sweet Mama smile of hers. She knew he had searched his heart and made good decisions, and that made her proud.

"Now, Mr. Ferguson, let's get back to our agreement."

"One thing we have learned in 4-H is how the reproduction of farm animals is the lifeline of continuing success. I propose that, should I actually win the $25.00 prize that you keep that money."

The congregation hung on to every word that was to follow.

"Mr. Ferguson, I would like to propose to you as one businessman to another that there will be more profit for you if you let Sylvester live; actually I done changed her name to Sylvia since she is a she, and she stands to become the best breeding sow in this county."

"She started out as a runt with not much potential, but with I what I learned in 4-H, and from the teaching of the best hawg raiser in this county, Mr. Bud Tyler, I met the challenge of 4-H."

"I learned by doing."

"And I applied the motto to this little runt of making the 'best even better.' I am proud of my work with Sylvia and feel that she will be more valuable in producing offspring than making pork chops for dinner."

"I figure she will produce mighty fine litters, and I hereby offer to care for her at my own expense and give you the first two litters, and that should more than make up for her worth by not being divided up and sold in pieces."

Billy Joe started to take his seat. From a hush over the congregation, there came a big rousing applause most of it coming from the members of the 4-H Club.

Mr. Ferguson walked up to the podium with a grim look on his face and stood beside Billy Joe. He put his hands on his shoulders and looked him straight in the eyes and said, "Well, Billy Joe you make a fine offer; and we all know that a man's word is his bond. I have tried to think honestly and fairly about your proposal. But… I must say…"

Everyone was holding their breath, and Billy Joe was bracing for the next words as he knew that Mr. Ferguson was a man of integrity. Mr. Ferguson stretched out his hand to shake Billy Joe's hand and said…

"As a fellow businessman, Billy Joe, I accept your business offer. And as the leader of the 4-H club in this here town, I call for a vote right here now on the presidency of the club. The vote can take place tomorrow as usual for the other offices, and the new president can handle what was previously planned. Billy Joe had not settled his brain around what had just taken place, and now he was unexpectedly facing the vote right then and there. If knees made noise when they shook, his would have been rattling.

Mr. Ferguson said, "But now, I call now for a standing vote for this here election. Those members in favor of Billy Joe Alrod remaining president of this here 4-H club let yor vote be declared by rising to your feet which will count as a vote. Those who remain seated will count as a vote for John Roberts."

There was no movement among the 4-H'ers to stand. The church was still and silent. The fear was still looming in their thoughts about the threat from John Roberts to expose secrets about their parents.

It seemed that John Roberts had won by fraud and intimidation. But then suddenly one member rose quietly and turned and looked directly at John Roberts and said, "I don't care what secrets you know about our town. We know our town better than you do."

"We know that these are hard working families struggle every day to make marriages, farms, and our community work. And as far as the quarter you promised if you got 100% of the vote, well kids you might as well stand because I vote for Billy Joe, and you won't git yor quarter anyhow."

And at that, each and every one of the other members stood. What did they have to lose? Nothing...but everything to gain.

Billy Joe paid little attention to all those standing, but his eyes were riveted to that beautiful young lady who stood on his behalf. It looked like they could go together as good as cornbread and turnip greens.

A few days later, everyone had a great time at the 4-H Club Fair, and several of them won blue ribbons and advanced on to the next level in the competition.

Sylva, the hawg, did, in fact, win the contest as everyone had suspected. Even though, she was by far the biggest pig there, they had to make it legal; so each one had to be weighed.

Billy Joe was presented the blue ribbon, and his deal with Mr. Ferguson stood except he was told that she would be not eligible to enter the state contest. When Billy Joe asked, Mr. Ferguson, why not; he leaned over and whispered in his ear, "Because she is about to deliver her first litter of piglets."

Chapter eighteen: The Unexpected

"Well....Mama, you shore do look nice today. You headed out somewhere?"

"I been doin' some hard thinkin'on old Granny Wilson now for the past few days and was just wondering how she might be gettin'on. That sweet old lady is shorely missed by the folks at church; but especially the young'uns."

"You want I should go with you? That is a pretty long trek up to the mountain side, and with you carrying' that extry load," he said as he carefully patted the baby inside her bulky abdomen.

He was greatly concerned for her. He was a little awkward about hugging her this late in her pregnancy. So he endeared himself to her by gently patting the baby to come.

He was as anxious as Mama was that the baby be born soon and come into the world healthy. Her last trip to see Dr. McPherson eased their minds somewhat as he felt she was not having twins. He did not detect more than one heartbeat, but he told her they could not be sure until the day of the birth.

He also told them that Mama seemed to have come about with her blood being so low, and it was well within reason then. But Herman worried all the same. His lifetime companion had been the only love of his life, and he refused to even think of a day without her.

In answer to his question, she said, "No, I don't think so… it's just a nice healthy walk for me and it'll do me some good to git out away from all the young'uns for a while and stretch my legs, and smooth out my mind."

"Besides, I got myself some thinkin' to do, and the beauty of the fall leaves will give me joy to behold as I walk along. It won't be long now before they will all be gone. I can feel ole man winter just creepin' up on us bit by bit."

"All right, do like you want. I done been married to you long enough to know when you have set yor bonnet to do something that is just about what you will do."

"It seems like there is a nice day a comin.' However, there was a red sky this morning. And you know what that could mean."

Papa replied, "We can learn a lot about our world if we just take heed to what God's Word says."

Mama continued, "I seem to recall that Jesus said something about a red sky in the morning and night!" Papa said that the sailors had an old adage that said, "Red sky at night, sailor's delight. Red sky in morning, sailor's warning."

"Maybe I ought to preach on that someday. Here let me get out my little New Testament and see exactly what it says."

Papa reached up into his shirt pocket where he always kept a little New Testament; for he never knew when he would need the Scriptures for himself, in planning his next sermon, or helping some troubled soul. Often times right in the middle of plowing or other chores, he would get an urgent need to look up something in it.

Opening to the very first chapter in the New Testament, and turning a few pages, he ran his finger down the page until he came to the scripture. He read it out loud so Mama could hear it as well. He said, "Now remember this is Jesus speaking when He was being confronted by naysayers."

> *"He, answered and said unto them, when it is evening, ye*
> *say, it will be fair weather: for the sky is red. And in the*
> *morning, it will be foul weather today: for the sky is red*
> *and lowering. O ye hypocrites; ye can discern the face of*
> *the sky; but can ye not discern the signs of the times."*

"We are all a lot like that ain't we Mama? We look for what we want to see while overlooking what God wants us to see."

He closed up the little Bible just as Mama reached up and kissed him good-bye, saying, "It is one thing for sure, we need to be aware of the times, and every day, for we know not when the Lord will come back; or call us home."

Papa kissed her back and said, "We never know what a day will bring so we just have to trust and obey, and in our hearts, keep saying every day, *"This is the day, the Lord hath made, let us rejoice and be glad in it."*

Mama put on her sweater and replied, "Well, if I don't get going, this day will be most gone, and this may be the last time I get to see Granny for a while. Late autumn is surely upon us. With the baby coming along, and with the cold weather, it won't be too long before the last of the leaves fall from the trees. And I do so love this time of the year. It will probably be several months after the baby comes before I could get back up there to see Granny again."

Herman had a flashback to the day when Mama passed out and scared everyone to death. Although recovered, she seemed somewhat different this time around; not like she did when the other children were born.

Papa looked at her with concern and asked again, "Are you sure you are feelin' all right? You look a little pale. You think that young-en will be here afore Thanksgiving?"

"Well, that is another reason I am going to see Ole Granny. While not doing midwifery anymore, she still knows more about birthin' babies than anyone in these parts. I suppose she knows more about this kinda stuff than the doc does; being he never had any young'uns."

"You showing any signs of feelin' poorly?" Her concerned husband asked again.

"Oh, naw, it ain't time for the full moon. I've got a while yet."

"Anyway, I mostly want to check and see how's she's doin' since Earl died. You know they were married nigh on to 68 years?"

"There was a time when every time the church doors were open; you could depend on them being there... and I hear tell it was always that way even when their children were little ones. It seems such a shame that she done outlived both her children don't it?" said Herman.

And Mama chimed in, "And now her beloved husband, Earl is gone, too."

The day had started out to be beautiful. Mama took her own sweet time walking along the crooked path that wound up and around to

Granny's cabin. It was nestled at the foothills of the mountains that set way off in the distance from the church and the Alrod home.

It would only take Mama a couple of hours or so to reach the cabin using the old time-worn path rather than the road. Feeling closed in and feeling uncomfortable about the coming birth of her baby, she felt a long walk would help her both mentally and physically.

Thinking about the times when she was a young girl and still living with her parents, her mind went back to the times they would hike up the little mountain. They would pick blackberries and sometimes wade in the creek that trickled down from further up in the hills. The walk, up there along the path, had always been as much fun as getting there. Granny and Earl Wilson always greeted them as family and insisted they stay for supper.

It began to get a little cooler, and wind began to stir up a little more. Mama kept a close look at the beautiful blue sky above. She knew that the weather could change quickly when a storm came over and across the higher mountains.

The surrounding oaks, elms, hickory and cottonwoods still had a lot of their foliage. The leaves varied from tree to tree, and the colors were breathtaking against such a blue sky. They were bright and beautiful in bold colors of red, yellow, orange and the different shades of brown. They looked as if they had been dipped in the one of the young'uns paint boxes.

She thought to herself, "There is no artist like God for He knows just the perfect colors to put together; both in creation and in our lives."

As she walked up the hill enjoying God's handy-work, she thought to herself just how blessed she was to have such a big family, a husband who loved God, and her.

Thinking about each of her children from the oldest to the youngest, Mama said a special prayer for each of them that they would grow up to be like their Papa; strong, faithful, and dedicated to the things of God.

She also said a prayer for the little one soon to come. She had this nagging feeling for a few days that something was just not right. There wasn't particular any signs; just a gnawing inside... a foreboding.

Nearing the crest of the hill, Mama could see the smoke coming from Granny's chimney a few hundred yards before she got to her little log cabin. It had been built many years ago by this old couple; who were then so young... and so much in love.

Their love had carried them through many trials, and together with God, they had turned their sorrows into joys. Their daughter had caught the measles when she was about ten. They settled somewhere in her body and Granny did everything she knew how to get them to break out again. She had fixed a special herbal tea for her to drink, and kept her warm.

Granny knew when the measles "went in" on you; it could be dangerous; if you didn't get them to break out soon. She kept the windows covered to keep the bright light out of her eyes, and sat keeping by her bedside for days. However, when the pneumonia set in there was just nothing could be done. That sweet child went suddenly to the arms of Jesus and left behind a sorrowing Mama, Papa, and big brother, Pete.

Mama was getting a little winded as she turned the bend in the road where the path meandered around the Wilson family graveyard. Glancing over in that direction, she could see the recently dug grave of Granny's husband Earl. The ground had not healed even though it had been several months since he died.

Granny Wilson had already grieved over two more graves there. Buried beside her beloved husband were her two children; one grave belonging to her little daughter and the other her son. Her only son, Pete, was one of the first soldiers to leave the mountain during the World War. The draft of 1917 included those 18 years old and older.

Peter George Wilson was anxious to go. However, he could have been deferred since he was the only male Wilson child to carry on the name. He made a joke that it was his duty to go and support President Wilson. He said, "After all, he might be kinfolk." They had no claim to that, but it seemed right to young Peter.

He was young and filled with all sorts of romance about being a soldier, and he wanted to see something besides the mountain. So off he went to war with a big fanfare from the village. President Woodrow Wilson and Congress had tried to remain neutral at the beginning of the war in 1914, but then almost overnight on April 17, 1917, America had been brought into it.

Germany continued to sink merchant ships traveling to England. And since England was one of America's closest trading partners, America became more and more sympathetic toward the war.

After the sinking of the Lusitania, a British ocean liner, killing over a thousand people, including 128 Americans in 1915, America broke off diplomatic relations with Germany.

Four more US ships were sunk by Germany and tensions grew stronger; finally America declared war against Germany.

The sentiment of Americans began to change about the war; although, in the beginning, most were against it. But the country gradually became more favorable. The British had intercepted a message from Germany intended for Mexico. Afraid America would enter the war; Germany offered Mexico lands in America if they would invade the United States.

There had been disputes and continued conflict between Mexico and America after the massacre at the Alamo when the Mexican province of Texas broke its ties to Mexico and eventually joined the United States of America.

In the message, Germany promised to return all of the territories that Mexico had lost to the United States. That built a fire underneath American citizens, and President Woodrow Wilson had little choice, but to declare war against Germany.

Young Pete Wilson had just turned twenty-three and was required to register for the draft. He was eager to go, and make his mark on the world. He could hardly wait to see the ocean and lands so far away.

The Battle of Cantigny fought on May 28, 1918 was the first American offensive of World War I. There were fierce battles between the American forces and the German army. While winning the battle, American casualties were high.

The Wilson's were told their son had died valiantly during that battle defending the world against the tyranny of German aggression. At first, he was reported as missing in action, but later they were notified that he was presumed dead and buried somewhere in Cantigny, France.

Thousands of families requested that the bodies of their loved ones, who died in that war, be brought home by ship. The war ended in 1918, but it was as late as 1921 before the first bodies were returned to America.

Those who were unidentified were presumed to be buried near where they fell or in an unmarked grave somewhere over there.

All the Wilson's had to show for the soldier they had loved and raised was a photo of him in his uniform, a telegram, a *Victory Medal* and a *Silver Star*. The *Victory Medal* was sent to them several years later after the notification of his death. It was designed after the war had ended and was presented to all men who served. The *Silver Star* was presented to those who served gallantly in the Army. It was pinned on the suspension ribbon which also held the *Victory Medal*.

Little comfort for their loss; but cherished none-the-less.

Granny Wilson and her husband Earl had gone to the city with Pete to see him off on the train. Pete began to have second thoughts when he saw what a brave front his parents were displaying. But those tiny tears that made their eyes glisten were a dead giveaway. Those forced smiles broke his heart, and on the ship all the way across the ocean to France, Pete could not get those faces out of his mind. Little did he know that would be the last time he would see them.

His father's explanation for the tears in his eyes haunted him remembering the last time he had seen his Dad. Earl Wilson, Pete's Papa, wiping away a tear said, "Must be some of that train smoke got in my eyes."

Pete and his Mama knew different. Just at that moment, Pete realized he had only been thinking about himself; and not them. Then he realized just how much he would miss them. None of the three realized that would be the last time that they would be together.

They did not know it then, but they later learned he was headed for France and training. They waited months without ever hearing from him. A few cherished letters came to them months after they had been written, and they were sparse in words, and they never really knew where he was.

Finally, unbeknown to them, the last letter arrived, and he told them how much he loved them and wished that he had not left them. He said that no matter what happened, he would one day see them again. They never heard from him again.

Months later, they received a letter from the US Army in the mail telling them that their son was missing and presumed dead. They were told that after a fierce battle, many young men had died and were now buried scattered all across the Western Front.

Many times fallen soldiers would be buried on the very battlefield where they were slain, and makeshift markers would be erected, and then later other battles would take place there, and the graves and markers would be trampled underneath the soil and mud.

While they could not say definitely where he was buried, they presumed he would have been buried with the rest of those lost in his regiment. Because some of the soldier's bodies were so mangled, they could not all be undeniably identified.

Grief stricken and no way to say goodbye to their son, they decided to have a memorial service at the little church on the hill. They even placed a tombstone at the head of an empty grave beside his little sister there in the family graveyard on the mountain.

Instead of Pete's body being buried in the pine box, they put in his fishing rod, his old hunting boots, a special plaid flannel shirt he had often worn. His Mama told those at the funeral that it had always been what he called his "lucky shirt" because once when he was wearing it he caught twenty-five huge catfish in one short afternoon.

That grieving mother drew the shirt up close to her face knowing it was the last thing he had worn at home. He had gone fishing with his Dad on that last day before leaving for the military, and she never laundered it.

A few of her tears went into that coffin along with the shirt. Granny sometimes regretted having buried the shirt, but she had to put something in there of him.

Sometimes when she would be thinking of him, her thoughts always came back to his shirt; Earl would try to comfort her when she would say, "If only he had been wearing it that day."

The agony of their hearts was that they did not know how or when he died, and if he had suffered before dying. These thoughts tormented them. Finally, they decided that the only way to turn it completely over to God was to have a burial service for him there on the mountain. It only helped a little.

Now there were three graves in the little family cemetery; for alongside the graves of his children, Deacon Earl Wilson was laid to rest there as well. Granny Wilson took care that not a single weed would grow on those graves, and she planted rose bushes and other flowers that would bloom most all of the year. Even though, she never had any grandchildren of her own, she was lovingly called, "Granny" by everyone who knew and loved her. She was "Granny" to a lot of adults as well as the children.

Granny Wilson was left alone to provide and "make do," for herself.

Granny Wilson was a rather large woman; strong and big boned. She had the strength of most men she knew. She worked alongside her husband on their little mountain-side home. She cut wood, brought water from the creek; and served for many years as a midwife to many of the women before they had a real doctor come to the mountain. She had delivered two of the Alrod children, Billy Joe and Sarah Louise.

As Mama approached the old sagging porch to the cabin, she felt a little bit of a twinge in her side. She stopped for a minute and took a deep breath and kept going toward Granny's closed door. The temperature had dropped considerably from when she first started up the mountain.

Mama felt a kind of chill run down her back. She should have worn a thicker sweater. Actually the one she was wearing was not hers at all; but Herman's. She had far outgrown the two that she had.

Approaching the doorstep, "Ole Rusty," Granny's hound, raised his head, twitched his ears back and forth in every direction, and then put his head back down on his paws to finish his nap. He must have figured she was safe enough.

Mama walked across the creaky old porch and gently knocked on the door. She waited. She knocked again, and there still was no answer. She began to feel a little frightened when she called out, "Granny, oh Granny; yoo-hoo, are you in the house?"

No answer. Her initial minor fright was now a full blown big fear. Stepping over the old hound dog, she went to the end of the porch and leaned over to see if Granny was anywhere near the house outside. There was no sign of her.

Concerned, and now with that little twinge bothering her again somewhat, she knew she had to find Granny. She would not have left her cabin with a fire in the fireplace and fresh laundry on the line blowing in the late autumn breeze.

The twinge became a little harder; she knew this was not a contraction, but it was unnerving anyway. However, she pulled Granny's old rocking chair around to sit down for a minute or two. The walk had taken more of her than she realized.

In so doing, she unintentionally rocked over the tail of the old sleeping hound. He was sleeping no more. He let out a howl that would wake the dead. Mama could not bend over too much because of her girth and the pain in her side. But she tried to reach down to comfort the ole hound. He wanted no part of her. He shot up and ran down the steps and underneath the house.

Hearing the painful howl of her old yard dog Rusty, Granny scooped up her herb basket and headed out of the woods and down the path…past the outhouse…to her little cabin. There was no need for her to try and hurry; for at age eighty-five, there was no hurry left in her.

Meanwhile, Papa back home was getting worried. The late afternoon rolled on, and the wind began to pick up, and the temperature began to drop suddenly. There was a fine misty and icy rain falling. And there was no sign of Mama coming back down the road from Granny's up on the mountain. He wondered what had been keeping her so long.

Feeling that something must be wrong, as Mama would never have stayed away that long, Herman rounded up the kids and instructed the older ones to keep track of the younger ones by feeding them and putting them to bed on time.

He went out across the sandy front yard and climbed into his old 1930 four-door Chevrolet Sedan. He had bought it secondhand in 1938, and he had already had it for a year.

But in inclement weather, and on trips to the city, it was a must. Papa was fortunate that the blacksmith in town had converted a portion of his place into a mechanic shop. He had kept the old nine-year-old car running over the past several years for the previous owner, and several times Papa had depended on him to replace parts. It was still a good running car… well most of the time. It was not often used around town; since it was walking distance.

But this was not one of those times. He got in behind the wheel and turned the switch…RRRRR… nothing. He tried it again RRRRRR… nothing. It would not start.

Worrying was not something a country preacher, who preached reliance on God, should have been doing, but he was beginning to falter when with one more turn of the switch, it whirled a little and then started. As he turned the car around, he saw all the children standing at the back door in the middle of the porch. They had not learned the rule, "Thou shalt not worry" too good either. It showed in the face of every one of them.

On the way to Granny's place, the sun was going down, and it became quite cloudy: like it was coming up a storm. He turned the lights on. Another mile or so, it began to drizzle, and the temperature began to drop rapidly.

All of a sudden the old engine began making a sputtering sound and then ended in total silence. The old Chevy had stopped about halfway to Granny's place.

If ever Papa needed the light of the full moon Mama had been talking about, it was now, but it was nowhere to be found.

Try as he might, there was no getting that car to start again. Papa got out and opened up the hood and looked around the engine and saw nothing he could fix or repair. The wind was beginning to pick up, and it was cold.

Exasperated, Papa crawled back underneath the wheel and slammed the door behind him. When he jarred the car from the door slamming, it made the needle on the fuel gage bounce. He took another look and when the needle settled back down it landed on the empty side.

He felt sick to his stomach for having not remembered siphoning gas out of the car to share with a church member who had given out of gas just as he drove up into the churchyard last Wednesday night. He had only left enough in the tank to get to the gas station in town. And he had not been back to town since then.

Earlier that afternoon, Mama and Granny had gone into the house after they nearly frightened each other to death as Granny came around the corner of the cabin. She had a hoe raised over her head in her bony hands. Even at eighty-five, she was ready to do battle to protect her hound and her home.

Later, Granny and Mama sat in front of the fire in the cabin and talked about the good ole days, their children, their husbands, and their lives. During all that time, Mama kept shifting in her chair to find an additional measure of comfort.

Granny asked her several times if she were okay, and she said she was. Secretly, she thought she had probably taken on a little too much with such a long walk. She wished she had listened to Herman.

After a short visit, Mama rose to leave and bent down to give Granny a big hug, and then it hit her right square in the back; her first labor pain. When she grabbed her back and then held her stomach up in the front, Granny knew. And Mama knew.

After five births, and delivering six children, there was no doubt in Mama's mind that her seventh was soon about to greet the world. But what to do?

It was too far to walk back down the hill, and Granny had never owned an automobile. She only had Brutus... her old blue nose mule, who in mule years was as old as she. To try and take Mama back down the side of the mountain on the back of Ole Brutus, it would have been a contest between her and Brutus as to who succumbed first. And, besides to do that would be foolhardy.

The fine rain was turning into snowflakes, and there was no way Granny could have ever gone for help.

Mama thought of a scripture that said folks should be thankful in all things and felt blessed that Granny had delivered many babies in her time. With the help of her husband, Earl, Granny had delivered her own two children there in that cabin

Mama trusted Granny because she had also delivered her first two babies, but that had been years ago. At Earl's funeral, Mama had noticed a big change in Granny since she had seen her the last time. Earl had been ill for quite a long time, and there was no one to help her. Granny looked as if she was just plumb worn out.

And now in this situation, it was hopeless to expect anyone from the outside to help way up there on the side of the mountain. There were no neighbors in hollering distance, much less in walking distance.

Up in the mountains, when the sun sets, the darkness quickly takes over. It was, as they say, "dark as night." The snowflakes began to increase, and the wind was howling; you could hear it making creaking noises about the cabin, but inside it was snug and warm.

Mama told Granny to not worry that Herman would see she had not returned, and he would be along shortly, and he could drive her right into town to the doctor's house. Mama continued to sit in one of Granny's old rockers, and they resumed their conversation as if nothing was going on. Granny put pillow to Mama's back and propped her feet up on a little footstool.

Trying to keep her wits about her by making conversation, Mama asked, "Granny, how have you been doing since Earl died? I know you must be lonely without him."

"I won't lie… don't take to lying… won't say it's been easy…'cause it ain't been easy. Losing Earl was like losing part of myself. He was my very soul. Him and me… well, we wuz partners in everything we ever did. I did what he couldn't, and he did what I couldn't, and between the two of us, we got it done; whatever it was."

"Losing my little girl… and then losing Pete…" Granny's voice began to tremble as she continued, "Now mind you, we wuz mighty proud of that young man… but he was so terribly young. We could've stopped him from joining up, but he said they'd draft him…come and get him anyway… so he thought he would just go ahead and join up and…"

"Ow," Mama said as she nearly rose up in the chair. She leaned backward holding her belly, and said, "Go on… I'm listening… that was a good one."

Granny picked up where she left off … "But losing Earl was different somehow. We had been married so long it was like sometimes I would forget where I left off, and he began. I was just seventeen when we married, and he was barely twenty-one and… …"

"Ow," came from the direction of Mama once again, and this time she did stand up.

Granny went into her little back room and turned down the covers on her bed. She reached up into a cabinet and took down some old blankets. She took a stack of old newspapers and wrapped them in a clean sheet to be used on as a pad to protect the mattress.

Returning to the front room, she tried the best she could to help Mama up. She had already sat back down in the chair. Mama unable to speak waved her off and struggled to get up on her own. Granny held Mama by her sides and helped her into the back room to the bed.

At home, Billy Joe and Sarah Louise had followed their father's instructions. There was leftover cornbread in the pie safe... a pot of beans on the stove that Mama had started early that morning in her black iron cooking pot. There was fresh buttermilk.

They fed the twins and LeRoy. They made sure they washed the bottoms of their feet. And after one or two tries, they got them to stay in the bed. They took turns telling Bible stories and singing hymns together; until they were finally asleep. Sarah Louise had rocked Baby James until he was out like a light.

But asleep, Papa was not. He was stranded on the road with the storm approaching closer by the hour.

Figuring the night was too dark, and since he had no idea how far he was from Granny's cabin, he decided to stay in the car. He figured getting lost in the dark of those mountains would not do anyone any good.

Trusting in God that Mama had not left Granny's cabin, he curled up in the front seat of his old Chevy with no blanket for his cover, shivering in the cold, in the dead darkness of the night. He knew that God would take care of them all, and he said this prayer to his Almighty God.

"Lord... it is me Herman. I know that You done said that You would never leave us nor forsake us, and that You know every time a little sparrow falls to the ground. You know when the wind blows in from the east or down from the north. You know all the stars in the sky and You know the predicament that we find ourselves in tonight. Lord, they just ain't nothin' that takes You by surprise. Nothin' is unexpected with You. Amen"

He would adjust his sitting position behind the wheel to try and lay back a little. When one position didn't work, he'd try another. Finally, he opened the door, stepped out on the running board, and got out. He crawled into the back seat. He kept trying to get comfortable. By then it was bitter cold.

As the darkness totally engulfed the area, it became even colder. He could hear the wind tearing through the woods. He was hoping none of the trees fell on him and the car.

He had thought to bring along a lightweight jacket, but surely wished he had brought a heavier one. Then like a sign from heaven, he remembered there were some old burlap croker sacks lying in the floor board. He wrapped them tightly around his body, tucking them in everywhere to shut out the air holes.

"Lord, I'm praying in faith… for it is faith that moves mountains. I am praying that Mama is still at the top of this here little mountain safe with Granny. Then the thought hit him…and he said, "Oh, Lord, please don't let Granny be sick."

Then he prayed that the children were tucked in bed fast asleep. "Lord, I don't ask for sleep for myself… but Yor protection through the night until I can see the first peek of that ole sun coming up."

Papa knew then it would be hard to put one foot in front of the other climbing up the rest of the way up the mountain in the mud, but he didn't know just how hard it would be.

He went back to praying, "I am thanking You in advance, Lord I'll be giving you some of yor Words right back; not that You forgot nary one of them; but that I need to hear them agin my ownself."

"When thou liest down, thou shalt not be afraid: yea,
thou shalt lie down, and thy sleep shall be sweet."
"I laid me down and slept; I awaked; for the Lord sustained me."
"I will both lay me down in peace, and sleep: for thou,
Lord, only makest me dwell in safety."

Then Herman prayed, "Now Lord, I claim all of these Your Words for all my family; and for Granny, too." The dark of the night prevented Papa from seeing anything; not even the inside of the car.

But he could hear the wind getting stronger and unbeknown to him even though it was early yet, this was the first freezing rain and snowflakes of the season. It soon blanketed the earth like the fluffy egg meringue on one of Mama's fresh baked chocolate pies.

Chapter nineteen: A Time to Be
Born and a Time to Die

Choking back tears, Pastor Alrod raised his Bible to read and said, "Today the church has gathered by this graveside for a most solemn occasion and our hearts are filled with much sorrow. While we mourn the loss of this dear one... we know that to be absent in the body is to be present with the Lord."

With shaking shoulders, he stifled a cry into his handkerchief. He began again. "A life lived long or short... is a life that has meaning and purpose. There are those who come into this life like a soft breeze against our cheek, and then they are gone. They are budded on earth to bloom in heaven, and they know no sin."

"And then there are those who come to this earth and give themselves for others as in war... and those who live long and fruitful lives serving family and others; all have a reason and a purpose."

"As we lay this dear one to rest, we come away from our thoughts of other things to share a sad and mournful time. But we know Who we have believed, and we know that this life is not a destination but a journey. And for this precious one the journey has ended."

There were sniffles heard from those standing around the open grave. The preacher went on, "She was a dutiful mother, a loving and caring wife. She loved her children with an undying love, and she cared for them diligently; as she did for so many here in this community."

"She will be missed for a while on this earth, but would never purposely leave her new dwelling; which is with Christ Jesus. She is not gone... but gone before. There is no way to preach the funeral of such a fine lady. Her life preached her own sermon. Let us pray."

The little congregation huddled a little closer together against the harsh, blowing wind; the icy rain and snow began to fall once again. These were folks whose hearts were heavy at the loss of this kind and wonderful lady who was a pillar of the community; and one so devoted to all who knew her. Those who loved her just could not believe she was gone.

They also felt a tug in their hearts for Preacher Alrod as he stood with shoulders back and head held high as he read from the Holy Bible. He shifted his weight from his broken leg with the cast to the other one making it hard for him to stand, even though leaning against one of his crutches.

There was a soft cry of a newborn baby wrapped tight in swaddling clothes and covered with a newly crocheted afghan made by the very hands of the one they were eulogizing. There was a brief pause in the sermon, and they all turned and looked in the direction of the new infant. They smiled at Sarah Louise. She was holding the infant close to her as if it was her very own.

❧❦❧

Could it have only been three days ago when Mama decided to pay a visit to Granny Wilson? She told Herman she just wanted to go for a walk and get away for a while. She wanted to enjoy the colorful panorama of God's world; so beautifully painted with the colors of fall. She knew it would be her time before long, and had felt a little uneasy about how she carried this seventh child.

Thanksgiving was right around the corner, and she would have a lot to do so that her family would have their traditional Thanksgiving Dinner. However, she needed the advice of another woman. Both her mother and mother-in-law had already passed from this world.

Hoping the long walk up the mountain would help to clear her mind and perhaps change the position of the baby, all too soon it made her realize that it had not a good decision to make. There was another reason for her trip as well. That was to check on Granny, who had not long before lost her husband of sixty-eight years.

She had passed the graves of Granny's husband, and her two children...a girl child who died way too early with the measles; and a

283

young son killed in service for his country. His body was not really there because he was buried in some foreign land, but Granny and her husband had made a place for him in their family cemetery. They wanted a place where they could come to pray and to honor him; a place to put flowers there on his birthday and holidays.

Mama began to have signs before she got to Granny's place, but thought it just a twinge from all the walking. But it was much more… much more to come. Not long after she reached the cabin, the labor pains began in earnest. She knew she would not be able to make it back down the hill, and Granny did not have an automobile.

But she rested assured that Herman would crank up the old '30 model Chevy sedan and would be fast on his way to fetch her.

Herman had indeed started on the journey; leaving the other six children behind. They had been raised to take responsibility. He trusted that the two older ones, Billy Joe and Sarah Louise, would take care of the other four.

And, now all seven children stood around the newly opened grave like little wooden soldiers standing at attention, listening to every word their father was saying.

⚜

Granny built a fire in the fireplace and put more logs in the wood stove. She wanted to make sure the coming storm would not find her too busy delivering the baby to keep the house warm.

Several pots were put on the stove and the water boiled. One of the boiling pots contained a pair of scissors and a length of twine. She opened a little handmade cabinet which stood next to the fireplace and took down some antiseptic. White strips of cloth, that had once been a bed sheet, were gathered together as well. Just about then Granny remembered her fresh laundry still on the clothes line. The clean towels would be needed as well.

Already sweating from the heat in the room and moving around so quickly, she hurriedly took her eighty-five-year-old body out into the cold to bring in the laundry. It had begun to snow.

Mama's pain was increasing, and knowing what was coming, Granny knew she had to be prepared. When she examined Mama, as she had for so many other patients during her midwife years, she realized that the baby was breech. This worried her greatly; but she tried not to worry Mama... so she did not immediately tell her.

Mama had delivered five other times... once with twins. However, she knew that something had been wrong for days. As the pain grew worse, she was trying to listen to everything that Granny told her, but it was hard to hear over her own screams.

It had been some time since Granny Wilson had delivered a baby, but she hadn't forgotten the skills she had learned over the years. She knew that the baby would have to be turned. She knew that, even though the baby was small, a natural birth might be impossible unless she could turn the child. She also knew without anesthesia, Mama would not survive if she took the baby directly from her belly.

She had assisted in such a procedure years ago with a doctor on hand. However, the circumstances were better than in her little dimly lit cabin. Not to mention there was a howling storm beginning to brew. She was also without the correct tools and medications. She knew the only way, for both mother and child to survive, would be for her to turn the child physically; while trying not to get the cord around its neck.

⚜

Several hours had passed. The snow had completely covered the windshield of the old stalled auto. Herman was alternating his worries with prayers for both Mama and the children.

He hoped the children had built up a good strong fire in the fireplace and remembered to keep the wood stove burning. Then his mind would drift off to the "What if's."

"What if they caught the house on fire?"

"What if Mama was having the baby?"

"What if he froze to death sitting there in the car?"

He had never seen such a snowstorm so early in the year. Not only was it snowing, but it was sleeting. The wind was howling as it whipped around his disabled car sitting there on a cold and lonely road. Nightfall had caught him, and he thought it best to stay in the car until daylight.

He prayed, he quoted scripture, and he sang some of the old hymns of comfort. He did everything to keep his body warm and his mind clear. He thought of the many sermons he had taught about not worrying. He reminded himself how Jesus even saw a little sparrow as it fell to the ground. He reminded himself of how God said *"I will never leave you nor forsake you!"* How well Herman knew that to be true.

That was good for his preacher side, but for his husband and father side; he would slip back into worry again. He would tell himself that it was not really worry...which he knew was a sin; but that he was only concerned. But as the hours rolled on, the "sinning part" began to win.

Billy Joe and Sarah Louse had gotten the children fed and tucked into bed, but they tried not to allow sleep to close their eyes. They sat at the kitchen table, keeping watch on the fires, and prayed for their parents, and their yet to be born sibling.

They often fought with each other about trivial things like brothers and sisters often do. But this was no time for conflict... but cooperation. Several times they bowed their heads and asked God's protection on them all.

The morning light shining through the kitchen window found them both with their heads down on the table when unintentional sleep had crept up on them. That same sun showing through Herman's car windows was like a glorious light reflecting through the ice crystals frozen to the windshield and side windows.

The daylight was so bright, it hurt Herman's eyes, and he thought about Paul on the Damascus Road and how God had blinded him to get his attention. Sitting up and stretching his muscles, he dreaded stepping outside the car knowing what a long, cold walk laid ahead; not knowing what he would find at the end of it.

He tried several times in vain to get the motor to turn again, but to no avail. He had only one choice now that he could see the road...walking. He would not expect anyone to be coming up the mountain that early in the morning even on a good day. His one thought was that perhaps if Granny had any mail, the postman might venture up there later in the day.

But he felt such urgency and could not take the chance of waiting any longer. Oh, how he prayed that Mama had not started walking back down the path and got caught somewhere in the woods in the storm. He prayed all the harder for both her and their unborn child as he made his way up the slippery, icy road.

The wind was still blowing, but the snow and sleet had stopped for the time being. With this first snow, the ground was still somewhat warm and each time he put his foot down in front of him, he made another track in the mud.

He slowly made it around the bend where he could see three mounds covered in snow with grave markers rising from underneath.

He paused for a second to catch his breath as the cold air stung his lungs. He looked at the burial site and fleetingly gave reverence to the scene. While looking over in that direction, his foot stepped on a stone underneath the thin layer of snow. He turned his ankle and down he went face first into the icy covering cutting a gash in his ankle.

Pushing up the best, he could with the mud shifting underneath his hands, he had almost made it to a standing position when he slipped and fell again. This time he heard a distinct crack; like that of someone stepping on a twig. He knew he had broken his leg.

❦

The little cabin was picturesque… a little brown log building… with a light snow covering on the roof and a thin trail of dark gray smoke swirling in the air against a cerulean blue sky. It was a tranquil site; one that reminded him of a *Norman Rockwell* painting on the front cover of the *Saturday Evening Post*. But looks can be deceiving.

It was anything but tranquil inside. Mama had grown weaker, and she could no longer push. Granny had tried several times unsuccessfully to turn the infant. Once, a whole foot and leg had emerged. She had managed to turn it enough to replace them back inside of Mama. Exhausted from the labor… both hers and Mama's… Granny began to feel weak and fatigued herself.

Her friend, who was also her pastor's wife, had walked all the way up that mountain to seek her help. And she could not let her down. Finally, when it seemed she had done all that could be done, she rubbed her aching left arm and knelt down on the cold plank floor at the foot of

Mama's bed and petitioned the aid of the Great Physician. She was going to try and pull the baby out.

She prayed, "Lord, this here is Granny Wilson. I ain't asked you for much since you took my man from me. I have just been content to sit and wait until you brought me along as well. I am old, and I am tired and I have lived my span of days, but this young mother has a passel of children to raise, and this one which she is trying to bear is already givin' her grief, and it ain't even here yet."

"Lord, if it be Yor will, and I ain't sayin' what that might be... could you just look a little kindly down here on earth this mornin' and hep us all out a little bit. Lord. I don't have to be tellin' you nothin' cause You got all-seeing eyes, and the all-knowing heart and all the power of the universe."

"Could You just please release a little power toward this here place and hep us out a little. Lord, I know You know the situation, so I won't be botherin' You anymore. But Lord You done promised You ain't ever going to leave me hepless, but what You would send Yor angels... if need be. Lord we only need just one...one that knows about birthing babies. Good mornin' to You Lord, and I'll be thankin' You beforehand. Amen"

A knock came so loud at the door; it startled Granny. She struggled to get up from the old plank floor. The pattern of wood grain was imprinted into the flesh of her knees. She could barely pull herself up.

She ambled through the door to the kitchen to make her way to the front door. She didn't bother to ask who it was; because she knew it was her angel straight from God.

At first she flinched to see such a thing standing in her doorway. It had a human form but was covered from head to toe in red mud; half frozen, and hardly able to utter a word.

It hobbled into the room and past her to the fire that was growing low to embers. She immediately lifted a chair to put under this creature, just as his legs began to give way. She threw a shawl over her bony shoulders and went out onto the porch to bring more wood inside for the fire. She chunked the wood on the fire and immediately began to tend to this "mud man."

Finally, thawed enough to speak, Herman asked if Mama were still there. She was. He shook his head in approval and relief.

Granny began to help him out of his mud covered outer coat and started to help him with his boots, and when she pulled on one, he let out a holler. His foot was so swollen the boot would not turn loose. She knew she had to help him because she needed him to help her.

From her kneeling position in front of him, she looked up, and she said, "Broken?" He nodded, "Yes." She took a sharp kitchen knife and struggled to cut the leather from the side of his boot so she could pull it off.

The gash in his ankle had bled a lot, but thanks to the cold weather, it had stopped until she took the boot off. She grabbed some kerosene from nearby the fireplace, and hastily poured it over his foot; and wrapped it tightly with a piece of white cloth.

A broken leg, gashed ankle, and frostbite were not very good for the circulation. She had to take the time to do it; even though she heard Mama moaning once again.

She grabbed another afghan from the back of the rocker and threw it around his knees and rushed toward the bedroom. Granny felt a little dizzy. She stopped for a moment to catch her breath and to steady herself. She looked toward the ceiling and said, "Lord, if this is an angel, please don't send the devil."

Finding little change in Mama's appearance, white to pale... sweating...barely conscious, she leaned down and told Mama, "With the help of God, I might be able to save one of you; you or the baby. Do you hear me?"

She gently shook Mama's shoulders and got her to look up at her. Mama nodded her head that she understood.

"Now the hard part," asked Granny, "which is it going to be?"

Mama whispered so low that Granny had to bend way over to hear her. She faintly heard her say "ba-by."

Granny knew that an incision would give the baby room to be born, but it would cause Mama to bleed to death. She just felt there had to be another way. This time without getting on her knees, she cried out to God. She looked around at Mama; she was unconscious. She had to act now. Whatever she was to do, she had to do it now when Mama would be feeling no pain.

Herman made his way to the bedroom door and asked "What's wrong?"

"Ain't got time to tell you... just come in here and do like I say."

He obeyed her like a little child. Hobbling to the foot of the bed, he asked, "What do I do?"

Granny said, "When I get up here and straddle across her, you get a hold of that baby's foot and pull with all your might."

Granny crawled up on the bed and straddled across Mama facing Herman at the foot of the bed. She started pushing against Mama's stomach with all her might, and she told Herman, "Pull!"

Herman had pulled many a calf from its mother, and he got the idea quickly. He pulled hard and Granny pushed so hard guiding the baby with each push... Herman fell backward on the floor with a tiny, but healthy baby boy, landing right on top of him.

Granny immediately ran around to see what damage had been done to Mama. Surprisingly enough, there was little outside visible damage, but she had no way of knowing what was happening on the inside.

She hesitated for a moment when she heard the familiar cry of a newborn infant. She looked up toward the ceiling; and said, "God forgive me. I won't ever distrust Yor choice of angels agin."

She looked at Herman and said, "Get up from there and take that baby in by the fire." She had to go over and pull him up while he barely held on to the baby.

"There is a little afghan on the side table, wrap him up in it, and hold him close to you to keep him warm while I see what I can do for its Mama."

Mama's breathing was very shallow. Granny raised Mama up in the bed while experiencing some pain of her own in that left arm again. She hoped that Mama would not come to until she had stopped the bleeding, but she had to get air into her.

She pushed gently on her chest, and Mama took a big gulp of air in and she seemed to be breathing better... but for how long? She propped her up higher with the pillows. Then she took a straight chair that had been sitting by the bed, and turned it up upside down with the legs toward the foot of the bed and raised Mama's feet high above her heart.

For what seemed like hours... Granny worked with Mama to stop the hemorrhaging; finally it slowed. Granny continued to wipe the sweat from her own brow, even though, the room was growing colder by the hour.

Mama began to moan a little and Granny wiped her head with a wet cloth. It was late afternoon. The fire had died down once again, and the cold cabin was eerily quiet. It was if there was no one inside.

Herman had managed to take the eyedropper Granny had given him, and he sat by the fire slowing dripping sugar water drop by drop into the little sucking mouth of his newborn son. When Granny last checked, they both were asleep; baby resting peacefully on his Papa's chest.

⚜

As the day had worn on, Billy Joe felt something had been terribly wrong. He hitched up the old mule and rode into town to Mr. Ferguson's store. There was no one out and about... the snow had begun to melt... the roads were massive mud trails. Slowly he and the old mule made their way down the road. He went inside the store and told Mr. Ferguson that he feared something must have happened. He asked him to drive up the mountain and check on things. He agreed.

A knock came loudly at the door of the cabin. Following the knock, there came a familiar voice from behind the door. It belonged to Mr. Ferguson. He had finally made it up the mountain in his truck and found an unbelievable scene when he got there.

Granny had left the door ajar when she brought in the last firewood. He slowly pushed it open. He did not know what to expect since no one had answered. The blood was rushing through his veins to his heart so fast he could hardly believe his eyes.

There sat a mud man holding an infant in his arms... a fire mostly gone out... a cold cabin and the exhausted voice of a woman calling from the bedroom. "Come quickly... I think she is dead."

Chapter twenty: A Time for Reflection and Thanksgiving

The house had a chill. The fire in the fireplace had been reduced to a few glowing embers. However, the fire in the wood stove was still burning enough to keep the house from being too cold.

As soon as Herman got inside the house, he went immediately to the back room to take off his Sunday clothes and to change into his working clothes. The children quietly did the same.

The breakfast dishes were still on the table… the scrambled eggs and gravy had fast-dried to the plates. A couple of the ladies who were at the funeral offered to come in and do the dishes, but Papa told them to go on home to their own families; they could handle it. He knew they were cold from standing out in the cold wind and needed to get home. Several of them had been there over the past couple of days helping out while Papa went into town to get a cast on his leg.

Pretty soon he had a roaring fire in both the fireplace and the stove. He put the kettle on for hot water to wash the dishes. Twelve-year-old Sarah Louise had been the perfect little mother holding Baby Wilson so close all during the funeral.

But she knew from having helped her mother so often with the other little ones that he would soon have to be fed. She set out to start making up his formula. If she seemed overburdened with the task of helping her Papa take care of him and five other siblings, it didn't show. She felt so grown up.

Mr. Ferguson had previously brought a half dozen empty *Coke* bottles with a box of baby nipples that could be stretched over the top so that Baby Wilson could nurse. He also brought a couple cans of Pet *Evaporated Milk* and a small bottle of *Karo Syrup*.

One of the women who had been there the day before wrote down the formula and had shown Sarah Louise how to sterilize the bottles and to boil the water that was used half and half with the canned milk. Sarah Louise put Little James and LeRoy down for a nap.

The baby had been very cooperative during the funeral... hardly a peep from little George Peter Wilson Alrod; only three days old. He was named after Peter Wilson, Granny's son, in tribute to her.

Sarah Louise had just finished making his bottles when he began to show signs of hunger; first with little grunting sounds and looking into his blanket; and then gnawing on first one fist and then the other. She fed him and wrapped him in the little warm afghan that Granny Wilson had made for him.

Some hours later, after all the children had left the kitchen, Herman stood looking out the back door window at the thin layer of snow that covered the earth; and took in the beauty of the scene.

The ground had been so evenly covered with the early snow the only ground showing underneath was where his family had trekked a straight line of footprints to the house when they returned from the funeral. Further down in the yard, there were tire marks in the mud from the old Chevy sedan.

He stood and looked at all those footprints belonging to such a big family. Even though Herman was a man of faith, he could not help but wonder what the future would hold for his children; with a war raging in Europe; the after effects of the Depression still evident across the land. The year of 1939 was fast-becoming last year with the new one of 1940 less than six weeks away. But no matter how hard the road seemed, Herman knew that God would take care of them.

Because it was the first snow and early in the season, the ground underneath was still warm enough for the grave to be dug. Herman tried not to think about the events of the past few days, and he tried not to blame anyone; especially God. As he had said at the graveside, *"The Lord giveth and the Lord taketh away."*

The snowflakes had stopped falling. Soon the afternoon sun melted most of the snow that lay on the ground, and it turned to slush. But later in the day when the temperature began to drop along with the cold blowing wind, everything quickly refroze.

For a while, the earth had been a pristine white and looked like a winter wonderland. There is always something so beckoning about a snowfall. It covers even the ugliest of scenes. Herman thought of the scripture that said, *"Though our sins are as scarlet, they will be white as snow."* Now the snow had a pinkish brown color since refreezing; now mixed with the red mud.

Herman knew he had to get better organized and had to help the older children take on adult responsibilities that would be difficult for them. His worries just began to pile one on top of the other, and then he caught himself. In comparison, to what was going on across the nation to other families, he began to feel guilty for not trusting in the divine care of God.

There was despair all across the nation where families had lost their land, their jobs, and many still standing in bread lines. There were strong men willing to work and couldn't find jobs. There were children going hungry. The nation was on the verge of another world war.

He was thankful that he still had his land and food in the cellar and pantry. God had blessed him in many ways. God had just given him another beautiful son, but with that broken leg, he just didn't see how they would be able to make it. Then he reminded himself that he was looking through his own eyes and not the eyes of God.

He could always tell when the folks in his congregation were having difficulties in the finance department for the tithes and offerings would go down drastically. They were a loving and caring group, but when it came to buying five pounds of beans or putting twenty-five cents in the collection plate, they had to feed their children.

Herman, like the disciples and Paul in the Bible, was self-employed. He did not depend on the meager salary that they paid him at the church, but it helped between planting and harvesting. The 1940 Farmer's Almanac had indicated that it would be a good season for growing corn.

He also knew that if the United States were to be drawn into the war, there would be a great need for lots of corn to feed soldiers, and to feed livestock.

Billy Joe, the oldest, was capable of not only taking care of himself, but had already jumped in to help care for all the younger ones. Two-year-old Baby James had been his responsibility at the funeral. He was older and heavier than the new baby.

Now Baby James would have to slide up a notch as he was no longer the baby of the family. Each of the children had been given a task and was told to be as quiet as possible in the doing of them. The twins would have to begin helping out more around the house as well. He knew it was just going to be a matter of organizing everyone, so they all knew what was expected of them.

Who knows... if just one little thing in the past could have been changed – what a difference it could have made in the present and the future. There was no use blaming anyone; things like that just have to remain in the hands of God.

"For when we are weak, He is strong," were often words coming from the mouth of this little country preacher to others, and now he had to apply it to his own life.

Regardless of how many newborns Herman saw in his own household or the homes of his congregation; he was in amazement that such a small, but whole person could be housed in such a tiny body... such a miracle. But death was a much bigger mystery.

How can it be that one moment a woman is living, breathing, and full of life and the next minute all signs of life gone? Death was such a mystery; but so was the birth of a baby.

He felt, and had often preached, that the little ones God sends to parents is only a loan for them to care for until they can be on their own. "They are not ours," he would often say; "but just wards for us to have for safe keeping until they are ready to be the people God created them to be."

When he looked at their little fingers and toes and their responses at such a tender age, it only renewed his faith in God. People have been amazed that God could make a tree... so much more a human being. It seemed the months of Mama's pregnancy had gone by quickly; maybe not to her... but to him.

He wished that she had told him about how serious her concern was that something was wrong this time. But he knew that she always wanted to spare him and the children any undue worries. What Mama couldn't handle; she took to the Lord in prayer.

As his mind drifted toward the unspeakable pain she must have endured, he could only wince at the thought... and would give little notice to the throbbing pain in his broken leg. It was his heart that hurt the most. She had suffered so terribly.

He turned from the window and looked over his shoulder at all seven of his children… from the oldest to the very newest. They were trying to be quiet, but he heard them as they came back into the kitchen. It was time to begin preparing supper.

He knew that no matter how dark the world could sometimes seem; God always promised that the sun would come up each day. He was thankful on this cold day that he had seven healthy children.

He was thankful for life and accepting of what death had taken away. It had not been long since he had lost his father, James Alrod; and only a few years before that his precious mother, Sarah.

Thanksgiving would be coming around in about a week, and without Mama to do all the cooking and planning, it would be hard, but he felt with the help of some of the neighbor ladies they would make it through.

Even with the harshness of the cold weather upon them, and their own families to think about, he knew there would be some of the church ladies there to help. He had been right.

On Thanksgiving Day, there were those who came by wagons and cars to bring the Alrod's Thanksgiving Dinner. He felt that many of them had taken things right off their own table to share. Some of the men had gone up on the mountain for a turkey shoot…and they got one for the Alrod family. It had been cleaned, plucked, and cooked by the time it reached their house.

There was plenty of good home-cooked food that would last for days. It was cold enough on the back porch to set some of the food out for safe keeping. The house was warm, and the children were beginning to get a little livelier. They had been penned up in the house for days but had done very well. Billy Joe and Sarah Louise kept them busy doing little projects, playing board games, and quietly listening to the radio turned down low.

Papa had to calm them down several times for those who were sleeping. He would only intend to get off his leg for a while, but would soon drift off to sleep himself. Having a new baby in the house left him and Sarah Louise exhausted. They tried to catch a nap to make up for those sleepless nights when they could.

Later on that Thanksgiving Day when the table was laden with food made by loving and giving hands, the Alrod family gathered around the table…each of the older children finding their own place… with Herman at the head and a vacant chair at the opposite end where Mama's usually sat. Baby James was napping.

First, he took out his old worn leather Bible. the one Mama had saved her egg money to buy many years before. He began to read, Psalm 100.

It had become their family ritual on Thanksgiving. Mama would read the verse…one line at a time, and Papa would either explain it or ask one of the children to do so. That was their "Psalm of Thanksgiving." But this year, he began to read:

~ Make a joyful noise unto the Lord, all ye lands! ~

He smiled as he looked up from the pages and said, "We sure got a lot of racket goin' on here don't we? And to my ears, and God's, it is joyful."

LeRoy spoke up and said, "We have even more now that Baby Will is here. He makes my ears hurt when the cries."

"Will?" his father said. "Who said we would be calling him Will?"

"Cause, Papa, Wilson is too big for him now. And besides you said he was born by the Will of God."

His Father smiled at him; surprised at the wisdom of one so young; to know that even in the midst of the cold wind blowing at the funeral, he had heard what his Papa had said at the cemetery."

"Point well taken, LeRoy; "Will" - it shall be."

~ "Serve the LORD with gladness"~

"Do any of you children know what that means?"

At first there was no answer and then Billy Joe, the oldest spoke up and said. "Papa, it is just like that other verse that says, *"Whatsoever you do, do it as unto the Lord."*

"And Papa, I want to tell you how sorry I am for complaining. And in the future, I will try harder not to gripe and complain when I am asked to do the chores; even when I don't want to do them."

"I know you will son. We have all got to stick together and see after one another, don't we?"

They all nodded their heads. But LeRoy was still eyeing the big ole drumstick on that bird sitting in the middle of the table. The chocolate cake already had a few finger swipes in the icing, but this was no time for whipping little ones, or giving them an opportunity to lie. But since there was more than one culprit, who could say which finger swipe belonged to which child; LeRoy and both the twins had tale-a-tale signs of chocolate on their faces.

~ *"Come before His presence with singing"* ~

Papa asked, "Sarah Louise, being that Mama ain't at the table today, would you sing the Thanksgiving song she always sang?"

"I don't know if I can or not, Papa, but I will try. I know Mama would want me to."

They all turned their eyes toward Sarah Louise as the sweet strains of *"Come Ye Thankful People Come,"* flowed in sweet melody from her heart. At twelve, she felt so grown up. She was going to have to be.

~ *"Know that the LORD, He is God"* ~

After reading that line of scripture, Herman said, "When a body really knows who God is, then they know that He is Lord, and until people make Him the Lord of their lives... it don't much matter what else they believe."

~ *"It is He who has made us, and not we ourselves"* ~

He paused for a moment, thinking of that new little creature in the cradle beside the big old wood stove. He marveled once again how intricately different God had made each of them; like the leaves on the trees and the snowflakes that fell; all, part of the whole; but so powerfully different.

~ *"We are His people and the sheep of His pasture"* ~

"Velma, why do you suppose God says we are His and we are like sheep?"

"I know," said the other twin, Verna.

Velma punched her and said, "Papa asked me not you?"

"Well, I know the answer because my Sunday School teacher told us we needed someone to look over us like the shepherds do for the sheep!" exclaimed Verna.

"I was going to say that," said Velma.

"You were not!"

"Were, too!"

"Girls," was all Papa had to say. They turned back toward the table with heads down a little saying in unison, "We're sorry Papa."

"You should be," said their Papa.

Looking to see if their racket had affected little Will, he said, "Remember today is a special day, and we need to keep quiet as possible."

They shook their heads showing they understood.

~ *"Enter into His gates with Thanksgiving"* ~

Herman said. "Notice that the Word says here… enter with Thanksgiving. That means we are to go to Him. We are to go with thankful hearts in all things. It does not say we have to be thankful **for** all things, but thankful **in** all things."

~ *"And into His courts with praise"* ~

"This means when we are in His court; we are in His presence, and we are to come to Him with praise and not complaints."

~ *"Be thankful to Him, and bless His name"* ~

"God is Holy and we should always remember that in using His name we are to be thankful and respectful and not use His name in the wrong way. That is so important that He wrote it on the stone tablets that He gave to Moses." *"Thou shalt not use the name of the Lord thy God in vain."*

~ *"For the LORD is good"* ~

LeRoy, spoke up barely taking his eyes off the turkey said, "Even when He lets people die?"

"Yes, LeRoy, even then."

"When we come into the world just like little Wilson...huh... Will... our very days are numbered from the beginning. We only have a span of time on this earth to be the person God created us to be. Then like the Bible says, there is a time to be born, and there is a time to die."

"Papa, Verna asked, "She was a good person wasn't she?'

"Yes, she was and loved by so many," was his reply.

"Death can come at any age, take Granny Wilson's family, for example. She lost a very little girl and a very young son; and yet her husband was old when he died."

They all looked at him with concern and pain in their eyes.

~ *"His mercy is everlasting"* ~

Reassuring the children once more, he said, "God's love and mercy know no bounds. And His mercies are not limited to time, age or purpose."

He said, "Remember Granny Wilson's little girl didn't live very long in years, but she lived forever in Granny's heart. It made Granny love all little girls. And while her son Peter only lived a short life as a young man, he gave his life for his country so that we could all be free."

"Remember Mrs. O'Brien lost a tiny newborn baby that didn't live very long, and we lost Grandpa, who had lived a long time."

"And look at this last verse."

~ *"And His truth endures to all generations"* ~

"None of us at this table know the number of our days, and we can make them shorter by living outside the will of God. For each person born, God has a plan for their lives, but He allows us to accept or deny that plan."

"But each generation is to give to the one coming after. That is why we should be careful that those who come behind us will find us faithful. We must learn and then teach our children so they in turn can teach their own children."

"Now let us bow our heads and thank God for all He has given us and show our thankfulness in days to come and toward one another."

Just then a noise was heard at the doorway coming into the kitchen, and a soft voice saying, "Not without me you don't."

"I may have to lie back down in a while, but I intend to share this Thanksgiving Dinner with my children, Mama said."

Papa jumped up and hobbled from his place at one end of the table and rushed over to Mama's side to pull out her chair. Sarah Louise ran into the back and brought out a pillow for Mama to sit on.

Mama was still weak and pale, but stronger than the day before. When he helped her into her chair, there were tears streaming from the eyes of the older ones and a lot of hand clapping by the smaller ones. LeRoy said, in a loud voice, "Do we still have to be quiet?"

Just then Baby Will began to cry a lusty loud and healthy cry, and Little James came running into the room, rubbing his eyes waking up from his nap. Billy Joe scooped him up before he pounced on Mama, and Sarah Louise immediately picked up Baby Will. There they were… all nine of the Alrod's sitting around the table on that memorable Thanksgiving Day.

Mama had been in the hospital for days, and now she was back up on her feet…for a little while anyway. Her recovery, according to the doctor, would be long and hard. He had told her there would be no more Alrod babies in this generation, but with seven children, she could look forward to lots of grandchildren.

Papa sat back down and reached for the little soft hand of Verna sitting next to him. That in turn caused a chain reaction of each one reaching for another hand. They knew it was time to thank the Lord.

Preacher Alrod began: "Lord, we come to you with praise and thanksgiving, and we know from whom all blessings flow. We thank you for all this here food the church ladies done brought."

"We thank you for sparing Mama's life and giving us Baby Wilson... and we thank You precious Lord for Granny Wilson, who gave her all to make that possible."

"We know that if she could speak to us from heaven, she would be saying, "Don't worry 'bout me... ain't nothin' to worry 'bout. I'm having Thanksgiving this year with my family....and Jesus."

"And oh yes, Lord, bless all the people overseas who are fighting against that evil Hitler. Help them to whip them evil folks and be able to be back in their homes and with their families by next Thanksgiving Day!" And Lord if it is according to Yor plan, let it end before any of our boys have to go over there like Pete Wilson and my father did in the last war."

A huge wind blew up there on that mountainside where a fresh grave had opened up the earth. The Wilson family was together once again. The wind blew so hard it created a whirlwind of snow on top of Granny's grave and drifted heavenward.

Epilogue

You have finished the first book about the Alrod's and the little church on the hill nestled in the valley beneath a small mountain range. We have celebrated the tenets of their faith and culture; as had their forefathers before them; as would their descendants after them.

Perhaps by now you have fixed in your mind the individual characters and how you perceive them to be. Don't you just love LeRoy; his innocence and inquiring mind?

You may have also noticed that Mama never has a name in the whole book. She is Mama, Mrs. Alrod or the "Preachers wife." This was on purpose and for a reason. It was the desire of the author to allow each reader to picture her as their own mother or grandmother.

Over the centuries in the history of America, many small churches grew into much larger churches. However, some would remain small country churches for many generations; some of them are still small and are still standing after a hundred years or more.

Such is a little church, Hopeful Primitive Baptist, located in Fayette County, Georgia, the author's hometown, that allowed their little worn out church to be photographed in order to give a visual of just how well built it was. It is still standing after one-hundred and ninety years. It was built in 1825 just about the time the county was established. It is being restored.

Another aspect of the story reveals that the little church on the hill does not reflect or represent any particular denomination in hopes that many would identify with the purpose of the church and not just a denomination. It lasted through seven generations.

The cycle of life, birth, death, and infinity will continue to rotate full circle in each generation as it has been since the beginning of time and will continue until the end of time.

New generations will come and go experiencing the same joys and trials of life; each in their own time and circumstance. Bit by bit with each new generation, there would be changes, and then there would also be great events that would make far-reaching changes; seemingly overnight. But never changing are the steadfast love and promises of God. God changes not... because He is the same today... yesterday,... tomorrow and... forever more.

The theory is that once you are born into the church, attended the church, married in the church and are buried behind the church; you became an integral part of the church; much like the timbers and foundation upon which it was built. For after all... the church is the people.

Book One of "Sunday Meetin' Time" leaves many questions; not the least of what happens to the church in later years when a young history teacher takes up the fight to save the 150 year old building.

He is the future that so many of the Alrod's worked toward in past generations. He is the seventh generation of Alrod's to live in the valley. Not until his ancestral history is threatened did he come to understand the importance of the past and those who came before him. They had been found faithful. Would future generations be found the same?

Now that you have spent time with the Alrod family and their friends and neighbors you will want to revisit them as the rumbling of World War II comes closer and closer to America and to their valley.

In Book Two, the Alrod's face turbulent financial setbacks and Mama deals with post-delivery depression. Christmas and the year 1939 passes into 1940 bringing tragic and mysterious events which impact the Alrod's and the whole community.

A suspicious stranger shows up under a cloud of secrecy, and two life altering unexpected letters come to the family. The circus comes to town bringing a dreadful event.

❦

"Happiness is when you finish reading a really good
book and then find out there is a sequel."
This is not "The End" of Sunday Meetin' Time but only the Beginning.
Available where Christian books are sold you will find:
"Sunday Meetin' Time"
Book Two: The Alrod's

The Leaves of our Family Tree

We are but leaves on our family tree...
One represents you and one represents me.
Some are larger and some are small...
None more important... but part of the all.

Centuries of family have come and passed on by;
All have lived... and all must die.
Many millions have come along before us;
Their Lives..."Our Heritage"...Our lives..."A sacred Trust."

Before the tree, there comes the seed;
The composition of life... previously conceived.
Before the leaf, must come the bud.
Like those before... who made the way for those they loved.

For me to tell our story from long. long ago...
So that all future generations will know...
Seems the very right thing to do.
To share the "How," the "When" the "Why," the "Who."

They lived, they breathed like you and me.
They are the leaves on our family tree.
They loved, shed tears and made the way.
They are the reason…. we are here today.

They are long gone from this earth that they trod.
They raised families, fought the wars; and worshipped God.
Their mission finished… the angel of death was given the nod.
They are gathered up… and returned to the land of God.

They answered life's call…
They gave it their all…their all…
And lived it by doing their very best…
They unlocked the gateway for all the rest.

Though dust lies in their graves of long ago…
Their stories should live on because they were so.
They should be remembered for all their worth;
For they were our doorway to this earth.

We owe them remembrance and should value their life.
Their lives were not easy. They also had trouble and strife.
The things they accomplished and the things that they fought for…
They endured for us… through hard work and even war.

Someday we will meet them on Heaven's distant shore.
We'll all be together and then we will learn more.
We'll have millions of years to share with them then...
About the **"How,"** the **"Who,"** the **"Why,"** the **"When."**

Like the faithful ones who came before...
Who left open wide... destiny's door...
Will we be found as faithful and will we do the same...
With the blessings God gave us.....
To preserve our heritage...our name?

Those in the garden were the first two of our clan...
They were the beginning of woman and man ...
From these blessed two came all of life...
God created the first man... and his wife...

Since then families have come and gone...
Some forgotten and some live on...
Our family is no exception of what is written above...
Let us remember our family...for family means love.

No matter where we find ourselves today...
We should all stand proudly and be willing to say...
That family..... Our family – is the best it can be...
Because this is the family...where God put you and me.

The leaves on the tree begin to bud in the spring...
As new life is given to everything...
Harsh sun, rain, winds and winter's cold air ...
Cause the leaves to disappear and are no longer there.

After the leaves fall, once again comes the bud... then to full bloom
The old leaves are dropped to the ground to make room...
For the leaves coming behind... for it will be their turn to live...
Their chance at giving... what they have to give.

We are like those leaves that bud, bloom, and too soon die.
They fall to the earth and there they lie...
But once on the ground, they continue to give ...
Nourishment for those who come after... to help them to live.

We are a part of a cycle from life unto death ...
From our first cry... to our last breath...
We live because of destiny's decree...
And others will live because of you and me.

So that is why I tell you this story...
One of hope... love...despair.... and glory...
So that those who come behind us will in God trust,
Will find that we, too, were faithful and are much more than dust. (c)
Written by Patricia (McCullough) Walston
February 6, 2005

Printed in the United States
By Bookmasters